The House of Baric

Part One:

Shields Down

D1562197

Jillian Bald

HILLWALKER PUBLISHING

SECOND EDITION

First Edition published 2015
Second Edition published 2018
This second edition has a revised, expanded ending, as well as reorganized, renumbered chapters. The glossary from the first edition has been deleted.

Printed in the United States of America

ISBN: 978-1-943594-07-8
ISBN-10: 1-943594-07-4

The Keep Tower

This book is dedicated to my family and friends who
encouraged me to give this a real try.

The House of Baric is a fictional story set in the real world of the past. You don't need to know a lot about the political circumstances happening in Europe in the 17th century to enjoy this book, but a little bit of background might help.

A VERY BRIEF HISTORY LESSON

THE THIRTY YEARS' WAR

Though the fighting was centralized in Middle Europe, this was a terrible period in all of Europe from 1618 until peace treaties were signed in 1648. It was the longest continuous war in modern history.

Religious intolerance between the Protestant and Catholic rulers within the Holy Roman Empire was the primary reason for the extended fighting. There was a constant series of battles taking place from Denmark to the edge of the Ottoman Empire. Power struggles for political territory and wealth were unrelenting. Army troops could number in the hundreds of thousands during one battle. Ruling powers went bankrupt from the enormous cost of waging war. Cities and fortresses were demolished. Crops and landscapes were denuded. Famine and disease epidemics killed unimaginable numbers of civilians and soldiers alike.

The mercenary soldiers in *The House of Baric*, led by the character Salar Nassim, were coming from the fighting in Bohemia. They fought in one of the last battles of this war in 1648, the siege of Prague by the Swedish Army.

THE MOST SERENE REPUBLIC OF VENICE

The Venetian Republic (or The Venetian Empire) lasted from 726AD, when the first Doge government in Venice was established, until 1796, when it was conquered by Napoleon.

The Venetian government was not based on a monarchy's authority, but was designed as an oligarch-democracy. The Republic was ruled by a Doge, determined by elected councilmen. The council was primarily made up of elite aristocrats from the privileged class.

The capital city of Venice was rich with galleries, theaters, operas, and renowned architecture during the Renaissance and Baroque Periods. The wealthy merchants traded silk and other high-quality fabrics, glass, armor, and gold jewelry. The Venetians were master ship builders. In its heyday, Venice commanded one of the most formidable navies in the modern world. It expanded and conquered territories from other

powers, including the Ottomans, Austrian Habsburgs, and the Spanish.

Most of the battles in the time of this novel were fought to protect the Venetian Republic's continued wealth and acquired territories. Venice also had a long rivalry with the Republic of Genoa, which helped finance the Venetians' enemies.

Plagues were the only real threats the city dwellers worried about. The large, merchant middle-class did not feel the direct effects of the wars going on around them in Europe. The wealthy nobility lived well off the labors of their conquered population and the underclass. The ruling elite became complacent and decadent in defending their Empire in the later years, which finally led to their demise.

THE HABSBURG EMPIRE

The House of Habsburg monarchy (also written Hapsburg) was one of the principal dynasties in Europe from their rise in Austria in 1273 until their defeat in 1918, at the end of WWI.

The territories they occupied were vast: Italy, Germany, Poland, Romania, Hungary, Prussia, and Czechoslovakia. The Habsburg Empire encircled Central Europe and was formidable. It claimed lands through marriages and assigned the new lands to sons and relations. Their Catholic ties to the Holy Roman Empire put them in constant battle with the opposing Protestant kingdoms of Germany, Sweden, and the Netherlands during the Thirty Years' War.

When the Habsburg Empire claimed Hungary, it had to contend with the Ottoman front along the Balkans, where this story also takes place. The Venetian Republic bordered Austria and Hungary, ruled then by the Habsburgs. The Venetian soldiers in *The House of Baric* are constantly defending against their intrusion.

THE OTTOMAN EMPIRE

Sometimes referred to as the Turkish Empire, this was a super-power from 1300 until the end of WWI, whose height of military domination occurred during the 15-16th centuries. The capital was Constantinople (Istanbul), but it controlled most of Western Asia, Southeast Europe, the Caucasus, and North Africa.

The government was an absolute monarchy. It was ruled by a centralized Sultan family, not branches of princes or other royalty, and was sustained by Islamic ideology. The Ottoman Empire had an excellent cavalry and a formidable navy until the 17th century. They were experts in gunpowder and musket weaponry. Much of its army was made up of slave tributes

from its conquered lands. The Ottomans had power over many important trade routes. Its wealth was concentrated with the Sultan family, who lived a decadent lifestyle while the rest of the population was exploited for its gain.

Its push into Europe through Hungary in the 16th and 17th centuries in its attempt to conquer Vienna brought the Ottoman Army up against the Croatian/Venetian Republic borders.

(In *The House of Baric*, the Kokkinos and Spiros families lived in Greece, an Ottoman-ruled territory.)

CROATIA

The Romans ruled this land for five hundred years until it came under the rule of the Byzantine Empire in the 5th century. Croat tribes moved in from Europe during the 7th century, and the first Croat king was recognized by the Pope in 925 AD. Power struggles ensued within the fledgling Croatian Royalty. (In *The*

viii

House of Baric, this is the point in time when Mauro's ancestors became a part of the new Croatian nobility.)

The Republic of Venice invaded Croatia and made its first foothold along the coast in the 11th century. Hungarian kings invaded the Croat Kingdom in 1091. A hundred years later, Venice waged war against the Hungarians. By the 13th century, Venice ruled the Croatian coast, Dalmatia, and its islands. Dalmatia was relinquished to Hungary again in the 14th century, but they sold Dalmatia back to the Venetians after the Hungarian king's death in order to raise funds for their new ruling nobility.

With the exception of the free and independent Republic of Ragusa (called Dubrovnik today), and some territory lost back and forth with the Ottoman Republic, the Venetians held a solid grip on the coastline of the rest of Croatia for another five hundred years, until the Venetian Empire's fall in 1797.

Shields Down

Part One of

The House of
BARIC

Chapter 1

Baric Castle, 15 August 1637

A strong tide after the summer storm swirled the usually placid water below the children's diving cliff, but Mateo had jumped anyway. The sea gods ruled the watery underworld there—at least that's what Mateo had told his younger brother, Mauro. Mateo had been bold and fearless at fifteen; the gods would have wanted him. Mauro wished he had jumped with his brother on that fateful day and died in the blue depths along with him. They never found Mateo's body in the choppy waters or on the pebbly shore, and Mauro was lost without him.

A year had passed since Mateo's tragic death, and it was decided Mauro would be schooled with other boys his age in the North. On the eve of Mauro's leaving Baric Castle, Idita came into his room one last time. The once happy boy had grown pale and thin in his self-imposed seclusion. She wanted to comfort him again, like she had comforted him after his brother's accident. She knelt next to Mauro, who lay on his bed staring absently at a glittering stone he held. She took his chin gently between her fingers and looked into the brilliant green eyes of the sad boy she had helped raise. She knew what she had to do.

"Mauritius," she said softly. "Today you are thirteen, and your father will take you to foster with your uncle at Toth Castle."

Mauro continued to stare at his rock, not caring what was planned for him.

"Do you want to be brave again, like Mateo wanted you to be?" The boy's eyes moved slightly, now seeing into hers. "I have a birthday gift for you, Mauro, which will make it so. But you must follow what I say."

Idita had been nanny to the two Baric brothers, and their father and his brother before that. She was an old woman who had lived to see many tragedies in the House of Baric. She had an authority in her status that was never challenged; the Barics respected her wisdom and felt her kind spirit.

Idita had brought a small chest with her to Mauro's room, setting it on Mauro's dressing table near the shuttered window. She opened the shutters and let in the remainder of the fading daylight. The room was on the east side, and it was now long past noon. She lit two candles to better see and took out the box's contents: a small, wooden mallet; several thin, sharpened sticks; two jars; and a golden plate. Idita opened one jar, sifted the dark powder onto the plate, and then mixed it carefully with spirits from the other jar.

"Mauro," she said to him across the room, "come sit on the bench by my side."

Mauro frowned but slipped off his rumpled bed. He had shared this room with Mateo, and his brother's matching bed was next to his. Mateo's blue cover was straight and smooth, the same as on the day he had died. Mauro walked slowly to his nurse, looking cautiously at the crowded tabletop.

"You will train to be a soldier, Mauro, and for that you must be brave. Mateo would have wanted you to be strong without him. I can pass his strength onto you today, but you must remain still. Can you do that?" He looked into her brown eyes with his cheerless, green ones and nodded that he could.

She assessed her young ward. "You will need to take off your shirt, Mauritius. Reach across the table and hold tight until I am done." He did as she required, resting his chin on his chest as he held fast to the other side. He wanted what she offered. He wanted to be brave.

Idita proceeded to ink a sharp stick, then transferred the black ink with the tiny hammer into the boy's pale skin. Somehow, Mauro managed to stay perfectly still, even as tears ran down his cheeks. She chanted a soothing song but did not speak to him while she continued her laborious, shallow taps on Mauro's narrow shoulder. When she had finished the design, Idita handed him a cloth to wipe his silent tears while she found his small looking glass.

Mauro's arms and shoulders ached from his clenched hold, and he sat up with effort to use the cloth she had offered. Idita smiled at her plucky boy, then tilted the mirror near his arm.

Mauro inhaled sharply—how could she have known? On the back curve of his left shoulder was the outline of his brother's resting palm and fingers, just as they had touched him before Mateo dove into the sea. Beautifully scrolled in the middle of the small handprint was the letter M. Mauro looked in the glass at the black markings for several moments until Idita interrupted his thoughts. "Are you ready to go to your uncle's now, Mauritius?"

He spoke for the first time in a year. "Yes."

Chapter 2

It was already dark outside when Demetrius and Castor Kokkinos walked up the torch-lit pathway to their walled courtyard in a quiet corner of the rambling city. Demetrius smiled at the sound of the family dog's welcome bark. It had been a twenty-minute walk to their small villa from the harbor, where Demetrius moored his three merchant ships, but it had not been enough time for Castor to tell his father all about his two weeks away, his first voyage fully in charge of his father's ship.

Castor had sailed to meet a Venetian ship in a designated spot in the southern Adriatic waters. His detailed recap of what had happened was interrupted when Alexis, Castor's wife, opened the front door and eagerly embraced her husband. The rest of the story could wait, Demetrius thought. He cheerfully made his way past the young couple as Castor warmly kissed his pregnant wife. Demetrius hung up his cape and bag on the pegs near the doorway, and the two followed him hand in hand into the house.

Demetrius Kokkinos handled special services for wealthy clients around the Aegean. He shipped their goods across the sea to the Near East, south to Africa, west to the Republics in Italy, and beyond to the Kingdom of France. Along with his Turkish clients, he had several foreign customers, including Baron Lorenc Baric, whose ship Castor had met with on this last journey. Demetrius had been Lord Baric's middleman for fifteen years, if one counted the six years he had been away, imprisoned.

Lorenc Baric was a Venetian aristocrat, a baron of the old Croatian line of royalty, and his monthly shipments were a valuable part of Demetrius' business. Demetrius had two other ships that sailed steadily as well. He captained one himself, and he had taught both his oldest sons to navigate the waters and learn his customers, so they could one day inherit his successful trading routes. Baron Baric had finally agreed to allow Demetrius to send his firstborn son in his place for the monthly rendezvous, and Demetrius was pleased that it had gone well.

Drawn by the delicious smell of their dinner roasting, the three went through the sitting room and into the kitchen, where his wife was waiting for him at the cluttered dinner table. Their younger children had already eaten their supper, but she had no appetite, and her plate lay empty in front of her. The smile left Demetrius' weathered, handsome face when he saw her grave expression. "Celine, my love, what has happened?" he asked.

She met her husband at the threshold. She kissed his cheek, then handed him the letter she had been holding the last hour. "A courier came a little while ago," she answered.

"Is it Patricius?" Demetrius asked. "Is there finally word about him?"

Their missing son was the first thought on Demetrius' mind. Patricius was the Kokkinos' second-born, barely a man at eighteen. He was strong-willed and had forsaken his father's offer to learn the family shipping business. He had left almost two months ago for Athens to join the Ottoman Army and become a solider instead. They had been informed by the army a few weeks back that Patricius had not arrived to finalize his enlistment, and the family had received no news from him.

"The letter is not from the authorities, Demetrius. It is from the Barics."

Demetrius looked at the sealed envelope. This correspondence was just as unwanted. "Why haven't you opened it?" he asked with a forced calmness.

"I was afraid of the answer," she replied.

Demetrius' only daughter, Terese, was promised to Mauritius Baric, the second son of Lord Lorenc Baric. It had been arranged long ago that she would be sent to their castle in the Venetian Republic when she came of marrying age. Demetrius had finally acknowledged in a letter to Baron Baric earlier in the summer that his only daughter was ready to marry. This letter today would explain their instructions.

Castor looked from parent to parent with his sympathetic, gray eyes. They had just lost one child to the Ottoman Army, and now they would lose another to this contracted arrangement. Demetrius opened the outer seal and looked at the sharp lettering of his name on the inner envelope. He handed it to his son. "You read it, Castor. I cannot bear it."

The short message was in a clear hand in Latin, and Castor read it through quickly before he reread it aloud with a smile. "I have received your letter and inquiry for a wedding date," he translated. "My son, Mauritius, has taken a commission as a captain in the Toth regiment of the Venetian Empire's Army. Please accept my regret that a definitive date cannot be planned for the wedding while he is on active duty in foreign lands. Upon his return, a marriage date can be finalized. I will send instructions at that time. It is signed Lorenc Baric, the 20th of August 1644."

"Another soldier," Celine said quietly to her husband. "Why do all these young men want to go fight wars?"

Demetrius tried to console her. "War has been going on all around them their whole lives, Celine. I suppose every young man must prove himself in some way. I went to sea to do that."

"Patricius did not have to go to war," Celine exclaimed. "He could have gone to sea like you. He should have gone to sea with your ship, and then he would not be dead."

"We don't know if he is dead, my love. The army may have found him. We will wait for that news as well. But you still have your daughter. Be glad that these wars will keep her here." Demetrius squeezed her hand across the table.

She smiled lovingly. "Yes. We still have our sweet Resi."

Demetrius looked across the room and saw Terese standing in the shadows of the doorway leading to the children's sleeping quarters. He could see by the expression on her young, pretty face that she had heard the good news. She was only sixteen and was too young to leave her family, he thought. He had talked about the love for his children during his time as a prisoner, and in the end that love had been used against him to leverage a deal. So now his daughter was to bravely fulfill her father's debt to the Barics.

Demetrius smiled over at his daughter. Resi, as she was called by her family, smiled back at him. She heard her little brother call out for her, and she quietly turned to go down the corridor to him. She was still free, for a little while longer at least.

Chapter 3

Habsburg Territory, 15 August 1647

The afternoon air was sticky and sultry on the shadeless edge of the woods. It could have been any other day of the three-week siege, but today was the Day of Assumption in the Catholic faith. It was a Holy day; a time to pray and feast for the blessed Virgin Mother meeting her son in heaven. But there would be no feasting for the Toth troops without the food wagons, and no praying, except the usual prayer for rain to cool them and fresh water to quench their thirst. So the men sat in the dust, as they had yesterday and the day before, waiting for something to change.

Something had changed for Mauritius Baric—he was a year older. The Day of Assumption was also Mauro's birthday. His mother had told him he was lucky, that Saint Mary would watch over him throughout life because of his special birth. His mother, the Baroness Johanna Baric, had sneaked out of her confinement in the manor house those many years ago to spend the day praying for her favorite saint in the family chapel. That is where they had found her, on the floor giving birth to her only child in front of the Virgin Mary's altar.

His mother always wrote to him in August to remind him of his fortunate birthday. Her unsettling correspondence usually arrived months late, but always managed to find him. He dutifully read the tedious letters, hoping she had something happy to write him from home; but they were always the same, always filled with her grief.

Mauro had another lucky charm tattooed on his shoulder from another birthday, which he put more faith in. From time to time, he thought of this special gift that Idita had given him, especially just before a battle. Whether it was the Holy Virgin Mother or his lost brother protecting him, Mauro Baric had survived five years of war to now turn twenty-three.

The letter Mauro was contemplating just then was not from his mother but from his uncle, who was just a few miles away and had been too busy to tell him the tragic news in person: his father was dead, the funeral had been arranged, and he was excused from his service as a captain in the Toth Army. That letter had arrived two weeks ago, and Mauro was still commanding his squad.

He sat against a downed tree in the shade of the woods and pulled out his uncle's letter from the pocket of his tattered military jacket. Mauro had not been close to his father. He had only seen him a handful of times since leaving home ten years ago. With his father's sudden death, Mauro was to be the new baron of Baric, and there was little chance of delaying the inevitable.

He looked around at his men cleaning their weapons, oiling their armor, and gambling at cards. Each attempted to find some distraction while insects feasted on their exposed skin in the late-August heat wave. Mauro decided he would tell his uncle his allegiance was to his men; the Barics would have to wait.

The white destrier approached the lounging men in the field. The troops came to full attention as Count Toth dismounted and looked across the crowd of soldiers, spotting his nephew. He walked toward him with a frown. Mauro stood up from the dusty ground and put the folded letter back in its place.

Count Vladimir Toth was not a tall man, but he had a presence that rattled even the fiercest of commanders. He became the Count of Toth through marriage, but had been born a Baric. A proud man, he had an ego as big as the Croatian territories he governed. The count always led his own army against their foreign foes, and he trusted no one else to negotiate the final outcome. Vladimir Toth had become quite powerful as he played the political games, protecting the wealth of the men ruling the Empire from the comfort of their grand villas in Venice.

Mauro walked through the crowd of his delegated soldiers and stood before his uncle. The commanding general was crisply dressed in his blue military jacket, brushed clean of dust and wear. His polished brass buttons were closed against his tanned throat. Mauro's matching overcoat was unbuttoned against the sweltering heat of the day, and he began to fasten it hastily to bring some order to his own appearance. He had left his hat on the tree stump he had been leaning against. Even without it, Mauro was still taller than the feather of his uncle's stiff woolen one.

"What are you doing here, Mauritius?" Count Toth demanded. His uncle called him by his given name when angry. "I wrote to you two weeks ago. Did you not receive my message?"

Mauro met his commander's eyes as he spoke. "Yes, I got your note, sir, but I will not leave my men until I am assured they will not be neglected. They are already half-starved, and without me organizing their rations . . ." Mauro looked around at his troops. Most were still at attention, watching their captain with the general, waiting for a sign from Mauro to organize into action.

The count assessed the squad of musketeers. "Are you their nursemaid now, as well as their captain? I told you to turn your command over to Petar."

"With all due respect, Uncle, my cousin already has two hundred pike men under his command, and I would not trust him to worry about the welfare of my extra hundred," Mauro challenged.

The count knew it was true and admired his nephew for his commitment to his regiment of skilled sharpshooters. "When do we attack?" Mauro asked in a quieter voice now. "I will agree to leave after the battle."

"You will leave when you are told," his uncle reminded him. He gave Mauro a stern look for his impertinence. "The battle will go forward in a few days. They have solved the problems with the heavy equipment. Captain Carrera sunk two of my cannons in the swamp, but we still have enough artillery to do the job. At least the gunpowder was not lost."

Mauro figured something had gone wrong with the artillery wagons. He had hoped his friends had not been attacked from behind while the infantry was gathered at the front lines. "I thought Captain Padovi was supposed to organize a bridge to be built over the marshes?" Mauro asked his uncle.

"His troops built a bridge, but it did not hold the weight of the cannons. Carrera's group lost three strong horses to the marshes as well. It took a week just to haul the trees in to fortify the planks," the count told him. "The good news is that they are only a day out now, and the supply wagons with our food are behind them."

"Good, because we have scavenged every barn within five miles of here. I think most of what we eat now is dog."

The count was not amused. "You will not die from eating dog, but you can die with no cannons for support," he said coolly. "This will be over soon, Mauro," he told him with a sigh. "The prince knows we are waiting in his woods with three thousand troops, and he barely has half that to defend his holding. They are probably without food themselves by now."

He walked back to his horse and Mauro followed him. "I am taking a party now to negotiate a settlement. I may or may not attack as planned, but either way, this will be over in a few more weeks," the count said.

Mauro understood the duty to family, but he was in no hurry for the title or the responsibility awaiting him. He would take his chances in battle. "Good," he said. "I will wait until then."

The count spoke to him as Mauro's uncle now, not as his commander. "I want you to leave, Mauro. You are more important to me back at home than here. Pick three good men to take with you. Your father's officers died of the same sickness your father did. It leaves you in a bad predicament for your Castle Guard. I will see to your men's rations personally. Ivan will lead them into battle, if it comes to that."

"What can two weeks matter, Uncle? I prefer to stay," Mauro said with one last, determined plea.

"Go home, Mauritius. Your duty is to the Barics now, not to me." Mauro nodded weakly. "And it is time you married the Kokkinos girl. Nestor will have the details of the contract," he added.

Mauro had not thought of this obligation in years, but he knew the full details already. He also knew there was no arguing the point either, and nodded again at the instructions.

A trickle of sweat rolled down the older man's temple under his wool hat. The stern Baric eyes held Mauro's own. It was always about business, but Mauro knew his uncle meant well. Then his glare softened, and the count told him, "I am sorry about your father. Lorenc loved you, Mauro; remember that. I will miss him, too." Mauro stared blankly ahead. "You are the last in the Baric line," Vladimir Toth said with seriousness. "He would want you at home to take care of your mother and the estate."

Mauro brushed off the sentiment and cleared his throat. "Thank you, Uncle. You are right. I already spoke to my squad and told them I would be leaving." With full command of his emotions again, he said confidently, "I will trust only Ivan with my men. I will take Vilim, Hugo, and Simeon back with me."

His uncle thought for a moment. These were his best sergeants, but he would not argue his nephew's choices. "As you wish; I release them to you. Get supplies from the wagons down the road. You will have a long journey home."

With that final order, the commander mounted his horse. Mauro gave one last salute before the general and his waiting entourage rode away in a cloud of dust.

Mauro said his farewells to his trusted soldiers and gathered his gear and weapons for the long journey back to Croatia. It would be a dangerous ride until they were back in Venetian territory. If the rains held off, it would take them three weeks to reach home. The long, dry spell of summer could not last much longer into September, so four weeks was what he wrote to Nestor, the Barics' steward, in an expedited message he arranged before finally leaving the battlefield.

10

~ * ~

A day into their journey home, Mauro and his escorts saw the dust cloud of the heavy artillery squad. Fabian Carrera and his line of cannons were where his uncle had said to expect them. Vilim and the others went to the supply wagons to collect what they would need for food and gunpowder until they came to friendlier lands. From there, they would treat themselves to meals and beds at the inns along the trade route.

"Hey, Mauritius, you are going the wrong way!" Fabian shouted from his horse near the middle of the pack of soldiers. "What are you doing here?"

Fabian Carrera had grown up in the aristocratic splendor of the Venetian capital. Even after the most dire of battles, he seemed to come through with his stockings pulled up tight and his plumed hat on straight. Mauro stared at the now muddy mess of his conceited companion.

"What have you been rolling in, Fabian?" Mauro asked as he rode up.

Fabian laughed, wiping the caked mud from his sleeve to no effect. "Is it that bad?" Mauro made a face that told him that it was. "I have lost my favorite hat, too," Fabian complained.

The line of soldiers and cannon carts continued to ride around them; the two friends took refuge on the side of the dusty road. "What happened back there?" Mauro wanted to know. "We have been waiting for you for weeks."

"We have had quite a time of it in the stinking marshes. I am surprised I still have any blood left. We have been sucked dry by these man-eating mosquitoes." Fabian's smile faded when he realized Mauro's stallion was loaded with all his provisions. "Did your uncle find you, then? I heard about your father. I am sorry."

"Yes, well, I am being sent home to become the new baron to the House of Baric," Mauro said with a frown. The reality was finally sinking in.

"You knew this day would come," Fabian reminded him.

"I never thought my father would die in the safety of his great hall sooner than I might on a bloody battlefield," Mauro said. They were quiet for a moment. "But I have some good news," Mauro reported with a forced enthusiasm. "My uncle says we will win this siege. We outnumber the prince's forces two to one. He told me they still need you and your cannons, but I myself am dispensable. Ivan will lead my musketeers in my place."

"Well, if everyone is waiting, I shall make haste and bring them the cannons," Fabian replied halfheartedly.

"We cannot eat cannons. The men are waiting for the food wagons. You will arrive to cheers, I imagine, but the applause will be for the casks of ale."

Fabian smirked at the teasing. The line of wagons lumbered past as the two men spoke. He could not bring himself to join them just yet. A group of riders coming toward them caught his attention. "You have escorts. I am glad." Fabian nodded a greeting to Vilim, Simeon, and Hugo.

"My uncle gave me free choice. They are good men and do not have any particular families to go home to. I am to make them captains of my new Guard," Mauro confirmed.

"And do you not want me to be your captain?" Fabian asked, trying not to sound disappointed.

"You are already a Toth captain with men to command, or I would have chosen you. These are my sergeants from my troops, so my uncle did not object."

"He must really want you out of harm's way to send you now." Under any other circumstance, the count would never have let an officer leave just before a battle, and especially not four of them.

"I asked to stay, but there was no delaying my return for him," Mauro said.

"Well, wish us luck that this siege is over quickly."

"I do. There is talk of a peace treaty, you know. You are not bound to the Toth Army after that, and I could always use your help in my Guard. Think about it when you get back, Fabian."

"Your uncle will not be pleased to lose so many trusted officers to the Barics, but I will gladly consider it. I could enjoy regular meals and my own bed again." The last of the cannons rolled by. "Our scouts have been tracking some Habsburg soldiers about five miles out," Fabian warned. "You had best change out of your Toth colors before you go any farther. And keep off the main road."

"We plan to do that," Mauro answered with a final handshake. "Goodbye, old friend. May God protect you."

"And you, Mauritius." He turned his horse and began to trot away, but turned back briefly and shouted, "I have considered it! Write to me if you need help, and I will come!" He then rode to catch up to the wagons lumbering along the road.

Mauro watched him disappear into the crowd of horses.

Chapter 4

They were still deep in Habsburg territory when they left Fabian's convoy, and safety was their priority over a speedy return home. The long summer drought finally ended a week into their journey, making the main route difficult for the horses to travel in the thick mud. When their gunpowder became useless in the driving rain, the men had to rely on bows for protection. Mauro was glad for his choice of company on the arduous ride home. His three companions did not complain, despite the hard trek.

Simeon was the oldest of the four soldiers at age twenty-six. He was dutiful and courageous, as well as being an excellent marksman. He was a proven leader of Mauro's men, even though the count had never promoted him to the rank of captain. Mauro would, though.

Vilim was Mauro's distant cousin near his own age. They had been together at Toth Castle since Mauro first arrived at age thirteen. Vilim's easygoing personality made him an agreeable traveling companion. He was a skilled strategist and could be relied on to make hard decisions when trouble found them. Mauro would need those skills to protect his own lands.

Hugo was a clever fighter. Mauro had relied on him in the past to lead small squads to assess tough situations. He was young, just twenty, but Mauro saw his potential. Mauro planned to rely on him again for his own Baric scouts.

As a boy, Hugo had spent many summers tending livestock in these border valleys, and he was familiar with the smaller passes. When Mauro and his companions met with enemy patrols for the second time before crossing into Venetian territories, the group took Hugo's advice to follow the herding trails through the mountains rather than the open trade route.

The mountainous trails were slower and harder on their horses than the Habsburg-patrolled wagon roads. But thanks to Hugo's connections, Mauro's party was welcomed with a bowl of hot stew and a night's sleep in a dry barn by several families along the way. They avoided trouble the rest of the crossing into Venetian territory. They traveled another two weeks through more familiar valleys to northern Dalmatia, then along the coastline. After five weeks of riding, weary and soaked to the bone, Mauro, along with his small band of men, approached the castle road.

"Well, Mauro, this is quite an ancient fortress," Simeon declared.

Simeon had been soldiering with the Toth Army since his wife died of the plague five years ago. He had said he would never find a woman as wonderful as his Elise, and Simeon had not been in one place long enough to try.

"It is not the imposing limestone fortress of my uncle," Mauro replied. "There is a manor house beyond the gate where my family and servants live, and the old Keep tower you see is housing for the soldiers."

The hulking structure stood two stories over the fortified, granite wall. The centuries-old, medieval tower was originally built more for defense than for comfortable living accommodations. Mauro's grandfather, Lord Fredrik Baric, wanted the comforts and grandeur a prosperous lord could expect in the modern age. It was he who built the manor house in the new style of the Italian villas. The ancient Keep tower remained in the center of the walled courtyard as a tribute to the generations of Barics who had protected their lands.

Vilim slowed next to Mauro as they trotted their tired horses around the final approach. He was a cousin on Mauro's mother's side, but was not of nobility. Vilim's mother had forfeited her status when she married a commoner. After his parents' tragic death in a brutal invasion when he was just a boy, Vilim was taken in to be fostered by the Toth family and came of age with Mauro.

"How many soldiers guard the Baric lands?" Vilim asked.

"That is what I will need to learn," Mauro answered. "After we arrive, I will have much to do. You know my family has a thriving salt trade, and there are many tenant farmers and merchants under the Baric banners as well. I will leave it to you to assess the state of the Guard and the armory," he said. "My father lost four of his officers, so I expect there will be much to organize with the remaining guardsmen."

The gate opened for them as they approached. "It looks like we are expected," Vilim said.

"It is always encouraging to be welcomed home," Mauro answered.

Mauro had been given his own home, a country villa, when he came of age five years ago. They had passed the turnoff to his estate less than an hour's ride from the castle. It was smaller and much older than the main manor house here. Fertile lands of cultivated orchards with nuts, figs, and grapes went with it. It had been a generous gift from his father.

Count Toth had also been generous to his foster son. He had sent Mauro off with his own sons to see the capitals of Europe and the Near East. Mauro and the other boys were tutored along the way in the languages and history of the kingdoms they visited, as well as the etiquette of the Royal

Court. It was during that time that Mauro first met Fabian Carrera and his friend Stephan Padovi in Venice. As their friendships grew, his new Venetian pals helped him finalize his decision to become a soldier.

During his education, Mauro had shown an aptitude for battle strategies and was well-liked and trusted by the other boys. At eighteen, Mauro accepted his uncle's offer to join the Toth Army and continued training to become an officer there. Lorenc Baric had been visiting his brother, Vladimir, at Toth Castle when Mauro told him of his decision. That was when his father gifted him the house and the land surrounding it to entice him back home. Mauro never went home, and he did not see his father again after that.

Mauro felt the weight of his new role shroud him as they rode through the wall's entrance. The sky was nearly dark now; the early October days were shortening. Large torches were ablaze along the front ramparts, and Mauro and his companions could see men moving about in the large courtyard in front of the Keep. They had ridden hard to spare them one more night in the cold rains, and their horses were lathered and exhausted. Mauro led them to the stables just beyond the closing gate.

A boy ran toward him and took the reins of Mauro's horse as he dismounted. "Thank you. What is your name, lad?" Mauro asked as he looked around at the sight of his boyhood home.

The tall, scruffy boy answered to his feet, "I am Geoff, sir. I am a stable groom here. At your service," he added, before he looked up at his new master with big, chestnut eyes. He seemed very young to Mauro, who had forgotten there would be children serving at his castle.

"How old are you?" Mauro asked the lanky, dark-haired boy.

"I am thirteen, sir," the boy stammered, not expecting to be asked more questions. Mauro remembered being thirteen once. It was the last time he was at Baric Castle.

He realized the boy might not know who he was, so Mauro made the introductions just as the stable master, Alberto, walked toward them. "Well, Geoff, I am your new Lord Baric. These soldiers are Vilim, Simeon, and Hugo. They are the new captains of our Baric Guard. They will need beds in the Keep and food and drink brought to them." He regarded the boy, wondering if he was a reliable messenger. "Can you fetch someone to arrange this? They will see to their own horses in the stable. We have had a very long journey."

"We were awaiting your arrival, my lord," the boy politely answered. "Nestor said their quarters in the Keep have been readied, but I will tell them that you are here." After a stiff bow for his new baron, Geoff ran off toward the servants' entrance at the back of the grand manor house. Mauro looked over at his men, who had overheard the conversation and were already leading the horses toward the stables.

Alberto bowed while he addressed the man who he had trained to ride ponies as a child. "Your lordship, I am happy to see you again."

Mauro patted the graying man on the shoulder to show his recognition and appreciation. "I wish it were under other circumstances, but I thank you, Alberto."

The horse master studied him and finally smiled. Mauro had passed his scrutiny. Mauro went on to explain, "We have brought you some fine horses to add to the herd, but they will need a good bit of care after what we have put them through."

Alberto took the reins that Geoff had let drop. "Yes, of course, my lord. You can trust me with their care." Alberto led the baron's horse away to be pampered.

"Now, I will be in need of Nestor," Mauro said quietly to himself, having been left alone in the courtyard.

His eyes followed where the stable boy had just disappeared to, but he knew not to follow him. It would be expected that he make his first entrance as Baron Baric through the front door. He walked across the wide expanse and up the path to where he found his father's steward waiting to greet him in the light of the open entrance.

"Mauro, so good to have you back home. We got your message weeks ago. I hope the traveling was not too formidable with the rains."

Nestor had been the castle's administrator for Mauro's entire life. Mauro regarded the older gentleman who stood before him in the same lacey, elegant clothes he remembered from his boyhood. Nestor had hardly changed, except perhaps he wore a better wig. Even as a young man, Nestor had never been handsome. He had tried to improve his appearance with an elaborate attire of petticoat breeches, and with brightly colored, silk stockings above his high-heeled shoes. He was nearsighted and in need of better eyeglasses. They were perched on the bridge of his pointed nose as he looked up at his new employer and informed him, "We have already finished our evening meal, but I will have some food brought to your room right away."

Mauro looked toward the familiar stairs, wondering if he would sleep in his old boyhood room tonight. He handed his sodden cloak to the young groom waiting at the side of the foyer as they entered. "Thank you, Nestor. I am famished. But first, I would like to greet my mother."

"I am sorry, Mauro, but your mother has already retired for the evening. I will tell her maid to expect your visit first thing in the morning, if you like."

Mauro did not mind waiting a day to see his mother. He was not looking forward to their reunion, but also hoped the delay would not weaken his resolve.

Nestor led the way up the wide staircase to the center of the second floor. At one end of the long hallway was his mother's room, and at the other end was his father's. Five chamber doors on each side of the corridor were in between.

It was an ornate hallway, with inlaid marble flooring and colorful, plastered walls. The staircase ran through the middle of the space. Its iron balusters were elaborately decorated with vines of enameled ivy and delicate flowers. The sconces along the walls of the passageway had been lit, and Mauro thought it had an inviting glow he did not remember from the past.

Nestor passed Mauro's old bedroom door and walked toward Lorenc Baric's room. "I thought you might be more comfortable in your father's chamber. It has been readied for you, if that is agreeable."

Nestor waved a hand in the direction of the tall, bowing groom standing at the doorway. "You may remember Jero," Nestor said matter-of-factly. Mauro genuinely smiled for the first time since the news of his father's death. Not noticing his new lord's reaction, Nestor continued, "Jero was your father's valet, and he will continue to be yours until your further instructions."

"Fine idea, Nestor," Mauro said. "You have thought of everything. You may leave me in Jero's good hands. I will meet with you in the morning to discuss how we will proceed."

Mauro strode past the silent valet and entered the room. It was a large space but quite spare, not as he remembered. It was as if someone had emptied all the memories out and left it blank for new ones. It was warm, though. The fireplace had been lit, and there were several candles burning on the larger table and nightstand. Bread and cold meats were already laid out on the table, as well as wine, ale, and water. Mauro smiled that his new valet had tried to think of all the options for him.

Jero spoke for the first time. "If there is something else you would like for refreshment, I will fetch it. Hot soup will be here shortly, sir."

His voice was deep and unexpected. Mauro didn't know why he wanted him to be the same thirteen-year-old boy; skinny, with strands of curls spilling from his tied-back hair. The brown, wavy hair was the same, but the free strands had been tucked behind his ear. Jero was smiling to match the grin on Mauro's face. The gaps from boyhood were now filled, with nearly straight teeth under a man's trimmed full beard and mustache. The green, embroidered silk waistcoat, flowing long over the matching Venetian breeches, was his father's preferred uniform for the Baric servants. Jero's smoky green eyes, looking into his at his own height, were the same as Mauro remembered.

Jero searched for his old friend in Mauro's eyes, too. Then he remembered who he was, and who Mauro now was, and lowered them.

"Is the wine French?" Mauro teased the uncomfortable man.

"No, my lord, it is from your harvest. But I can see what is in the cellar, if you like."

Mauro laughed heartily, interrupting Jero's extended effort to please. "This is more than satisfactory," Mauro told the blushing servant. He looked down at his muddy clothing. "I should change, but I have not eaten since last night." He sat at the table and began to help himself to the food laid out there.

A kitchen maid stood nervously at the door with the soup. Jero took it from her with a smile and set the small tureen on the table. He poured wine into Mauro's glass and asked, "Will that be all, sir?"

Mauro studied him for a minute while Jero waited patiently. Mauro had not thought of Jero in years, and seeing him now changed everything he had planned during the journey home.

"No. Shut the door and sit with me a moment." Jero followed his orders and sat across from his new employer, his old playmate, Mauro. "I will be making some changes tomorrow, but first I have some questions that you might help answer."

Jero sat silent while Mauro ate and contemplated his new valet. Mauro was tired, and the wine and the heat of the fire added to his sleepiness. He would be direct. "What did my father teach you about the Baric business, Jero?"

"Why would your father teach me about the business, my lord? I was only his valet."

"When we are alone, you may call me Mauro." Jero shook his head in agreement.

Mauro stood up from the table and paced the length of the room, uncomfortable in his new role and the conversation at hand. He looked out the window into the black night, seeing only the mirror of the room in the glass instead. Jero was too familiar sitting at the table by the fire, looking like a ghost in the reflection. Mauro shook off the shiver that ran through him.

He turned back to his old companion. Ten years was a long time, and Mauro hoped he could trust the man at the table. He would take that risk. "I have not seen my mother in a very long time, Jero, but she was a frequent letter writer. I learned from her that my father took a special interest in your education."

Mauro turned away, unsure how he should continue. After a moment he said to the window, "My mother is not your champion. I think it could be said that she has a great dislike for you, but she enjoys gossiping about such things." Jero looked uncomfortable in the reflection, but Mauro was unsympathetic. He walked back to the table and sat down across from Jero again. "I will need you to tell me everything my father taught you about the estate and the trade accounts," he said directly to the startled valet.

Jero stepped back from the table, his eyes at his feet and hands solidly behind his back for support. "I am sure I am not the one to be asking. Nestor can tell you all that there is to know."

Mauro tried a different approach. "Maybe I should tell you that I am happy that my father took an interest in you, Jero. I do not begrudge you that you were his chosen confident." He poured a glass of wine and offered it to Jero, who had no choice but to accept it. "It is no secret that I was asked to come back to the estate after my fostering. My father gave me a house and some land in my own name. I chose to stay on with my uncle instead."

Jero watched Mauro pour more wine into his cup. "I did not expect my father to die so suddenly," Mauro told him quietly. "My biggest regret is that I am here now without his guidance," he confessed. "Jero, I need to trust that our history together might mean something to you. My father thought highly of you, Jero. He trusted you. Now I will trust you."

Jero stared at the embers in the pit of the fire grate. "Yes, you can trust me, my lord. Mauro, I mean," Jero corrected himself. "But I do not know what you want from me."

Mauro told him, "As my steward, Jero, you will be entrusted with the affairs of my estate while I am away. If you believe I am wrong, and you are unsuited for the job, then I shall release you from that position. You can remain my valet, as you first assumed. What do you say, Jero?"

Jero took a deep breath and let it out again. "I did spent a lot of time with Lord Baric, and he did talk about his business. Your father showed me detailed accounts of his trade. I did not know if that was unusual for valets to be in such confidence. I will tell you all that I know about his affairs, but I do not think I am qualified to replace Nestor."

"Did my father say he mistrusted Nestor?" Mauro asked calmly.

Jero thought about this and shook his head. "No. They got along quite well."

Mauro had decided on the trek home that he would not trust the old Baric steward because of one unresolved question. "How do you suppose Nestor survived the plague, while my father and the other four died of it? They all shared their last meal together."

"Lord Baric never said anything against Nestor. For all appearances, Nestor has always been loyal to your family and performed all the duties asked of him. I believe Nestor to be a good man, Mauro."

Until recently, Mauro had also believed it to be so. "I will continue this conversation with Nestor in the morning." Mauro yawned unwillingly. "I realize now that I was wrong to press such an offer on you. I would like your decision tonight, but if you need to think on it, we can talk again in the morning."

Jero seemed to gain his composure for the first time since shutting the door. "I do not know why you want to give me this honor, but I will be your steward."

Mauro's smile carried to his tired eyes. "Good man, Jero! I am very glad you have answered yes."

It had been months since Mauro had slept on a mattress, and his bones were aching to lie down. He stood from the table and walked casually to the large, feathered bed. He plopped down upon it with a sigh. "That will be all, Jero. I have a lot of work to do, and I am glad to have your help."

Jero blew out the melting candles in the holders on the table. He turned back to tell Mauro good night, but the man was already fast asleep. He pulled the baron's boots off without stirring him. Jero threw a blanket over Mauro's sprawled body and extinguished the remaining candles before quietly closing the door to the dark room behind him.

Chapter 5

When Mauro woke, it was well past dawn. He had not slept this long into the morning in years; the burden of soldiers waiting for his instructions each day had never allowed it. The freed feeling was fleeting when he remembered that he was in his father's old room back in Croatia. He was now Lord Baric, and new responsibilities were waiting on the other side of his chamber door.

It was a cool morning, and a servant had already lit the fire while he slept. He sat up and stretched his aching body. He was still dressed in his muddy riding breeches and the sweat-stained shirt he had worn for the second half of the journey. Nestor would have kept some of his father's clothes for him to be presentable on his first day as baron; he would call Jero to find them.

There was a screen in the room, and a pail of warm water was on the floor behind it. He filled the basin on the grooming table and found the pot of soap nearby. He stripped his shirt off and scrubbed the layers of dirt and sweat away. In the solitude, he thought about how life might have been different had Mateo lived and they had grown old together. Mateo would be the new Baron Baric, and what would Mauro be? Anything else would be fine, he decided.

There was a knock on the door and a young man brought a tray into the room. "My name is Davor. I am at your service as your new valet, my lord. I have brought you tea, sir. If you prefer coffee, Suzana says she can make you some." Jero had already taken charge in assigning a new valet, and Mauro could not be more pleased to be relieved of this decision.

"Tea is fine today, but I prefer coffee in the morning. Is there water in the pitcher? This is the only castle where I will drink it," Mauro told the servant.

Davor poured water into a mug for his new master. "Shall I help you dress, sir, or would you like to eat first, my lord?"

Mauro found a linen towel and dried his torso. "Do you know if they have left my father's clothes in this room?"

There was a large trunk near the window, and Davor walked over and opened it. "Yes, my lord. This is filled with shirts and breeches. I have not been in here recently, but the wardrobe should still hold the baron's jackets and more formal attire."

"Thank you, Davor. I do not need assistance dressing, but I would like more hot water to shave." Davor nodded. "My own trunks will be sent from my uncle's castle. Until then, is there a tailor in the village who can alter these?"

"There is, sir. Jero will know. I will bring the hot water for you right away, my lord, and then inform him about the tailor," Davor replied with a bow, leaving Mauro to his breakfast.

Mauro considered Jero's choice of valet. Even as nephew to Count Toth, Mauro had not been given a personal groom during his time there. His uncle felt all his wards needed to be self-sufficient. As baron, Mauro was expected to have a valet to assist him, but he was not so sure whether such a young groom was suitable. Mauro eyed the tray of sausages and ham next to the toasted bread, and he decided his stomach would come first.

Mauro had just finished eating when the valet returned with more hot water and fresh linens. Davor cleaned up the breakfast tray and set the looking glass on the same table, along with the basin of fresh water. Davor then cleared his throat and asked awkwardly, "My lord, I do not have experience as a valet, so please excuse my ignorance. I mean no disrespect in asking, but shall I shave you, sir?"

"Well, Davor, I do not have experience as a baron, either. I have shaved and dressed myself all of these years. I think I will continue to do so." Mauro considered the young man trying to keep composed under his master's scrutiny. "How old are you, Davor?"

"I am seventeen, sir." He looked up at the baron for the briefest of moments, and chanced to offer more information. "I have been a house servant for two years now. My family farms one of your tenant holdings." The servant glanced up again, and then lowered his eyes. They were dark blue; not like the azure sea, but blue like the deep mountain lakes. They stood out against his fair-skinned cheeks and fine, blond hair. He would be a handsome man, when his spots cleared up and his thin shoulders filled out.

"And here you have a room in the servants' quarters?" Mauro asked absently as he sorted through the trunk and considered the contents. He found something to his liking and closed the trunk.

Davor stood at attention and said to his feet, "Yes, my lord. I am very happy living here at the castle."

He told him with authority, but not unkindly, "I would prefer you look at me when you speak to me, Davor. My soldiers do when I give them orders, and so shall you."

The servant stood a little taller, being put in the same class as the baron's soldiers. "I am sorry, my lord. I did not know what was expected, sir.

I shall in the future, always." Davor smiled for a brief moment, flashing his white teeth, the two in front slightly crossed.

Mauro studied him for another long moment, then said, "I think we will get along fine."

Mauro put the starched shirt and velvet breeches he had chosen on the chair, then went to the table to shave before the water turned cold again. "Do you know if my mother is up this morning?" he asked as he lathered his whiskers.

"The baroness doesn't come out until at least noon, sir, so I haven't seen her. I saw her maid bring her ladyship's breakfast tray to her room a short time ago, though." Davor remained by the door, waiting for further instructions.

The waiting valet made Mauro uncomfortable. "That will be all, Davor. I will be gone to the village later. Jero will assign your duties today."

Alone again, Mauro stood in front of the long looking glass when he had finished dressing. His father had an elegant taste in clothing and had kept current with the fashion. There was a collection of various stockings and cravats in the trunk as well. He was pleased that the shirt, waistcoat, and breeches were already a good fit. He had always thought of his father as being larger than him, but maybe it was because he always felt so small in his presence.

Mauro had not seen his father in years, even though the Toth lands were less than a week's travel from Baric Castle. His uncle came through the region often enough, so conducted any business with his brother from here. Mauro could have accompanied his uncle, but his father could have also traveled north to see him. It was now too late to ask him why he had stayed away.

Mauro looked around for his boots and found them by the door, cleaned and polished. One benefit of being Lord Baric, he reflected as he pulled them on. He was not looking forward to his plans for the morning, but he knew he had made the right decision, especially after talking to Jero last night. He would visit his mother's room first. It was not too late to reconcile with his mother, and that is what he hoped to do.

~ * ~

Mauro did not know why he should dread seeing his mother again. He stood in front of her solid door at the other end of the corridor and willed himself to knock. He was saved the trouble when the door opened, and out came a girl with a tray of empty breakfast dishes in her arms. She gave a little screech and stopped in front of him. "Pardons, my lord, I didn't see you there!"

"I would like to see my mother. Are you her maid?" Mauro asked the servant girl flatly.

"I am Natalija, my lord. I am the baroness' lady's maid since this summer," she answered timidly. She was a thin girl, but tall, and her light brown hair was tucked neatly under her small cap. Mauro thought she had a familiar look but could not quite put his finger on it.

Mauro noticed Davor coming from the servants' staircase and called him over to collect the tray from the girl's wobbling arms. Once her burden was lifted, he asked, "Are you from the village, Natalija?"

"I am, sir. My father is the tanner."

He remembered the village tanner, and that he had a son his age; he could see the resemblance now. Mauro wondered why his mother sought out the tanner's girl for her personal lady's maid; but there was a lot he did not know about his household yet. He dismissed Natalija and went through the open door.

Mauro expected to find his mother in her bed and she was, having just eaten her morning meal there. He took a deep breath and said, "Mother, I am so pleased to see you well." He walked to her bedside and bent to kiss her cheek. She was in her dressing gown, propped up on several colorful pillows, looking curiously at the man in front of her. She took his hand and squeezed it tightly, finally realizing it was her Mauritius.

"Look at you, my son, so grown up! So handsome, too! I will be glad to have you at home again!" Mauro had forgotten that his mother was so excitable. But this would be normal, he thought; the reaction one would expect from a mother missing her only child. Maybe he had been wrong about her.

Mauro had not seen Lady Johanna since he had left home at age thirteen, although there had been plenty of opportunities for her to visit him at Toth Castle. Her sister was his aunt Renata, the Countess of Toth, and the two had been very close when they were younger. It was the countess who had insisted his father, Lorenc Baric, marry her sister. Lady Johanna Toth had a fragile disposition, and Renata wanted Johanna to be closer to her childhood home, instead of being sent to a distant kingdom to marry.

"I am so glad to have you here. Is it not a shock, my dear? A terrible, terrible shock! I am not yet over it!" she exclaimed, reaching for her handkerchief. "The surgeon said it was an ague, and so sudden, too!"

"Yes, it is all very terrible," he agreed, watching her odd expression. He would have to get used to his mother's emotional tendencies again.

"And you have come back to take care of me and to take your rightful place as baron, my sweet boy!" Her need for him took him by surprise.

"Yes, Mother. I am back to take care of things," he assured her gently. "I am glad you did not catch this ague, as you call it. It took the lives of several others in the castle, I understand."

"Oh, yes, Mauro. Lorenc's four captains all perished from the fever. Poor Lorenc. My dear, sweet Lorenc," she said through tears.

His mother's new fondness for himself and his father was unexpected. He was uncomfortable with her sudden sentiment. He freed his hand from her grip and moved away from her bed. "I met your lady's maid outside the door. Is she a girl from the village?" he asked, changing the subject.

"Yes, she is such a pleasant girl, too, little Natalija! She has been good company to me these few months since Lorenc passed. She is only fifteen, but the last girl Renata sent my way was a loathsome creature, just like the one before." His mother dropped her handkerchief onto her lap and pulled out her fan from between the bedcovers; she batted it furiously in front of her face. "I decided I would not tolerate any more contemptuous girls from Renata's flock. I told her not to send any more lying, wicked Toth handmaids to vex me," she hissed through gritted teeth. This was the mother Mauro remembered.

"If you are happy with your new lady's maid, then I am pleased for you," he said, dismissing the subject.

He brought a chair over to her bedside. He would need to be seated before raising the topic he wished he could avoid. Mauro began cautiously, "Mother, I have hired a new steward."

She looked at him with concern. "Oh? Is Silvijo leaving us? Does he not want to work for you?"

"Silvijo Nestor will not be leaving. At least I do not think so." Mauro suddenly regretted talking to his mother before he talked to Nestor about the changes. "Jero will be my new steward, Mother. I have already asked him, and he has agreed."

Lady Johanna stared at her son with complete disbelief. "Jero? You want to replace Silvijo with the bastard boy?"

"Mother, it is not kind to call him that. He came to us as an orphan, and he has served Father well," Mauro said softly, trying to calm her.

"What was your father thinking, bringing such a worthless child into the house? What a nuisance he is to live with."

Change upset his mother, but Mauro was not asking her permission. He spoke firmly. "Jero is no longer a child, Mother. He is a man, like me. He is not a nuisance. He is quite capable, and he will be our new steward."

She looked at him as though seeing her son for the first time. She smiled. "Yes, of course, Mauritius. There is no need to shout."

"Of course not, Mother. I am sorry." He had not been shouting, but she seemed to have already forgotten the argument.

Mauro ventured to tell her his other difficult announcement. "There is something else I wanted to talk to you about. Uncle Vladimir said I will need to marry now. I am to honor the marriage contract Father made for me. Do you know about this arrangement?"

"Oh, yes, my dear," the baroness said with a broad smile. She looked at him with the keen eye of a matchmaker. "You had the choice between the two Dubovic daughters, but I am afraid the eldest could no longer wait; she has already married. The second daughter is not as pretty, but she is of age and will be quite suitable for you. It will be a pleasure for me to have grandchildren at the manor house."

Mauro closed his gaping mouth. He had never known his mother to enjoy the company of any children—certainly not her own children, and probably not his. But it was the comment about marrying a Dubovic daughter that surprised and troubled him more.

Baron Dubovic was a neighboring aristocrat with a significant estate, twice the size of the Baric lands, bordering them to the north. His forefathers had formed an alliance with the Dubovics long ago, and Mauro had not heard of a need to marry between the two families to keep it.

"Mother." He waited until he had her full attention again. "Did Father not tell you about the arrangement with the trader in Thessaloniki?"

"No, there is no arrangement with any trader," she exclaimed. "I told Lorenc he should tell Vladimir to mind his own business. He is always meddling in the Baric affairs."

"Uncle Vladimir governs the region, Mother, and the Barics are included in that. I do not think that could be called meddling," Mauro explained calmly.

She looked at him with disdain, but he was not shaken. "Do you remember when I was eleven, Mother, and it was decided that I would be betrothed to the daughter of Demetrius Kokkinos? He was the Near East trader that Father did business with. Is the name not familiar to you?" he asked.

"I have heard the name Kokkinos," she admitted. "Vladimir had no right to bind *my* son to the contract."

"Then you do know of the arrangement?"

She smoothed the covers on her bed as she composed herself. "Yes, now it is coming back to me. But that trading business is all in order again," she said with certainty, still fidgeting with the lace and satin coverlet. "You do not need to marry this Ottoman girl. You can marry the Dubovic girl in place of Mateo."

Mauro flinched. "Mother," he said firmly, "there will be no marriage with any Dubovic daughter. The Kokkinos contract is what *keeps* our trading affairs in order. I will have to marry this Ottoman girl, probably in the spring. Do I have your blessing?"

He wanted his mother's understanding. It was important that she accepted the changes to come and welcomed his new wife. His eyes told her so. "Of course, Mauro. Whatever you want, my son..." Her voice trailed off.

Mauro kissed her on the cheek again and put the chair back with the others at the polished table. His mother did not look over at him. Instead, she picked up the fan and waved it absently in front of her. Natalija was waiting outside the chamber, and she bobbed a curtsy as Mauro held the door for her to enter. Before the door closed again, he heard his mother ask her maid for her writing table, paper, and ink.

Chapter 6

Mauro took his time going down the stairs and listened to the various voices in the house. Too many were unfamiliar, he thought. Curious to put faces to the new voices, he rounded the corner at the end of the foyer to the kitchen entrance and looked in. The room stood at attention when they realized their master was at the open door.

"Where is Cook?" he asked the quiet room.

Nela had been the family cook Mauro's entire life and was the first face he noticed missing. She was loved by all of them, just like Idita was. She was older than his father, but Mauro would have been told if she had passed away.

"I am your cook, my lord," said a much younger version of the cook Mauro remembered. "I am Suzana, sir; at your service."

He was about to ask why Suzana was the Baric cook now, but at that moment Nestor came into the room behind Mauro. "Ah, yes," Nestor interrupted. "I was going to explain that there have been some changes in the kitchen. If you will come with me, my lord, we can discuss this in the study." Mauro took one last look at the nervous kitchen staff and followed Nestor back out the door.

The study had been Mauro's father's sanctuary. When Mauro's grandfather first built the manor house, there had been no study. Lord Fredrik had wanted to conduct business in the open, and he built the great hall to be the one grand room for both entertaining and negotiating. Lord Lorenc was not fond of endless entertaining like his father had been. He did not expect to host many balls and gatherings that would fill the great hall. Half the space was still larger than any castle hall in the region, so Mauro's father took it upon himself to make a new floor design when he claimed the barony.

Lorenc wanted intimacy in his home life—privacy, actually. He walled off the southern half of the great hall to make a sitting room, complete with a small terrace at the back of the house for his first wife, Margaret. The front entrance no longer opened directly into the great hall. It was walled-in to make the new foyer, with new double doors leading into the diminished great hall. Across from these doors, his private study was constructed. It was the only room that had just one key.

Nestor turned the lock on the heavy oak door, and Mauro instinctively took a seat at the long, waxed table near the entrance. Mauro had spent little time in his father's study as a boy, but when he was called there, it was to sit across from his father in this same seat.

"Has something happened to Nela?" Mauro demanded when Nestor took his father's seat across from him.

Nestor put his spectacles on and leaned in across the table. "I believe your father and his captains were poisoned," Nestor announced bluntly.

There was a rumor of this theory, but Nestor had also been the first suspect. He had been at the fateful meal and had survived. Mauro looked at the old man with disbelief. "So you replaced Cook, because you believe she poisoned my father?"

"It was actually the baroness' idea to dismiss her, not mine," Nestor defended himself. "Your mother had the entire kitchen staff replaced. Geoff and Verica were sent to work in the stables and as a housemaid, but all the others are gone."

"I have a question for you, Nestor. If you believe they were poisoned, how is it that you ate with the five men and yet did not become ill? Why should I not think you poisoned them?"

Nestor did not flinch at the direct accusation. "Yes, I ate with his captains that night. We had a merry meal, with a lot of wine and conversation," Nestor explained. "But I do not partake in alcohol. They all drank the wine, and I drank only water. I have come to the conclusion that the drink held the poison, not the food. That is why I was spared."

Mauro was still skeptical.

Nestor insisted, "I did not kill your father, and I do not believe the cooks did either. I told the surgeon that they were poisoned, and it was he who diagnosed them with a sudden ague just before they all died."

"Poisoned or plagued, I want the old kitchen staff reinstated," Mauro declared. "Find a place for Suzana if she stays, but I want Nela brought back."

"Of course, Mauro. I will do my best to find her."

Despite this new turn of events, Mauro was still determined to carry out his decision. "Nestor, I do not doubt your theory or your ability to manage this household. I am, however, relieving you of your duties as my steward."

The old steward's face went white with shock. "I have played no part in whatever crimes have been done here. I loved your father like a brother, Mauro. I would never hurt him."

Mauro poured Nestor a cup of water from the crock on the table and waited for him to recover. "I am sorry, Nestor. I want to believe you, and I will talk to this surgeon. If they were poisoned, someone must pay. But that is not why I am replacing you." Mauro continued his rehearsed speech before he lost his courage. "My father chose you as his steward when he was a young man, Nestor. I have struggled with this decision, but I am appointing Jero as mine."

"Jero? Do you realize—?" Nestor stopped short of explaining. He slumped back in the chair. "You are right to relieve me, Mauro. I am an old man, and I can understand your desire to have a younger steward to grow with you."

"Thank you, Nestor. I am glad you see it my way." Nestor rose from the table, but Mauro had more to say to him. "I have something else to ask you."

Nestor took his seat again.

"Your value to this family, and especially my father, is enormous. I will make Jero the new steward to the Baric estate, but I am asking you to stay on as my business advisor. I need you, Nestor." Mauro waited for a reaction, but Nestor stared at him blankly. "Jero is a clever man, and you can teach him what he needs to understand about the affairs of the estate. I will need to be taught everything, too." Mauro reached over and patted the elder man's hand as it rested next to his water glass. "Will you be my advisor, Nestor?"

Nestor's lips curled into a smile over his stained teeth as the words sunk in. He stretched his arms to his wigged head, the long lace from his sleeves floated down onto his upturned face. Mauro impatiently waited for an answer.

"I will stay on," he agreed, relaxing his arms at his sides again. "Yes, of course, I will." It was Mauro who now leaned back in his chair, unable to hide his relief. "You are right, Mauritius. Jero is a capable man like you are. I will help you in any way I can." With a regained vigor, he added, "Your father was a wealthy man, you realize. The tax debt is substantial this year, but so are the profits from the salt trade."

Nestor's passion came out when he spoke of business, and Mauro smiled at his new advisor's commentary. Feeling lighter now, he told Nestor, "I am glad to hear the House of Baric is prosperous. I have spent the last five years earning silver as an army officer, and I have not had much time to spend it. It is comforting to know I can leave it in the bank for now."

They both stood, and Mauro patted Nestor on the back in appreciation. "There is much I must learn about us," Mauro told him. "I have some other urgent business in the village today, but I would like to start with the account books first thing tomorrow."

"That is an excellent idea. I will send word to get the kitchen staff back and then sort out the account logs to go over with you in the morning."

Nestor settled in at the desk near the sunny, south window to begin his new role as advisor.

~ * ~

With two things accomplished, Mauro felt good when he walked out the front door and into the fresh, autumn air. The sky had cleared into a fine day, and the October sun gave heat to the late morning. He looked over at the green houses behind the Keep and saw his mother through the glass. She was inside with the gardeners. Other men were moving the tender citrus trees back into the green houses in expectation of the coming winter. Mauro decided against looking in on her project just now. She had a passion for flowers that was the opposite for people, and he expected she would still be there when he returned from the village.

Mauro continued on to the Keep tower to find his soldiers. Their assignments had been quickly completed earlier that morning, and they were waiting for him on the benches outside the great studded doors of the tower armory.

"Do not start thinking you will be sitting around sunning yourselves every morning. I have plans for you," Mauro called over to the three men.

"Mauro," Vilim shouted back, "we were just contemplating the same for you. You are usually an early riser. We expected to see you hours ago." Simeon and Hugo nodded in agreement.

"You know me well. It will not happen again," Mauro told them, smiling in return. "Have you had the chance to talk to the other soldiers? I hope they gave you your due respect."

"They seem like good men, Mauro," Simeon reported cheerfully. "We introduced ourselves, and they accepted it as fact, but of course it will make a difference if you give them instructions personally." Mauro agreed. "We found there are about thirty soldiers living in the quarters here on full duty as your Castle Guard. Another dozen or so live outside the walls in the cottages," Simeon added.

"They have had no regular training since the baron died three months ago. One older soldier, Eduard, has taken over their leadership, but he told us he is not trained to lead troops into combat," Vilim explained.

"You will need more officers," Hugo asserted. "Simeon and Vilim can lead the soldiers, but I am no good at commanding men."

"You will do fine as an officer, Hugo. But you are right, and I have already anticipated this news. I will ask Fabian Carrera and Stephan Padovi to come help me. They are experienced in training soldiers for warfare."

The men agreed that they would be the best choices.

Mauro went on to ask, "Have you found the lodgings suitable in the Keep? I must admit that I do not know the condition of it."

"It is quite suitable, especially after sleeping on the ground for three months," Vilim said. "The armory is just inside on the ground floor. That seems well-supplied with weapon of all kinds for about fifty men. There is an open sleeping hall with beds for your soldiers on the first floor."

"There is a special room upstairs for shitting. Did you know about that? Very fancy, Mauro," Hugo said with a chuckle. "You don't even have to go outside."

"I do know about that," Mauro said, laughing with the others. "We can thank the old Romans and the mountain springs for that Baric specialty. We have the usual outhouse with holes in the ground over there, if you prefer something less fancy, Hugo." He pointed to the back of the Keep.

The men rose from their bench in the warm sunshine. "Your man Nestor came to show us to different quarters this morning," Simeon pointed out. "Your father's officers had sleeping chambers on the second floor, and we have each been given a private room there."

Mauro acknowledged, "I am grateful you have seen me safely back to the castle, but you are not bound to stay. The general's order was to escort me home, and you have all done your duty well. You have now seen my castle. I am offering each of you a place here as an officer, if you want to stay on to join my Guard. General Toth has released you from his service. But if you want to go, I, too, will release you."

The three men had already talked of this choice earlier, and all three had come to the same decision. They were free men, but each had no home except the army barracks to go back to. They respected the baron as their commander and as a new friend. "We will stay on," Vilim answered cheerfully for the group.

Mauro was pleased and it showed in his broad smile. "Excellent. I would like you to come to the village with me this morning," Mauro said. "I have a few errands and could use the company. I remember it being a busy place, and you may find it to your liking."

Vilim spoke for all of them. "Then let us get our horses and have a look at our new home."

Chapter 7

The village had an official name: Solgrad. No one there had used the village's proper name for generations. The people of the region called it "Barics' Village," and those living there just called it "the village." It had once been a larger town with a thriving river port. There had been a boating channel to the sea, with open trade between the neighboring republics across the Adriatic. That was before the wars and plagues had reduced the prominent town's population to a small village again. The traders were long gone, and their vital river port had been left neglected, overgrown again by nature.

This place had always been the Barics' land, ruled by Baric ancestors, who had been in Solgrad for centuries. From the castle, situated on the western slope of the mountain range, the village was a quick, ten-minute gallop toward the Adriatic Sea on the guarded castle road.

The road to the village itself had been paved at one time, a souvenir from the Romans who had lived there for hundreds of years before the Croats arrived. Time and wear had taken its toll on other unmaintained roads, but the cut stones beneath the shallow, dirt covering kept the way smooth, even in the winter rains.

Salt had always been a part of life to the Barics, and it continued to be a profitable trading commodity. Along with their prized sea salt, the Barics sold fish and fruit, wine and olive oil, and wool and hides, too. The river provided as much bounty as the sea, and waterfowl and fresh fish were abundant at the local market.

Before the Venetians conquered the region, the town had been ruled by the Ottoman Empire. Trade among neighboring republics back then had not been forbidden, like it was under the Venetian law now. The Muslims built their mosques and brought their culture, soldiers, and unbending authority; but they let the local farmers and herders continue their traditions. More importantly, they allowed the Catholics continue their prayers. The town's people were a devout group, and through the rough times of plagues and occupation, they prayed to God for respite.

Lord Fredrik Baric, Mauro's grandfather, constructed the new church in the center of the village after the new manor house had been completed. The stone masons had built his villa with quality workmanship in record time, and he decided to keep them employed. They had plenty of stone from the nearby mountains, and there seemed to be endless funds at the time to pay for it.

The new church was modestly designed, like his manor house, not grand and complicated like a cathedral. It was spacious, and the inside was richly painted in the baroque style. Lord Fredrik had also commissioned a small school to be built next to it for the village children, and the citizens erected a statue in the town square to honor him for his noble generosity.

With all this activity, the Venetian councilmen began to make inquiries as to how Baron Baric was funding the elaborate civic projects. Lord Fredrik was motivated to subdue their unwanted attention to his quiet corner of the Empire, and nothing was built in the village after that. Lord Fredrik tragically died a short time later.

Life had its rhythm in the village, and today was market day. The streets leading to the town square were full of merchant carts. The main market square was halfway between the crossroad and the decaying river port. Few residents recognized their new lord as Mauro rode through the market-day crowd. The curious villagers knew he must be a nobleman from his finely groomed appearance, the rich fabric of his clothing, and the three armed strangers who flanked him. He had his favorite sword belted at his side and wore his tall, black riding boots, distinguishing him as a soldier of high rank.

Mauro's first stop that morning was at Constable Radic's office, situated just before the village square. The constable was called only by his surname, even by those who knew him well, and almost everyone in the village did. Radic had been chosen by his father nearly ten years ago. Mauro had only met the constable as a boy, when Radic had been the village bailiff. Mauro wanted an impression of the man's character and allegiance to decide whether he would need to choose a new one.

The constable was an important man in the village and to the Barics. He had jurisdiction to jail any person he deemed needed to be held until the matter could be resolved by the governing Venetian authorities. The Count of Toth, Mauro's uncle, was the regional judge for civil matters, but maritime crimes were handled by the Venetian Navy. Mauro had been warned by his uncle to make it a priority to learn the temperaments and personalities of the other Venetian agents he would have to negotiate with as the new baron, and Mauro took his advice to heart.

It was nearly noon, but there was little light coming from the open door to Radic's office. The shutters were closed on the building's windows. "Constable Radic?" Mauro said as he entered the dark room.

"That is me. Do I know you, sir?"

"Yes. But it has been a good ten years, sir."

Radic was a well-proportioned man with a full, unkempt beard and mismatched jacket. Seated at a plank table, he stared at the baron for a moment. "Ah, the young Lord Baric! I'd heard you had arrived yesterday, sir. It is good of you to come here so soon, my lord. I was going to ride up to the castle tomorrow."

He stood and shuffled his table clean of the scrolls of papers and dirty plates. He motioned to his new lord to take a seat on a low stool across from where Radic had been sitting. "Some wine, Lord Baric?"

"Do you have your own scouts then, Radic, if you already knew of my arrival?" Mauro asked as he sat down and accepted the mug of dark liquid.

"I know of everyone who enters your lands, sir. They are your scouts, my lord, but they report anything important that comes along the trade route. Your own Guard catches those entering from the east."

Radic looked like a man one would not want to deal with when angered, but who would happily cradle a babe on his barreled chest if a woman asked. Mauro liked his commanding appearance already, despite his disheveled attire. Radic was between wives, which was the reason for his sloppiness. His second wife had recently died giving birth to his third child.

Mauro took a swallow of the sour wine. Regretting it, he set the cup down. "I need some information on the particulars of the docks and the Venetians policing there. I have some other questions I hope you can answer as well, Radic."

"Let me get some light in here, my lord, and I will pull those books for you."

He went to the shutters and folded them back; a current of muggy air moved through the crammed space. The light from the opened windows showed the small room was lined with shelves of maps, scrolls, and log books; a bolted door along the wall hid a holding cell for any criminals. Radic looked out the open door and remarked, "I see there are soldiers outside. Are they yours, sir?"

"Those are my new officers. I will introduce you before I leave. They soldiered with the Toth Army and are excellent men," Mauro proudly informed him.

"Very good, sir." Radic set down the entry journals and log books. "Here are the current records, my lord. Where shall we start?"

"Who is the bailiff in the village now? I heard Grgur was killed," he asked straight off.

"Aye, my lord. I am sorry to tell you that you heard correctly. Old Grgur passed last year."

Grgur had been a soldier in his father's Guard before taking the bailiff job of managing village disputes for the Barics. He had also been with Mauro on the day Mateo had died.

Radic went on to explain, "Your new bailiff is Anton, sir. He is a trustworthy man. There has not been any trouble this year to report. He collects rents in October after the harvest, so is meeting with several of your tenants this week. I will have him call on you at the castle, if that is to your liking, sir," Radic proposed. Mauro agreed.

After elaborating on the Venetian inspection protocol, Radic and the baron went over the security procedures in place for the village; they scanned the log book of the residents; and they discussed past troubles on the public roads crossing the Baric lands. When Mauro was satisfied he had learned what he had come for, he introduced the constable to his new officers.

"You have been most helpful to me today, Radic," Mauro said. "Come with Anton when he visits the castle. I may have thought of more questions by then." Mauro had already mounted his horse when he remembered to ask, "Where can I find the surgeon who doctored my father?"

"That would be Signor Sandrigo, your lordship. He has been here only a few months, so I have not had many dealings with him. His office is above the apothecary." The constable directed him to cross the bridge and follow the street to the end. "I look forward to our next visit, Lord Baric." Radic bowed respectfully and Mauro tipped his broad, felt hat to the constable.

The four men slowly rode through the crowd and across the bridge. Word had passed through whispers up and down that the new baron was visiting the constable. Within the hour that Mauro had been sequestered with Radic in his office, the entire village knew who he was.

The four took their time looking in the merchant windows and making light conversation with the goods handlers on the main street that led to the market square. The soldiering men were not used to a leisurely pace, but quickly became accustomed to the friendly manner and cheerful greetings they received.

The scent of roasting meat made them put aside the apothecary for a noon meal. The sign over the door of the sprawling, two-storied tavern depicted an image of a green goose. The main floor was crowded with hungry customers, so they made their way through the tables of whispering onlookers and found an empty one at the back near the kitchen door.

The owner, a short, plump woman with a starched apron and brightly colored skirts, came with a pitcher of frothy ale to greet them. She had a booming voice, since she was hard of hearing after having worked in such a noisy place for most of her life.

"Hello, gentlemen," she said cheerfully. "I have not seen you in my tavern before. Welcome to the Green Goose. Can I bring you four meals?"

The men were not particular about what they would eat for lunch and nodded their agreement. "Yes, thank you, good lady. I am the new Baron Baric, and these are my officers, Simeon, Hugo, and Vilim. If your food tastes as good as it smells from the doorway, you may expect to see us again."

She stared openly at the Baric men with more than a passing interest. It meant good business to have gentlemen patronize her establishment, especially Lord Baric himself. The tavern woman managed a small curtsy with the limited floor space and her ample skirts. She quickly found her tongue after having so casually addressed the new baron, and introduced herself with as much grace as she could muster.

"I had not heard you had arrived, your lordship. Welcome to you, sir, and to your officers, too," she said excitedly. She looked from face to face as she poured their drinks, thinking these were fine men, to be sure. "My name is Andrea. You will find, Lord Baric, sir, that this is indeed the best eating establishment in the region. And should you need any other services, gentlemen…" She let her words hang in the air, winked at Hugo, whom she considered the most attractive of the three young soldiers, and then cocked her head in the direction of the bar being tended by two pretty women busily serving the local men leaning against it.

"Thank you, Andrea. For now we shall just require a meal," Mauro said with a dignified expression. Andrea left with a whoosh of her skirts as Mauro watched his companions glance eagerly at the women behind the bar. He was not so certain his men would have answered the same.

The kitchen was a small building just outside the back of the tavern. Andrea rushed to her daughter, who was tending the grilled meat. "Tatjana, my love, take a quick peek through the door at the four gentlemen sitting at the third table."

Tatjana did as she was told. "Who are those gentlemen?"

"The clean-shaven one is the new Baron Baric himself. You can bring them their lunches and have a better look. Make a good impression, Tatjana dear, and we will have some new customers," her mother counseled. "Let me fix that smudge on your face first." Andrea took the corner of her apron and blotted her daughter's rosy cheek.

Tatjana was about to go through the door but shut it again. "Drat! Lord Dubovic is just walking to their table," she hissed back to her mother. "I will bring their food after he leaves them, or I won't have a chance to get their full attention."

A well-dressed gentleman approached Mauro's table from the other side of the room. "Mauritius Baric, is it not?"

Mauro was not certain, but he guessed the man to be Baron Dubovic, whom he had discussed just this morning with his mother. It was not by chance that the neighbor was at the Baric village. He, too, had scouts.

Mauro quickly scanned the confident, stout man of his father's age. The neighboring lord casually held a large, double-plumed hat in one hand and a silver-topped walking stick in the other. He was wigless, with a thick mane of dark, gray-streaked hair tied back with a velvet ribbon. A flourish of pale lace was ruffled high on his collar, making him look as though his head were perched directly on his deep purple waistcoat, which was covered by his long, gray taffeta jacket. The same pale ivory lace of his collar flowed out from his sleeves, covering his jeweled hands. He did not look like he would be traveling the dusty roads by horse; he looked to be dressed for a visit to the Royal Court.

"Am I correct in addressing Lord Dubovic?" Mauro replied. Dubovic bowed slowly to indicate Mauro had guessed correctly. "I am glad to meet you, sir. I just arrived home yesterday, and I am acclimating myself to the village once again."

"If I remember, you were just a boy when you left, Lord Baric. I am sure you have forgotten your little village in all your travels. It is unfortunate to come back under such circumstances. Please accept my sympathies for your father's sudden, tragic death. He was a good man and a good friend to my family." The aristocrat's words were silky and convincingly heartfelt. "I would wish to invite you to my manor for dinner soon, but unfortunately I am heading to Zadar on business. That is the reason I am in your village for my lunch. I was just leaving when I noticed your party coming in."

Lord Dubovic looked around the table at the three military men, expecting an introduction. Mauro caught the subtle request. "Ah, may I introduce my new officers: Vilim, Simeon, and Hugo. They were with me in the Toth Army, and they will be leading my Castle Guard." The men stood with the introductions, and each gave a short bow to the stranger before taking their seats again. "We have much to talk about, Lord Dubovic, and I would be glad to dine with you when you return."

"My daughter would dine with us, too, of course. She is yet unmarried and is living with me at our home this winter. I have recently spoken with your mother, the Lady Baric, and she thought you might be considering marriage, now that you are settling down." Baron Dubovic smiled slyly, showing two gold teeth along one side of his grin. He waited for Mauro's affirmation.

The three soldiers listened with hidden amusement. Mauro was not amused. He did not want any misunderstanding, so told Dubovic the truth of his arrangement. "I am to marry, sir, but it was arranged years ago by my father. In her grief, my mother may have forgotten the fact that I am betrothed going on twelve years now, and my bride will join me in the spring."

Baron Dubovic masked his disappointment. "Well then, I wish you congratulations and much happiness. This does not affect my dinner invitation, of course, Lord Baric." He chuckled lightly, but Mauro saw the look of contempt show through. "I will send a messenger when I return." He bowed again at the table in general.

"I look forward to it, sir. I bid you a safe journey, Lord Dubovic." He watched the man with curiosity as he left, meeting his two escorts by the door. An odd feeling washed over Mauro as he watched the door shut behind them.

The food arrived at that moment, and the visitor was quickly forgotten. Tatjana politely reached across each one, exposing the tops of her full breasts as she refilled their mugs. She had made her desired impression. That was all the convincing the soldiers needed to return to the Green Goose later for a second visit after dark that night.

It was all falling into place for Mauro's first day as baron. After the satisfying meal and rounds of ale, Mauro managed to find the tailor's shop and also expedite his messages to his friends, Fabian and Stephan. He sent the letters to Toth Castle, where his friends' whereabouts would be known and his correspondence forwarded. The surgeon's shop, however, was closed. The keeper of the apothecary below the shop did not know where Signor Sandrigo had gone so hastily with his packed bags that morning. Mauro would not get his answers.

With the other errands accomplished, the group made the easy ride back to the castle just a few hours later.

Chapter 8

It took a few days for Jero to adjust to his role as managing steward. He was given a private chamber on the floor with the Baric residents, instead of a bed in the servants' dormitory. Mauro had insisted Jero wear his own wardrobe rather than his assigned servant's uniform. Jero had confided to Mauro that beyond his two valet costumes, he had only one change of clothes for Sunday Mass and one for riding. He had no other clothes and no money to purchase any. Mauro decided the easiest remedy was for the visiting tailor to fit three new ensembles from his father's trunk for Jero as well. Jero was grateful for Mauro's generosity and promised to work hard to repay the gifts.

Mauro and Jero spent the next few weeks confined in the study, poring over the account books with Nestor. Mauro was impressed with his new employee. Jero already knew quite a lot about the trading routes and the markets for the produce they sold, in addition to the special shipments with Demetrius Kokkinos. Nestor familiarized both of them with the names of the various customers and their particular payment schedules. Some customers traded other valuable goods for the Barics' commodities—some paid with lire, and some transactions were not on the books at all, but recorded in another account log not given to the taxman.

The taxes owed to the Empire were negotiated by Signor Rosso, a stout man who rode up and down Dalmatia on behalf of the Republic. Rosso was a Venetian bureaucrat, but had lived in Croatia for many years collecting and recording the landlords' debts to the government.

In the feudal days, it was enough for an aristocrat to provide the realm with an army and manage the lands for the Empire. But the Venetians did not consider themselves a kingdom in that sense. They were a governed democracy. Each must pay their share; even the aristocracy. In addition to his duty to help protect Venetian lands, Baron Baric also owed a hefty monetary contribution. Whether the baron collected all of the taxes from his own population or paid it from his pocket was not the Empire's concern.

On this day, they met with the tax collector to introduce the new baron and his newest steward, as well as to confirm that the rules for the late Lord Lorenc Baric applied to the new Lord Mauritius Baric. Signor Rosso sat at the long table in the study. Nestor and Jero were across from him, and Mauro paced at the window. "You know that we will have to draw up new documents, Signor Nestor. This will not do at all," the taxman reminded him.

"We shall copy these documents with the new names and be done with it, Signor Rosso. What could be simpler?" Nestor insisted.

Rosso shook his head. "Any time there is a change like this, the entire estate must be reviewed. And for that, we will have to send new documents to Venice." He put down his quill and waited for Nestor to agree. Nestor did not.

"I understand there is protocol, but nothing has changed except for the first name of the baron and to record a second steward's signature. I assure you, the business and the estate are exactly as they were under Lord Lorenc Baric." Nestor leaned across the table and picked up the man's quill. He held it out to him.

"Your horse looks tired, sir," Mauro said from across the room, staring out into the courtyard. "Perhaps it is time for a new one. Maybe one with a new saddle as well. That might make your trip here more comfortable next time."

Signor Rosso thought about his offer. "Yes, it might, sir," he agreed. "Especially, Lord Baric, if the saddle had an extra pouch." Rosso took the quill and gave the smiling Nestor a hard look.

"Done, sir," Mauro told him, turning from the window. "Thank you, Signor Rosso. I shall leave you and my stewards to finish the paperwork. I must step out for a moment."

Mauro met the three men at the stables an hour later. Alberto had helped him choose a gelding from his herd with a strong back and a gentle reputation. He had picked out one of his father's extra saddles and had it readied with a pouch of silver coins and a bottle of their finest Italian wine in the side saddlebag. Lorenc Baric was thought to be one of the lesser noblemen of the Royal Croatian line. His contributions to the Empire had not been scrutinized during his tenure, although he earned a substantial income on the side. In the end, Signor Rosso agreed to extend Lorenc Baric's lower tax burden for his son. Signor Rosso rode off smiling and waved back as he left on his new horse. Mauro had gotten off cheaply today.

With that behind them, the three walked casually back toward the house. The tax duties and customer accounts had been thoroughly considered, but there was one other urgent matter that Mauro's advisor wanted to discuss today.

"The count gave me orders to arrange your marriage, Mauro. You are aware of that, I hope."

Mauro was aware; the requirements of an unmarried nobleman were very transparent. Mauro paused under the large oak on the path that led to the front door as Nestor explained, "The Kokkinos girl is nineteen now, and her father is waiting for your instructions. Have you contacted her?"

"I have not had any correspondence with the Kokkinos family at all. I suppose I should have. To be honest, I was hoping the entire thing would go away."

Jero did not know the details of the betrothal and was curious about it. "I am sure she is a pleasant girl. Have you ever met her?" he asked.

"Yes, in fact I have," Mauro told him. "I was sixteen and traveling to Athens with my cousins to visit the ancient monuments. My uncle thought it would be good that we meet, since it was only a slight detour to Thessaloniki." Mauro had an odd look on his face as he recalled the visit. "Our planned detour had not been announced to them, I think, because they seemed very surprised by our arrival. There were several boys playing in their courtyard, or at least they were all dressed like boys. One of them was my future bride."

"Your bride is surely a girl!" Jero said, laughing nervously.

"Oh, I am sure she is. Later that day she was formally presented to me, dressed as a pretty girl of course, but under layers of silk robes and a veil hiding her face. I do not know what she is like now. She was only twelve at the time, so she did not make much of an impression on me. By what I could tell, I did not impress her either. I do not think it was love at first sight, Jero."

"You do not have to marry for love. You marry for posterity," Nestor told both young men. "You should write to her family today. The weather will begin to turn soon, and the message may take a while to arrive. I suggest you go there in the spring."

Mauro had already thought of the wedding and replied, "I do not think I can manage a voyage to Greece and be back for the salting season. It is important to me that I supervise the first shipments. She will have to come to me, and we will be married here."

Nestor considered Mauro's idea. "Most women want their family at the wedding. Would you welcome them to come with your new wife?"

"If it is necessary, yes, they could come. Of course, they are welcome." Mauro tried to sound convincing. "I suppose I could send the request for her hand and not mention any specific invitation for the family. It would be assumed, would it not? I will leave the details to you, Nestor."

"As you wish," Nestor replied, unfazed by the task. "One last detail to consider would be a gift for your bride. It should be something personal, something significant. Sometimes these gifts must be planned ahead."

"I will consider it, Nestor. Thank you. That is good advice," Mauro said cheerfully, now that the burden of wedding planning had been assigned to Nestor.

~ * ~

Mauro had a new appreciation for his father and his uncle. Besides running an estate with all the problems that arose in the village and with the many tenants working his land, there were still wars being fought and bandits causing trouble on the trade route. He knew he had to get his castle army organized.

Vilim, Hugo, and Simeon had been good choices to lead his Guard. They were already respected and well-liked by the Baric guardsmen in just their first few weeks there. Mauro wanted to have a trained militia from the village men, as well, but that would have to wait for now. He had not yet heard back from Fabian or Stephan as to whether they would join his small army. Had his friends even survived the last siege?

The highest priorities had been marked off the baron's list. Mauro and Jero were confident that Nestor had covered all the facts and details for the running of the house and the Barics' business. The letter had been sent to Thessaloniki instructing Terese Kokkinos that the marriage would take place in Croatia, and, in the end, invited her family to attend the ceremony with her. To everyone's relief, there had been a happy ending to Nestor's search for the dismissed kitchen staff. The Barics' old cook, Nela, and Franja, her assistant, had been found working at a distant castle to the south. Suzana, feeling affronted by the search, decided not to stay on. Nestor reported that the same baroness who had released Nela back to them had hired Suzana in her place.

When Mauro learned Nela had arrived home, he anxiously went to greet her. Nela was standing with her back to him, sorting things in the kitchen, but he knew her right away. She always wore brightly colored skirts of red or orange, with a white cap over her thinning, gray hair. She was energetic and moved about quickly, despite her age of sixty and her plump, round size.

Nela was unloading her basket of vegetables when Mauro declared, "I have waited years to have supper with you again, Nela. Of course, you will have to make it." She turned and gave a low curtsy to her new lord, then walked over and gave him a lingering hug that he returned, sinking into her motherly arms.

Nela stepped back. "Praise be to God, your lordship. I am overwhelmed by your loyalty, and don't know how I can ever thank you. I was beyond myself to have to leave. I have lived at this castle for fifty years, my lord. I loved the baron. To think they thought I would poison him." She dabbed her tearing eyes on her clean apron.

Mauro was sincerely moved to see old Cook in tears. "I know, Nela. I am sorry you were sent away. It was a mistake and a misunderstanding. No one thinks that anymore."

Nela sniffled to stop her tears, then grinned a toothy smile. She had her hands on her hips, looking the young baron up and down. He was head and shoulders taller than Cook, but he felt like a little boy again standing there under her gaze. "You have grown into quite a sight for these old eyes," she proclaimed. "You were always the handsome one, sir. I am glad to see you safe at home again."

"And I you," he told her with a relieved smile. He looked around the kitchen, then said, "I have not met the other cook."

Franja had been standing back in the shadow of the pantry door. She was tall for a woman, with few noticeable curves under her layered skirts, considering she worked in the kitchen where the servants were well-fed. She had plain features, with light brown eyes, a smallish nose, and pale skin, but she was pleasant to look at. Her long, brown hair was carefully pinned into a swirling bun at the base of her neck, and she wore a crisp linen cap on the top of her head.

She stepped out into the room and curtsied with her eyes downcast. "I am called Franja, my lord. I was here for eight years, and I, too, thank you for the second chance, sir. You will not regret it." She finally looked up at him.

"You can thank the soldiers, Franja. They told me that you are the best baker in the entire Republic, and they must have you back." Franja smiled brightly with her crooked teeth. Mauro looked over at Nela and asked, "Is that true?"

"I will say nothing, my lord, or you will send me away again and only keep Franja," Nela boasted about her young assistant. She busily pulled onions from her basket while she talked. "I let her do all of the sweets and bread baking now, if that is all right. I keep to just the savories and puddings. Franja will put five pounds on you this month with her cakes and pastries."

"I shall look forward to that. But there is one thing I must ask of you." She set her onions down. "We are still mourning my father's death, but it was suggested that we have a feast to celebrate my arrival."

"That is a lovely idea, my lord. When will the feast be held?" she asked.

"In two days, Nela." He saw her eyes widen. A grand meal for an extra hundred people took many days to prepare. "I am sorry it seems hasty. I will be taking a group of soldiers to tour the estate the day following the feast, and we will be gone for at least ten more."

Nela sighed but told him, "I worked in the kitchens when Lord Fredrik, God bless his merry soul, had three feasts a week and a gala ball once a month, sir. The hunters could hardly keep up with the butchering for the roasting pits. You shall have your grand feast in two days, my lord, or I am not worthy of your kitchen." With that, she took out her knife and began chopping.

~ * ~

The banquet was an elaborate celebration, and Cook outdid herself with a multitude of platters, puddings, and roasts to feed more than could fit at the tables in the great hall. Noblemen and landlords from the neighboring estates came to meet the new Baron Baric. The constable, bailiff, wealthy tradesmen, and anyone of importance in the village all joined the Baric household in officially welcoming him. Even Lady Johanna, who no longer enjoyed gatherings, came down in her splendid aristocratic pomp, bejeweled despite her black gown of mourning. Casks of ale and wine had been opened hours before, and the drunken group pranced and danced jigs to the local musicians' tunes well into the night.

The traveling party left later than their planned dawn departure for their ten-day tour, but the merriment of the night before had been a welcomed release. Mauro had talked to every visitor and was spared the hangover, since he was forced to converse more than drink. Vilim and Hugo were not so lucky, and the ride the next day was not an easy one for them.

"We will just go to the salt fields for our first stop," Mauro told them as they galloped south from the village crossroad to the next turnoff toward the sea. This was the guarded road to the tidal flats along the shallow seashore where the salt was harvested. Mauro and his entourage waved to the soldiers as they passed the first gates.

Mauro pitied his youngest captain, who swayed uncomfortably on his horse. "How much wine did you drink last night, Hugo? Find a spot in the shade somewhere while the rest of us have a look around."

Simeon explained, "Hugo discovered brandy, Mauro, which he thought he liked very much. I think he is still drunk on it." The other soldiers chuckled along with Simeon at their friend's misery.

Fortunately for Hugo, Mauro spent several hours inspecting the salt operation and talking to the Huzjak family, who had been the Barics' lead salt miners for generations. Jakov, the family patriarch, and his five sons worked the brackish fields and dried the piles of salt all summer. October had ended with crisp, dry weather, and they had been able to glean the last of the salt harvest for the season. They already had it packed and stored before the first November storms would arrive.

Mauro was satisfied with the workings of the production. He trusted the Huzjak's loyalty for now, because his father and his grandfather had trusted them. Mauro believed they were loyal not because of their fondness for their employer, but because the Barics had always paid them well for their services and their discretion. Mauro would continue to do so.

From there, Mauro and his group of nine guardsmen traveled in a large loop through his lands, stopping to meet each of his tenant farmers and inspect the fields that they worked for him. The mountainous land boasted productive orchards with apricots, almonds, olives, and grapes in the fertile valleys. The main harvests had finished for the year, and the fields had just been readied for the winter. The farmers had time to discuss their needs for the next planting and growing season. Mauro was glad for the chance to put faces with the names he had read in his account journal. He also got the opportunity to recruit a few young men for his militia, should he need to call for more soldiers to fight for him one day.

The weather was still pleasant for November, and Mauro's company was able to camp out each night, even though they were politely offered accommodations at each farm they visited. At the end of ten days circling the tenant farms, Mauro decided they would enjoy one night at the small villa given to him when he had come of age. It was in a valley at the far eastern boundaries of his estate, near the territorial border now controlled by the Habsburg Empire. The neighboring land owners were old family allies, and they did not care which empire collected their taxes. Truces were still respected, and Mauro was not concerned for his safety as they rode along the border trail.

The villa house had a permanent keeper, Erwin, who readied it as needed. Nestor had sent a message earlier to notify him of the baron's possible arrival in the coming week. Mauro and the soldiers rode through the low mountain pass, chatting of the pending pleasure of a warm fire and sleeping under a roof that night. Mauro had not considered that traveling on his own land could be dangerous to him after years of dodging musket balls in foreign fields. They never made it to his villa. In the dim twilight, just a mile out from their destination, the Baric soldiers were attacked by unseen raiders among the cliffs. Two of his men were badly injured from the fighting, and Mauro himself took a bullet in his left shoulder. He did not remember anything after that.

~ * ~

Mauro was in his own bed sleeping when his two friends came bursting into his room. Idita had sent them in to see if they could finally wake their drugged friend. Fabian jostled the bed as he plopped down next to Mauro. "Mauritius, you lazy dog," Fabian said loudly, "is that all you can do is sleep, now that you are a wealthy baron?"

Mauro opened his eyes and focused on the intruders. Fabian smiled down at him. "I am glad to see you open your eyes. We have been here two days already, and you have been out the entire time," Fabian said softly now. "You cannot die on us, now that Stephan and I have come to rescue you."

"What day is it?" Mauro asked. He had a hard time getting the words out of his dry mouth. His head was foggy, and he didn't know if he had actually spoken or had only dreamed the question.

"It is the sixteenth of November," Stephan replied from the side of the bed. He handed him a cup of water, and Mauro tried to sit up to take it. "We arrived just in time to watch your nurse dig the bullet out of your shoulder, old friend. Here, let me help you." Stephan propped the pillows behind his friend and put the cup to Mauro's lips.

"The wound did not look too awful, Mauritius. It was a clean shot, and your brother's hand caught it. You will live to fight again," Fabian assured him.

"I suppose that is good news, Fabian. But I did not expect to be attacked on my own land," he said hoarsely. "I cannot remember what happened after I was shot, though." He took a long drink.

"We talked to your man Jero," Stephan began. "He told us there was an ambush. One of your soldiers is dead." Mauro shut his eyes at the news; he was not ready to ask who had lost his life. Stephan went on to explain, "The others are recovering Mauro, but your mother took ill when she heard about your injury."

Mauro felt the pull of responsibility and tried to get out of bed. "Careful, my friend! You are not strong enough to get up," Fabian warned. He helped Mauro steady himself on the edge of the bed.

Stephan sat on the other corner of the bed next to him and finished explaining, "They called for a physician. It was only the shock, and he expects her to recover quickly."

Mauro nodded groggily. "I am glad you have come."

"Do you want to get dressed?" Fabian handed him a shirt, but Mauro was unable to take it.

He winced in pain at the attempt. "I cannot move my arm."

Fabian helped Mauro guide his good arm through the loose sleeve. Stephan filled glasses with the wine from the bottle there on the table. He passed one to Fabian as Jero entered the room apprehensively, not wanting to disturb the reunion. Mauro managed a weak smile. "Come in, Jero."

Jero approached the bed and handed him an envelope. "A message arrived from Thessaloniki this morning, my lord."

Mauro held the letter in his good hand for a moment and stared at it pensively. He handed it back to Jero. "Will you read it to us?" Mauro asked him quietly.

Jero unsealed the papers. He was worried it might be in Greek, but it was written in Latin. "It reads: 'To His Lordship, Baron Mauritius Baric. I humbly accept the invitation of marriage for my daughter, Terese Helena. You can expect her arrival by coach in the month of May, 1648. She will be accompanied solely by her trustworthy friend and companion, Ruby Spiros. Please confirm and acknowledge the timing is to your satisfaction. Your most humble and obedient servant, Demetrius Kokkinos. Thessaloniki, 25 October 1647.'" Jero set the letter down.

The three men all looked at Mauro, who had shut his eyes again, sinking back onto his pillows. He had not told his soldiering friends he was doomed to finally fulfill the contract to marry the girl he had met only once. Fabian poured wine into Mauro's cup and held his own out to him.

"To your wedding," Fabian toasted his friend, looking at him with a solemn expression. Mauro held up his own wine with his sleeved arm. Fabian drank his down in one gulp, then laughed heartily. He passed the bottle back to Stephan, who helped himself to more.

"I am sorry I find this so amusing, Mauritius! Three months without us, and look at the troubles you have—a bullet in your shoulder and a bride on her way. We won't leave your side again, or who knows what might happen to you. Cheers, Mauro. All will be well."

Mauro felt better already. It would all work out. He looked up at his grinning companions standing over him and began to laugh, too. The new mood was contagious; Jero joined in the celebration, and the bottle was soon emptied.

Chapter 9

Baric Castle, May 1649

The steam rose in threads of shimmering gray around her as her lady's maids giggled and swam in the hot bath. She smiled at their pleasure, wishing her heart was light again. It was nearly summer, and she should be splashing with her little brothers under the Aegean sun. She was now the Baroness of Baric; she could never go back to her old life. She wished she were still just Resi, the daughter of Demetrius and Celine Kokkinos, loved in their crowded villa in Thessaloniki.

She looked over to Ruby, her best friend since childhood, who was lounging with the two servant girls in the large pool. Resi did not know how she would have coped the first months here without her dear friend. Ruby was to be sent back to Thessaloniki sometime soon, but she wished it could be never.

Resi's husband had built her this bathhouse on the grounds of the Baric estate. It was an elaborate wedding gift, she knew, and she was grateful for it. Resi tried to convince herself that it had been given out of love, but there was little love in her husband's company. Her simple wedding had taken place in the small Baric chapel, performed by the village priest one week following the funeral of her future mother-in-law.

Resi and Ruby had been en route to Solgrad, halfway through the month-long journey by carriage to her new home, when a messenger delivered the news of the baroness' death. She had never met Lady Johanna Baric, but she was sad for her new husband and wanted to hurry to be there with him. They continued their journey north, and the marriage went on as planned shortly after her arrival. But there were no festivities surrounding her wedding, and there had been little joy at the house since then. That was almost a year ago.

Despite their shy first weeks together, her husband shared her bed for a time, and he seemed to find pleasure in her and in his new situation. Resi found him to be a quiet man, contemplative and occupied during the day with his endless duties as a baron. She longed to know more about her new husband, but the baron's world included more than a new wife to focus on. He would be gone for weeks at a time without notice. Some trips were short, to neighboring estates for political meetings. Some were extended; he and his entire Guard had been called to faraway battles several times this year already. When home, he often slept on a spare bed in his study, instead of sleeping with her in their private chamber. It was to finish estate business without disturbing her, he had told her, but she did not believe that was the reason. It had been a lonely first year together with Mauro.

The servants were teaching Ruby to speak Croatian, and their laughter at her efforts lulled Resi back to the present. She thought about the day ahead of her and the plans she should be making, if she was going to finally do what she had been too afraid to do all these months.

"Are you unwell, Resi?" Ruby asked as she stepped out of the pool. She wrapped a linen drape around her and sat by her friend on the marble bench.

"No, Ruby. I am feeling exceptionally well today. I think I am finally over my queasiness. I am ready to go back inside, though," she told her. Resi stood up and reached for her silken robe hanging on the wall peg.

Resi and her lady's maids were certain she was pregnant, since two months had passed with no courses. They told her to wait for a quickening to be sure, but she knew the feeling of being pregnant already. Resi had lost the first child she was carrying just before November. She had wanted to be the one who told him, and Resi was heartbroken when he had learned the news of their loss from the servants. Her husband had looked at her with such disappointment, like she had chosen not to give him an heir.

Her mother had warned Resi that a marriage such as hers was a contract, and sometimes there would not be love between a husband and a wife. Resi thought she could love Mauro. He was physically pleasing; his tall, trim figure was masculine and satisfying for her to lie with. She found him attractive with his neatly cropped, sandy locks that framed his strong face and striking green eyes. When she caught him smiling at her, his stare would be warm, and she knew he could love her, too—one day.

The marriage arrangement was to provide Baric children, but she had failed at the first try. He did not come to her bed again until Christmas, and after that only on a few occasions because of the escalating conflicts that called him away. The last time she saw Mauro was a little more than two months ago, on the eve he was to ride out with his soldiers to join with his uncle's army. She thought back on their quiet evening together before he had left. They had dined alone in their chamber, and he had made love to her tenderly by the lit fire. She remembered fondly how he had held her close in bed that night while she fell asleep. The next morning she woke feeling a new connection to her reserved husband, but he had already departed.

Mauro must have known he would be away for so long, or he would not have made such a special effort that last night. She had been worried for him and the other Baric soldiers. This morning a messenger finally came with word that the fighting was over, and they were expected to be home in two weeks. She felt a rush of excitement thinking about his arrival. She would make him happy with her news that she was with child again.

Back in her bedroom, Resi watched her maid fold the garments and hang the still clean gowns in the wardrobe. Verica liked to leave her mistress with a tidy room, and Resi never argued. She was grateful to have her help.

Verica was one of the servant girls who had grown up at the Baric estate. Resi's husband had chosen Verica as her lady's maid to help his wife quickly learn all about the castle and her new household. Verica was young, just sixteen, but Resi was glad for his choice and enjoyed the energetic girl's company.

Over their year together, Verica had slowly taken charge of her mistress' appearance. Resi had a simple taste in clothing. Her life in a Greek shipping family with only brothers had been quite different from that of a gentlewoman in a castle. She was not used to dressing in the full, stiff skirts and plunging bodices that were the normal attire for aristocrats here. She liked her loose, flowing robes and belted waistcoats.

Resi continued to wear her long, wavy hair tied with ribbons straight down her back, and not curled and pinned high on her head, as was the fashion of a noblewoman. Verica had tempted the baroness to let her create something different each evening, even if it was only for her to see in her looking glass. She took pride in styling Resi's flowing locks to enhance her striking light eyes and soft features. Soon Resi agreed to wear these styles during the day as well.

Resi's mother was from the Kingdom of France, not the southern lands of the Ottoman Empire. The Kokkinos children all had light olive skin, soft brunette hair, and gray-blue eyes, a blend of the mother's fair complexion and their father's dark features. Her father's family was Salonikan for generations, until his fateful voyage around the Atlantic landed him in France for several years. There, he had met her mother, the daughter of a sea captain, and they had fallen immediately in love. He took her back to his ancestral home to continue the successful trading business of his own father.

"Will you be needing anything else, my lady?" Verica asked as she picked up the tray of used teacups from a small table.

"No, Verica. I think I will read a little while by the window before the light is gone. I will see you at supper."

Verica ventured to ask, "Was there good news today? Are the soldiers coming home soon?"

Many of the Baric soldiers were friends that Verica had grown up with, and Resi forgot that she would be worried for them, too. "Yes. All is well, Verica. We can expect them back in a few weeks' time."

"Is the war over?" Verica lingered to ask.

"I don't know. One battle is over and another starts. I think my husband must be a good commander if his uncle keeps calling him away to fight his wars. I hope he stays."

"I will leave you to your reading now, my lady," Verica said softly and closed the door.

Resi leaned against the cushions of the window seat and opened the book she had recently bought on the recommendation of the village bookseller. It was by the Englishman William Shakespeare and was a collection of his poems. She loved poetry and loved to read. She had been taught to read in Greek as a girl with her brothers. Her father had let her continue sitting in on their lessons, and she learned to read Latin and Ottoman Turkish as well. She did not think to bring many books with her when she packed her possessions for her new life. She was disappointed when she found only old, cracked history and religious volumes on the shelves of their sitting room. She began going once a week to the village to visit the book merchant, and after a year had a fine collection hidden away.

In the quiet of her room, Resi found she was too restless for even her wonderful poems. Mauro would be home in a fortnight, and she was both anticipating and dreading his return. She wanted to make some changes, but did not know how to go about it. Resi needed some advice, but had not yet dared to ask the one person in the castle who might be able to help her. She summoned her courage and slipped on her shoes to visit Idita.

Resi had never been in Idita's private chamber. She hesitated as she rapped on her door and opened it. The room was smaller than the Barics', but identical to Ruby's chamber just next door. Where Ruby's room was sparsely furnished and airy, Idita's was filled from floor to ceiling with a lifetime collection of small furnishings, rugs, and tapestries. A trunk near her narrow bed held fifty years of memorabilia from the Baric children she had raised, and one little baby gown from the child she wasn't able to.

Resi looked around the room, not sure if the nanny was even to be found among the treasures. The room faced west, and Resi finally saw Idita sitting on the window seat with her sewing in her hand; she was enjoying the last of the early summer daylight.

"Your ladyship," Idita exclaimed with surprise when she looked up from her work. "This is an unexpected pleasure."

Idita was the oldest person in the castle, but still had a sharp eye for her embroidery. She put her needle down and stood to make a small curtsy to her young mistress.

"Am I disturbing you, Idita?" she asked as Idita sat down again. "I have something I needed to discuss with you in private."

"Please, my lady, sit with me." The sun was warm at the window seat, and Idita had opened the first of the three panes to let in the sea air. From this floor of the house, one could see the distant Adriatic; Resi found herself lost in the view for a moment before she sat down. Idita looked at her with concern. "Are you well, my dear?"

Resi drifted back to the present and smiled at the gentlewoman. Idita was also a healing woman who many sought out for her medicines. "Thank you, I am quite well."

Idita beamed a smile back that made it to her deep-brown eyes, and it gave Resi courage to continue her plan. "It is about my husband," she began. "I know it is wrong of me to ask you, Idita, but a message arrived today. He will be home shortly and I . . ." Resi was now unsure how to explain it to the old nurse. She had thought about what she wanted to say, but the words were lost again.

"And you want to please him," Idita finished her sentence for her. Resi let out her breath and looked with pleading eyes at the small woman.

Idita set her embroidery on the carpeted floor and sat closer to Resi, taking the space of the basket that had been between them. She told her, "Mauro sat right where you sit now when he was a little boy. He would bring me the treasures that he found on his adventures with his brother, Mateo, and with Jero." She pointed to some sparkling rocks and colorful shells displayed on the small table near the window seat. Resi turned to look at the pretty stones and sea shells, but then gave Idita a questioning look.

"Your husband has not mentioned his older brother. I can see it in your face," Idita said. "Mateo drowned in the sea when Mauro was twelve. Mauro took it very badly; he loved his brother more than anything. Shortly after that, he left to be fostered at the Toth Castle."

Resi knew he had been away for many years. He had visited her in Greece during that time. She listened as Idita revealed her husband's past to her.

"The first time Mauro came home after that was when his father died. The boy who left and the man who returned bore little resemblance to each other." Idita reached over and took Resi's hand from her lap and quietly told her, "When I first came to Baric Castle, I rocked Lorenc as a babe on my knee long before I had charge of Mauro and Mateo. I saw how Mauro's father built a shield of armor over his own heart with Mateo's death. Lorenc shut his living son out in his grief."

Saddened, Idita explained further, "Mauro has done the same as his father. I believe the happy boy who played in that courtyard below us is still under the grown man's armor. Be patient, my lady. Lord Toth trained Mauro to be a commander of soldiers, but no one has taught him how to be a husband. He will let his shield down soon enough. I think you might find you will like the man revealed there."

Resi felt herself blush that the old nanny could read her worries so well. "I will try to be patient."

Idita smiled brightly again and patted the hand she was still cradling with hers. "In the meantime, custom dictates that the house mourns one year for the dead. Lady Johanna was buried a year ago, and her soul is with God." Idita crossed herself solemnly. "You are now the baroness and the lady of the house." Idita waited for the words to sink in. "Your husband has seen much death, but you can show him that there is life here again."

She let Resi's hand free and stood up to signal she had said all that she had wanted. Idita looked out onto the view of the sparkling sea. "The sun is sinking. Shall we go together to see if Cook has made good on her promise of fish stew for our supper?"

Resi found she had an appetite again, and the thought of Nela's stew sounded delightful.

Chapter 10

Today was about new beginnings. The visit with Idita yesterday had given Resi a new determination. She had been timid and had felt foreign in her new home for a long time, but she did not know how to change those feelings. Mauro did not stand in her way, but he had not helped her take charge of her new role as baroness either. Jero was polite and considerate, but he was busy with his own duties while Mauro was gone. Any time she would ask his advice about something, he had none to offer her. Resi knew she had gained the respect and trust of the castle servants, but she had no authority.

Now she walked the manor house with a renewed interest and confidence. She opened doors she had been too insecure to venture behind, and she even sat in the lady's chair that had been reserved for her dead mother-in-law. Lady Johanna had been a force in the castle for over twenty years, and Resi needed reassurance that the role was hers to take over now. She knew who she would have to ask this time.

Resi had not been raised in a typical Catholic home. Religion and politics were two subjects that Demetrius Kokkinos avoided. The ruling Ottoman Empire was tolerant of its conquered Christian citizens, as long as they paid their heavy tax burden and dressed according to the law. Demetrius traded with anyone who paid his price, and he did not differentiate too much toward one side or the other. Not choosing a religion was as important for business as not choosing a side in war.

Resi's mother was Catholic, having grown up in France. She taught her children her faith as best she could in the privacy of their home. Unfortunately for her mother, Resi was an energetic child. In her youth, she could not be convinced that kneeling silently for long periods could be beneficial for her soul. Her mother could rarely get her to pray. But now, when she was missing her mother and needed to feel a connection from afar, Resi tried praying again in the Baric chapel. She found comfort in her short visits to the small church when she could not find peace otherwise.

The chapel was near the front entrance of the walled compound. Resi walked along the south wall from the manor house, keeping to the shade on the walking path. The sun was not yet a quarter in the sky, but May had already proved to be as warm as full summer. The courtyard was quiet, with only a few men working their various duties. Most of the soldiers had been called away with the baron; those who remained trained mornings in the sparring fields outside the north wall.

Resi thought again about the Baric estate and how its size had surprised her when she first arrived. Resi had been told by her father that her new husband was from an old, aristocratic family with a relatively modest barony in Croatia. She had not imagined the land holdings included a walled castle, a village, an inlet with salt mines, along with miles of orchards and tenant farms. Her own family lived in a luxurious but unassuming villa near the sea in Greece, and they owned several ships that made up her father's profitable trade business. She had grown up with house servants and a gardener at her home as well, but only a handful to maintain her family's basic comfort. She had always thought they were rich, but now she understood what wealth meant.

The actual compound was surrounded by a high, granite wall that matched the mountains. She was used to the scale of it now and found comfort in its massive presence. The gate house and the Keep were the original and oldest parts of the property. The manor house—said to be modest compared to the stately manors of other baronies—had been designed by Mauro's grandfather and built from blocks quarried from the mountains. The protective walls had been extended to the eastern cliffs as far as could be managed for the new villa house, and the space left within the walls had dictated the villa's restrained size. Resi thought it was a marvelous design that let in the light and the fresh, sea air. She could not imagine what life would be like living in the Keep tower, where the Barics had lived just a generation ago. She judged by its small windows and thick, solid walls that it must be cold and dim.

The old chapel had been constructed at the time of the original castle walls. The pretty, whitewashed structure was built into the south wall and, as it had been explained to her, frugally saved the first owner the cost of one side. The little church had once been used regularly by the inhabitants of the castle, but now they attended services in the larger church in the village.

Resi had not been taught her faith with sermons or congregations, so she felt at ease in the quiet intimacy of the small sanctuary. It was the building closest to the gate, and she decided the chapel had been placed there so the souls laid out in mourning could escape the Baric grounds into heaven more easily. Resi felt the urge to escape through the open gate herself today, but she instead turned toward the door of her destination and went inside.

The chapel was just one stone room with small, stained-glass windows set high on one wall. The inside walls were plastered and whitewashed for brightness, and there were soft cushions on the wooden benches for its visitors to sit in comfort. Resi sat on the front bench before the statue of the Virgin Mary and contemplated what her request would be. She chose a brief prayer instead of a long appeal for answers. "Mother of Perpetual Help, please ask for me whether the Lady Johanna Baric was received into heaven and her soul is at rest with God." She bowed her head and waited for a sign.

Resi had not asked her husband about the events that had led to his mother's death, and he had not given her an explanation. Natalija was with her mistress, though, and said Lady Johanna had not died peacefully. Natalija thought she was crazed in the end, but Verica would not let her elaborate.

Kneeling before Saint Mary, a surge of air moved upward around her bent shoulders. It was an unmistakable signal that the prayer had been answered, she decided. Lady Johanna's soul had not lingered, but had moved on and up into heaven. Resi was pleased her errand had been so quick. She crossed herself, and then rose to go back out into the bright May sunshine as Baroness Baric.

~ * ~

The next two weeks were filled with bustling enthusiasm at the castle. Verica and Natalija were instrumental in helping Resi find the tapestries and cushions and carpets that had been stored away on the top floor of the main house. What had once been the children's nursery was under lock and key, and within it was all the color that had been missing this past year. The black draperies of mourning that had hung for almost two years were put away. In their place were the elaborate hangings and decorations from the days of Lord Fredrik. The great hall was dusted and cleaned from top to bottom by the industrious house servants, equally ready to see new life come back into the house. The legacy left in Lady Johanna's flower garden was used to supply the house with fragrant arrangements that were the final touches to make the great hall welcoming.

There was a consensus among the women of the house that there should be a celebration when the Baric men returned. Resi did not have any idea how to go about planning such a party, but Jero and Nestor made the banquet arrangements and sent invitations to neighboring lords and village dignitaries. For days, the kitchen bustled with preparations. Hunted fowl and rabbits were hung for stuffing, and a plump pig was chosen for roasting. Dishes of savory puddings and aspic were readied, mountains of mushroom and kidney pies were planned, and dried fruits were soaked in wine for tarts and custards. Breads would be baked, and casks of beer and wine were already being sorted for the occasion.

The message received from Mauro's company on the road had said they expected a two-week journey home. Jero scheduled the feast for a week after their expected return, just to be sure. As the promised reunion date came and went with no new message, the cheerfulness of the Baric household was stifled. They began to fear the worst when five more days passed with no word.

Resi had been sitting in the great hall after dinner when the gate was finally opened to the dusty, exhausted Baric troops. Mauro rode in with his soldiers to the stables and handed over his horse to Alberto.

"Your arm, my lord!" Alberto exclaimed when he took the reins. Mauro had forgotten about the dirty bandage wrapped thickly around his sword arm. It had begun bleeding again during the ride home, and the wrapping was now stained red. "Shall I send for the surgeon?"

"No, Alberto. Send for Idita. Tell her I will be in my study," Mauro instructed him, and then walked toward Stephan and Fabian, who were just dismounting from their horses. They also saw the soaked bandage, but did not comment on it. Geoff ran by them on Alberto's errand to find the Baric nurse.

Mauro regretted having sent word to the castle to give them false hope of their safe arrival. To his surprise, he had thought often of his bride during the lonely nights away. He knew she would be worried for him, especially now that they were a week overdue. He told his captains, "The terrace doors to the great hall might be open. We will go in through there, and maybe we won't be noticed right away. I need this arm tended to and a strong drink before I face my other responsibilities." He gave them a weary smile, and they nodded and followed him to the house.

It was after nightfall, and Mauro hoped his wife was already in their chamber. He didn't know whether she had feebleness for bleeding wounds, and he was in no mood for a fainting woman tonight. She would understand not seeking her out first.

Mauro hurried through the great hall with hardly a glance around him. He did not notice his stunned wife, sitting on a new chair next to the hearth. She eagerly greeted him, "Husband, you are home!" Then her lovely face went pale with panic. She touched the bloody bandage in alarm. "You are hurt!"

He covered her hand with his own and was sorry that he had to meet her like this. "I am fine," was all he could think to say in that moment. She was radiant, and he dared not look into her eyes or he would have lost his last ounce of strength.

58

"I am going to my study now, Terese," he told her weakly. "I have called for Idita to tend to my arm. I will come up to you later." He gave her a small kiss on her forehead, then walked away from his bewildered wife.

"He will be all right, my lady," Stephan and Fabian murmured together. Each gave her a small bow and forced a smile in an attempt to soothe her. They followed Mauro out into the foyer and across to the study, leaving his wife alone again. Resi was suddenly exhausted by the dramatic arrival and departure of her missing husband. She dutifully went upstairs to her chamber to wait for him.

Once in the study, Fabian protested, "Why not let your lady take care of you, Mauro? We could all see how concerned she was for your welfare." Stephan looked at him with the same questioning expression.

"What would you have me do? When the bandage comes off, you, too, might be faint. I do not want my wife to be ill on my account. You know Idita is the best choice for doctoring the wound," Mauro said in defense of his actions. "Besides, I admit I am feeling a bit ill myself and prefer not to have an audience for that." He sat down at the table with his head resting on his good arm in front of him.

Idita entered the study and gave a slight curtsy to Fabian and Stephan. She set down her basket with medicines and supplies to treat the baron's arm and waited.

"Do you want us to stay, Mauro?" Stephan asked sympathetically.

He raised his head again and noticed that Idita was there. "No, there is no need now, Stephan. I will be in good hands. See that the men get any attention they require. Send for the village surgeon, if they want, but Idita can check on them when she is done stitching me up." She nodded to Stephan that she would. "Everyone should rest tomorrow," Mauro managed to add.

Fabian and Stephan, too, were exhausted from the difficult ride home and left the room with a pat on Mauro's shoulder and a respectful bow to Idita.

Idita set her medicine basket on the long table. It was packed full with small bottles of potions and tins of powders that she had learned to mix in her father's apothecary in her youth in Venice. She unpacked what she would need.

"You have been gone two months, Mauro. We are happy to have you back home." She spoke in a comforting voice.

"I am relieved to be back. It was not meant to be a long campaign. We ran into the most trouble just before we were back on our own lands," Mauro explained. She gently lifted his arm on the table and unwound the dirty bandages. Mauro watched her through tired eyes. "The sword sliced through my jacket sleeve."

"I can see that. The jacket probably saved your arm, but it will need stitching. I hope you can stay in one place and rest while it heals properly," she warned. He nodded that he would, but was not so confident that he could.

Idita efficiently went about cleaning the inflamed wound. "It is a straight cut," she reported, "but deep enough. How long has it been festering?"

"I am not sure. We were attacked a week ago," he replied. "I had it cleaned with some brandy and wrapped it myself. It has been tormenting me almost as long."

He shut his eyes while she cleaned the cut down his forearm. He felt stronger when he talked, so continued to tell her, "We traveled far north with the Toth soldiers. We were spared most of the fighting by the time we arrived. It was not until we were back to the Venetian border that we were ambushed."

She held her needle against the flame of the candle and chose a sturdy thread. "Why didn't you have it stitched earlier?" Idita asked quietly.

"I thought we would be home sooner," he confessed drowsily. "Several of us were injured, so it was a grueling ride back. I lost two men along the way; they bled to death, I think. I decided dying at your hands would be the least risk." He managed a weak smile despite enduring the stitching through his flesh.

"I won't let you die today." She returned a weary smile as she continued her task.

She finished the last knot and examined her work, then began rolling fresh linen around the cleaned arm. "The arm will hurt you tonight, maybe even worse than before. I would like you to drink a sleeping draught; you look like you could use the rest."

Mauro nodded; he wanted some relief and some sleep. She began to mix some powder with water in a cup.

"Should I send for your wife?" she asked.

He considered her suggestion. "No, I will rest on the cot here and see her in the morning." Mauro still was not used to the notion of someone caring about him. He drank Idita's potion.

When Idita had finished packing her thread and bandages, she studied Mauro for a moment. She decided he would want to hear some good news today and said quietly, "Your wife is pregnant, Mauro." His stunned expression made her chuckle. "I am sure it is yours, dear Mauritius, if that is what you are thinking. The timing would be from before your departure."

"Yesterday I was not sure I would make it back to my doorstep, and today I learn I am to be a father. This is welcome news, Idita. Thank you," he said as he leaned on the table.

"You know, Mauro," Idita continued, "Lady Terese is stronger than you give her credit for. But you must let her prove it."

He didn't know where she was leading, but he knew better than to dismiss her opinion. "Is that right?" he wondered. "And do you think she can bear me a child this time?"

"I do, if you treat her with care," Idita replied provokingly.

"Are you saying you think I do not care for my wife?"

She had expected to incite such a response. "It is not so obvious that you do. You have been given a beautiful gift, Mauro, and this is her second try to give you a son. She needs to succeed."

Mauro stared at Idita with worried eyes.

"You have been away a long time, but you must show restraint. God has set the rules how a man should behave with his wife. You should know that already, Mauro."

Such audacity would not be tolerated from a servant, but this was Idita. She had given him counsel and courage over the years when he could not muster it himself. He could not be angry at her.

"I do appreciate my wife, and I want her to succeed," he finally acknowledged drowsily. His brow furrowed with indecision before he continued, "I do know what is expected of a husband, from God and from myself. I will not share her bed until the baby is born, if that is what it takes. It would be too painful for her if she lost a second child." Painful for Mauro, too, but he could not bring himself to say those words out loud.

She touched his bandaged arm once more to see that it was secure. The sleeping draught began to take effect. Idita blew out the candles on the table. Just the torchlight from the courtyard shone into the room. "You will heal, Mauro," she promised.

He lay down on the cot and looked up at her through half-closed eyes. He knew she did not mean his arm. "I know I will."

Chapter 11

Mauro slept like the dead through the entire next day. Come evening, Idita was worried for her recovering patient, and she asked Jero to try to wake him. When Jero entered the study, he was relieved to see Mauro already sitting up, unwrapping his bandages.

"I thought maybe Idita was our murderer after all," Jero said with a forced cheerfulness. He set the tray of bread and soup down on a stool next to the cot. "You have been sleeping almost a full day. How is your arm?"

Mauro lifted his heavy head to focus from his arm to his steward. "The bandage is clean, so the stitching held," Mauro began, "but my head is splitting from the powder. I am afraid to stand up, or I might fall over."

"Idita said food will clear your head and make you feel stronger. I brought you some broth to begin with." Mauro stretched his wobbly legs and leaned in to smell the steaming soup. "Mauro," Jero continued cautiously, "Ruby told me your wife has been pacing the gardens for hours. Should I send her to you?"

Mauro did not like to see Jero look so concerned, but just the same he answered, "No, do not call her in."

Jero could not hide his disapproval. Mauro told him, "My wife will be doubly frightened if she sees me now, would you not agree? I will eat first and then find her when I am cleaned up a bit."

"Yes, you do look a bit rough," Jero acknowledged. "I will send Davor with some clean clothes."

Mauro awkwardly tore a piece of the fresh bread with his good hand and dipped it into the soup to eat. He looked at his bloodstained hands. "I suppose I need to wash up, too. Have him bring some hot water first."

Jero was about to close the door when Mauro called out, "Wait." Jero peered back into the room. "Tell her that I am all right."

"Of course," Jero assured him and then left to find Davor.

Mauro looked out the window and watched the last of the sun's rays disappear over the castle wall. He thought of the uneventful journey back from the campaign in Habsburg territory and the unanticipated trouble so close to home. Who would want to attack them on friendly soil? It was plain that his men flew the familiar Baric banners. He was deep in those thoughts when Davor knocked and entered the room.

"Shall I light some candles, my lord?" Davor politely asked.

Mauro hadn't realized he was sitting in the dark. "Light them all, if you will," Mauro instructed him. "I do not normally ask this of you, Davor, but tonight I will need your help dressing. I am afraid I cannot use this arm."

Davor regarded at his master with sympathy. "Gladly, sir. Aron is bringing more hot water for washing up. Shall I shave you tonight, my lord?" He had never shaved another man before, and the baron knew this.

"Yes, I think it will be necessary tonight. I hope you have practiced on yourself at least; otherwise, you should tell Idita to be ready with her sewing needle, in case I need more stitches," Mauro managed to joke. Davor laughed nervously at the truth of it. He was a late bloomer at almost nineteen. In the past months, he had given up on growing his scraggly beard and had begun to shave his sparse whiskers.

"I have practiced on myself, my lord, even when there was nothing to cut. You will be clean and handsome for Lady Baric when I am done dressing you," Davor boasted. Mauro was grateful for that luxury tonight.

~ * ~

Feeling stronger with warm food in his belly and the grime from his travels gone, Mauro wanted to find his wife. It was now fully dark outside, but the torches had been lit on the terrace and the evening air was comfortably warm. He was sure he would still find her in the gardens.

As he walked through the great hall toward the open terrace doors, it struck him that it was all different. He paused on the landing and looked around. The tables in the room had been rearranged, there were colorful tapestries on the walls again, and new chairs and cushions had been placed near the hearth for intimate seating. It was a woman's touch, and Mauro was pleased.

He stepped out the double doors onto the terrace. Where had the plants come from? And the fountain was running again. He had not noticed any of it last night. Whatever had happened while he was gone was a rewarding delight. Then he saw his wife; the bride he had been neglecting was looking back at him in the moonlight. A hopeful smile was spread across her face, and he realized now that he wasn't ready for what he would say to her.

Resi did not seem to notice his hesitation. She walked up the terrace steps from the path and greeted him. "Jero told me you are feeling better, Husband. I was so worried for you."

She reached out and took his uninjured hand in hers. She looked beautiful in her rich saffron robe, the one that accentuated her tan skin. Her flowing, soft curls lifted in the light breeze, and he ached to touch them. Had she always been so enchanting?

He found his smile again. "Idita says I will live. That is good enough for today," he added.

Resi laughed sweetly at the hopeful statement. "You look much better than you did last night. I was distressed to see you hurt and bleeding," she said softly. "I thought you would come upstairs to me."

"I am sorry that you worried. I was given some sleeping powder, and it put me out right away."

Mauro continued to stare into her deep gray eyes—or were they blue? It was the evening shadows that changed them. He remembered now; they were dark blue like the angry sea, with a touch of gray like the Baric mountains. Beautiful.

Sensing that her husband was not yet fully fit, she tugged his hand and brought him back into the great hall to sit near the fire. He sat on a soft armchair, and she sat next to him on a cushioned bench. "Have you noticed a change, Husband?" she asked anxiously.

Mauro looked up at the banners he remembered from his youth and noticed the fresh flowers on the tables. "The house was in mourning for my father when I arrived almost two years ago. We left it that way for my mother . . ." Mauro did not continue his speech, and Resi was afraid she had done wrong to change the tone of the house without his permission.

He sensed her apprehension and said reassuringly, "I am pleased you have ended our mourning, Terese." He looked around again, taking in the changes. "I am very pleased, indeed." He reached over and gave in to the urge to touch her soft hair.

"I need to tell you something important, Husband. I hope you will be happy about it." He smiled, thinking she would tell him about the baby. Instead, she announced, "We have arranged a sort of banquet."

Resi had hoped for a joyful reaction, but his expression remained questioning. "I, um, we expected you sooner, or the date would not appear so sudden. We have invited the neighboring lords and village merchants to a feast tomorrow night at sundown. Everyone will be here."

"Tomorrow?" Mauro repeated with irritation. He stood up and paced to the fireplace. Resi held her breath. "The first harvest begins this week. We passed the orchards, and they are ripe and ready," was his immediate objection.

"All the preparations are made, and the invitations were accepted, Husband. The harvest can go on during the day. I just require that you show up at sundown."

He knew he had not been good at informing his wife of his departures, and was usually days behind his planned return. "You look at me as though that would be difficult. Am I always so tardy?" Mauro teased her.

She looked at him hopefully, and he felt the overwhelming urge to kiss her. She had gone to so much trouble. "I will be there tomorrow at sundown. I promise you. Now, show me all that you have done while I was away." He held out his good hand for her, and they strolled around the great hall and foyer while Resi proudly pointed out the changes made for his arrival.

It was late in the evening, and the servants were saying their good-nights in the foyer and taking leave to go to their sleeping quarters. "Are you tired, Husband? Shall we go to bed, too?" she innocently asked.

Mauro thought about what he had promised Idita and himself. How was he going to get through the months of sleeping in the same bed with this sensual woman and not have her? He would take it one night at a time. "You go up without me. I have slept almost a full day and am wide awake. I need to talk to Stephan and Fabian about an important matter before they retire. I will come to bed after that."

She was disappointed, but this was how it always was. "May I ask one last thing?"

Already at the door to leave, Mauro turned back to his wife, who was standing gracefully on the marble steps in her silk robes. He fought the urge to follow her after all. "What is it you need, Terese?"

"May I take an outing with Ruby to the harvest tomorrow?"

"An outing? Yes, why not," Mauro agreed quickly. "I will see if Hugo can escort you. He hurt his shoulder, and it will do him good to take another day off. I will see you later, Terese." She nodded and then continued up the stairs to wait for him in their room, and he went out the foyer door.

~ * ~

Fabian and Stephan were walking their saddled horses out the stables door as Mauro crossed the courtyard in the torchlight. "There is our wounded leader," Stephan shouted. "We were just going to head out for some drink and company." They held their horses and waited for him to catch up to them.

"You look surprisingly good after the sleep of death. I heard they were worried Idita had given you too much powder," Fabian told him. "Are you recovered enough to ride?"

"My arm only aches when I move it, so that is an improvement. And my improved appearance, I owe to Davor. It is nice to have a valet sometimes," Mauro acknowledged. The men were amused that he would finally admit this.

They had grown up with personal grooms and did not mock the luxury like Mauro did. "I came out specifically looking for you both. If you are not in a great hurry to your pleasures, I think I can manage to ride at a slow trot. We can talk along the way. Let me get my horse saddled."

He glanced up at his lighted window, where his wife was waiting for him. He would only be gone a few hours. Maybe it would be better if he found another way to relieve his burdens tonight, he thought.

~*~

The three riders encountered no other travelers on the moonlit road. They were not worried about an ambush here, but they were conscious to look for trouble in their path as they rode. This caution did not prevent them from their jovial conversation.

Mauro told his companions about his wife's homecoming banquet the next day. "Without excuse, everyone will be in the great hall at sundown. It is very important to my wife that we all attend, and on time," Mauro said with emphasis.

Stephan poked fun at his friend as they rode alongside each other. "Ah, now we are the ones scolded for being late. We shall not fail her, but you are a different matter, Mauro. She is growing on you, isn't she?"

"Of course she is growing on him," Fabian goaded him playfully. "She is growing on all of us. What is not to like about Mauro's wife?"

Mauro shot him a look of caution. "You like everyone's wife, Fabian, and I would rather not hear that mine is growing on you. That is exactly your weakness and the cause of all your troubles. You love too many women. They torment you with their emotions."

"Maybe that is your problem, Mauritius. You do not want to feel anything. You might do better with a little more torment," Fabian advised his friend. "My problem might be that I *want* to feel something. One woman does one thing that gives me such pleasure; another has other tricks and talents that keep me coming back. They are magical creatures, really."

"As I said before, that is why you will never settle down with one woman," Stephan reminded Fabian. "You will always need more 'magic', as you call it. As for me, I will ask for Mira's hand as soon I can leave this bloody fighting for half a year."

"Marry her, Stephan," Mauro encouraged him as he trotted alongside. "You are a free man and a wealthy man, at that. Give up soldiering and take your bride. I do not hold you captive to your post in my little army." Mauro looked kindly at Stephan and added, "Tonight, my friend, we will toast to your future wife."

Fabian burst out laughing. "Aye, we will! But do not tell the girl he takes upstairs!"

Stephan gave him a feigned scowl, but was quickly laughing at the truth of it when Fabian nudged him nearly off his horse.

They rode in silence for the next few minutes until Fabian asked, "Mauro, if you are not interested in Tatjana tonight, might I take her upstairs? She is always your favorite at the Green Goose. Does she have some special, um, talent?" He gave Mauro a teasing wink.

Mauro was surprised by the question, but he considered it a moment before replying. Tatjana was a young, pretty widow who ran the Green Goose with her mother, Andrea. She was a barmaid, but on occasion would take a special customer to her bed, like the baron or another wealthy patron; they usually treated her well and paid her fairly. She had married young, but her husband died in a mishap in the blacksmith shop. She had been his wife for three years, and it was said that she was barren. So the reassurance that no bastard would be left on the nobleman's doorstep was especially attractive in bedding her, as were her full breasts and curvaceous hips. She was admittedly desirable to any man, but what made him go back to her? Mauro thoughtfully answered his friends, "I think I enjoy her company because she expects nothing in return from me."

Stephan and Fabian had not anticipated Mauro to admit this, and they both hooted with laughter. Fabian could not resist provoking his dignified friend. "She has no pleasure with you, then; is that it, Mauritius?"

Mauro laughed, too, finding the unintended humor now in what he had answered. "I would say she finds pleasure in bed, maybe even because of me. But she is quiet about it." Fabian gave Stephan a nudge to poke fun at his friend's reasoning. Mauro ignored him and went on to say, "I have been with enough women to fairly judge her talent. She has skills, but that is not what makes me choose her."

"Oh? Then, what makes her special?" Stephan asked again, looking over at Fabian, who was struggling to hold back his laughter.

"I think I prefer her, Stephan, because she does not talk to me."

Fabian found Mauro very comical now. "Are you admitting that you demand silence from your lovers, just like from your soldiers? Taking a woman to your bed is not a battle, my friend. It is the surrender after the battle to get there, and the cries for mercy should be mutual."

Mauro took the friendly bantering lightheartedly. "You can be assured, Fabian, that I know the difference between making love and making war."

"We have had too much of one and not enough of the other these last months. Let us have a merry time at the Green Goose tonight," Stephan said cheerfully.

"I will leave your quiet girl for your taking, if you are up to it," Fabian told Mauro. "I prefer noise in my bed tonight."

Mauro considered his friends' remarks as they rounded the corner to the tavern. He would just have a drink or two, and nothing more. He was surely in need of some merriment, but a few drinks would suffice. They found the stable boy, left their horses in his care, and then entered the rowdy ale house. Mauro's mood was already lifting. "Barkeeper, a round of drinks for everyone," he shouted to the cheering men inside.

Chapter 12

It was well past midnight when Mauro slipped fully dressed into bed with his wife. She breathed small, steady breaths as he crawled in close to her for warmth. He could lay with her now and just sleep. He took in her scent; it was orange blossoms. She always came to bed smelling of flowers, he thought. He noticed she was wearing her prettiest silk shift, and her sewing basket was on the edge of the bed. She had waited up for him.

His head was still reeling from the ale and the noise of the tavern, and his wound was throbbing. He should shut his eyes and catch a few hours of rest, but he was drawn to stare at this exotic woman who belonged to him. Did she love him at all? He fought the urge to wake her and ask. Instead, he touched her gently on the round of her trim hip and thought of how enticing she felt, how delicious she smelled. He felt ashamed that just an hour ago he had been in another woman's bed. He had wanted the release, but not the woman. He was sure of that now.

Terese stirred, but her sleep was still peaceful. Mauro could wake her and see her face, tell her how much he wanted and needed her. This was the woman he longed for. He slowly lifted the silken cloth covering her and was easily aroused by the touch of her smooth skin. Then Mauro thought of his child she was carrying and the vow he had made to Idita. He would not be able to sleep in here after all; he knew that now. Carefully, he rose from the bed and crept to the door. He walked candleless to the end of the hallway, to a place he knew would be empty.

His mother's chamber was musty and dark, but there was a comfortable bed, and the servants would not intrude on his sleep as they went about their duties in the morning. Guilt grabbed him as he crossed the room to the closed windows to let in the night air. He had not been in there since her sudden death a year ago. Her possessions had not been removed from her room, and he felt a sense of trespassing. The large chamber had been cleaned after her wake, but it was the son's duty to give the instructions to empty the room. Instead, he had abandoned it. He began to regret choosing this place for stealing some sleep and feared that his dead mother's ghost would not grant it. He shut out the memories, crawled under the cold covers, and let the eerie quietness take him.

~ * ~

Resi lay awake in their bed. She had been briefly startled from her slumber when Mauro dropped his boots near the door coming in, and she had fought the urge to open her heavy eyes. She was angry at her husband for shutting her out of his life, and she would rather sleep now than face him. She did not know what to expect from a marriage, but after a year she had hoped to love her husband more than she did now. Her parents loved each other openly, and she yearned for that same open love and affection from Mauro. But her parents had married for love, not for a settlement, and that was the difference that changed everything.

Just now, when Mauro slunk into bed alongside her, she could smell the road dust mixed with sweat, ale, and other scents that could only come from a woman. Did he not love her at all? But then he had touched her so tenderly in her dreaming state that she forgot for a moment that she was cross. She had begun to allow herself to wake fully. She had nearly turned to him just then, but he took his hand back and went away too quickly. She had stayed motionless out of regret. He did not love her; she knew that. She would bear and love his children, but there did not seem to be any way to love Mauro. She turned to feel for any warmth left where he had just lain, but it was already gone.

~ * ~

Before falling into bed, Mauro had left the glass windows open, knowing the noise of the courtyard would penetrate his dreams. Morning came too early for him; it was punishment for his adultery. He was married and had said his vows before God to be a faithful husband. He had not thought of it that way before last night, but there was no other way to see it. The day was not beginning well: his arm hurt, his head hurt, and now his conscience pained him too.

He got up and tried to salvage his disheveled appearance with his one good arm. The stone floor felt cold as he stood at the small grooming table and looked into the mirror. He didn't need to shave again, but he regretted the lack of water to help him wake up. He stared at his reflection and thought of his dead parents. He did not resemble the Barics as much as he did the Toths. His hair was a light brown, not a darker shade like his father's. He had a square jawline instead of the oval faces of the other Baric men. This gave the impression of sternness without meaning to. It had been an advantage as a commander. Despite the fistfights while soldiering, he still had all of his teeth, nearly straight behind his full lips. His eyes were the only real feature he had inherited from the Barics. They were green like his father's, not blue like his mother's. This morning there were dark circles under them. It would be a long day with the extravagant banquet planned for this evening, but he would get through it.

He sensed that the castle was in full motion preparing for the festivities, but he lingered in his mother's quiet room, looking around to chance upon a memory. The apartment was well furnished with a large curtained bed, now rumpled from his use, an elegant table with four femininely upholstered chairs, as well as fine Oriental rugs that covered the floor and paintings that adorned the walls. There were several trunks and chests around the room filled with his mother's final possessions that still needed to be dealt with.

Out of curiosity, Mauro opened one and began rummaging through the bundled papers and odd women's accessories. He pulled out a pale blue silk scarf and kept it to the side. He would have this sent to Tatjana for her attention to his needs last night. Looking down again, he noticed a small, jeweled chest under the scarf covering. He brought the interesting box to the table and set it down, thinking it might contain something special he could gift his wife. Inside the unlocked chest were squares of folded papers that had once been sealed letters. Each had "Lady Johanna Baric" scrolled on the outside in a masculine hand that he did not recognize. Mauro was intrigued, but would look at the letters in detail another day. He put the small chest back into the larger trunk, picked up the silk scarf, and left the room.

Davor was waiting for the baron outside Mauro's chamber. If Davor was surprised when the baron came from his mother's room, he did not show it. Mauro's own chamber was vacant, his wife having gone about whatever duties Mauro imagined filled her day. He was glad he would not have to see her just now.

"Good morning, my lord," Davor addressed him with a bow, then followed him into the room. "Hot water is ready for you. Can I help you dress this morning, sir?"

"Yes, I will need your help again, Davor, but I am in a hurry. I will eat here, if you could arrange that first." Still holding the scarf, Mauro gave his valet instructions for the gift and then set it aside for him to organize later. Davor went to order the breakfast tray.

Mauro was just picking out his wardrobe for the day when the maid came in with his breakfast. "Tell me, Natalija, where is my wife this morning?" he asked her as she set down his meal.

"She left earlier with Lady Ruby and Verica to help with the harvesting." Natalija saw the questioning expression on her lord's face and tried to explain. "Her ladyship told Hugo that you had given her permission to join the villagers in the apricot orchard today. I saw them leave with the wagon over an hour ago."

His face softened. He had forgotten their brief conversation yesterday. "Yes, that is right. Thank you, Natalija. You may go."

She bobbed a small curtsy and crossed paths with Fabian as he entered the room. Fabian was dressed for sparring in his thick doublet with full leather sleeves, doeskin breeches, and his over-the-knee boots. The leather made a soft crinkling sound as he sat down on the chair across from his friend. He watched as Mauro attempted to cut his breakfast with his left hand.

"Good morning to you, Mauro," Fabian cheerfully greeted him. "Are you going to be here all morning trying to feed yourself with your bad arm? Let me help you with those sausages." Fabian picked up one with his fingers and bit off half with a grin. Mauro scowled at him, but then picked up his own with his good hand.

"You are dressed for swordplay. What do you have planned for the day?" Mauro asked Fabian, who was now helping himself to toast as well.

"I thought I would work with the new group of soldiers on the sparring fields, if you have no objections."

Outside the north walls, the trees had long ago been cleared. The land was not good for farming because of the boulders, but the ground was even enough for horses to gallop across. Mauro used the spacious fields to keep his soldiers in shape for battle.

"Simeon and Stephan have already ridden off to talk to Radic, as you suggested. I hope the marauders left some clues as to who they were working for," Fabian said between sips of Mauro's coffee.

"Have you eaten your fill yet?" Mauro asked with annoyance as Fabian took another sausage. Fabian bit into it and winked. Mauro was not hungry anyway. "I have some duties on the south fields and will not be able to join you," Mauro said. "I expect to be gone all day. Do not forget to be on time to the banquet tonight, for my wife's sake."

"For your wife's sake, I look forward to it with pleasure."

Fabian stood and made a mocking bow with a grand swoosh of his elegantly plumed hat, leaving Mauro to finish what was left of his breakfast in peace.

~ * ~

The apricot orchards were not far from the castle, just twenty minutes south of the walls by wagon and even less by horseback. The laden trees went on for acres in the river valley. Picking had started at first light, and the villagers had already collected several cartloads of the ripe fruit by the time Resi's party had arrived. The fragrant apricots reminded Resi of home, and she was glad to be in the middle of it today.

The apricot harvest was a communal affair. Women from neighboring tenant farms joined the village women to get the hard work done quickly. The produce belonged to the baron, but each family was entitled to a portion of the pickings. Later, the individual households would sort the baron's apricots on great racks for drying in the sun. There were many children put in charge of bringing full baskets to the carts, and most had eaten their fill of the juicy fruit by midmorning. Resi, Ruby, and Verica were eager to lend their help, and Hugo took shelter in the shade of their wagon. He watched the activities for a few minutes before shutting his eyes to nap.

Near noon, when the early summer sun began to shine too hotly, the women stopped for the day and went over the hill to wash and refresh themselves in the river's cool water. Verica had joined her village friends along the shoreline. Resi joined Ruby, who had settled in under a willow tree near the edge of the stream. A pleasant breeze blew across the river and cooled them nicely in the shade. The village women had stripped down to their shifts at the river's edge, where they splashed and relaxed after their long morning working in the heat.

Resi was not used to such activity after her leisurely year in the castle, and she decided the water would be a wonderful relief for her sore arms. She stood and stripped her layers of robes and pulled offer her thin cotton stockings until she was immodestly clothed in her gauze shift. She knew Mauro would not approve of showing her bare legs, but there were only women nearby to see them. She pulled the ample skirt of her shift up between her knees, tied the billowy fabric with a sash around her waist, and ran down to the water. Ruby watched her, laughing, as she plunged in to a deep pool that formed near some boulders. Resi loved to swim, and it felt good to be free in the open water again.

Hugo, sound asleep beside the wagon, was woken by a kick from the baron. He had ridden to see how the harvest was coming along and to find Terese. "Where is my wife, Hugo?" he demanded of his young captain.

Startled from his deep sleep, Hugo struggled to remember where he was. "She is . . . um . . ." he stuttered, looking around for her, not knowing how to answer. Mauro left him still sitting against the wagon.

Seeing the empty rows of trees, Mauro knew the women must have already finished for the day. He rode up the knoll that overlooked the river to search for his wife. Resi was easy to spot, wearing a pale purple undergarment that stood out among the drab linen of the village women. Even from a distance, his wife was exotic. Idita was right. Why had he not paid more attention to his fortunate gift that was his wife? She was the spice added to the Baric salt, and he felt a jolt that was a mix of pride and lust for her. He wanted to gallop down and take her in his arms. Instead, he turned and rode back over the hill before he could see Resi looking up at him, watching him leave her again.

Chapter 13

He was late! Most of the guests had arrived more than an hour ago. Nestor had ceremoniously introduced the baroness to each unfamiliar face while they waited for their host on the terrace. Resi wandered inside to see if her tardy husband might have come in through the foyer doors instead. She was disappointed. Fabian, Stephan, and the other officers had all arrived within the last half hour with damp hair and ruddy faces from a quick washing for this special occasion. Casks of home-brewed beer and local wines had been tapped under shading canopies, and the invited guests noisily mingled with the Baric Castle residents. The bright colors of the richly clothed men and women made a vibrant display against the setting sun as they sipped refreshments on the warm May evening.

Mauro rode through the gates with his escorts just as the sun was sinking. He knew Resi had gone to a lot of effort to make this homecoming special for him. He hastily washed the sweat of the day off in the Keep and ordered fresh clothes rushed there from his chamber to change into. Mauro hoped his wife would not find fault with his hurried achievement to look like the lord of the castle.

"Here he is," boomed Simeon, "the man of the evening." The crowd turned toward the announcement. Mauro quickly stifled his discomfort at being spotlighted and forced a smile as he strode up the terrace steps.

"Right on time, Mauritius," Fabian congratulated him. "You always liked to be the last one to the party. Here, you will need this for when you see your wife." Fabian handed him a glass of brandy before Mauro made his way across the terrace, greeting his visitors as he went. At the open double doors, he scanned the great hall for a glimpse of Terese. He was rewarded by a surprising vision.

The two Greek women had spent last week trying on variations of their same, tired gowns they had brought with them from home, hoping for some inspiration. Ruby tried on Resi's dresses, and Resi Ruby's for a change, but they knew they would still be out of place with the stylish women at the party. Neither of them had cared much whether they were fashionable or not before; but now that a year had passed, Resi decided it might be time to try to look the part of a baroness.

Mauro's aunt had sent a dressmaker months ago to the castle, but the delivery of the new wardrobe had not yet arrived. Lady Johanna had many gowns in her trunks, but she had been a much shorter woman than Resi. Besides, most of what she wore was either sorely dated or moth eaten from the years of storage. Verica was hesitant to suggest that her mistress trust her to cut and remake the precious gowns. She found the courage to share this idea when the baroness seemed so unhappy with her circumstances. Resi decided to trust her maid's instinct, and all the servant girls were put to the task of stitching the new gown to be ready in time for the banquet.

Verica had convinced the baroness that the summer fashion required more skin be exposed. When the baroness finally agreed, Verica removed the sleeves from the original dress and added a trim of frilly, yellow lace to accent her mistress' slender arms. With no corset to aid her design, Verica stiffened the bodice of the new gown to lay flat against her chest, as was the fashion, and lowered the neckline to accentuate the baroness' growing bosom. The effect was perfect. The maid kept the flowing sheer silk of Resi's own preferred style for the outer skirt of the billowing gown, but added extra layers of stiffer satin she took from Lady Johanna's wardrobe as an underskirt to lift the floating silk around her hips.

Once dressed, Verica had taken special care to pin her mistress' long hair with jeweled combs from her mother-in-law's collection and added yellow ribbon through her locks of high curls. Resi looked stunning in the rich, poppy-colored dress that complemented her smooth, olive skin. They all agreed before she descended to the party that they had never seen a baroness look lovelier. Resi felt like a princess, and she hoped her prince would be happy with Verica's effort.

Mauro stood at the doorway to the great hall staring at his wife until he remembered to breathe again. He had always thought she was a striking woman—lean and long, but with enough curves to be femininely seductive. She muted her beauty by covering herself with modest but colorful robes and simple ornamentation. With her adorned hair piled high, she looked almost regal, and he noticed several men waiting for a turn to meet her.

Fabian whispered to his friend as he joined him at the edge of the room, "I have never seen your wife's, um, *shoulders* so exquisitely revealed." Mauro gave him a warning glance. Fabian patted him on the shoulder in reassurance and chuckled. "Relax, Mauro. I am paying you a compliment. We can all see now what a lucky man you are." He walked away to the group of soldiers calling to him across the room. Mauro went over to interrupt a flirtatious guest talking to the baroness.

"Excuse us, Viktor," Mauro politely said to the leering older gentleman leaning into his wife. He casually pulled Resi away to the side of the hall. "My dear, Fabian just paid you a fine compliment."

"Did he? Fabian is always so gallant," Resi said coyly to her protective husband. "I am glad you made it on time. Thank you."

Mauro looked into his wife's sparkling eyes. "You are lovely in your new gown, Terese. Perhaps your maid could fetch you a shawl to wear with it?" He raised his brows in emphasis as he spoke.

She held her gaze and flicked open her new fan in front of her exposed bosom. "For your comfort or mine, Husband? It is a rather warm evening and stifling in this room."

"As you wish, Terese," Mauro conceded with a smile. "Have you met everyone? If so, then we can begin the banquet." Resi took his good arm, happy she had gotten the reaction from him that Verica and Ruby had promised.

~*~

Dinner was a boisterous affair. Every house servant was employed transporting the multitude of trays and platters to the long buffet tables. The lined-up guests picked through the delicious choices, then found their seats to enjoy it. Resi was placed next to Lady Nikolina Leopold, the wife of Baron Neven Leopold, Mauro's friend and neighbor to the south. They were involved in their own cheerful conversation.

Leopold Castle was a half day's wagon ride from Solgrad. Resi had visited Lady Nikolina twice since coming to Croatia. She was ten years older than Resi, but they found they had a lot to talk about, and Resi enjoyed her companionship. Lady Nikolina had three children and was also newly pregnant again.

"The food at the Baric manor is always so delicious," Lady Nikolina declared. "You are so fortunate, Lady Terese, to have a kitchen staff that can prepare a banquet. Your cook Nela always outdoes herself. I myself have such a hard time keeping good cooks." Resi politely nodded her sympathies, having no experience to go by.

"Where is your husband tonight, Lady Nikolina? I am sorry he could not attend," Resi said sincerely. She liked Neven Leopold; he was a jovial man and a good friend to her husband.

"Well, Neven wanted to come, of course, but we have had guests at our castle all week. It has been really quite boring for me. They are here for a hunting party and have left their wives at home. My mother-in-law is there to organize the household. She loves that sort of business. I told Neven that I would not miss the chance to see you again, though, Lady Terese. You must come to visit soon while we are both able to move about." She looked over to the young woman seated to the left of Resi. "Poor Elizabeta," Lady

Nikolina continued. "She looks enormous. I am surprised she is not in confinement already."

Elizabeta Radic was the young bride of the village constable. She was a year younger than Resi and had become the constable's third wife last summer. She continued her buoyant conversation with the two baronesses while pacing the table; she couldn't stay seated on the cushioned bench for any length of time. Her midwife suspected that she was in her last weeks of pregnancy, but since Elizabeta had not realized she was pregnant until just a few months ago, no one could be sure.

Resi enjoyed the interesting gossip and general entertainment of the women adjacent to her, but she found she was also becoming uncomfortable seated in her tight, new gown. She was about to excuse herself from the ladies to get some air when Mauro rose to make a speech.

The men seated around the baron banged their mugs on the plank table to gain the crowd's attention. "Before we retire for the evening, I would like to give my appreciation to my Guard and soldiers," Mauro said proudly to the hushed room. "We returned home this week with two less men and several more wounded. We are all grateful for your strength, bravery, and sacrifice to protect my lands and those sitting here who live in it." The crowd applauded loudly at his words, and more mugs were banged on the cluttered tables.

Mauro continued, "I lift my glass to my tenant farmers for completing the first planting this spring with limited men at home to help in the fields. May God grant us the right rain and fair weather for the growing season." There were more cheers and applause for a successful harvest, and Mauro continued on with his gratitude.

Resi listened to her husband and predicted it would be a long speech, with so many dignitaries in attendance to thank. The heat of the room and the smoke from the burning torches were beginning to affect her vision. She concentrated on the new tapestries on the walls to keep her mind in the present. Mauro continued talking, but the words faded as she struggled to breathe the stale, hot air.

". . . and finally," Mauro said to the room, "I raise my cup to your baroness, my beautiful wife, Lady Baric." Mauro extended his arm toward Resi; the faces in the room turned her way as she looked around the crowd. "Thank you for this wonderful feast tonight, and God's blessings on our one-year wedding anniversary."

Mauro smiled broadly at her while holding up his mug; the cheering crowd followed with their glasses and mugs held up toward the baroness. Lady Nikolina and Elizabeta prodded Resi to pick up her own. She looked to

Ruby across the room for support. Her laughing expression beamed in Resi's direction, and Resi lifted her glass in appreciation of the honor. Mauro sat down again, and the murmur of voices resumed its natural thrumming in the great hall.

What had just happened? Resi was floating in a dream. It had been a coincidence that the day of the feast was the same as their wedding date. She only realized this after the invitations had been delivered. She had not dared to expect Mauro to remember the significance of today with all the important things he had to keep track of. But he had announced to the entire party that it was important to him. It was a start, she decided; a very good start, indeed. Resi smiled with joy.

With the speeches concluded, the visitors began to depart. It was already hours past sundown, but a few of the gentlemen, Mauro's officers, and his stewards retired to his study to discuss more private matters. Mauro caught his wife's eye as he escorted his male guests into his sanctuary. He gave a nod toward the stairs to indicate that she should go up to bed without him. Resi was so tired that she did not think to argue.

She said her last goodbyes to the departing guests, and she and Ruby climbed the stairs to their own quarters. Verica had returned upstairs earlier and was there to help her mistress undress and brush out her pinned hair. Resi thought back on the day that began in the apricot orchards, then swimming in the river, and now her husband thanking her for being his wife. She would wait up for Mauro to finally tell him her other news. She knew tonight was the perfect time to announce she was having his child, and he would be so pleased with her.

"The gown was a complete success, Verica. Thank you," Resi told her maid as she finished dressing in her sleeping robe.

"Thank you, my lady, for letting me join the festivities. I have never seen such a merry crowd. I had a wonderful time," Verica said. She tidied the forgotten clothes littering the floor, opened the shutters, then bid her mistress a good night. The evening air was warm, but Resi crawled under the bedcovers for comfort and, despite her best intentions to stay awake, fell fast asleep.

~ * ~

When Mauro woke that morning, it was before daylight, as usual. The first birds sang out that dawn was near. He had accepted an invitation to hunt with Lord Leopold, but in the rush of the past few days, Mauro had neglected to tell his wife. Mauro would already be late; the others would be waiting for him in the courtyard just after sunrise. The traveling party would accompany

Lady Nikolina's carriage. She had spent the night in one of the Barics' guest rooms, and an early departure was the small price she had agreed to pay for the security of the soldiers' company on the trip home.

Mauro groaned softly as he lifted his head to see the other side of the bed. His body told him to stay sleeping, but he had been trained that duty came first. To his relief, his wife was deep asleep. Her peaceful face had the shadow of a smile across it.

He had only been home again three days, but there was too much unspoken between them. He had a duty to make that right, too. He had not had a real conversation with her in months. Watching her now, he realized that he knew little more about her than what he knew when they first met a year ago. In his heart, Mauro regretted he had been gone from her so often. In their first brief weeks together, Mauro was pleased to have such an attractive and attentive bride. But then political conflicts had taken his small army away for several months shortly thereafter. When he returned in the autumn, she had told him that she carried his child. He had been filled with pride and happiness at the news.

After months of war, though, he had been lustful and needy, and she had been so willing to please him. When she lost the first child soon after his return, he could not bring himself to touch her again out of guilt. She had recovered quickly from the early miscarriage and, as a dutiful wife, came to him again. He did not understand how she could have forgiven him so easily.

And now she carried his second child, and he faced the same constraints again. In the dimness of the growing dawn, Mauro appraised her trim body, now exposed to the morning air. He could not deny that he felt a passion for her. He reached across the bed and pulled the coverlet over his peaceful wife. He smiled at the funny frown it caused. No, he decided, as he sat on the side of the bed. He would not touch her these next months. He made his choice with a sigh, tugged on the breeches that he had dropped earlier on the floor, then tucked in the shirt he had changed into before crawling into bed just a few hours ago.

Davor had already packed his hunting clothes yesterday; the traveling bag was downstairs. Mauro crept out of the room with his stockings and boots in hand to finish dressing outside the door. He would eat his morning meal in the Keep with his soldiers. Mauro told himself he would make time for his wife when he returned in a few days.

Chapter 14

The sun shone brightly through the open shutters onto Resi's pillow. She reached her hand out across the mattress and felt that she was alone in her bed. At least Mauro had slept there in the night, she thought. His side of the bed was crumpled and still smelled musky with his familiar scent. She rolled to where he had lain, lingering there as her maid entered with her breakfast tray. Verica smiled at her mistress, thinking she had interrupted a dream. "Have you seen my husband today?" Resi sleepily asked.

"I have not seen his lordship, but I asked for you in the kitchen." She set the tray of food and hot coffee down on the large table in the corner. "The baron left earlier this morning with a hunting party and isn't expected back for several days," Verica said.

Resi clutched the pillow, still faintly warm from Mauro's recent presence. She was now wide awake and realized nothing had changed after all. "Unbelievable. I thought we would have some time alone, some time together, just the two of us today." She got up and went to the table to have a drink of the coffee Verica had just poured. "What is so important about a hunting party?"

"I am not the one to ask, my lady," Verica replied. "I have no experience with men to understand how their minds work. Noblemen are especially complicated, if you will forgive my impertinence."

Resi thought the same and agreed with her maid, but said no more while she quietly ate her breakfast. Verica finished laying out the clothes her mistress would choose from, and then excused herself to fetch hot water for her grooming.

Ruby knocked and entered her room, dressed for the day. Without Ruby, Resi would have felt very alone in the strange land with a husband who did not include her in his life. She had felt the urge to run away many times, and had written to her family saying so. They returned words of encouragement, but told her she must stay, no matter what.

In her own self-pity, she did not notice that Ruby had not said a word to her. Resi finally looked over at her friend, standing by the open window. "What are you looking at down there, Ruby?" Resi put on her dressing robe and joined her at the window.

"I am just looking out," Ruby said with a pink blush, having been caught.

"Yes, I can see you are looking out. And now I can see who you are looking at."

Jero and the gardener were talking by the cutting garden below the window. Resi said with new insight, "You favor Jero, don't you? I saw that you were sitting with him at the banquet last night."

They were speaking in Greek, but Ruby shut the window so he could not hear her say his name. "I don't favor anyone," Ruby said too sternly. "Jero is a nice man, and I like talking to him. He is kind and, well, handsome and ... All right, I find him appealing. Why shouldn't I?" She was no longer stern, but looked defeated instead.

"Because he is my steward, Ruby." Resi knew this did not sound like a good reason, so went on to explain, "I like Jero, too. He is a good man. But he cannot provide for you the way you are used to living."

"You know I don't care about money," Ruby argued. "I want to fall in love. And I could with him."

Resi wanted her friend to have the love in a marriage that she didn't. "Yes, love is better. But so are clean clothes, and fresh bread, and a tasty stew to eat. You don't know the first thing about keeping a house or cooking a meal." Ruby was still staring down into the garden through the shut glass. "If you married Jero," Resi continued, "Mauro would give him a nice cottage with a little vegetable garden for you to grow your cabbages in. There would be no servant or cook to prepare it for you."

"We could live here, like we do now," Ruby said hopefully.

"You could not stay in the manor house married to Jero. It doesn't work that way. Jero will marry a girl from the castle or the village who will be glad to have the little cottage. Besides, you know you will probably marry someone your father arranges. You cannot fall in love here." Ruby was near tears, and Resi put her arm around her shoulder. "There, there, Ruby. Let him be kind to you, admire you. You can have that much before you go. But do not fall in love with him, because he cannot have a chance to love you back."

Ruby fought the brimming tears. "Am I to go home soon, Resi?"

"Mauro will not send you away, if that is what you are worried about. He does not care one way or another, I imagine. It is up to your father, whether he calls you back home."

Ruby sniffed back the last sob and quietly watched Jero out the window as Verica returned with a steaming pail of water.

~ * ~

The ladies passed the day in the garden helping Ranko trim the first faded roses and peonies. The early summer weather did not hold, and the day was cool and cloudy. "I wish I could go riding," Resi told Ruby, as they put the rose petals into a basket to keep for making scented soap later. "I had such a perfect day out in the fields yesterday. I have the urge to just ride beyond the orchards until I am lost somewhere."

"You don't mean that, Resi. Besides, you cannot ride now that you are pregnant again. You don't want to risk losing the baby." Ruby waited for her friend to reply, but Resi continued her pruning. "You will have this baby, Resi, and then you will be so happy. You will never want to leave the castle walls again."

Resi finally looked up at her companion and tried to smile. She knew that pregnant women had blue moods with the cheery ones, and she vowed to be cheerful today. "I suppose you are right. Maybe I can't go riding, but I wish I didn't always need to be escorted everywhere. We cannot even walk to the village alone without my husband being afraid for us. We have no freedom here."

"I am sure he has good reasons for it. Even if the castle road is guarded, the village is not. He is the baron and was attacked himself just outside his own lands. These are not safe times, Resi. Besides," Ruby added, "when it is Hugo's turn to escort us, we always have some laughs, don't we?" She nudged her friend.

"Yes, I like Hugo. He is good company compared to the others," Resi agreed more cheerfully. She looked up at the sky as the first drops of rain fell down on them. "I think we have enough petals to make some nice soaps and rose water. Shall we go in?" They collected their baskets and hurried back indoors.

~ * ~

The evening meal was quiet in contrast to the lively festivities of the night before. Most of the soldiers were away from the castle. Fabian and Vilim were spending a few days at the salt mines supervising the next transport in Mauro's place. Stephan and a handful of men had joined Mauro on the hunting expedition. Hugo and Simeon ate their meals that evening in the kitchen, flirting with the kitchen maids. Idita had taken her light supper up to her own chamber that night, but Jero and Nestor had joined the ladies and the house servants in the great hall.

Ruby broke the silence after they had finished their meal. "Resi, should I fetch the harp and lute? Maybe we can play a song or two tonight." This caught the attention of the group around the solemn dinner table.

The eager expressions on her servants' faces cheered her. "All right, Ruby. I think we left our instruments in the sitting room." Ruby wasted no time finding them.

The party moved to the new seating area near the hearth, and the two women began to strum a tune to the small group. Both had melodic voices that blended well when they sang their native songs. Even though their audience did not understand the words that they sang, they enjoyed the serene entertainment. The music resonated through the open door to the servants' hallway, and soon the soldiers and kitchen maids came out to listen to the performance.

Simeon had a great baritone voice and later sang several rowdier songs for the household, while Hugo strummed along on Ruby's lute. Verica and Natalija danced a jig together to the lustful songs, and even Nestor stomped and clapped to the music. Geoff had sneaked in from outside and stood at the corner of the servants' doorway, but the girls pulled him into their circle to dance, too. The small, impromptu party went on until well after dark as the rain thundered outside.

Chapter 15

The next morning started gray and dark to match the baroness' temperament. She lingered in bed with no particular plans. The castle ran itself in a businesslike manner, organized by the competent Jero, who seemed to know just what was needed before it was needed. There were dozens of servants working at the Baric compound like a busy beehive. Resi knew all of the house servants by name and most of the estate keepers. Their duties were specific in the kitchen, chambers, pantries, stables, gardens and grounds, kennels and livestock, buttery, armory, greenhouses, bathhouse. There was always someone performing some activity quietly around her, yet Resi felt very alone at the large house today.

After her noon meal, she left her room for a change of scenery. She thumbed through the books she had recently organized on the shelves in their sitting room. Her maids did not disturb her when she was alone in there. They were mystified she could enjoy the bound pages of long words they saw in her books. The girls only had the basic education to read simple words themselves.

Resi chose *The Iliad*, one of the few books she had brought from home, printed in her native Greek. She had read this song of war and unhappiness before, but it had been long ago, and Resi wanted to feel the emotion it had brought. The threat of a new storm appealed to her, and she hoped it would rain again to wash away her gloominess.

It had rained hard during the night, and the terrace was still soggy with the drying puddles. Despite the dampness, Resi moved outdoors and found a dry seat under the eaves of the house as the sun tried to break free of the clouds. She enjoyed reading on this inviting terrace compared to the one off the great hall. It was small and intimate, set at the back of the house near the corner of the east wall. The noises of the courtyard and its activities were muted here, and she soon became lost in her book.

"My lady," Verica interrupted the spell. "A messenger has just arrived with a letter for you. Jero said it was urgent that I bring it."

Resi felt a twinge of panic. What was so urgent? Was her husband injured? Was someone in her family gravely ill, or even dead? She opened the letter and recognized the careful script of her brother Patricius.

"The messenger is waiting for a reply, if you would like me to bring out ink and paper," Verica told her when she thought the baroness had finished reading the one-page letter.

"Thank you, but I fear I cannot reply until I speak to my husband." Resi set her book down on the table next to her. "I think I will walk the grounds before it rains again," she told her maid with an uncharacteristic calmness.

Verica curtsied politely, but wondered whether her mistress was distressed, and whether she should find Lady Ruby, who could offer her company on her walk. Resi did not give her the chance to ask. She picked up her letter and stepped down the short terrace steps to the path that led away from the house.

Jero was in Mauro's study recording figures in the account books when he heard the dogs barking. He looked out the study window, which had a view of the Keep and the yards around it, and watched the baroness walk away with the brown hound wagging its tail at her side. Not again, thought Jero. Roko, the kennel master, would complain again that the baroness was making his best guard dogs into tame house pets. Roko had insisted on telling the baron of the incidences, but Jero had convinced him it would not happen again. Jero set down his quill, took his coat from the chairback, and left the house to find the baroness.

Resi was sitting on a bench under the rose arbor near the bathhouse when Jero found her. The dog was at her side, and she absently stroked its scruffy fur. When Resi looked up, Jero's heart sank. She was crying, and he did not know if he would be able to find any words to comfort her.

"My lady, I am sorry to disturb you. Did you receive bad news, then?"

Resi set the letter down on her lap again, noticing him for the first time. She wiped her hand across her cheeks to catch the tears. "No, Jero. It is happy news. It is from my brother Patricius, and he tells me he is nearby and asks to come visit me."

Jero stood in front of her and smiled as best he could to his distressed mistress. "That is excellent news." He tried to sound enthusiastic.

"Of course, I will need to ask my husband's permission, if he is ever home long enough. The letter seems to say that the messenger will know my brother's route. He will be able to find him with my answer, if Patricius is not too far away when he finally receives my reply." She started crying again, this time with deep sobs.

Jero regarded the miserable woman in front of him with pity. If he wasn't her servant, he would have acted to comfort her in her grief, but the impropriety of touching Mauro's wife would not so easily be forgiven by the baron. He looked around the path and saw that they were alone. He sat on the bench next to her, his side touching hers, hoping that his closeness would be enough to console her without being noticed by a passing servant.

"I don't know why I am crying," she finally said.

"That is normal for ladies in your condition," Jero began soothingly, and quickly realized his mistake when she gave him a shocked glance.

"Condition?" She looked at him for a long, uncomfortable moment while she continued to stroke the peaceful dog. "You know I am pregnant, don't you? Of course! There are no secrets here. I haven't even gotten to tell my husband! I suppose the entire castle knows I am with child. And my husband, too?"

Jero was nervous, sensing the baroness was about to become hysterical. He would have to find a way to calm her, and he hoped his words were the right ones. "Yes, my lady, it is known that you are with child. I am sorry you could not talk with your husband first. I hope I am not being presumptuous to tell you congratulations, and we at the castle all wish you and your baby well."

She sniffled loudly, but Jero was relieved that she had stopped crying. It took all his concentration to keep from reaching out and holding her hand. He looked over to the bathhouse at the end of the path. "I have an idea," he went on to say. "I will take old Brownie here back to the kennels before Roko has a fit, and you, madam, shall go have a lovely soak in your bathhouse." The raindrops had started to plop softly through the rose vines. "I will tell Verica where she can find you, and then notify the messenger that he must wait until the baron returns."

She looked up at him, nodding between sniffles, and then released the dog into his hands. "Thank you, Jero." She stood and began to walk the short distance to the small building, but turned to add, "You will not tell my husband that I am such a crybaby, will you?"

Jero looked at his mistress with admiration. He gave her a hopeful smile. "No, my lady. It would be a lie for me to say so."

She was better now, and she let out a small laugh at his kind words before she disappeared through the door.

~ * ~

The bathhouse was the only place on the estate that was just for Resi. Mauro had told her that no one was to use it without her permission; it would be her refuge. She walked through the entrance, past the fountain with its cool water. A lattice screen had been designed into the wall for a separation from the bathing pool. She passed the arched entrance there and set her brother's letter down on the marble bench near the opening to the round room.

The interior was not large, but it was covered in enchanting mosaics depicting Greek scenes and lovely gardens, surrounded on all sides with smooth benches. It was well lit from the glass dome above, but there were no windows along the walls. Small vents could be opened and closed to bring in fresh air, depending on the heat of the room, and she shut these now to let the steam from the hot bathwater rise. The bathing pool was built with benches within the pool for reclining and soaking, and the middle was deep for standing submerged.

Mauro had explained that Turkish architects brought in from Budapest had designed the domed structure. The mountains just above the bathhouse had both hot and cold springs that were piped in to keep the bathwater fresh, and a building master had been hired to stay on to maintain it. There was a bolt on the door, but Resi had never thought to use it.

The baroness took her time undressing and hung her clothes on one of the many pegs along the tiled wall. Her tears were dry now, and she took pleasure in soaking the rest of herself. It was a wonderful solution, to steam away her unhappiness.

Resi thought about Ruby's feelings for Jero, and she understood why Ruby found him so appealing. He wasn't the most handsome of the men at Baric Castle. He was obviously not a wealthy man, with only a modest income befitting his station in life. He chose his limited attire well, and his tasteful clothes highlighted his athletic build and lean frame. He reminded her of a softer, kinder Mauro, although she had not really thought about it until today. Her husband had golden brown hair that he kept short, whereas Jero's was a longer, darker brown that curled when it came loose from its binding, which was almost constantly. Jero preferred a trimmed, full beard to perhaps hide his weak chin, but had full lips and a bright, straight smile under his long nose. Mauro's clean-shaven face let his square jawline compliment his chiseled features, with a narrower nose that pointed to his full lips and prominent chin. Both had green eyes, although Mauro's were a little lighter, and Jero's a little grayer. Resi brushed away the comparisons. Maybe she wished it had been Mauro who had found her beneath the roses and not Jero. She leaned back and decided she would think no more of men. They only brought her sorrow today.

Chapter 16

The noblemen and their entourage returned early to Baron Leopold's castle on the second afternoon away. The hunting outing in Leopold's forest had to be cut short due to the steady downpour. Mauro was now anxious to return to his own home. The remorse of leaving his delicate wife for a second time without notice was unexpectedly gnawing at him. He was sorry to put his men through another miserable ride, but Mauro decided his own party would ride directly back to Baric Castle that evening.

The roads were thick with mud from the ceaseless rain, and the horses were lathered from the extra effort it caused. When they finally rode into the courtyard, all the windows of the manor house were dark. It was nearly midnight. Mauro thanked Stephan and the others for enduring the wet, hard journey, when they could have slept one more night in comfort at Lord Leopold's castle and ridden the same road easily in the daylight.

Josip was the stable groom on duty that night. He woke when the guards opened the heavy castle gate. He came with two lanterns to greet the tired riders; a sleepy Geoff trailed behind him with a third light. They all worked quickly to dry their steeds and unload their hunting bounty. Then the group eagerly went off toward the Keep to their dry, warm beds.

Mauro was still standing under the shelter shaking his dripping cape when he had second thoughts about going to his own bed. "Geoff," he called to the stable groom. "Take your lantern and go wake your sister." Geoff nodded. "This is important now: Tell Verica to wake my wife. The baroness is to bring me clean clothes directly to the bathhouse. You will escort her just to the bathhouse door, is that understood?" He smiled encouragingly at the sleepy boy, who stood before Mauro with an opened mouth, trying not to forget his instructions.

"To the bathhouse door. Directly. Yes, my lord. I will wake my sister," Geoff repeated, then he hurried to the servants' entrance of the main house. The disappearance of his swaying lamplight in the dark storm let Mauro know that he had made it inside.

Verica had a small room off the Barics' bedroom. It had an entrance door to the hallway and one to the couple's chamber. The servant's room was meant to be convenient, so the groom or maid could serve the nobleman or his wife at a moment's notice. Lord Lorenc had decided long ago that his father's design for convenience was instead a disruption to his privacy, and he had a heavy wardrobe placed in front of the maid's entrance on his side of the door.

The maid's room was not much bigger than one of the privy rooms downstairs. But with the second door on the longer wall blocked off, there was space for a small table with a washbasin, a chair next to it, along with Verica's bed and an extra storage chest in the cozy room. She had six pegs along the wall where she hung her change of clothes, her aprons, cloak, and linens for washing up. She kept her treasures in her trunk, neatly tucked away. Verica had few possessions except the small gifts she had received from the Barics over the years. Her mistress had given her an oval-looking glass and an elegant hairbrush last Christmas that she kept on the table next to her candle holder.

Verica was still not used to sleeping alone. She did not remember their family's cottage before her father died, but knew she had slept in a small bed with her brother. Her widowed mother gave up their cottage and came back to live at the castle, where she had been employed in the kitchen.

When their mother died, the children were adopted by the kitchen maids, and they slept on a pallet there by the hearth. When Verica was thirteen, she was allowed to have her own bed in the female servants' dormitory. The baron gave her this empty room when he married her mistress.

Verica sometimes left her door open to the hallway at night. Not to better hear her mistress, if called, but because she did not like to be alone in the dark room. There was one small window above her bed that let in a little light and just enough breeze to stir the stuffy air in the summer. On this night, she had left the door open, but did not hear her brother until he was right up next to her ear. She almost cried out, but he had the lamp near his face, and she saw it was only Geoff.

It was somewhere closer to morning when Verica shook the baroness to wake her. Verica was dressed in her night shift and looked white with panic; Resi was terrified to know why. "My lady, Geoff has been instructed by his lordship to take you to the bathhouse. The baron is back and wants dry clothes, my lady. He said that only you could take them to him."

"I don't understand. My husband isn't coming home for at least two more days," Resi stammered as she tried to clear the sleep from her thoughts. "He is in the bathhouse? Are you sure?"

Verica had lit some candles and was already gathering garments from the baron's trunk that she thought he might need; she hoped she had not forgotten anything important. "Geoff spoke to him at the stables. They came back early because of the rain. Hurry, my lady, let me help you dress."

Resi slipped on a satin robe over her sleeping gown, then a long cloak over that to keep her dry in the pouring rain. Verica handed her the stack of clean clothes, then followed her with her candle down the hallway to meet Geoff at the stairs. He was crouched on the top step holding the lantern in the dark hallway. The baroness left down the stairs with him in silence.

~ * ~

Mauro had never bathed in his wife's bathhouse. He had wanted Resi to have some place private to call her very own at her new home. He lit the wall lamps when he came in and found the glow of the room sensual and seductive. The colorful walls and the sound of cascading water added to the allure of it. He was pleased with his final gift to her.

Mauro sat on the first bench near the paneled entrance and removed his cape and boots. That was when he noticed the papers on the end of the seat. He reached to examine what his wife had left there. He read the brief letter, then set it back down where it had lain. He would wait for Resi to broach the topic of her brother, but was glad he had time to first contemplate the request.

Stripped and feeling already warmer from the steamy air, Mauro stepped into the bath and sank to the middle of the pool to free his clinging hair of the rain and mud. This was very nice indeed, he thought to himself, and he took a seat on the bench built into the pool wall to wash with the scented soap left near the ledge.

Mauro remembered when he had first seen the construction plans that winter before his bride came to him. The architects were very insistent that the pool be designed at the right height for the baron. He told them that the bath would be for his wife, and he did not expect to use it. He smiled at his own ignorance and closed his eyes, enjoying the liquid heat.

"Am I disturbing you, Husband? I brought your clean garments you asked for."

He had not heard Resi come in. She was misty from the walk through the rain and clutched the pile of clothes to her chest. Her hair hung loose around her shoulders from the hastily tied ribbon that had come undone in the wind, and she had a worried look across her pretty features.

"Set them down over there." He pointed to the first marble bench. "I am sorry I woke you." Mauro watched her as he continued to lean nearly submerged along the pool wall. "I wanted your company, but I see that I should have let you sleep."

She put his things on the bench across from him in the pool and then sat down next to them. "Have you bathed today?" he asked lightly, feeling thoroughly relaxed from his half hour in the warm water. "Do you want to join me?" She released her breath and a small laugh, staring at him in the pool. Mauro smiled at her, too, in his steamy drunkenness.

"If you count yesterday as today, then I have bathed today. I came in here earlier by myself and had a very peaceful bath." Resi continued to look at him. "Thank you for my sanctuary," she added sweetly.

"Ah, and here I am using it without your permission." He sat up and smoothed his hair off his face with his hands. "I may ask you again another time, and I hope you will grant me permission. I find it surprisingly enjoyable." He stood up and looked at his palms. "But I am turning into a prune, so I will get out now, if you could hand me a linen from the stack beside you?"

Resi continued to stare at the marvelous creature climbing out of the water in front of her. She had never been in the room at night with the dim torches glowing. It made her husband look like a statue from her father's courtyard, with swirls of fine hair plastered against his chiseled muscles. She snapped back to the present as he walked toward her and was, unlike the statues, unashamedly aroused.

He suppressed a grin at her discomfort as he leaned past her and took two linen drapes; he wrapped one around his waist and with the other began drying his hair. He stopped his chore, stood just a breath away from her, and bent to kiss her parted mouth tenderly. "Are you happy here, Resi?" he asked casually, as though asking the time of day.

She was fully awake now, but this scene in the steamy room still seemed unreal to her. "You called me Resi. You have never called me by that name before," was all she could say in her foggy state of mind.

"I did, and I would like it very much if you would call me Mauro." He kissed her again, softly brushing her lips as he said, "You have not answered my question."

Was this a trick? How should she answer? Was she unhappy, really? She was trapped in a loveless marriage, and she was a month's journey from the home that she craved to see again. But there was the beginning of change, and she was hopeful that, in time, maybe her husband could learn to love her.

"Yes," she replied. "I am happy. Mauro."

He took her two hands in his and pulled her to her feet to look into her eyes. He did not believe her, but he was glad that she had told him yes. He leaned down and kissed her softly above her brow this time. He could feel her exhale. She had been holding her breath. Her answer was meant to please him, and he smiled again in earnest. He moved to the pile of clothes she had brought him and began dressing in silence.

Resi sat back down on her end of the smooth bench and realized, for the first time in three days, she had his undivided attention. "I am pregnant, Mauro," she blurted out. He stopped buckling his belt and looked at her. "I know that you already knew, but I wanted to tell you myself," she said shyly. She looked sad, and he pitied that it was not a surprise to him.

"I wish more than anything that you had been the one to tell me first. That does not change how happy you have made me with this news," he whispered.

He reached across the bench to touch her cheek. He felt an odd emotion tug at him, but his words did not express it. "We have both had a long day," he said. "Shall we go to our room now?" She nodded and silently watched him pull on his muddy boots and soaked cloak again, leaving the other things scattered on the floor.

The clouds had blown clear, and the stars shined brightly against the black sky. They walked side by side in silence to the servants' entrance at the back of the house. They took the servants' stairway up to their bedchamber, where they disrobed unceremoniously. The couple quietly slipped into bed together, each lost in their own thoughts at the late hour.

Mauro thought Resi was asleep when he slid closer and gently pulled her warm body to him. He wrapped his one strong arm around her waist. She had not taken the time to bind her hair again, and he buried his face in it beside her neck, breathing in the fragrance. She felt him relax, and his breathing slowed. He was asleep against her. She took his hand from her waist and placed it across her breasts, enjoying the sensual touch that she longed for again. She fell asleep a moment later.

Chapter 17

The sheet next to Resi was already cool, and she panicked. It had been a dream, and Mauro was not home. She opened her eyes and saw her maid sitting on the window seat looking out. "Verica, I had the strangest dream last night," Resi declared. Her maid looked up from her own daydream.

"My lady, you are awake," Verica said in a startled voice. "I was told to be near you when you woke. His lordship did not want you to think he had left you again, but he did not want to disturb your sleep, either." Verica smiled as she considered how romantic his instructions had seemed. "Come, my lady. The baron asked that you see him in his study as soon as you are dressed."

The maid opened the wardrobe and pulled out several garments for her mistress, not knowing which she might choose. Resi sat up and smoothed her tangled locks, thinking about what her servant had just explained. "In the study?" Resi mumbled as she rose urgently from her warm bed. "How late is it?"

"It is well past dawn, Lady Baric," Verica answered in a rush of energy. "Which would you like to wear? You always look very pretty in the green." She held up the choices of gowns for her, then frowned suddenly, noticing the baroness' tangled tresses for the first time. "I'll have to take extra care with your hair this morning. Shall I call for your breakfast?" She did not wait for an answer, but left in a hurry to find Natalija in the corridor.

Natalija brought Resi's morning meal a few minutes later. She was confused by the obvious anxiety of the two women and the piles of robes scattered around the room. She ran down the corridor to inform Ruby of Verica's odd distress getting her mistress ready for the day. Ruby immediately came to hear what had happened that morning.

The three women quickly finished dressing the baroness. In the end, they all agreed that the pale blue robes matched the light of the morning better than the green, gauze gown. Even though Ruby was only half-dressed herself, she stayed to help Verica add the finishing touches to Resi's ensemble.

No one spoke of why they were so anxious to highlight Resi's beauty; it was only a request from her husband to come to his study. But the women sensed that something had changed in the house last night, and they were not going to waste this opportunity for the baroness.

After all the extra attention, Resi found she was nervous walking down the stairs and crossing the wide foyer to her husband's private room.

~ * ~

Resi knocked lightly on the sturdy wooden door and entered. Idita was just packing her medicine basket. Resi watched Mauro pull his shirtsleeve down over his arm. She had noticed the stitching last night in the bathhouse, but had forgotten it was still fresh and raw. "Resi, come in," Mauro said as he stood from his chair and replaced his doublet. Idita turned and gave a small curtsy to her mistress and a short glare back at Mauro.

"I will check your arm again tomorrow. No more baths until the stitching is out," Idita scolded her patient. "Will you keep your promise?" she added with a softer stare now.

"You know best, Idita. I promise to rest the arm," he said kindly as he took her wrinkled hand in his and kissed it lightly. "And no more baths."

He looked up from his old nurse and winked at Resi, who was still standing by the door watching the domestic scene. Resi tried to picture the little boy who needed strength from Idita. She wanted to know more about that Mauro. She only knew the capable man who, until yesterday, was as cool as the rainstorm that had ruined his hunting party. But he was warming to her, and she was grateful for the opening in his heart.

After Idita left the room, Resi looked around with curiosity. She had never been in Mauro's study. It was his sanctuary, a place for men and the affairs of men, and it had never occurred to her to disturb that world. It was a large room that took up the front southwest corner of the house at the foyer entrance. The space was filled with masculine furnishings that reminded her of the worn usefulness of her father's favorite ship. A rectangular writing table near the furthest window was piled with leather-bound ledgers and scattered parchments. There were two, heavy chairs with crumpled cushions next to it. Closest to the door was a larger, long table where Mauro and Idita had just been sitting; a dozen chairs surrounded it. The massive table was scrubbed and smooth, like it had been used for a hundred years by a thousand people. There was a map she recognized from her father's shipping business, and other sketches and documents rolled and unrolled next to it.

Despite the dark furnishings and faded tapestries, the room was bright with windows to the west that overlooked the courtyard and the Keep. The south windows overlooked the kitchen gardens and the wall. Resi instinctively walked to a southern window; Mauro watched her in silence.

Danica was out there with Franja collecting the first fresh herbs for drying. Resi enjoyed collecting from the gardens, but it had never occurred to her that she might have had an audience from the study watching her. She turned back to the room and was startled that Mauro had moved next to her. "I have never been in here," Resi said, almost to herself.

"My apologies for that," Mauro answered. "Nestor works here, and Jero uses this room when I ask him to tend to special affairs for me. Otherwise, I keep the room locked."

By her curious expression, Mauro decided he should explain further. "My father was a secretive man. I am not so much, but I suppose I understand the need to keep some places under key. We are salt traders, Resi, and it was quite profitable the way my father did business. I do not agree with everything he did in the past, but I have continued in his footsteps. We are under pressure from the Venetians to sell all our salt to just them." He paused and looked at her as she listened to his story. "We sell to others as well," he confided. "So, to protect the business, there are some secrets. My estate is well-guarded, but I would not want important information leaving this room."

Wanting to lighten the mood away from business, Mauro changed the subject. "Come, sit down, Resi. I wanted to talk to you about other things."

Resi sat on the chair that had just been occupied by Idita, and Mauro sat across from her. He had shaved this morning, and his tanned skin was smooth along his jaw. She liked looking at his light eyes and was lost in them for a moment.

"Wine?" He offered her the goblet of wine he had just poured. He took a gulp of his own and considered how he would begin the speech that he had practiced in his head that morning. "Are you well, Resi?" It was a start.

"I am. Thank you, Mauro," she countered. She held the goblet, but did not think she could manage to swallow any wine, so she set it down in front of her.

He took a breath and another drink before telling her, "I am not very good at this. I have mastered a lot of things, but I am finding I am not good at this."

Resi waited a moment, hoping he would clarify exactly what 'this' was.

Mauro saw in her face that he would need to do better. He tried again. "There is nothing more important to me than to see you happy." He stood up and walked to the west window to open it, in need of air. Resi watched him as he closed it again, distracted by his own thoughts. "I asked you last night if you were happy. I think I really wanted to know that you are. Why did you lie to me?"

Resi felt a jolt as the accusation sunk in. She looked at her husband's softened eyes, and unguarded tears began to form in her own eyes. She had to think quickly while he waited for her answer.

She shook her head. "I didn't lie, but I didn't tell the whole truth, either. I have been treated kindly here, and for that I am grateful and happy." She tried to smile as a tear dropped onto the table. "I have no right to expect more than that, and it should be enough," she confessed.

Mauro sat down beside her and took her hand in his for the first time. "But," he prompted. He was sincere; she could see it. She would be honest.

She wiped the corners of her eyes with the lace on her sleeve and gathered her strength. "I thought I was prepared to come here," she began, looking out the window, not daring to look at his face. "I had been taught what I should expect about your customs, your language, and dress. My mother told me what she knew about men and what to expect in our marriage bed." Mauro watched her, listening. "But no one could have prepared me for you."

She looked him in his eyes, willing herself to confide what she needed to tell him. "I need to know why you find me so revolting. I must be, or you wouldn't keep other lovers." Having said the words out loud, she was angry now. "Why will you not come to me, not share your life with me?"

"Resi, please . . ." Mauro began, trying to cover his panic at this unexpected turn in their conversation.

Once started, she could now finish. "If you cannot love me as a wife, then I must find a way to be happy without your love. I will bear your children, and I will try to be a good wife to you." Then Resi dared to ask what she really wanted to know. "Tell me, Mauro—why are *you* so unhappy?"

He wasn't prepared for this question and looked back at her blankly. He could not sit next to her now; he was stunned that she could see it. He was unhappy, but she was not the reason. "I do not know," he lied. "And you are not," he stammered, "not revolting. You are lovely and charming. You are more than I ever expected for a wife," he said to her from the other side of the room. "I did not mean to hurt you, Resi. You lost the first baby, and I won't put you through that again."

She went to his side, as close as she dared stand without touching him. "Mauro—" She began to protest, trying to understand his reasoning.

He interjected, "You are right, you know. I did not want to bring you here. I married you out of duty to my father, because of the arrangement he had made for us. I did not think I needed anyone in my life, really. It was easier to not have to worry about anyone else, or have anyone worry for me. But then they gave me you." He was barely audible as he concluded, "And everything changed."

She reached out, and he let her take his hand this time. "It was a silly arrangement made long ago." Resi tried to sound comforting. She tried to be agreeable, even though her heart was ready to break. "Of course you don't need me."

Slowly he twined his fingers to hers and brought her hand up to kiss it. He looked in her eyes. "I am glad for this silly arrangement. I want you to be happy with me. I want to make this right. Can we try?"

His eyes pleaded for understanding. Unable to find any words, she nodded that she would. How could she not?

He pulled her close. "Thank you," he whispered.

A startling knock came from the closed door and time began again. Mauro kissed her where his chin had rested and walked across the room to open it. It was Jero, and they spoke in hushed voices for a moment before Mauro came back to her side.

"Resi, I am very sorry. I must leave you. Something urgent has happened at the salt mine, and I must go out for a while." He fought back the urge to take her into his arms and carry her upstairs right now, but he could not change so quickly who he had been trained to be. "I will be back before the evening meal. I promise." He kissed her again, this time softly on the lips to seal his promise.

They left the room together. Mauro left through the front door to the stables, and Resi climbed the stairs back to her chamber. Even though the weight of her world seemed to have been lifted, she felt very tired. But she did not want to be alone just then, so went instead to Ruby's room.

Ruby was at her window seat. It looked out to the southwest, over the apricot orchards by the river. Resi sat down next to her friend without a word of greeting. Ruby looked into her eyes with concern, not knowing what her odd expression could mean.

"I have so much to tell you, I hardly know where to start," Resi finally told her worried friend. "I have a wonderful feeling that everything is going to be different now."

~ * ~

Mauro's horse stopped at the edge of the slope that overlooked the white plain of shallow water that was the Baric salt mine. Generations ago, Mauro's ancestors learned how to coax pure salt from the sea for trade. The production was now in the able hands of the skilled Huzjak brothers, who had learned the mining tradition from their forefathers as servants of the Barics.

The hot May weather had made it possible to begin production for the season, and the first shipments had been loaded in his ship and onto the wagons for deliveries this week. Under the precarious Venetian rule, there were no more foreign markets. The baron's salt was to be sold to the Venetian customers at regulated prices. It was an open secret in Solgrad that not all of their salt production made it to Venice.

The Barics' salt was of an exceptional quality, with the purest grade of each batch sent by boat in sealed urns to Demetrius Kokkinos' waiting ship off the Ottoman shore. Demetrius would transport the urns and other sought-after commodities to the Barics' customers—the Dutch, the French, and the other Italian Republics who sailed the Mediterranean trade routes. It had worked successfully this way for years until Demetrius Kokkinos double-crossed the Barics.

Lord Lorenc thought he could lock up the Greek thief and let him rot in his brother's prison. He soon discovered that Demetrius Kokkinos was the best of the corrupt Mediterranean Sea traders, and the Barics could not continue their profitable black-market business without him after all.

So Kokkinos was released, but under special terms: his only daughter, who meant the world to him, would be promised to Lorenc Baric's son. Despite Demetrius' fees and the need for heavy bribing at the port, the profits for the Barics were still substantial—if they were not caught.

For years, the authorities had been persuaded to look the other way. This changed when the Venetian Navy took charge of all the small ports that had once been overlooked, monitoring all vessels that came and went out of Croatia. The region's new commander, Lieutenant D'Alessandro, would not play by the old rules. Under his command, the navy relentlessly watched the Baric salt production and its comings and goings. Last night, Mauro had lost the game of cat and mouse with the lieutenant.

Mauro guided his horse down the wide trail to the brackish water and his docks below. Fabian had just saddled his horse again to ride back to the castle. "There is nothing to be done now," Fabian shouted over to him. Mauro rode closer before he dismounted, then approached his friend at the dock.

"Jero said the ship was confiscated," Mauro said without a greeting. "Tell me what happened."

"It is a tricky situation now," Fabian explained. He took off his hat and shook the salt dust from it. "Did Jero tell you D'Alessandro has your crew, too?"

"Damn him to hell," Mauro shouted and threw his own hat.

"Mauro! Language!" Fabian chided.

Mauro gave him a cross look, but he knew Fabian was only trying to offset the grave circumstances with a bit of humor. In the Toth Army, the count did not tolerate cursing from his high-ranking officers. He found it vulgar and beneath their position, as well as a bad example to the soldiers. As a result of his training, Mauro never cursed. Fabian, on the other hand, was the worst offender and had often been reprimanded for his poor self-control.

"Did you send Anton already?" Mauro questioned him.

"Yes, your bailiff and Vilim went by horse together to sort it out. The bastard lieutenant was here himself," Fabian said. "I had to stay behind. There is nothing I hate more than the fucking Venetian Navy."

"I thought you hated the Habsburgs more?" Mauro asked absently, not needing an answer. He paced the dock, thinking about the seriousness of the situation and how to remedy it.

"Yes, number one: the Habsburgs," Fabian agreed, holding up one finger as he began to count out a list that Mauro had heard many times before. "And after them, number two: the Ottomans! A close third are the Spaniards, who are financing the Habsburgs with their stolen gold! But today, I put Lieutenant D'Alessandro and his *fucking navy* on top!"

Mauro stood by him again, now that he thought his ranting was over. Fabian declared more calmly, "The commander is impossible. Have you ever talked to the man, Mauro?"

Mauro had met with D'Alessandro on a few occasions, and he did not like the flashy overachiever. "Yes, and I am afraid I will have to talk to him again to get my *fucking* ship and crew back," he said with an emphasis to match Fabian's.

Fabian laughed. Mauro managed a small smile despite his rotten predicament. "If you were not my best friend, you would be a fucking nuisance. Did you know that, Fabian?"

Fabian slapped him on the back good-naturedly, then mounted his horse to leave. "That is what I live for, Mauro."

Mauro mounted his horse again, too, and continued to ask about the details as they rode away from the inlet. "Why did we miss the rendezvous with Demetrius' ship?"

"Because of the high seas," Fabian explained. "Your crew had to weigh anchor just offshore to wait out the storm last night, or the salt load in the hold would have been flooded. Your captain thought he was in Ottoman waters outside Tirana. I cannot understand how the Venetians could have followed, but your ship was boarded by the navy while it was at anchor, and then they confiscated it and took it to port. The lieutenant came here in person to gloat about his victory."

"This will cost me a fair amount to get the crew back. At least it was not a special shipment, so the navy cannot charge me beyond the fines for smuggling, right? I might be able to negotiate this with lire."

"They have elevated smuggling to more than a fine. They are jailing now. Who knows what he will write up this time," Fabian warned him.

"I will ride down to talk to Neven first thing tomorrow, and then go to D'Alessandro's office myself," Mauro decided. "Neven knows the man better than anyone, since the navy is stationed on his land."

They rode in silence as their horses negotiated the uneven terrain back to the main road. "I have one piece of different news that I wanted to discuss with you," Mauro announced when they were side by side again.

"Oh?" Fabian waited for him to continue.

"My wife received a letter from her brother Patrik, which might interest you. He was in Vienna and appears to be traveling back south. He wants to stop here to see his sister." Mauro looked over at his friend for his reaction.

"At least he knew better to send word first. And what did you tell your lady?" Fabian wanted to know.

"She has not had an opportunity to ask me. I expect she will find time to tell me about the letter tonight."

Fabian considered Mauro's statement. "Then how do you know all of this?"

"The letter was left on a bench, and I read it." Fabian raised his eyebrows, and Mauro continued to tell him, "He wrote that he will be coming with his small band of mercenaries."

"I remember them," Fabian said seriously. "They are excellent soldiers. Do you not trust them?"

Mauro considered whether he did. "I trust no one who switches alliances as readily as you change hats."

Fabian frowned at his teasing. Mauro did not approve of Fabian's choices of impractical headwear. "So, will you tell your wife yes?"

"I will. She will want to see her brother, and I have no good reason to deny her."

"Except her brother and his companions are dangerous men," Fabian reminded him.

Mauro nodded grimly. "From his letter, they predict to arrive in a fortnight."

"Perhaps they will not stay long." Fabian tried to sound encouraging.

"They won't," Mauro assured him.

Chapter 18

Resi woke from her restful nap with one, panicked thought: How could she have let him go without asking?

She had been pacing the great hall when Mauro returned several hours later, dusty and tired from the ride to the salt flats. She knew this would not be the best time to talk to him, but she found that there was never a good time for a private word with her husband.

"Mauro, I have something urgent to discuss with you," she began to explain as she walked toward the front door he had just closed. "It will only take a minute."

He knew what she would ask, but played along. "Come with me then, Resi. I would like a drink, and you can join me."

He unlocked the study door, and she went to the table she had sat at earlier that morning. He poured two mugs from the water pitcher and offered her one; he then sat down with an exhausted thud. He downed the cup's contents, then filled his mug again with wine from the open bottle on the table. Mauro looked at his wife and hoped his face did not show how miserable he felt.

"I received a letter from my brother Patricius," she said to him right away, before she lost her nerve. "He will be traveling south with a small company of four, and he wants to stop here to see me. A messenger is waiting to take my reply. May I tell him to come, Mauro?" She took a drink from her cup, expecting a long discussion and much pleading on her part, but she was hopeful she could persuade him to agree.

"If it pleases you, yes; of course he may visit," Mauro replied quickly, to her astonishment.

She beamed with excitement at the thought of seeing her favorite brother. "I don't know how long he will stay, but any visit will please me immensely. Thank you, Mauro!"

"Do you know these companions who are traveling with him?" Mauro casually asked.

"I am not sure who the four are. Unless there has been some tragedy, Salar Nassim is part of his company. He comes from Persia originally, but one can say he is from many places. He is very elegant and plays several musical instruments." She smiled as she described the most dangerous man Mauro had met in recent years. "He does cheat at cards, though," she added.

She went on to say, "Soren is likely with him. He is my brother's best friend, like Fabian is yours. He is from Denmark. I remember that he was a quiet man, but I suppose that was because his brother, Niels, did most of the talking for both of them." She chuckled at the memory. "Niels and Soren are twins. They claim they are not identical, but I think they look very much the same, since they *are* brothers and were born at the same time. You will like them. I remember they were both quite tall, even taller than you." She held her hand over her head when she mentioned their size. "Both are fair-haired, with broad shoulders." She motioned to the sides of her own shoulders as she described their physique. "And they have clear blue eyes." She smiled to herself as she recalled their faces.

"Resi, if you like them, then they are all welcome. I met the messenger waiting in the Keep. Go write your letter telling your brother to come. Give it to Jero, and then the man can be on his way with it."

"I will, right now. Thank you again, Mauro." She bounced up from her chair and kissed him quickly on the lips. She hurried out the study door to the sitting room to find some parchment.

Mauro watched his wife leave and let the warm touch of her lips linger on his thoughts. He had felt an unexpected pang of jealousy listening to her describe the mercenaries. At first, he could not understand his own reaction. She was an attractive woman, and he accepted the fact that she would be desirable to other men. But then he realized that the thought of her desiring another man was unacceptable to him. He hadn't considered until just a moment ago that she might have had possible suitors before she married him. He would have to keep an eye on her while the mercenaries were at the estate.

At least it was reassuring that she believed the only notable dangers they brought were the Danish brothers' killer-blue eyes and Salar Nassim's card cheating. For her sake, her brother's gang might be civil company while here. Mauro would make an effort to be a good host in return.

He could not dwell on this problem, with so many other troubles that needed to be tended to. He would write to Neven Leopold immediately to warn him of his urgent visit tomorrow. D'Alessandro's headquarters were at Baron Leopold's port town, and Mauro needed an ally to help him clear up his mess. He would also need money to save his ship and crew from impounding. Any large fees and penalties to the Venetian Empire could be handled with a promissory note through his banker. But he would need coins, and perhaps even some gold, to grease the palms to get any agreement signed.

Most of the gold and valuables kept at the castle were locked in the treasury room on the second floor of the Keep. Only Mauro and his stewards had access, but it was well-guarded, since it was located in the hall where his officers lived. He took a look around his desk to see how much silver was available there first. Jero kept his wife's allowance fund somewhere in the study. He searched the shelves and in the drawers, but there was no money to be found.

The door to the foyer was still open, and he called out, "Jero!"

Natalija was dusting the stairs just then. It was unusual for the master to shout in his house, so she stuck her head in the doorway to ask if she could be of assistance. "Thank you, Natalija. Find Jero and send him to me," Mauro ordered, and she hurried away.

It was part of his wife's contract to be given an annual allowance for her personal needs. It was kept in cash to purchase small items in the village as needed. Mauro had been quite generous with her, and he guessed there would still be plenty in her safe box, if he knew where to find it. He kept searching.

"Ah, Jero, there you are," Mauro said when his steward came into the room a few minutes later.

Jero had hurried from the cellar, where he was inventorying the wine after the banquet. "Are you looking for something, Mauro?"

"My wife has her clothing allowance somewhere here, and I will need to take some money from it. Where do you keep it?"

Jero opened a side drawer in the desk that had a false bottom. He pulled out the small, locked chest. He unlocked it and handed it to Mauro.

Mauro was perplexed. "I expected more. What has my wife been buying beyond stockings and ribbons?"

Jero sighed, then explained, "She has not been buying incidentals; she has been buying books, Mauro. I had no idea until recently that she was using her allowance for her reading passion. I think she thought that she should keep it secret, for fear of you not letting her purchase any more."

Mauro thought about this odd indulgence for a woman, but he could not be angry. If his wife wanted books to read, she should have said so. The Baric men were all literate and well-educated, but they did not use their leisure time for reading, so few books had been purchased in the past to make a proper library.

"How many books did she buy?" Mauro asked.

"Quite a few, it seems. She put them on the shelves in the sitting room when she redecorated this month. Have you not seen them in there?"

"I have not been in the sitting room," Mauro replied with annoyance. "I have barely been to my own chamber since my return."

Mauro looked pensively at Jero. He had not opened the door to a friendship with Jero when he returned after his father's death. Mauro did not ask Jero his personal thoughts about the servants, and he had never asked him his opinion about the baroness, outside her general requirements as mistress of the house. The two freely discussed opinions regarding the running of the estate, but Jero instinctively knew where the line between his role as steward and a personal friendship with Mauro had been drawn. He had been careful not to cross it. Now Mauro moved the line.

"What else goes on here while I am away? Roko talked to me this morning, Jero. He is concerned about the guard dogs and his hunting hounds. He said my wife is interfering with them. Do you know what he is talking about?" Mauro asked with irritation.

"You should ask the baroness yourself, Mauro."

"I will ask her, Jero, but I am also asking you."

Jero took a seat at the desk and picked up the quill for something to hold in his nervousness. "She is a complicated person, but I say that in the most complimentary way." He had Mauro's full attention with his remark, and he went on to explain, "She is the only one besides Roko and Daniel who can control the dogs, and I know Roko does not like it. He has spoken to me, but your wife is doing no harm that I can tell. She only takes the brown hound, and sometimes the spotted one." Jero paused a moment, then added, "I think she gets bored being confined to the gardens. Maybe she is lonely, and a dog keeps her company."

Mauro took a deep breath. "Yes, I suppose she is lonely. It was not my intention to marry and then be gone from her so often. I will trust that you are doing right by things while I am away. Thank you for watching out for her, Jero."

Mauro turned back to the opened box with the coins again and counted them. "I will still need to put together a few purses of silver. Can you take care of that?" He was the baron again.

Jero answered politely, "Of course, Mauro."

Chapter 19

The great hall was noisy with lively conversation at the communal table that evening. The baron's seven officers had joined the manor house residents for dinner at Mauro's earlier request, but he was too preoccupied now with his troubles to join the jovial discussion. He had known more leisure time as a captain in his uncle's army than in the past year as baron, and he found it difficult to hide his weariness tonight. He was worn out.

Resi and the others retired to their rooms directly after dinner, while Mauro and his captains met privately in his study to discuss his strategy for Lieutenant D'Alessandro. When he was satisfied that they had planned the best course of action for tomorrow, he too went upstairs to bed.

Resi sat in front of her looking glass while Verica finished unpinning her mistress' hair, which she had taken such care to make pretty that morning. Mauro motioned to Verica when he came in, and she curtsied and hurried out of the room. Resi had learned to not disturb her husband when he had a scowl on his face like he did now. She began brushing her loose hair, quietly watching his reflection in the mirror on the dressing table in front of her.

Mauro kicked off his shoes at the door and sat on the bed to undress. Despite his fatigue, Mauro was a man of habit, and he went through the motion of his nightly grooming. He stepped behind the screen, where the servants placed pails of hot water each evening for the couple.

When Mauro was a boy, he used to fight his nanny's attempts to get him to wash. "Why should we wash our face and clean our teeth when they will just get dirty again," he had always asked. It was in this rebellious time of age nine or ten that the Baric sons were to learn with a new tutor from Italy, Meister Uberti. He was a very worldly and learned man, and he came highly recommended to Lord Lorenc. His education, however, had not extended to his hygiene. His rotting teeth gave him a sour, foul breath that the boys endured as he leaned over their schoolwork. Idita took advantage of this new revulsion and warned the boys that they, too, would begin rotting if they did not clean themselves properly every day.

It had worked. Even on his long journeys, Uberti's plagued smell haunted Mauro. He always packed a small tin of the special paste Idita made for the Baric household, a mixture of fine salt with ground sage and mint, to clean his teeth. Resi made her own tonic of cinnamon, cloves, and other exotic spices mulled in white wine that she kept bottled for a sweetening rinse to wash away the salt.

Behind the screen now, while the burning cinnamon tonic subsided in his mouth, he washed the dust and sweat from the rest of him with the cooling water. Mauro was not a modest man, but he slipped on a clean shirt when he had finished and then stepped back out into the drafty room from behind the screen.

Resi sat on the bed now with a roll of linen next to her. "Idita heard that you are leaving again tomorrow, and she left this with me to bandage your arm."

He joined her sitting on the bed and pulled up his loose sleeve. She leaned over him and unwound the soiled wrapping. He smelled fragrant from the lavender soap the women had made during the winter, and Resi tried to concentrate on her work. She was glad the stitches were no longer inflamed, and the healing skin around them was new and pink. She unrolled the clean linen around his forearm. "How long will you be gone?" she asked.

Mauro inhaled as she pulled the wrap tight against the still tender stitches. "I hope just two or three days. The port is not far, only a few hours' ride. It may take a few days to negotiate the crew's release, though. I wish I did not have to be the one to go, but this could be disastrous for us." He looked at her worried expression and explained, "The new lieutenant is truly difficult to negotiate with. I may come back empty-handed earlier than that."

She tied off her wrapping and patted his arm. She did not ask for any more details. It was already a step forward in his trust that he had wanted her to understand the seriousness of it.

Mauro was anxious to change the subject and asked, "Did you get your message off?"

"Yes, I believe so. I gave it to Jero, like you said. Thank you again for welcoming them."

Mauro did not want to go to sleep with his mind still swarming with his ship troubles. He had never asked his wife about her family, and he was curious to know more about them. "You miss your brother, I am sure," he said.

Since Mauro had no brothers or sisters, she considered that maybe he could not imagine how much she did miss and love Patricius. "I miss all my brothers. And my sister. I have four brothers, you know."

Mauro saw her face brighten when she mentioned them. "No, I did not know that. Tell me about them." He genuinely wanted to hear.

"My oldest brother, Castor, is twenty-seven. You must have met him. He is the captain of my father's ship that meets yours."

"I met him only once, I think. My captain meets the ship outside Venetian waters, and I do not go with the crew."

"Well, Castor has been married seven years now," she continued. "He has three little children. They all live with my family in our villa. I miss his little ones dearly." She was lost in the thought of them for a moment, then continued, "Patricius comes next; he is twenty-two."

"I know him as Patrik. That is what he goes by as a soldier," Mauro informed her. "We fought together on the same side once. His group signed on in my uncle's army for a battle."

She had not considered that Mauro and Patricius could be enemies. "Good, then you will have something to talk about," she said playfully. "He and I were very close growing up, since he is less than two years older than I am. I played with his friends, too, when they let me."

Mauro recalled the memory of Resi when he first saw her out playing with the boys in her family's courtyard. Mauro never played with little girls growing up, but then he did not have any sisters to influence that. He looked at her soft features in the candlelight. She was very different from that twelve-year-old girl now.

Focusing on her and not her words, Mauro almost missed her telling him, "Patricius spent a lot of time helping at the docks growing up, but he didn't want to be a sea captain. That is when he became an army soldier."

Mauro was curious about this. He never knew Patrik to be tied to one army. He and his companions were sellswords. "Did he train with the Ottoman Army?"

"He did at first, but he was not bound to them like many Greek boys are. There are only four sons in our family, so we do not owe the Ottoman Army a tribute. That comes with the fifth son." She became serious when she told Mauro, "We never asked him why he left the army, but I am sure he had his reasons. My father thought he would forfeit his life for leaving, but he must have been clever and escaped that fate."

"It is usually impossible to get out of the army," Mauro said solemnly. He knew many clever men who never escaped such a fate. "And your other brothers? Are they soldiers or sailors?"

He was surprised by her sudden laugh. "My other brothers, Hector and Lander, are ten and seven. My baby sister, Phyllis, will turn three this year. She was just beginning to talk when I left. My father was gone for many years, as you know. He could not sire children from prison, so there is a bit of a gap between me and my younger brother. I was not even two when my father was taken away."

It was difficult to broach the awkward topic with her husband of her father's detention, but she felt the dispute between their families needed to be in the past. She was careful not to say more on the subject, though. She did not want to spoil the bit of ground she was gaining tonight.

Mauro proceeded with the same caution and avoided the topic of imprisonment. It was his uncle Vladimir who had held Demetrius Kokkinos at Mauro's father's request in the Toth prison. A dungeon cell there was a dreadful place to spend six years.

Mauro changed the subject and quietly asked, "Do you want me to bind your hair before we go to bed?"

Resi nodded, and he went to pick out a pretty ribbon from the pile on her table. He sat behind her on the bed and reached around Resi to gather her flowing hair. It was soft and light in his hands, despite the thickness that fell around her shoulders to her waist. He took his time wrapping the pink ribbon, enjoying the closeness of her.

He opened a new subject in a roundabout way. "Your mother had six children, then. That is wonderful," he remarked.

"Yes, I love our big family, but I think she will not have any more." Resi explained, "My mother told me that she was pregnant eight times. She lost two babies in the beginning."

Mauro had finished tying her hair, and she turned around on the bed to face him. His expression was puzzling, and she guessed correctly why. "Are you worried that I cannot carry a child? Is that why you are interested in my siblings?"

"I am genuinely interested in your family, Resi. But if a mother has many children, then usually the daughter can too. That is good to know."

"You said something today that I want to talk about," she said with a new seriousness.

"What was that?"

"You said that you were ashamed that you had hurt me. In what way?" She had thought about it since then, and knew that he was wrong.

They were face to face on the bed, but he was still barely audible when he answered, "When you were pregnant the first time, I still took you as I wanted, and that was wrong of me."

"I told you my mother lost her first two babies. She believed that sometimes God is not ready to have a new baby come into the world, so he takes it back for a while. I believe it, too."

"If God took our baby back, then I blame myself," Mauro insisted.

Resi was desperate to help her husband understand that there was no blaming anyone. "I never blamed you. You did nothing wrong, Mauro; nothing at all." She curled up next to him as she explained, "You did not hurt me with your passion; I enjoyed it. The baby inside me died because he wasn't meant for this world yet. This one is. I know it."

Mauro lay back on the bed and looked up at the ceiling. "I cannot touch you until after the baby is born."

She whispered, "I want you to touch me, Mauro. I am your wife."

She leaned over him and kissed his mouth slowly, determined to kindle a flame that she knew she could spark. She then softly kissed his face, then continued down his neck, stopping with a final kiss on the curve of his throat.

He looked up at her with misty eyes, but was not convinced. She brought his hand to the soft curve beginning on her flat stomach. "The baby hardly takes up any room now, Mauro. He won't be born until winter. That is a long time to wait," she told him quietly.

He caressed her smooth bulge. "The baby must be very small," Mauro murmured.

"Yes, and he won't mind sharing me," she said, enjoying his gentle strokes along her silky nightgown.

"Would it not hurt him?"

"No, a baby so new is very deep inside its mother. A man cannot get that far into a woman."

He had to chuckle at her certainty. Mauro sat up on his elbows and looked into her eyes again. "Can you feel him yet?"

"No, I have not noticed a quickening," she admitted.

Then it was not yet a sin, he told himself. His touch became playful this time and slid his hand slowly down her belly to her thighs. She let out a soft moan as his hand went under the light fabric to her bare skin, caressing her there. He eased her down onto her back and kissed her deeply, like he had wanted to all day.

"I won't mind sharing, either," she said hoarsely.

"Mmm, for sure I will not mind," he added to the word game.

He reached for the ribbon holding the bodice of her gown closed and tugged, opening the loose fabric around her throat and exposing her warm, scented skin. He took his time and kissed the soft curve of each breast tenderly. "Well, if we are all in agreement," he managed to say.

He moved to spread her exposed legs and looked up at her mystic blue eyes. She was ready for him. After months of being apart, their bodies were naturally one again. Mauro thought no more about his promise. This was not sinful. It all felt so right.

~ * ~

At first light, Mauro woke Resi in their bed. He was dressed for travel, with his packed saddlebag on the floor near his booted legs. "I vowed I would not leave you again without saying goodbye. I will be back in three days at the most," he said confidently.

"I wish you could take me with you," she told him, holding his hand tightly.

"Not this time. When the reason for the journey is friendlier, I will."

She accepted that answer and released him. He bent to kiss her soft mouth one last time, then turned to go. She was going to miss her new husband. Three long days—how would she ever fill that time without him?

Chapter 20

Anno Domini 1595 was scrolled across the stone casing above the wooden double doors of the manor house entrance. The house was built by Lord Fredrik Baric and took a decade to complete to his satisfaction. Lord Fredrik wanted a modern house with a grand room for hosting other members of nobility and the living space to welcome them for extended visits. He designed a top floor with several small but elegantly appointed rooms, one large apartment reserved for honored guests at one end of that floor, and a large apartment for his and his wife's own sleeping comfort.

Life was lively in the new manor house for many happy years, and they lived in peace and harmony in their lands. Lord Fredrik's wife, Lady Anica, had given him two strong sons who were his pride and joy. The joy ended when his beloved wife died giving birth to their premature twin girls in 1601. Lord Fredrik was never the same after their deaths. He chose not to remarry. Instead, he focused on playing the political games with the ruling Venetians. Before long, he wielded a great deal of influence in his region of the Empire.

His two remaining children learned from their shrewd father. They were desirable suitors among the eligible aristocracy. In 1612, Lord Fredrik arranged for his firstborn, Vladimir, to marry the eldest daughter of Count Dominik Toth. Lady Renata came to Solgrad and lived together with her new husband's family at the Baric estate until Dominik Toth succumbed to a sudden fever in 1613.

With no sons and just two daughters, Vladimir's wife inherited the title and was now the Countess of Toth; her new husband was appointed as the new count. They moved into the Toth Castle in the northern Venetian Empire. Lord Fredrik did not live long enough to enjoy the new political edge his son had brought him. He died tragically after a hunting injury in 1614; he was forty-seven.

This left Lorenc to inherit the Baric estate after Lord Fredrik died. Lorenc was a young, attractive man of twenty with a new lordship title and no arranged restrictions to his marriage choices. He was not looking for political advantages in his new wife, like his brother. Lorenc wanted a pretty face to look at.

He set about gaining the favor of a young Austrian woman, Margaret, whom he had met at Court the year before. There had been amorous flirtations on both parts, but at the time Lorenc was not a titled aristocrat. With his new wealth, her family readily agreed to his proposal of marriage, and the lovers began their new life together that year as Baron and Baroness Baric.

It was Lorenc Baric who had expanded the house upward in 1616 and added the second floor under the roof. In contrast to his gregarious father, Lorenc was a reserved man by nature. As the new master of the house, he preferred to walk his halls at night without stepping over sleeping servants scattered about the corridors. He built the top floor with new servant dormitories for the house staff and a nursery for his growing family; Margaret had given him four children in eight years. Margaret and their oldest three children died from the plague that had ravaged the region in 1622.

In happier times, before tragedy struck the House of Baric, Lorenc had renovated the south side of the enormous great hall into a study for his private use, with a smaller sitting room next to it for more intimate gatherings. In the sitting room, along with several finely upholstered chairs and a long lounging couch, was where Mauro kept his collection of swords and various blades mounted along the tall walls of the entrance to the comfortable chamber. He displayed a giant, two-handed longsword passed down from his grandfather, as well as broadswords he had purchased during his travels. Mauro's father had collected rare, single-handed dueling swords before him, and those were mounted there as well. It was an impressive wall of ornate steel, many decorated with jewels and gold inlay. Mauro kept his favorite fighting swords with him or in the armory, ready for his immediate use, but the ones that hung on the wall were also kept sharp and oiled. This was where the baroness was searching when Jero entered the foyer.

Today was pastry day; Jero could smell the delicious fragrance from across the courtyard. Franja baked fresh bread every morning for the castle's needs, which was a daily mountain of loaves for the residents of the house and the Keep. But once a week, the women would bake sweet breads and cakes for the manor house. This was always a stressful time for Cook and Franja, and Jero did not like to disturb the bustle of the kitchen on this day, even though the smells were tempting.

With the terrace doors closed, he came into the manor house at the main entrance. Scenes depicting the occupations of the Barics—medieval battles, the salt fields, the orchards, and the sea—had all been chiseled into the dense oak structure. The regular waxing had made the wood a rich, dark color over the fifty years, set against the gray stone of the manor house. When both sides of the double doors were opened fully, one could drive a carriage through and into the grand receiving room in front of the marble staircase. Walking through the smaller door cut into one of the massive halves still felt wrong for Jero; until he became steward less than two years ago, he had only accessed the house through the servants' entrance.

He regretted that Mauro had left today, because a special order from the village tanner had arrived in the late morning. Jero had accepted the cartload of goods with no particular instructions from the baron. Jero had worked three years in the estate stables, so was familiar with the quality of leather expected by the Barics. But there were several new saddles and a stack of tanned hides that were not on the order papers he had found in the study. Mauro would have to settle that with the tanner himself when he returned.

Jero took his time inspecting the new inventory and then washed up at the communal basin of the Keep to rid his hands of the fresh tanning oils. Mauro was very particular about his account books, and Jero did not want to leave smudges on the pages when he copied the figures. He looked down at his oil-streaked breeches, which would have to be changed before dinner, but he would finish the bookkeeping task first.

He was just unlocking the study door when he heard a loud scraping noise in the otherwise quiet foyer. The sound seemed to come from the open door of the sitting room. He walked to the end of the hall beyond the stairs and peered in. The baroness was standing on a heavy chair in front of the wall of swords, trying to pry one free. "There is a latch, my lady. Here, let me show you how it releases," Jero said as he rushed to her side.

He helped her step off her perch. She watched him take the chosen sword down. Jero could not imagine what the baroness wanted with the blade, but it was not his place to object. "This one is beautiful," his mistress pointed out. It was a long, single-handed sword in the Italian style, with a gold-leaf twisted hilt.

"You have a very good eye, my lady. It is actually my favorite of these swords," Jero told her. "I have used this myself before. The balance is excellent."

Jero watched the baroness as she held the sword at length and swung it several times with expertise. He smiled brightly at her when she handed the blade back. "Forgive me the impertinence, but I did not know you were a swordsman, Lady Baric."

"I have had a little practice," Resi said mischievously.

Jero went on to explain to her, "Lord Lorenc brought this sword from Florence several years ago. I was with him when the sword-maker fit the hilt to his hand." Jero took it into his own grip and held it out.

She admired his tall frame holding the slender, pointed blade. "It fits you well, Jero. Do you spar?"

"No, madam; not recently," Jero answered as he set the sword down on a side table. "Lord Lorenc did teach me to use most of these weapons." Jero immediately regretted having divulged that to his mistress. He did not want to have to explain his friendship with Mauro's father.

"Why don't you continue to train?" she prodded.

Jero wanted to direct the conversation away from him, but could not be rude to the baroness. "I have been busy as steward these past two years, my lady," he answered.

"If my husband knew that you desired to practice your sword fighting, I am sure he would take you to the fields with his soldiers."

"Perhaps," Jero replied vaguely.

He looked along the wall and took down a smaller sword, then handed it to her. "This is an excellent sword for a small hand. Mateo used this when he—" Jero cut his words short. He had not thought about Mateo in many years, and the sorrowful memory made him suddenly pause.

"You were friends with Mateo, weren't you, Jero? What happened to him?" Resi asked.

Jero had not talked about Mateo's death to anyone, but enough time had passed that he decided he could speak of it now. "Yes. Mateo and the baron were both my friends when we were little. He was just two years older than me. It was a shock to all of us that he could have died so young. Mateo was so full of life." He turned back to the wall, awkwardly admiring the remaining blades that he had recently cleaned and oiled.

She took her time browsing the other swords as well, not looking his way. "Were you with him when he died?" she pressed.

"No, I did not leave the estate at that age. I had duties at the castle. They were with some of the village children, I think." Mateo's sword was still in his hand, and he felt melancholy as he held it. "I remember it had been a very hot week in August, and Lord Baric, Lorenc Baric, let his sons spend that week at the seaside for some relief from the heat."

Resi waited. When he did not continue, she asked, "And he drowned there?"

Jero took a deep breath and let it out. He decided he could continue his story. "Yes. Mateo and his brother were lodged at an inn. There had been a violent thunderstorm." He turned to look at her, wishing she were the baron instead of the baroness, so Jero could ask what had really happened on that tragic day. "I was told the two brothers went to the diving cliffs after the storm passed. No one knows what happened for sure except Mateo dove from the cliff, as he had many times before, and his brother watched him disappear into the foaming sea." Jero yearned to sit down just now, but stood silently looking at the baroness.

"I am sorry. I didn't know how he died," she said solemnly. "Mauro doesn't talk about his brother."

Jero looked at her sympathetic face and was compelled to tell her, "Mauro, I mean the baron, came back to the castle and was never the same, you know. He was twelve and I was thirteen. We were too old to be playmates, but we had been for as long as I could remember. I had just moved from the house to the stables to train as a groom there." Jero was staring ahead now, recalling those days. "I never saw him again after that. He did not leave his room for the year of mourning. Then Lord Lorenc sent him to Lord Vladimir in the North. The next time I saw your husband was when he came back as the new baron."

"Thank you for telling me, Jero."

He took another deep breath and forced a smile across his face, feeling self-conscious in front of her. "Shall I hang these back up?" He pointed to the two swords on the narrow table.

"This one can go back, but I will take the other one with me," she said, keeping Mateo's blade.

Jero did not think his mistress should be taking any sword, but he could not refuse her. "It is not my business, my lady, but what do you propose to do with it? It is very sharp, and I would not want you to injure yourself."

"We all have untold stories, Jero. I will not ruin the sword, if that is your concern. If I injure myself, I promise that you will not be held responsible. I would prefer to keep this between ourselves, though. I will be practicing with it in the old drying room upstairs." She took the weapon from him. "Thank you, Jero. I will not need any further assistance."

Jero heard the clicking of her shoes on the marble as she hurried up the grand staircase.

Flustered from the encounter, Jero shut the sitting room door behind him and walked to the study. He had not had many conversations with other women beside the Baric servants. They were like his family; his mothers and sisters he had grown up with. He never had an awkward moment in their presence. Lady Johanna, on the other hand, had paid him little attention as a boy, then later ignored his presence entirely as a man. She was reclusive in the end, and Jero thought perhaps all royal women behaved that way. But the new baroness was not easy for Jero to understand. She wanted to talk to him about everyday things and learn his opinion on them. She did not care that she was superior to him in rank; he was only there to be of service to her husband and to the household. Talking to the baroness always left him confused.

Jero could not tell Mauro about his predicament, or Jero might be blamed for provoking her attention. Mauro might also accuse his wife of showing an improper interest in Jero, and he would lose her confidence. He unlocked the study door and shut the thoughts out for now while he settled Mauro's account log and tidied up the room.

~*~

Resi climbed one of the two staircases to the top floor. At each end of the elegant first floor hallway was a servants' stairway. These stairs were not the grand, marble steps that connected the main foyer to the first floor; just a set of simple, but broadly built, wooden ones that went from the ground floor, to the Baric residents' floor, then to the dormitories under the roof.

The old nursery was located on the opposite end from the dormitories, above Mauro and Resi's large chamber. It went from the front of the house to the back, at the end corners of the building. There was a beautiful view of the village and the Adriatic Sea from the western windows, and the other set of windows looked out over the mountains to the east.

Lorenc Baric must have planned for many children when he designed this room, Resi thought. It was a big nursery for only Mateo and Mauro to sleep and play in. She had never been told that Lord Lorenc had been married twice, and that he once had several other children with his first wife, Lady Margaret.

The room was still used for drying flowers, herbs, and laundry. The heat from the west windows under the tiled roof was stifling on a warm afternoon such as this. She opened the row of windows to the east, and those across to the west, to draw the sea breeze through the large space. There was little furniture in the room except a few long tables for sorting and cutting, and she left these in place as training obstacles. Resi did not expect any interruptions, but she locked the door with the key to be sure of her privacy. If she injured herself, she hoped Jero had a second key to open the door from the outside.

Her brother's visit was the motivation for this folly. She had an illogical need to impress him again with her skills. Patricius would have liked another brother instead of a sister, she had always thought, and had treated her as one growing up. He taught her what the other boys had learned: to sail, swim, and play-fight. When he left for the army, she was barely sixteen and just blossoming into a woman. Before that, she could be dressed to look like any boy, and sometimes did.

She set her fine weapon aside, then stripped off her waistcoat and the top layer of robes. She drew the remaining underskirt between her legs and tucked the long fabric into her sash to free her movements. Next time, she would sneak a pair of breeches from Mauro's chest to wear instead. She picked up the fabulous sword and began her practice.

~ * ~

Jero had performed all the duties that he found needed his attention for the day. He decided to take some private time to change his oil-stained clothes and wash up before the evening meal. When Jero became Mauro's steward, he had been given private quarters next to Nestor's chamber on the east side of the first floor. Idita and Ruby had small rooms across the hallway. The large staircase opening cut through the middle of the floor, separating the two sides with beautifully decorated banisters of polished wood and enameled iron. Before going to his room, Jero took a short detour to the top floor and listened at the nursery door to hear whether the baroness was still occupied there. The faint banging noise confirmed that she had not yet had enough practice for the day.

Back in his room, Jero began to think about his conversation with his mistress and his own untold story he kept hidden in his chamber. He pulled clean garments from the large trunk against the wall and took out the ebony case that he kept tucked away under them. He set the well-worn box on his neatly made bed, and then slipped out of his dirty clothes. He washed in brooding silence over his basin, looking occasionally at the case with guilt. The swords were not his to take, but he did not think they would be missed. He had been right about that.

Jero had been given the task to clean the baron's room after his funeral. He had grown to love the baron, and it was a heart-wrenching chore for Jero to look through the dead man's possessions. When he learned that Mauro would come to claim the manor and all of Lord Lorenc's possessions, Jero wanted to have something of his to remember him by. So he took the ebony box to his own room and hid it. As a trained soldier, Mauro would not have a need for it, and he probably would not have known it even existed.

Now freshly washed and nearly dressed, Jero thought about the first time Lord Lorenc had shown him the marvelous weapons in the case. His lordship and his soldiers had been in the courtyard sparring, and Jero had been leaning against the horse rail watching them. The baron joked with Bruno, one of his captains, that Jero would make a better sparring partner than Eduard, who had been fighting poorly on that day. Jero was eighteen then, and he was already tall and strong from working with the horses. A wager was set betting that after one month's training, Jero could beat Eduard in a sparring match. Jero was anxious about their bet. He did not want any part of it; but his lordship said that he would train Jero himself, and assured him that it would be an easy victory.

That was the first time Jero had used the blunt sparring swords held in the long case on the bed. They were perfectly balanced and beautifully crafted, but were not honed to cut flesh with contact. Jero did prove to be a good student and did indeed win the bet against Eduard for the baron. After that, Lord Lorenc made him a regular sparring partner and showed Jero how to use the larger broadswords and double-handed longsword as well.

Jero was excited when he was finally invited to practice horse combat with the castle guardsmen later that year. They were kind to him and showed him special tips and tactics that he excelled at. Jero had begun to have hopes of being asked to join his lordship's Guard after the praise he had received, but it was not offered. Lord Lorenc continued to challenge him to private sparring duels, but he was never given a real sword again, and his summer with the guardsmen was not spoken of.

Jero decided he would return the elegant case and its contents to the baroness. He was certain she would keep it her own secret. The swords would be put to better use with his mistress, and then she was sure to not injure herself with Mateo's blade. Jero seldom used them now. He only brought the blunt swords out to practice alone when Mauro was away; when Jero's presence for a few hours would not be missed.

Dressed for his evening duties, Jero discreetly covered the case with his linen towel and walked the short distance to the baroness' empty room to place it uncovered on her table by the fire. Later that night, when Jero was extinguishing the last candles left burning in the house, he found Mateo's sword on the side table in the sitting room. He returned the boy's weapon to its place on the wall, and he did not see the ebony box or its contents in the baroness' room again.

~ * ~

Resi had practiced alone for several hours in the nursery before realizing that the sun was already setting. She left the sword locked in the room and came downstairs intending to sneak into her chamber to change her clothes. That was not to happen. Ruby was anxiously waiting in Resi's room. She feared that her friend might have had some sort of accident when no one could locate her. Resi brushed off Ruby's concerns and made an excuse of walking in the gardens and falling asleep in the shade, as she did from time to time.

She would not confide even to Ruby that she was going to challenge her brother to a sparring match when he visited. Ruby was already worried that

Resi did not spend enough time resting with her pregnancy, although Resi had never felt better than she did now.

Ruby left the room when Resi convinced her she would eat her evening meal later, after a visit to her bathhouse. Resi had just tossed the waistcoat she had been holding over the chairback when she noticed the beautiful, black box on the table next to it. Someone must have brought it to their room for Mauro. Curiosity got the best of her, and she looked inside it. Jero! She closed the special gift and slid it behind her dressing table until she could take it up to the nursery for safekeeping. It was an extremely kind gesture for him to bring it to her in secret, and she would keep it that way.

Chapter 21

Baron Neven Leopold's castle was a small fortress perched on the cliffs overlooking a wide bay and the port town built around it. South of the seaport, the land flattened out and tenant farms stretched to the next lord's landholding. To the east, beyond the Leopold's miles of dense forests, was the border of the Ottoman Empire. To the north was the Barics' barony.

The Leopolds had not always had the best relationship with the neighboring Barics. Fredrik Baric was a generous and boisterous man that most aristocrats found to be good company. Neven Leopold's grandfather, Cedomir, thought Lord Fredrik's lax use of his noble position was dangerous and irresponsible. He did not approve of the banquets and balls the Barics held for the Empire's leaders. Why should the Croatian noblemen wine and dine the ruling councilmen who cared nothing for their homeland, except for the profits it brought to them?

Lord Fredrik lived under the guise that he was friends with everyone. To some, like Lord Cedomir, he appeared careless and too agreeable with his political principles. But it was Cedomir Leopold who lost control of his ancestral town when his port was requisitioned to the Venetian Navy, not Lord Fredrik. A good politician like Fredrik Baric knew that it was after the dancing and music had stopped that the real decisions were made when it came to war and power. He had spent years securing discreet alliances with those who were truly influential in the capital in order to promote his family and their security as colonial nobility.

Lord Neven Leopold inherited his title ten years ago directly from his grandfather Cedomir, who had lived long into his late sixties. After a prosperous nobleman's life, and surviving battles and plagues, Lord Cedomir Leopold died in a most unexceptional way: choking on a prune pit at his breakfast table.

Neven's father had met with an early, unexplained death. He had disappeared while traveling horseback to a council meeting in the south five years before Cedomir's death. They never found his father's body or those of his escorts. It was presumed that he had been robbed, and their bodies thrown into the sea.

Neven's mother, Lady Eleonora, was the efficient matriarch of the Leopold family. She took the lead in running the household affairs with their long-standing steward, and had endless energy, like her son. His wife, Lady

Nikolina, managed the growing Leopold offspring; she was expecting their fourth child. Neven directed his time keeping up with the politics between the navy and town merchants; their likes and dislikes for each other seemed to change with the wind at his port.

The harbor had always been a thriving fishing and trading port. It was a deep, natural bay that allowed for the larger shipping vessels to dock close to shore. There was usually a multitude of ships and galleys anchored offshore in the open, protected waters as well. The centuries-old fishing village had grown into a vital town, with tradesmen catering to the sailors and the ships that they sailed.

It was only in the past decade that the Empire anchored more and more naval ships in what the Leopolds considered ancestral waters designated for fishing and merchant trade. The escalating conflicts with the Ottomans and the current war in Candia had made his seaport an official station to launch naval ships to war. All of this change was still tolerable until Lieutenant D'Alessandro took charge in the autumn of 1648.

Mauro met with his friend Neven at his castle, and the two continued on to the town together without delay.

"Are your houseguests still with you?" Mauro asked.

"My guests left the day after you left. We had such dreadful weather for the last day of hunting, but they were satisfied with their catches the few days we went out before."

"I hope this is not too much of an imposition, Neven. I know you already have a lot of your own difficulties with the navy as it is."

"I am always happy to help you, Mauritius; you can count on that," Neven assured him as they approached the overlook to the harbor.

Lord Leopold pointed to Mauro's ship moored at an isolated pier at the end of the harbor. "I asked my contacts earlier, and your ship is still loaded," he said. "The navy has thoroughly searched it, but there did not seem to be anything they could complain about. There may not be a penalty beyond your fine, but the lieutenant does seem to stretch the law for these things."

They left the main highway now and rode down to the port. Any road off the main north-south route led to the harbor. The waterfront was a great, half-moon shape, and the streets were like rays of moonbeams, all leading toward the harbor road that flanked the piers.

They rode along the row of small cottages and stone houses that filled the higher streets above the port to reach the main street, a block off the harbor itself. Baron Leopold had taken charge of planning proper granite buildings for his townspeople to do their business from, replacing the wooden structures that were first hastily erected during the boom in commerce that the escalating naval presence had brought.

The naval office was located on the harbor street at the far south end of the waterfront. It was an imposing, two-story building constructed on a small knoll, with four cannons protecting its entrance and the harbor. Vilim and Anton were on this knoll below the steps leading to the entrance. They were lounging in the shade of a large tree, with little else to do but to wait for the baron to arrive. Mauro's captain and his bailiff had spent the night in the local lodgings and looked a little worse for wear; but the lack of sleep was only from the drinking and card playing into the night, not the accommodations.

"Mauro," Vilim shouted and waved to the two barons to catch their attention. Mauro and Neven rode up to the Baric men and tied their horses to the rail there. "We were not sure when you would arrive, but we thought you would come down here first thing. We wanted to talk to you before you went in," Vilim told him with concern.

"What have you found out for me?" Mauro asked as he and the other three stepped away from the flow of men entering the building for a more private exchange.

Vilim and Anton explained all that had happened since yesterday and then told Mauro, "We saw the crew. They are being held in the temporary cells in the basement." He pointed to the naval station. "We brought them some food and drink last night. The navy is not so generous with the meals, but they are being treated fairly and are getting by."

Mauro was glad for this. "Good, thank you. You can head back to the village and give Radic your report. Have him draw up an official complaint against the navy to send to my uncle. I will see what can be done here." Mauro gave them some coins to pay their tab at the inn, and they took their leave to ride back to Solgrad.

"Shall we get this over with, Neven?" They went into the navy headquarters in search of the commander.

Lieutenant D'Alessandro's spacious office was on the top floor of the building. He had just finished his noon meal at the table near the window overlooking the harbor and had noticed Lords Baric and Leopold on the courtyard below. He emptied his glass of wine to wash down the last of his fried sardines and wiped his greasy fingers with an embroidered towel. His long, laced sleeves were tucked into the red fabric of his military jacket, and he set them loose again. D'Alessandro was adjusting the tall, curled wig that flowed down beyond his shoulders when his clerk, Orlando, escorted Mauro and Neven into the room. The gentlemen bowed politely to the uniformed officer, who looked up at them from his cluttered table in the corner.

"Ah, Lord Baric. I was expecting you. Please take a seat, won't you?" D'Alessandro moved away from the small table with the scattered platters and sat at his large, orderly desk, motioning for the two noblemen to sit across from him.

Mauro knew this would be a game to the lieutenant, and he made his first play. "We will not take much of your time, Lieutenant. I have come for my ship," Mauro said confidently.

"Have you, Lord Baric? I am afraid you have wasted your time coming here, then. I have begun compiling the list of rather serious crimes you have committed against the Republic of Venice, sir."

"Crimes, Lieutenant?" Mauro began his defense. "I think you exaggerate the unfortunate misunderstanding, sir. My ship got tossed in the storm and ended up off course. That is where you found them, practically marooned in an unknown location. Since when is that a crime?"

"Then you have an extremely incompetent captain sailing your ship, my lord. He was at least two hundred miles south of his origin. If his destination had been Venice, like the papers indicated, then he sailed in the wrong direction from the beginning." D'Alessandro shook his head, showing his disapproval. "It is time to hire a new crew, sir, because this is the third occasion this has happened, is it not?"

"It is not, Lieutenant, but if you would show me the list of crimes you claim against me? In any case," Mauro continued, "there was no need to take my property. I am filing my own complaint against your malicious act. You have caused me a great deal of inconvenience to come here, and more than that, great financial loss to have my ship and my men held without cause."

Neven Leopold took the uncomfortable lull in the conversation to defend his friend. "Lieutenant D'Alessandro," Lord Leopold began, "the Barics have been trading in these waters with the Venetians for decades with no recorded protests from the Republic. Certainly no crimes have been committed here."

Lieutenant D'Alessandro stared back blankly, used to dealing with men from dockhands to dukes. "Lord Leopold, sir, your concern for the Barics is indeed honorable, but it does not change the facts."

Leopold countered, "Given the family's excellent reputation with the Republic, is there not a way to expedite Lord Baric's case and let him, his cargo, and his crew be on their way? Surely there is no need to inconvenience the gentleman?"

"You both speak of inconveniences, but I am fighting a war and you engage in your continued smuggling, Lord Baric. I am the one inconvenienced. This is a serious crime against the Republic, and it cannot be brushed away, reputation or not. You did not have the proper order documents stamped by the local authorities before leaving your waters, and the manifest was sorely inaccurate. The navy has no records of your captain being sanctioned to move unofficial goods, and that is what we found in your ship. Each of these alone is finable under the law. But together, well, I understand that you are a busy man, sir, and your family's standing may be stellar, but the regime cannot tolerate such incompetence from you, Lord Baric."

Mauro was a patient strategist, but the man had almost pushed too far with his insults. He knew the commander would not dare imprison him should Mauro not be able to resist punching him in the face, but the baron would never see his ship again, and his crew would rot in jail.

Instead, Mauro answered calmly, "Lord Leopold and I have some other business to attend to in town. If it is *convenient*, Lieutenant D'Alessandro, we shall return in two hours. Surely that will give you enough time to pen a complete list of the charges for my review."

Mauro stood and bowed diplomatically, not giving the lieutenant time to argue. He walked out the door with Neven Leopold following closely behind.

The two men had no other business to attend to, but they needed time to discuss the charges and Mauro's options to remedy them. They went into one of Neven's favorite establishments and settled in a back-corner table.

"What is your plan, Mauritius?" Neven asked after the barmaid left their mugs of ale.

"You heard the charges. All petty documentation fines, and he cannot prove that the storm did not blow them miles off course. He wants to make me sweat, that is all. I cannot wait months for the officials in Venice to review the documents. The man must have a weakness, Neven."

Mauro stirred the steaming bowl of mussel stew just placed in front of him. Neven considered what might be the best course of action.

"Every man has his price, but I have not yet found his," Neven admitted.

"We know already the man does not take monetary bribes," Mauro said.

"This surprises me, though. I am told he is newly married, and he cannot make enough as a naval officer to keep a proper house for his wife in Venice. He must have some other funds." Neven thought for a moment. "To his favor, he is well-respected by all of the upper officials. He runs a tight port that is efficient and profitable. His naval ships are clean, equipped, and well-manned. There is no faulting the man's administrative talents." Neven went on to say, "He is an odd one, though, to be sure."

"There must be some angle we can use to our advantage," Mauro contemplated.

"He is a grand manipulator, as you know by now, Mauritius. Like all gamers, he plays to win," Neven declared through bites of his stew.

Mauro thought this might be helpful. "What kinds of games does he prefer, do you know?"

"He is very good at cards, and I am told he has a reputation for seducing women. Well, particular women, which is why it is also a game to him. My officers tell me that he has a preference for the young girls," Neven clarified.

"I thought there was something distinctly depraved about the man. To take young girls to your bed is repulsive," Mauro hissed with disgust, blowing on his own bowl of steaming broth.

Neven looked up from his meal with surprise. "Oh, I did not mean to make it seem so offensive. He only takes flowered maidens; those of bedding age. The talk on the docks is he will soon run out of bottles in this town to uncork, if you know what I mean." Neven laughed at his own joke. "Just last week, he won a maiden for the night in a card game. The gentleman playing did not have enough in his purse to pay the final wager he had lost, so he gave the lieutenant a girl from his household to take to bed."

"Neven, how can you say that so lightly? Are you telling me, if I offered an unmarried daughter for him to violate and ruin, he would give me back my ship and my crew?" Mauro was appalled at his friend's casual statement.

"No, good God! I have a daughter of my own! The man did not give his daughter, Mauritius, if that is what you thought I meant. I believe she was just a servant girl, a young woman in his employment."

Neven was unaffected by the possibility, but Mauro contemplated the indignity of paying a card debt with one of his servant's maidenhead. "Well, I have no available maidens for him to defile, so I will have to find another way to get my property back," Mauro concluded.

The two pensively finished their lunch. Mauro finally broke the trance. "You have given me an idea, Neven."

Neven was encouraged by the expression on his face. "Go ahead, Mauritius."

"He is a very flamboyant man for a seaman, with his powdered wig, fashionable neckwear, and court breeches. He is from the capital itself, is he not? I am sure he is used to a more refined company than one finds at the port."

"I see what you are getting at, Mauritius, and you might be on to something. I know he has accepted every dinner invitation extended to him this past year without fail, war or no war. Do you think he could be corrupted with an invitation to a party or something?" Leopold had confirmed Mauro's thoughts.

"I am not saying he can be corrupted. I am just thinking that if he is taken away from his desk and made to understand that we can offer him some sort of other repayment. Not virgins, mind you." Mauro liked the idea more and more as he formulated it.

"It is worth a try, since he will not take a gold bribe," Neven agreed.

"It could be an elegant affair where the lieutenant could see that we are worthy of some extra consideration. I could invite just the regional noblemen and their wives and have a more aristocratic evening of drink and cards, dressed in our finest costumes; maybe with a little music and dancing."

"A proper ball, Mauritius? You are sounding like old Fredrik Baric now," Neven declared with a laugh.

Mauro chuckled at the realization. "Yes, I suppose I am. But my grandfather usually got his way in the end."

Mauro felt more confident. "It will have to be within a fortnight, because I am expecting visitors myself after that," he said. "Let us return and make the offer to the lieutenant. This might just work."

~ * ~

Two hours had not yet passed when the gentlemen arrived at the naval station again. "We have a little time, so I thought we could talk to my crew before we go in," Mauro suggested.

"Certainly," Neven agreed. "Captain Toselli, a word please, sir."

"Good afternoon, Lord Leopold, sir. How can I be of service?" the young second-in-command offered when they approached his desk near the jail entrance.

"We need to see the jailor. Lord Baric's ship captain and his crew are being detained in your cells. He would like to speak to them," Baron Leopold explained to the attentive officer. Neven Leopold had had dealings with Toselli in the past and found him to be an agreeable man to negotiate with, compared to the other Venetian officers.

"I can take you to them, sir. I have been assigned as warden for a time," Toselli told them. He took the large ring of keys from behind the desk, then led them down the corridor to the staircase that led to the holding cells below.

"Captain, I noticed you are missing your boots," Lord Leopold ventured to say.

Captain Toselli was dressed from hat to stockings in his crisp, navy garb, but wore brown shoes on his feet instead of the polished, black knee boots of his uniform. "Yes, my lord. It is a rather embarrassing story, and part of the reason I am on duty in the prison instead of at the pier."

Both barons listened to the captain's story as he led them down to the row of doors in the basement. "You see, sir, I was with a woman last week and fell asleep in her bed. When I woke, both the woman and my boots were gone." He looked ashamed that he had lost his precious footwear.

"Oh, that is unfortunate, Captain." Lord Leopold sympathized; Lord Baric as well. It had happened to other soldiers on many other occasions. It would seem to be a humorous story for an officer to confess, until one remembered that sometimes the stolen boots were the soldier's only footwear. Captain Toselli had found something else to cover his feet in their place.

"Yes, the lieutenant was not pleased. He put me on prison duty until I can replace them." The men nodded disapprovingly at the harsh punishment.

"Captain Toselli, how long will my men be detained?" Mauro asked before the captain unlocked the door.

"As long as the lieutenant says, sir. There is really no reason to keep them, though," Toselli added.

"I do not understand, Captain. No reason? Why would you say that?" Mauro asked.

Captain Toselli looked around to see that they were alone in the passageway. "I am not really authorized to say, my lord. I could get into a lot of trouble," he whispered to the two barons. "It is just, um; I read the holding orders for your men, and there is a problem with them." Toselli tempted them with this bit of information. It was clear that there was more to the story, if he could be encouraged to tell it.

"I would be interested to hear about it, Captain Toselli, but I am on my way to the boot maker to have a pair of black boots fitted. This boot maker is a friend of mine and is very quick with his service. I usually get my boots the next day. Maybe I should introduce you," Lord Leopold enticed him.

"I would appreciate that, sir, but I haven't the means for such a meeting with your friend," Toselli said casually, understanding the offer.

"Such small details are easily dealt with," Leopold promised.

Baron Baric nodded his agreement to pay the price and said, "You have not finished your story, Captain Toselli. Please continue."

"Yes, sir." He smiled at the barons. "Well, I read the documents, and only Baron Baric is solely mentioned by name on all of the charges. Under the law, it would only be the baron who can be held until the crimes are proven, but not the sailors found on the boat."

The captain was uncomfortable suggesting that the baron should be arrested, but Lord Baric did not seem offended. The captain continued, "Unless they, too, are charged by name with a crime, then they cannot be held for any length of time once your charges are recorded. Of course, without knowing the particulars of the law and reading the specific wording of the documents, you could not know that." The captain was pleased to have easily earned new boots by pointing out these small details.

"And now we know, Captain Toselli. Thank you for clarifying that," Lord Baric said. "I shall speak with the shopkeeper myself, and he will be expecting you later today, if you are available."

"I am, sir. I thank you." He unlocked the door to the cell.

~ * ~

The two noblemen were led back upstairs to D'Alessandro's office following the brief visit to his jailed crew. The commander stood as they entered and gave a small, respectful bow to each baron.

Mauro got right to the point. "Lieutenant, I hope you have had a chance to finish the documents."

"I have them right here, Lord Baric. You may review the charges. They are all stamped and authorized. They shall be sent to Venice for a ruling, once I have your signature."

He handed Mauro the sheets of neatly penned parchments, and Mauro glanced through the pages looking for names. Mauro signed the paper declaring him a criminal without further discussion.

"Thank you, Lieutenant. Now, if you will release my crew to me, I will leave you to your busy day," Baron Baric asserted.

The lieutenant regarded him and Lord Leopold with confusion. "I told you earlier, sir, that I will need to hold your ship and crew until a judgment has been decided in Venice," the commander said with authority.

"But without being charged, the men you are holding must be released. I have just agreed to your assessment of the crimes you allege against me and will wait for the decision. But the law states that without being specifically named, the crew cannot be held. You will discharge them today, Lieutenant."

Mauro waited for the commander to regain his composure. D'Alessandro quickly softened his angry expression and stood to walk to the door.

"Orlando, release the Baric men from the holding cell. They have not been charged and can go free." The lieutenant returned to his desk and said, "I must retain your ship and cargo as evidence, Lord Baric. You do understand that part of the law, I presume, sir."

"You must do what the law requires, Lieutenant D'Alessandro," Mauro answered smoothly with a trained smile. "I cannot find fault with that. As a matter of fact," the baron continued, "I think we can put this whole misunderstanding behind us. I am having a small gathering in ten days' time at the Baric manor. It is a party, rather. From time to time, we gentlemen from the region like to powder our wigs and dance with our wives. I would like it very much if you could join us."

The lieutenant was already snared; Mauro could see it in his face. "There would be tedious navy business for you to discuss with my guests, but I hear you enjoy a good game of cards as well."

"You have heard correctly, sir." D'Alessandro smiled for the first time. "And I would be pleased with the opportunity to clarify current regulations with your neighbors. There may be questions I can answer for all of the lords at one sitting." The lieutenant was now rosy with excitement at the prospect of mingling with the aristocratic class. "Thank you, Lord Baric. I accept your gracious invitation."

"Excellent, Lieutenant! Plan to make it a long night and stay on as my honored guest. My steward will send you the details. Until then, sir," Mauro concluded. He stood and tipped his broad hat to leave.

Lord Leopold patted his slick friend on the back once they were outside again. "I did not think you could get him to accept, but I am now as convinced as you are. I think we have found his weakness. Congratulations!" he commended Mauro. "Will you be heading home with your men now?"

"No, Neven. I think I will send them ahead and stay on another day. I have left something with the goldsmith that will not be ready until tomorrow. I was actually expecting this to take more time than it did."

"Stay on at my place, Mauritius. You are very welcome," Neven told him wholeheartedly. "While you are here, you must have my mother help you with your party list."

"I could not impose on her time, Neven. That would be asking too much."

"Nonsense, she loves this sort of challenge, and you know it. She knows everybody who would want an invitation to come. You cannot exclude anyone important from a Baric ball, and she would never forgive you if you did."

Neven was enthusiastic now. "It must be grand, if you are to make an impression on the commander. He must learn that you are a man of importance not to be bothered again. And you know my mother knows how to do things grandly. Let her take charge," Neven insisted.

"If you think she will not find it bothersome, I will gladly accept her help. This must be just right, and my wife has no experience to pull off such a gala evening."

The two barons were still out in front of the naval station. "If you will allow me, Neven; I would like to retrieve my men personally and get them on their way. Can you see the boot maker in my place and meet me back here?" Mauro suggested.

"Excellent idea," Lord Leopold agreed. "An hour should be long enough to arrange your new knee boots, Mauritius. Then we can return to my home and get started on your plans."

Chapter 22

The clear weather had returned to the Adriatic and the sun shone brightly, warming the Greek women at their small breakfast table. They were sitting on the small terrace savoring Franja's sweet rolls, deliciously stuffed with wild cherries and goat cheese.

"What shall we do this morning?" Resi asked. After the thrill of practicing with her swordplay yesterday, she was in the mood for something adventurous to do today.

Ruby poured a cup of the Turkish coffee for each of them while she thought about the limited possibilities. "We should go to the stables. Natalija told me there was a foal born last night," Ruby replied cheerfully.

"Yes, I would love to see it. Mauro will be so pleased to know that it all went well."

They hastily finished their breakfast and then took the sunny path through the castle gardens to the stables. They stopped for a moment to watch the efficient removal of an old privy house to cover a newly dug pit. Several soldiers were carrying the intact structure the few yards, and other workers were filling in the old hole with the dirt from the fresh dig.

The outdoor privies were used mostly by the men serving the castle. The Keep tower had remnants of Roman plumbing from the original settlement there. The tower residents had the luxury of open seats built over a piped gutter to satisfy their requirements. The manor house had two modern privy rooms on the main floor copied in the Roman-style plumbing of the Keep; but the upstairs chambers and the servant dormitories were provided with pots that had to be emptied daily into one of the cesspools in the far corners of the walled compound.

The women continued along the path by the greenhouses to keep out of the way of the industrious activity. When they arrived at the paddock, Resi and Ruby found that they were not the only ones who had come to admire the new colt. Daniel and Eduard were there giving suggestions to Alberto about the baby stallion's future potential based on his parentage. The sire was from Lord Leopold's stables and was a fine warhorse. Mauro had not said his preference for his favorite mare's offspring, but a strong, new steed to add to his herd would always be welcomed.

Resi leaned over the railing beside Alberto to get a good look at the new addition. "If the new foal had been a filly, would the baron be disappointed?" she asked Alberto quietly.

"Disappointed to have a new mare? No, my lady," the stable master reassured her. "Now that men don't wear so much plated armor into battle, mares can make superior warhorses. They are intelligent and easier to train than stallions."

He gave his mistress a knowing look. Alberto had six children of his own, four of them girls, and his wife had once asked him if he would have wanted all boys. "His lordship would be content with many females in his herd. Have no worries, my lady," he said with an encouraging wink.

She gave Alberto a thankful smile. "He is a beauty with those markings, is he not?" The newborn was a gleaming chestnut color, with black boots on all four hooves, and a silky black mane and tail.

"He is indeed," Alberto concurred. "Those long legs were holding him back for a while last night. He made us work hard to bring him into the world, but he is fine and healthy."

Alberto watched Ruby reach in between the rails to pet the irresistible colt. "Careful, Lady Ruby. The mother is protective of her newborn," Alberto warned. "She will be friendlier the next time you visit." Ruby stepped back to stay clear of the mare's reach.

They lingered in the stable yard for a while longer and fed Resi's horse oats and apples before going back out into the warm sunshine. They noticed Geoff crouched down against the stable wall near a big rain barrel. He was hammering a rock with a good-sized mallet as the ladies approached.

"What do you have there, Geoff?" Ruby asked him; the rock had finally split from his effort.

Resi picked up the broken half that had rolled across the ground and examined the sparkling crystals inside the flat gray shell. She recognized the crystals from Idita's collection in her room. "This is beautiful. Where did you come across such an unusual stone?"

"I, I, um, didn't steal it, my lady." He looked from one pretty face to the other and confessed, "I found it in the cave, madam. I didn't think it would be wrong to keep it." He stood up to meet his punishment.

Resi saw the defeated look on the boy's face. She was not concerned that he had the small stone, but she wanted to know more about the cave he had just mentioned. "Where is this cave, Geoff? Is it far?"

He waved in the direction of the mountain behind them. "No, just outside the walls, my lady, but you can get there from the cellar." He put his hand over his mouth; he had said too much.

"Were you in the wine cellar, Geoff? You know only Jero has permission to go in there," Ruby scolded him.

Geoff cracked under pressure. "There is a trap door in the pickling room. You can get to the caves through a tunnel there," he blurted out. "I ran errands for the kitchen maids bringing up supplies from below, and I found it. His lordship doesn't know that I have been outside the walls. It is against the rules, and the baron will be angry with me."

Resi tried to soothe his obvious fears. "Why would the baron be angry? You have lived here all your life and are bound to discover some secret passageway. Besides, my husband will not need to know. I will keep your secret," Resi assured him, but he shook his head in disagreement.

Resi decided this was just the adventure that she needed today. "Listen, Geoff. If you have no duties to attend to, I want you to show us this tunnel," she insisted with authority.

"I cannot take you, my lady. You will have to crawl before the stairs come out of the old well and ..." Geoff wasn't making any sense to her.

"Out the old well to where? To the cave?" Ruby prodded him when he did not finish his thought.

"You don't understand, my ladies. You will ruin your fine robes," he stammered, finding no better reason.

"Well, if that is all, then it is settled. We will change into something sturdier and meet you in a quarter hour in the kitchen. Then you can show us this secret passage out the cellar," Resi cheerfully announced. She handed back the broken stone and walked away from the stunned boy. Ruby hurried along at her side.

~ * ~

"What have you come to the kitchen for, Geoff? Are you hungry already?" Franja asked him. Geoff slept in the stables, but took his meals with the house servants. Geoff had a bottomless stomach, Franja always said, and he came to the kitchen between meals quite often. She handed him a soft apple she was peeling for her tart, and he accepted it with a smile.

The kitchen was the only home he could really remember. His father had been one of Lord Lorenc's soldiers. He had been fatally wounded during a battle when Geoff was only three, and his sister, Verica, was four. His mother did not want to marry again after her husband died. She gave up their cottage house and moved back into the manor house quarters and began working in the kitchen; the children could be watched there and put to use for simple tasks. Geoff's mother died six years ago of an infection after she cut herself preparing a hog shank for curing into ham. Geoff and Verica were adopted by the kitchen women when his mother died, and the children had worked for the Barics ever since.

"I am waiting for her ladyship," Geoff began to tell Franja. He didn't get a chance to explain the foolishness he was charged with, because at that moment the baroness and Ruby entered the kitchen from the foyer.

"Hello, Franja," Resi greeted her. "It smells lovely in here. Is that cinnamon?"

"It is, my lady," she answered with a curtsy. "I am making tarts for dinner." Franja was puzzled that the ladies would be dressed in wool jackets and their twill riding skirts on such a warm morning. "Are you going riding, Lady Baric?" Franja boldly asked.

Resi hesitated for a moment, but Ruby answered for her, "We are going to count and record the wine for Jero, and we expect it to be cold and dirty in the cellar. Geoff will be assisting us, should we need anything moved." Resi was pleased with her friend's quick thinking and nodded in agreement.

It seemed an odd assignment for the baroness and the stable boy. "Of course, my lady," Franja quietly acknowledged, but gave Geoff a look of doubt. He smirked at her before he disappeared with the ladies through the cellar door.

The deep cellar had been built during the construction of the new manor house and was efficiently laid out for the servants. Fresh vegetables were orderly stored there, as well as cured meats, cheeses, pickled goods, and other preserved staples. There was a cellar entrance from the outside for deliveries as well. Expensive bottled wine and spirits were stored farther back in a separate room. The kegs of locally made wine and the house-brewed ale were kept in the buttery, a stone room on the other side of the kitchen. It had an outdoor entrance near the terrace for quicker access for the daily drinking needs at the castle.

The wide corridor of the main portion of the cellar narrowed into a long hallway, with small nooks in the walls for storage, and ended at the pickling room. The women had helped the maids with the cabbage preserving in this room last autumn. They did not remember noticing the small door built into a wooden paneling at the end of the room.

"There is no handle to this door. How does it open?" Resi asked after she pushed on the frame.

"It has a hidden keyhole here, madam, and the key is kept behind the torch on the wall. I found it by accident one day when my own torch went out. I had taken the torch off the wall to relight mine, and the key fell to the ground," Geoff explained. He reached along the wall and presented a small ring with a key. He unlocked the secret door.

"What if it locks after us? How will we get back in?" Ruby wondered out loud.

"I thought of that before, and I was afraid to venture out through the tunnel the first time. This key works on both sides. I left it on the outside of the door, but then I discovered a second key was already out there." He hung the ring back in its hiding place behind the torch. "I'll light another torch in case this one goes out," he said. He took a second one from the wall before shutting the door behind them.

"Can we leave it open a bit, Geoff? I would feel better with a little light marking the cellar," Resi requested. Geoff found a small stone on the ground and propped it between the door and the jamb.

They waited a moment to acclimate themselves to the darkness, then started along the dim path. "How long is this tunnel?" Ruby asked him.

"Not too long, Lady Ruby. We are walking toward the east wall above us," Geoff answered. "It will start to get a bit rough here. When they dug the storage cellar, they also found this cavern. It was an old water source. The way out of the tunnel is through the old well itself."

"Who told you all of this, Geoff?" Resi asked as she stepped carefully over the scattered stones, trying to stay within the light of the torch.

"I asked old Tomas about it when I first found the tunnel. He told me he was just a boy when Lord Fredrik built the new house. Tomas has passed on now." Geoff bowed his head and crossed himself, surprising the two women with his sudden, pious gesture. "Tomas told me that before the Keep was built, there had been a small settlement here, and this was their old well. When the water dried up, they must have moved down to the river where the village now is, instead of digging a new well, like we have," Geoff explained. He was pleased he could share so much information about the history of the castle. "Tomas said Lord Fredrik kept the connection open because he liked the secret tunnel, but he insisted the door be bolted on both ends to keep his enemies from discovering it."

They continued to move toward their destination at a steady pace while Geoff held the torches for them. "Who else knows about this tunnel beside you and Tomas?" Ruby asked.

"The baron surely knows everything about his castle. Jero and Nestor must know everything, too. But I don't think anyone else does. Servants are not supposed to go through any locked doors without permission, my lady. I did not want to admit that I had, so I never asked anyone if they had either," Geoff declared. "I saw Tomas come out of the pickling room one day when I was down here, and he gave me an odd look. I decided to tell him I knew about the door. So he sat me down, and we talked about the tunnel."

"Why did Tomas say he was in the tunnel?" Resi was curious to know.

"Lord Baric had given him a task, was all he told me. If he wanted to tell me more, he would have. Tomas was the baron's trusted soldier. It was not my place to ask," Geoff stated emphatically out of respect for the late captain.

The women were thrilled to learn these new details about their castle. "Look, I think I see some light up ahead," Ruby announced, crawling at Resi's side.

Geoff took the lead now. He was relieved the two gentlewomen had managed the narrow path without complaint. He soon forgot this was forbidden and began to enjoy the adventure himself. "There are a few steps dug into the abandoned well here, so watch your footing, my ladies. I'll unlatch the iron grate overhead."

It took some effort to move the rusted hinge on the screen covering the tunnel hole. It had not been opened in years, it seemed, and was partially blocked by broken branches. At last they stepped up through the opening and into the bright sunshine, surrounded by shrubs that disguised the barred entrance.

"This is not far at all. Right there is the wall," Resi commented as they climbed their way out of the brush.

"Where is the cave, Geoff?" Ruby asked.

"Just here, between the two pines. Do you see it?" He pointed in the direction of the mountain. "It has a shadow from the rocky ledge, so it is hard to detect. You can perhaps see the small path leading to it."

They followed this path and were quickly up the steep trail, through the trees, and in the dim light of the cave opening. The smooth entrance dropped quickly into the mountain.

"I hear water. Is there a spring here?" Resi asked the boy. He handed her a torch, and she moved toward the sound.

The walls narrowed in on them, and Geoff's voice echoed as he explained, "There are many small springs that seep through the cracks in the rocks, my lady. You may get a little splashed, but there is no pool that I have seen," Geoff confirmed. "Did you know, Lady Baric, that the water for your bathhouse is this same water? It is tapped outside the east wall. And the Keep has its own spring running under the foundation."

They walked for a few more minutes in silence. "The cave branches off soon, but I think the rocks that I found were just over here." Resi brought her torch closer to where Geoff directed and was not disappointed. The walls sparkled with the glittering veins of quartz.

"Oh, it looks like diamonds!" Ruby exclaimed. "This is so lovely." Her eyes were bright with excitement in the torchlight.

"I don't know what diamonds look like, Lady Ruby, but they cannot be prettier," Geoff agreed with a chuckle. "Tomas told me these are only crystals, so they aren't precious, like real gems."

He picked up a round, gray stone and told them, "I found the rock that I broke today right here several years ago. This is what it looks like before it is opened. I could never hit it hard enough without a tool to break it, but I borrowed a hammer this morning from the blacksmith."

"Here is a broken one. I am going to take this back with me," Resi proclaimed as she studied her find.

"Where does this go?" Ruby pointed ahead along the path.

Geoff held his torch high to light the area better and told them, "I did not go much farther than right here because of Tomas' warning. He said bears and wolves might use this cave, but he may have just been trying to frighten me." He felt a little ashamed to admit he had been scared. "I was alone when I came before, but he told me there would be a split in the trail, and I was never to take the left tunnel." The women peered into the darkness with awe at what might be down there.

Resi lifted the torch toward her friend, who was crouched down, searching the edge of the cave for more sparkling treasures. "I don't want to meet a bear in the dark cave, either. I have seen enough, how about you, Ruby?"

"There are some small bones here on the cave floor, but I don't think it is from a bear. They would eat bigger animals, wouldn't they?" Ruby realized the bears would eat people, too, if given the chance. "I am ready to return, if you are," she easily agreed.

The three explorers made their way back out along the uneven path; their pockets were filled with the glittering stones. They had left the iron covering to the old well open, and Geoff closed it and bolted the grate again before they inched their way back down the dark tunnel toward the cellar door.

Chapter 23

Franja greeted Jero with a friendly smile when he strode into the kitchen. The other maids were setting out plates for the servants' noon meal. "Have you come looking for the baroness?" Franja asked Jero as he picked up a slice of bread from a platter on the long, block table.

"I have come looking for food, Franja. I am starved and it smells delicious." He winked at Cook, who was just turning around to greet him. "Why?" he asked Franja casually. "Was the baroness asking for me earlier?"

"Well, she's been in the cellar with Lady Ruby and Geoff for over an hour." Franja told him matter-of-factly. "They were on an errand counting the wine for you, Jero." She studied his expression, convinced there was more to their assignment in the cellar than they had divulged.

"Oh, yes, I see," he answered her as steadily as possible. But he did not see at all, and he wondered what nuisance the baroness was creating for him now. "I will go check on them. I forgot they must be waiting for me." He managed a smile for Franja and turned to leave down the cellar stairs.

There were always a few torches lit at any given time in the cellar, because the kitchen was busy long hours of the day. He walked the cool corridor and turned the corners, but the baroness and her companions were nowhere to be found. A pang of anxiety came over him when he finally opened the door to the pickling room and saw a streak of light through the cracked door in the panel. Jero knew this secret doorway; it should be shut. At closer inspection, he saw it was propped open with a small stone, and he peered into the dark tunnel. What was Geoff doing in the tunnel with the baroness?

He and Mauro had secretly explored the forbidden tunnel and the cave outside the walls as boys. Jero was not surprised that Geoff would also know about it, having worked in the kitchen and cellar for so many years. But where did he get this foolish idea to take the baroness and Lady Ruby through it?

Jero heard voices and saw a light grow brighter from the other direction. He pushed the door back to a crack against the stone and formulated a plan as he hastily made his way back to the kitchen.

"Did you find them, Jero?" Franja asked suspiciously.

"Yes, indeed. They should be here momentarily," he answered, forcing a pleasant smile on his otherwise tense expression. "I forgot I will need to speak to Geoff again, though. Could you send him to the study when he has dusted off? I am afraid they will be dirty coming up."

The cellar walls were finished with smooth stones. Although it was not clean like their scrubbed kitchen, it was not especially dirty, either.

"Yes, Lady Ruby told me they expected to be dirty from the wine counting." She cocked her head in a mocking sort of way. With no satisfactory reaction from Jero, she let it go. "Will you and Geoff eat with us in the kitchen?" she asked.

He smiled genuinely at her this time. "We will. Send the boy to me so I can go over the wine count, and we will be back to join you shortly." He hurried out of the room before the others complicated his lie with their arrival.

Nela had watched Franja and Jero from the hearth, where she was supervising the roasting meat that would be their noon meal. She instructed the kitchen maids to take the pork off the fire and then went to Franja's side and quietly said, "You will not find a better man than him. What are you waiting for, Franja?" They'd had this conversation several times before. Nela wanted an answer to her motherly question.

Franja had taken the position as a kitchen maid for the Barics nine years ago. She was just fifteen, and her parents needed the extra income for their growing family. Nela had known Franja's mother growing up. Lord Lorenc continued to house more and more soldiers at the castle to guard his lands, and Cook recommended hiring her friend's daughter for extra help with the bread baking. Franja proved to be a talented baker, and those who lived at Baric Castle approved of her delicious contributions. The young, single guards also immediately began coming around the kitchen to court her.

Women of marrying age were difficult for young soldiers to meet at the castle, and any pretty, new face was always noticed. Jero was no exception. He had just moved from the stables back into the manor house again, and he had more opportunities to get to know the kitchen servants than the soldiers did. Eventually, Jero convinced Franja to meet him in the hay barn one night; even though she knew her reputation would be spoiled if they were seen. She was curious about men and didn't know quite what to expect when meeting a young man in secret.

Jero was almost her same age, and he did not seem as intimidating to her as the men in the Guard did. Franja had never been kissed before, but she liked it quite a lot as they experimented in the dark. She did not like being pawed under her skirts, but that had not lasted too long as they rolled around in the hay together. Jero had apologized to her the next day in the kitchen, but it took a while for her to figure out why he had been so embarrassed over their midnight encounter. After meeting another young soldier in the hayloft, she soon learned what had gone wrong with Jero's awkward attempt at a courtship. She and Jero had worked through the uncomfortable transition after their failed romance, and they had remained good friends ever since.

"Jero is one of my favorite men at the castle, make no mistake, Nela. But he is not the right man for me. I don't know if any of the men at the castle are right for me." She took a lump of butter from the large crock and scraped it onto a dish at the table. "I have already explained it to you, Nela. If I marry, then I cannot work in the kitchen with you."

"You will have your own kitchen, Franja, and little babes to take care of. Don't you want that?" Nela whispered to her.

"And socks to mend, and cloth to weave, and goats to tend—I don't want to scrub floors and grow beans. I like my life now," Franja hissed back.

"Don't make the mistake I did, and then you are an old maid with nobody looking your way anymore. You are twenty-four, and they won't come calling much longer." Nela took her aside so the other maids would not overhear, "I am not your mother and you have no father any more. The baron will not force you to marry, but he has asked about your intentions."

Nela looked at Franja's disappointed expression, then to the cellar door as it suddenly opened. Franja turned away from Nela to greet the laughing trio with a curtsy.

"We can have a tray sent up for your lunch whenever you are ready, my lady," Franja announced. Nela walked away to organize the maids to ready the baroness' lunch tray.

"Thank you, Franja. We will take our meal in the sitting room," Resi said smiling, still glowing from their exciting adventure. She locked arms with Ruby, and they walked out into the foyer and up the stairs to change out of their dusty clothes.

Geoff was nearly out the door behind them when Franja grabbed his arm by the jacket sleeve and pulled him back into the kitchen. "Not so fast, Geoff," she told him.

Geoff did not look at her as he said, "I will wash at the well first, if that is all right."

"Jero would like to have a word with you in the baron's study, if that is all right. Jero went to the cellar to find you, Geoff, and he wants the wine count," Franja answered. Geoff went pale.

She let his dirty jacket sleeve go, and he nodded to her that he understood all too well. "I don't know what you were up to, but don't be repeating it," she warned him with a pat on the back as he left the kitchen.

~ * ~

Jero had been pacing the room when Geoff knocked on the door. He let the boy in and closed it again. Geoff's dusty appearance told him all that he needed to know. "Why, Geoff, would you take the baroness through the tunnel?"

The boy looked distraught. Geoff was a tall boy for fifteen, but he suddenly seemed small to Jero. He would not have told the women about the tunnel except under extraordinary circumstances, and Jero tried to imagine what those circumstances had been. "Sit down and tell me what you did," Jero said to him with a sympathetic voice this time.

Geoff stayed frozen by the closed door. "I didn't mean to do anything wrong. It just sort of happened."

"What exactly sort of happened?" Jero asked. "Franja said you went to count the wine with the baroness. Lady Baric told Franja I asked her to. Why would I ask the baroness to inventory the cellar?"

"We were in the cave," Geoff confessed quickly.

Jero walked to the window, not knowing what to say to the boy at that moment without yelling. All the servants knew it was forbidden by Baron Baric to venture beyond the east wall, and nobody questioned why. The punishment was immediate dismissal. Geoff would be sent away.

"It isn't my fault, Jero," Geoff pleaded. "Her ladyship was talking to me out at the stables, and the next thing I know she tells me to meet her in the kitchen."

"Start at the beginning, Geoff."

Geoff cleared his throat as if to keep a sob from reaching his mouth. "I was up all night helping Alberto with the foal, so he let me have the morning to rest. I went around the stables to take a nap in the shade, but Karl was hammering in his shop, so I couldn't sleep. That made me think of borrowing a tool from him to open a rock I have been trying to crack. He gave me one, and I set about hammering it open."

"What kind of rock did you want to crack open?" he asked. "Have you been to the cave before today?"

"I found the key to the door when I worked in the kitchen. This was before the new Lord Baric came to stay. I used the key to see what was there behind the door. Tomas was coming out of the tunnel one day when I was fetching supplies for Cook, and he told me where the tunnel led. He is the one who showed me the cave, but he warned me to never go in it again."

Jero knew that Tomas had been one of the few people who knew the reason it was forbidden. He was dead now. He had died of the same illness as

Lord Lorenc and the other officers. Jero needed to be sure no other servants had gone there with Geoff. "And did you go again?" Jero asked.

Geoff began to cry. He knew he had done wrong. "I only went back once more. I got scared by myself, but I took some of the glittering pieces and a round stone from the floor of the cave. I hid them in my clothes chest." He was barely understandable through his sobbing.

Geoff had remained by the door while telling his story, and he slumped against its sturdy frame. Jero walked over to the pitiful boy and put his hands on Geoff's shoulders. He seemed fragile under Jero's large grip. Geoff finally regained control of his wits and looked up at Jero.

"Did you go again with someone or show anyone what you had found?" Jero asked him softly.

"I promise you, Jero, I never told anyone, not even Verica. I didn't think I was stealing anything. I have three rocks, plus the one I split today. If I give them back, will you not punish me?" There were still tears in his soft brown eyes.

"That is what I need you to do. I will come get them from you tonight, and I will not tell the baron that you had them." Geoff nodded and breathed an audible sigh of relief. But Jero was not finished with his questions. "Why would the baroness ask to go to the cave?"

"She isn't like other ladies who just walk past you without looking at you. She is curious about everything going on at the castle, and there I was, just splitting the rock and couldn't hide it. She got me so flustered, Jero. I don't know how it happened."

Jero listened to him with sympathy. "So, she asked you where you got the stone, right? And you told her from the cave?"

"I don't know! Half the stone fell to the ground. Lady Ruby was there and they admired it; and then I just blurted out about the secret tunnel. I figured she was the baron's wife, and she might already know about the cave." Jero nodded sympathetically and waited for him to continue. "I could not lie to the mistress, but I told her it was very dirty for fine ladies to crawl around in. I was worried, because noble ladies are delicate. But the baroness and Lady Ruby can climb like nanny goats, and they didn't complain or get scared in the darkness. I didn't have to help them but one little bit," Geoff proudly told Jero.

Jero was no longer angry at the boy, knowing firsthand how persuasive the baroness could be. "I don't think our mistress and Lady Ruby are like other aristocrats," he confided to Geoff. "But you cannot take them anywhere without the baron's permission. Ever! Do you promise me?" Geoff shook his head in agreement. "I won't tell his lordship, since no harm has been done, but you might still be punished for this if he finds out." Jero looked seriously at the rattled boy. "You must be very careful, Geoff. If the baroness asks a favor of you again, you must come tell me first."

Geoff had already turned to open the door, but Jero wanted to be sure the boy understood the consequences Jero had protected him from. He held the door shut and said, "This is your home, Geoff, and it has been for your entire life. But you could be sent away, never allowed to return, if Lord Baric decided you had done wrong with the baroness. You are nearly a man, Geoff. There are rules to follow, and you need to remember your place."

Jero did not like to reprimand any of the servants, especially not Geoff. He patted the boy on the back and walked out the door with him. "Franja has lunch ready for us, if you are hungry," Jero said, as though he had already forgotten about their serious exchange.

Geoff easily grinned again. "I'm starved," he replied and sprinted toward the kitchen while Jero locked the study door.

He would not bring up the subject with Mauro, he decided. If the baroness told her husband, then Jero would defend Geoff. But from the secrets Jero knew the baroness already kept from Mauro, he guessed she would keep her adventure today hidden as well.

Chapter 24

It was another fine day for the middle of June, and Resi had worked all morning in the kitchen garden with Danica. She was the wife of the Barics' head gardener, Krsto. Along with her various kitchen maid duties, Danica was in charge of harvesting the vegetable garden. Resi, in her linen overdress and starched canvas apron, joined her along the rows of leeks.

Some noble ladies were known to tend their gardens, mostly lending their opinion in their choice of colorful flower displays. Resi did not manage well with the extensive flower garden Lady Johanna had cultivated, but Ruby had taken an interest in it when she first arrived at the castle. Ruby was occupied with the flowers that morning with Natalija and Ranko, tying the climbing vines to the trellis along the greenhouse path, while Resi dug in the dirt with Danica.

"Nela needs a good stack of readied leeks this morning. I think that should be enough, Lady Baric," Danica said. "The maids set up a table for us under the arbor to wash them. The carrots are already there."

"Did the boys catch all the wild rabbits?" Resi asked.

"It has taken a week, madam, but Krsto tells me no carrots tops have been eaten in the last few days. I hear enough of the little pests are readied in the Keep's pantry to feed the entire castle."

"Then we'll get these cleaned, so Nela can get started. I do love her rabbit pie."

Resi rinsed the dirt and sand from the vegetables, leaving the leeks to soak in basins of water. She was not a natural gardener; she had never grown anything herself back in Greece. But she enjoyed the time working in the sun, even though Idita warned her it would spoil her pretty complexion.

Resi felt she and Danica had accomplished quite a lot for one morning, and they carried their proof to the kitchen. She was just thinking how Nela would turn these vegetables into a delicious meal when she saw a large wagon pull up to the front door. Most deliveries stopped at the Keep for inventorying and storage, and any cart that brought supplies for the kitchen would drive directly to the cellar door at the back of the house.

"That is strange," Resi said to Danica, who was loading her apron with cleaned carrots to take inside.

"I see Jero is coming from the stables to meet the driver, my lady," Danica pointed out before she went around the corner and into the kitchen with her own delivery. Curious, Resi bypassed the kitchen and left her basin of leeks on the steps for a maid to retrieve. She walked around to the front of the manor house to meet Jero.

"This wagon is from Toth Castle, Lady Baric," Jero shouted to her as she approached. He read through the delivery note that the driver had handed him. "I think it is for you, madam!"

She looked at the four chests being off-loaded. "The countess wanted to send me a new wardrobe, but I never imagined she would send so much. I actually thought that she had forgotten," Resi replied when she was nearer to the wagon. Jero stepped inside the front door briefly and called for two grooms to carry the delivery upstairs to the baroness's chamber.

"One of the cases is wine and spirits from Count Toth to your husband, but the rest are addressed to you and Lady Ruby. The boys will bring them to your room right away."

"Thank you, Jero. This *is* exciting."

Resi went in through the front door and quickly climbed the marble steps. Verica was already outside her door, pacing and wringing her hands in excitement while the servants put the trunks in the baroness' chamber.

At the end of winter, after Resi's first pregnancy had failed, Countess Toth had sent her favorite seamstress from Venice to the Baric house to measure her for a new gown. Resi had never met the countess, but Lady Renata had written a letter to say that she thought a new wardrobe befitting a noblewoman would help her recover from her loss.

Mauro had spent a great deal of his youth with the Toths, and Resi thought it was more an act of kindness toward him than her. It had been three months since the fitting, and she had only expected one new gown. Ruby had been measured for a new dress as well, but even two new gowns, no matter how extravagantly the underskirts were made, would not need three wardrobe trunks.

"My lady, what have they brought?" Verica asked eagerly. "Is this the dress from the countess?"

The young men finished unstrapping the chests and left the room with a respectful bow to their mistress. Ruby had run from the greenhouse when she saw the trunks being brought in and came breathlessly into the room, followed by Natalija.

"Shall I open them?" Verica asked, although she was already lifting a lid without waiting for a reply. Verica gasped at seeing the contents of the first trunk. "Oh, this is too lovely," was all the young servant could utter as she pulled the first garment out of its wrapping. The green satin skirt was fully decorated with fine embroidery and delicate lace.

Resi took off her muddy apron and smoothed out her own dress, noticing for the first time the state of her appearance. "My hands are black with dirt and I am soaked in sweat. I will already ruin the fine fabric just trying the gown on," she fretted to Ruby, who examined her own green-stained fingers.

Resi did not know what was coming over her; she felt the twinge of excitement building looking at the filled trunks. She had never been interested in finery before, but in her heart she thanked the countess for understanding how special this would make her feel. It was going to be an amusing afternoon for the girls, too, she thought with a smile.

"Verica, if you could unpack the new wardrobe, I will clean up in the bathhouse and hurry back to see what was sent. Natalija, will you come help me?"

Verica had barely noticed her mistress had spoken to her. She loved the clothing of the wealthy ladies she had encountered at the castle and in the village, and could think of nothing better to occupy her afternoon than to sort through the delivery.

"Oh, yes, with pleasure, my lady," Verica mumbled in reply, and Resi hurried out the door with Ruby and Natalija on her heels.

Verica noticed now that the three chests were labeled; two had her mistress's name scrolled on a tag hanging on the front, and the third was marked for Lady Ruby. She opened them all.

In the first trunk addressed to the baroness were three new gowns with additional brightly colored, stiff underskirts. The maid took each out and laid them carefully across the large, canopied bed. She thought the colors would be perfect for her mistress and imagined the fabric must have cost a small fortune.

In the second trunk, there were embroidered, heeled shoes; ornate, flat slippers; silk and wool stockings; lace partlets for modesty, if the gowns proved too revealing; two elegant shawls; and undergarments that she had never seen the likes of, many light and airy for summer. There was a stiff corset and a pair of pink, silk lady's drawers that fascinated her. She held them up against her own plain dress. Verica unpacked the undergarments and put them on the empty breakfast table. Ruby had also received a new gown with full underskirts, a corset, silk stockings, and finely decorated, heeled shoes. She called the two servants back to move Ruby's trunk to her room so they would not mix up the two.

Resi and Ruby did their best to hurry through their quick bath, and then rushed back to the manor house to try on their new gifts. Verica and Natalija enjoyed the excitement of their fashion show, for they had never seen such fine garments up close. In her room, Resi was oblivious to Mauro's early return to the castle.

~ * ~

Mauro left his horse with Josip and went looking for Jero. He found him at the front of the house sorting through the crate of wine for the baron and loading the bottles onto a small handcart. The wagon drivers had been sent to the Keep for a meal before they headed back on their way north.

"Whose wagon is this?" Mauro asked Jero as he came up the walkway.

"Mauro! I did not notice you had arrived home. Welcome back," Jero exclaimed; he stood up and stretched from his chore. "The gowns for the baroness finally arrived from your aunt, and she sent you a nice supply of fine wines and spirits along with them. I was just unpacking the crate to move the bottles into the wine cellar."

"Good timing all around," Mauro replied cheerfully. "We are going to host a ball, Jero, and we will need all the wine and elegant costumes to make it memorable for my honored guest."

"And who is this honored guest for your first ball?" Jero asked.

Mauro did not have to pretend with Jero, and his face showed that it was not a pleasant undertaking for him. "Well, my honored guest is the bastard Lieutenant D'Alessandro. Lady Eleonora and I have already worked out the invitation list, and I dispatched messengers to relay them to the neighboring lords this morning. In ten days, we will have a grand ball like the Barics have not put on in thirty years. I am glad my wife has her new gown for the party. But you and I and all my officers will need some new fittings as well."

"You are serious, then? It will be a real ball? We are not to just dust off our Sunday best and polish our favorite boots? Am I to come as well?"

"We are to seduce the good lieutenant with our charms and wealth, so he will show us a little more respect the next time he sees my ship in open waters. Lady Eleonora convinced me that the neighbors would all enjoy such an occasion, and I would like you and my officers to add to the parade of eligible dance partners for their daughters." Mauro smiled in amusement at Jero's stricken expression. "Tell me, did my aunt send an invoice with her delivery, or was it truly a gift? That will determine what I will spend on you." Jero finally smiled again.

"There is a letter here addressed to you. That may answer your question." Jero handed him the parchment with the blue Toth seal on it.

Mauro read it through and laughed.

"Does she write you flattering compliments?" Jero asked.

"No, she is scolding me for neglecting my beautiful wife. Her seamstress reported that my wife is sorely under-clothed and fully out of fashion." He took a deep breath and smiled again. "She is rectifying my poor management of my wife's situation, and she is sending 'supplemental necessities to round out her wardrobe.'" He looked up at Jero again. "How many boxes came for the baroness?"

"Three wardrobe trunks. I had them brought upstairs an hour ago. The ladies should have unpacked them by now."

Mauro imagined the spectacle of the four women with three trunks of dresses strewn about the room.

"I will go over the details for our own wardrobes later today. Can you find Fabian and tell him I am back? I did not see him at the Keep." Mauro picked up and examined a bottle of brandy his steward had just unpacked.

"Fabian is with his new group of guardsmen in the field. I will send Tin to get him. Are there any further details I can help you with?" Jero asked.

"I am going to go check on my wife. My curiosity is too great; I would like to see what 'supplemental necessities' the ladies are uncovering," Mauro said with a sly grin. "Have Tin tell Fabian I will meet him in the great hall." He turned and went through the front door and up the stairs, two at a time.

The door to their chamber was partially opened, and Mauro listened in for a minute before he peeked his head around the corner of the door into the room.

"It looks like the breeches tie in the back, my lady. There should be a quicker way to get them off for when—" Verica looked up from her work in front of the looking glass and said, "Your lordship!"

She stepped away from her mistress and curtsied. Mauro walked into the room to find his wife in front of her long mirror in a stiff corset and an unusual kind of pink, puffy breeches.

"Mauro! When did you return? No one was expecting you until tomorrow," she exclaimed, seeing his reflection in the looking glass. She turned to greet him, forgetting she was barely clothed.

"So everyone has told me. But I believe I have exceptional timing today." He noticed for the first time that Ruby and Natalija were also in the room. "Ladies, will you leave us now, please?" Ruby and the servants curtsied to the baron and hurried to the door, giggling to each other as they shut it.

Resi instinctively put on the silk robe that went with the new breeches for modesty, but didn't realize that it only heightened the effect of the seductiveness. Mauro surveyed the room; the bed and table were covered in colorful gowns and flowing fabrics. "Are those leggings meant for women?" Mauro asked, as he came closer to her from the door.

"Your aunt's note said they are riding breeches that the French princesses are all wearing now." She held out the puffy fabric of the ornately decorated bottoms and smiled at her husband's odd expression.

Mauro shook his head. "Maybe French courtesans are, but I do not think you will be wearing them out on your horse. They show the shape of your legs, and my men do not need to notice your legs along with your pretty face." He made his way to her, touching the satin of an emerald green gown that was on the pile on the bed.

Mauro ran his finger along the top edge of the tight corset Resi wore under the open silk robe. It covered just the bottom half of her breasts and had delicate ribbons woven along the trim. "This, though, you may wear for me any time."

He reached to her robed shoulders, slid the loose garment off her, and let the new robe drop to the ground. "Do you know," he said leisurely, admiring her standing uncomfortably in front of him, "that I have never seen a corset on a woman?"

This broke the tension, and Resi laughed. "I thought you spent time at Court. Surely the elegant women there wear corsets?"

"Surely they do. But it is always under their gowns, and even then your imagination cannot know how impractical"—He paused his comment to stare at her at arm's length. He turned her sideways to see the back, then he finished his thought—"and yet, wonderfully designed they are."

Resi was warming to his playful talk and took a step toward him. "I am afraid I will not be able to wear it for much longer. It is very tight, and I am growing round too quickly."

"Wear it today," Mauro told her. He bent down and kissed the top of her left breast, feeling the wild beating of her heart.

"You have not even kissed me hello yet," she replied after his amorous gesture. She bit her bottom lip after she said it, not knowing how this moment would evolve or how she wanted it to. Mauro had already decided.

He bent and kissed her tenderly on the mouth, holding her warm body firmly against his. She responded as his kiss became more urgent and hungry. He smelled masculine, of fresh sweat and horses, and she put her arms around his neck to embrace him closer. They had not kissed with a heated passion in many months, and she felt lost in the sensation of his searching lips and tongue. She could feel him harden against her through her thin, silk layers. Mauro stepped back, panting, but still held her about her waist.

"Resi, we, um . . ." he began to say, looking around the room, trying to make a decision. "You do not make it easy for a man. I would hate to ruin your new gowns before you even wear them." He finally decided he didn't need the bed.

He began kissing her again, running his hand down the small of her back, feeling for a clue as to how the pink leggings could be untied. Caught up in the passion, she managed to unfasten his belt. She felt her way down the front opening and began firmly caressing him. He abandoned his struggle with his wife's confining breeches, distracted by her detailed attention to his own. He moaned in frustration and gave in to the pleasure. He began to laugh softly, and she began laughing with him.

"I was worried about ruining your new garments and was not thinking I would ruin my own," he said shyly as held his forehead to hers. He stepped back from her and kicked off his shoes, then let his breeches slip all the way to the floor. "I am sorry that was over so quickly, Resi, but your new wardrobe is very appealing. I will make it up to you tonight."

"I was only expecting a kiss, Mauro. I am not sorry for anything," she said.

She sat on the chair next to her grooming table, catching her breath. She glanced into the looking glass and saw that her face was flushed and her lips swollen from their passionate encounter. Mauro busied himself at his own trunk and chose a fresh shirt and clean breeches. She watched him while he dressed, enjoying her own fashion show.

"Tell me, Mauro, did you get your ship back?" she asked him hopefully.

"No, but my crew has been released, so that is good news. I could have come home a day earlier even, but I had something I needed fixed and it was not ready until today." Mauro reached for his doublet, fumbled in the inner pocket, and brought out a ring. "I wanted to give you this on our wedding anniversary, but then realized it would not have fit you. It belonged to my grandmother, and she was a tiny woman. Will you try it on?" Mauro asked. He went back to her, took her hand gently in his, and slipped the jeweled ring onto her finger. It fit perfectly.

Resi stared at her hand for a long moment. She admired the delicately cut but sizable gemstone inlaid in its ornate, gold band. "It is very beautiful. It matches your ring, doesn't it?" Resi asked.

"Yes, mine was my grandfather Fredrik's. Both rings were fashioned from the same emerald. It looks lovely on your hand," he told her. "I know you do not particularly care for extravagant jewelry, but I hope you will wear it." He held her hand and bent to kiss it tenderly on the top of her ring.

"I will wear it with pleasure. I never had any gems before, so I never missed wearing them. I will treasure this, Mauro. Thank you."

Resi did like jewelry, even though she rarely wore more than a few pieces at a time before coming to Croatia. She routinely wore various gold earrings and strings of gold chains. She always wore the gold wedding band that Mauro had given her at their ceremony. It was scrolled with an intricate design that reminded her of old Greek runes. Mauro had considered having a new ring wrought for his wife before their wedding, but he had seen this ancient ring in the goldsmith's shop and bought it for her instead. She loved it and had not yet taken it off.

Mauro liked jewelry on women and for himself. He would often wear small hoops in his ears when he had leisure time at home or wanted to dress elegantly. He also wore three rings since becoming a baron: the large emerald and gold ring from his grandfather; his signet ring, bearing his own emblem, with which he sealed his documents; and the smaller, gold ring with the Baric crest that his father had given him before he fought in his first battle. His father was convinced that his only son would die in war, and he wanted to be sure they could identify Mauro's body to bring him home to bury with his ancestors. He had worn it during battle out of duty to his father, but now Mauro wore it daily because it felt like a part of him.

"I need to go, my dear," he said when he had finished putting his shoes back on. "I asked Fabian to meet me downstairs, and he is probably waiting. I will call your maids back, and you can finish trying on your other gowns. Oh, and there is more news." He remembered what he had really come upstairs to tell her. "We will be having a ball here in ten days' time."

"A ball, Mauro? What brought this about? That is not like you." She looked distressed and began to agonize, "I don't even know how to dance properly."

"You just have to show up, Terese," he teased her, remembering what she had told him before the last banquet she had hosted. The comment did not put her at ease.

He explained, "We are going to convince the naval commander that we are too important to harass any longer. Well, we can try, anyway. All of the invitations were written and sent while I was at the Leopold castle yesterday. Lady Eleonora took full charge of the details and has written a list of what preparations should be done before then." Resi still looked worried, and Mauro assured her, "Jero and Nestor will take care of these details. You may organize the meal with Cook and Franja, if you want. And we will both get a dance lesson or two before then." He raised his eyebrows, trying to get her to smile again. She finally did.

"If that is all I have to do, then I will not worry," she said with confidence again, and he kissed her to show his approval of her willingness.

Mauro looked at the gowns displayed on the bed as he walked toward the door to leave. "Wear the green one to the ball," he suggested. "It is the same color as your new ring. It will bring us luck."

She watched him leave and then went to the bed. Yes, she thought to herself as she held up the gown and looked at her reflection in the mirror. Green was the Barics' color. It would be perfect.

Chapter 25

Mauro was nearly at the bottom of the stairs when he noticed Davor heading toward the kitchen. "Davor, I will need to speak to you," Mauro hollered uncharacteristically down across the banister.

Davor hurried back to the foyer. "Your lordship, I did not know you were back. Welcome home, sir. What can I help you with?"

"Come with me first, I want to see if Fabian is waiting." The two stood at the entrance and looked in, but the great hall was empty. The door to the study was open, though, and Jero sat at the writing desk finishing the day's entries. "I wanted to talk to both you and Jero, so this is an opportune time." Mauro waved to Davor to follow him into the study and shut the door after him.

"Ah, how was the delivery, my lord?" Jero asked him formally with a bright smile. Jero always addressed Mauro with respect when they were with the other servants.

"To my satisfaction," he answered with a grin, still thinking about his wife's new pink ensemble. "But I must organize our own formal attire for the ball. I will be sending you both to acquire fashionable clothing suitable for the occasion. I want you to take Vilim, Simeon, and Hugo with you as your escorts."

Davor was unsure what his master was talking about. "Is there to be a ball here, my lord? Am I to attend?" he asked timidly. Mauro shook his head that he was. Davor smiled broadly at the news. "A new ensemble for me, sir? That is very generous of you."

Mauro replied, "Well, Davor, if I have to dress like a peacock, then so will the rest of you. We will show the Venetian snob that we Croats are not the drab fishermen they accuse us of being," Mauro declared with a chuckle. "We only have eight days, really, so you must leave first thing in the morning for Rijeka."

"Rijeka? Would Zadar not be closer, my lord?" Jero asked.

"Yes, but I do not know the shopkeepers in the cities to the south. I know Rijeka is a full day's journey at best, but there is a fine wigmaker there who knows Nestor and a reliable gentleman's clothier I have purchased from previously. There is no time to have you all tailored, so we will have to do with what they can fit you for quickly. Then have them deliver the finished garments to the castle. I do not want you waiting around all week for the order," Mauro instructed.

Jero still looked puzzled. "My lord, do you not want me to stay and help you with the preparations?"

"Lady Leopold has graciously taken charge of the invitations already, and she made a list for me to follow with other details I might otherwise neglect." Mauro rattled off the thoughts that had filled his mind for the past day. "Nestor can manage any other particulars and arrange the rooms for the guests here and at the inn. My wife will work with Cook for the food preparations. As a matter of fact," Mauro spontaneously decided, "you five should stay on an extra day after all. You have not had an outing in too long, Jero, and Davor can have his first." Mauro gave the young valet a wink. "My treat for all the good service you have both given me."

Davor was overwhelmed at the adventure the baron offered, and he sat down on the baron's chair without asking.

"Is that not too long, my lord?" Jero asked. "I calculate that we will be away four, perhaps five days."

"No, Jero, it will be fine. Everything is planned. You *are* indispensable here, but we can spare you both for five days. I shall be here, and I have Stephan and Fabian to lead my Guard, if needed."

Mauro thought there was something he had forgotten to mention. Now he remembered: his own attire. "You know my measurements, Davor. I suppose I will need something lacy and colorful for the ball. My wife will be wearing green. Choose something that will not clash with her. I will need some matching shoes as well."

He thought for another minute while Davor gave him his full attention. "You know it is not my style, but I will wear a wig for the occasion." Mauro frowned involuntarily at the thought. "Should you write this down?" he asked Jero.

"No, I will remember it," Jero told him. "Thank you, my lord. We will go talk to the captains now and plan our departure. Come with me, Davor."

"Very good," Mauro said as he opened the door again. "Where is Fabian, do you know?"

"Here I am," Fabian said; he had just come through the front door. "I thought I would do you the honor and clean up a bit before our meeting." His bound hair was still wet, and he had on a clean cotton shirt under his red, velvet waistcoat.

Jero and Davor bowed to the captain and went out through the doorway to find the rest of their company for tomorrow. Mauro and Fabian went back into the study.

"You look to be in a good mood. Were you successful then, Mauritius?" Fabian asked as he poured himself a glass of wine from the table and sat down. Mauro stayed at the window; he thoughtfully watched Jero and Davor walk across the courtyard.

Mauro turned back to Fabian as he answered, "Yes and no. The ship's crew is back, but I am charged with several petty documentation and smuggling crimes. I am not too worried about that." Mauro poured himself a glass of wine, too, and sat across from him. "Leopold and I formulated a plan that is chancy to succeed, but costs only the price of a grand ball if we do not."

Fabian stared at him with a confused expression. "Are you organizing a ball, Mauritius?"

"I am, Fabian. We are gambling that D'Alessandro is corruptible; not through money, but through status. We are going to bring him into our level and let him enjoy the company of the regional nobility."

"And you think that will be enough?" Fabian was doubtful. "A party with Croatian nobility is not quite the same as a courtly ball."

They drank their wine, and Fabian thought about it some more. "If he has not been to a true ball, and I doubt that he has, then he may not know the difference." He finally smiled with approval and told Mauro, "I have not put on makeup in quite some time. Will it be appropriate for your ball?"

"I insist. And you should wear the rose earrings you stole from your sister. It can be as grand as you like, Fabian. I will leave it to you to be our courtier." Mauro chuckled and Fabian joined in.

Mauro described his plans. "We will arrange musicians and dancing. There should not be more than sixty or so coming, so it will be an intimate affair. Jero and Davor will go with Vilim, Hugo, and Simeon to Rijeka to buy themselves some formal clothing. They have already been told the details; I will tell the others at dinner tonight."

Fabian remembered some other news that had arrived while Mauro had been away. "Mauro, you will want to know that Stephan heard back from his father. His proposal has been accepted, and he wants to leave this week for Venice to marry Mira."

"What? That was far quicker than he expected." Mauro had not anticipated his friend would really make good on his ten-year plan to marry his first love. Stephan had been pining for the only daughter of a distinguished nobleman since their youth, and he had talked about marrying her as long as Mauro had known him. "I am sure he is excited to get back," Mauro said enthusiastically. "We will celebrate his engagement tonight after dinner."

Fabian poured more wine. "Should we celebrate at the Green Goose?" Fabian asked him casually.

"No, I am done with the Green Goose," Mauro said sheepishly. "I will be celebrating only here from now on."

Fabian stared at his friend a moment. "You have finally done it, Mauro. Congratulations! You are in love, and with your own wife, too. I did not think you had it in you! Mauritius Baric, in love!" He held up his filled glass and toasted his friend.

Mauro blushed uncomfortably, but still smiled at the truth of it. "Did I tell you that you are truly a nuisance?"

"Yes, but I believe your word was a bit stronger than 'truly'." Fabian told him grinning. "Such a shame for me, though. I shall have to find some new drinking friends to while away my bachelor days with."

"Or, we shall have to find you a wife, and then you will no longer delay the inevitable. You cannot hide in my Keep forever," Mauro told him half seriously, finishing his wine.

"And why not? I love my life as it is. Your Keep caters to all my needs: I have my meals, private quarters, my washing done. Why complicate things?"

Mauro frowned at his answer, but Fabian smiled back, unaffected by his friend's disapproval. He stood to leave. "If I see Stephan this afternoon, I will tell him to be sure to come to dinner tonight. He went to the village earlier to dispatch his reply that he is returning home."

The smell of delicious food permeated the foyer from the kitchen. "Speaking of dinner, I forgot how starved I am for lunch. Have you eaten?" Mauro asked, and Fabian shook his head. "Let us go see what Cook is offering today, and we can have our noon meal here."

~ * ~

Resi kept her promise to wear her corset for Mauro that day, and Mauro kept his promise to give her a more pleasurable homecoming that night. The two of them together found the best way to undress from her confining clothes, which added needed mischief to their time alone in their bedroom after dinner.

Still nude from their lovemaking, they lay across their rumpled bed. The candles lit earlier were nearly spent. Resi rested her head on Mauro's firm chest and stroked the fine hairs that ran down his tight abdomen. He quietly enjoyed her attention, thinking that Fabian was right. This was what it was like to finally be in love.

Resi broke the silence. "That was a nice tribute you made to Stephan tonight. Will you go to the wedding?"

"I would like us both to go, but it depends on a lot of other things. We will plan on it, though," he explained while he absently twirled her long, loose hair. They were quiet again, and Mauro was drifting off to sleep. When he allowed himself, he could fall asleep in an instant.

"Mauro, I was wondering something." She looked up to see if he had heard her.

"Yes," he whispered with his eyes shut.

"Is it, well, fair?" she began, not sure if it was her place to complain to her husband over such a matter.

"Fair?" he repeated sleepily.

She continued to ask on her servant's behalf. "Is it fair that Davor comes to the ball and not Verica? She would be so excited to dress up, and she has been a wonderful maid to me this year. Wouldn't it be a treat for her, too?"

Mauro turned to her, leaning on his elbow to see her face better. How should he explain his reasoning to her, he thought? "I suppose it seems unfair to you, and to Verica, too. I agree that she has been a good companion to you and does her job well. I am just trying to protect her."

Resi frowned at this, so he explained, "Our honored guest has a reputation for seeking out young, attractive maidens. I do not want him tempted by any of our own servant girls, is all. I am not even sure I trust Ruby to be at the ball."

Resi sat up and protested, "Mauro, you cannot deny Ruby the chance to dance at the ball. She has a new gown and everything. She would be so disappointed."

"I am serious about this," Mauro told her quietly. "Neven said D'Alessandro needs to win at his seduction, and if he sets his sights on one of our castle girls, we may have to lock his bedroom door to keep him from seeking her out."

When it was clear that she still did not fully understand the danger to the girls, he told her plainly, "He has a fancy for bedding virgins, Resi. After a night of dancing and drinking, most men want to have a woman in bed with them. He would plan to take one of ours."

"Then what shall you offer this immoral man, this honored guest of yours? Will you find some sacrificial virgin in the village for him?" Resi wanted to know.

"I have not thought that far ahead, but it is on my list. I am open for suggestions," he teased as he rolled over to her, now feeling awake again. He began stroking her uncovered breast. Resi was distracted by his touch, but perplexed about this new dimension to the upcoming festivities.

"Mauro, would you prefer to bed a virgin over a woman who knows what to expect with a man?" She hoped for an honest answer to her awkward question.

Mauro took her inquiry seriously. "Well, I have only been with one virgin, and that was on my wedding night." He kissed the breast that he had been toying with and then sat up to look at her. "Believe it or not, a woman can be a virgin and still know quite a lot about making love to a man. But I prefer you in my bed, Resi."

She smiled sleepily at his last remark. "You are a diplomat, aren't you, Mauro. But you weren't a virgin on our wedding night, isn't that right?"

The night air chilled Mauro's skin. He got up and closed the glass and came back, offering the coverlet that had fallen on the floor to his wife. She pulled it up around herself and Mauro, and they settled back into bed. She looked at him and waited for him to answer her. "You weren't, were you?" she asked again.

They had never talked about these personal details before. She hardly knew anything about Mauro and the life he had led before marrying her. "No," he answered unapologetically. "That should not be a surprise to you. I am twenty-four, Resi, and have had a lot of opportunities to be with women."

"And have you been with many women?" she asked quietly.

He answered, "A few." She cocked an eyebrow at him. "Several, maybe," he corrected his answer.

Resi risked that she might spoil the light mood of their pillow talk and asked, "Who are the women in the village you were with?"

It was not a secret to any of his soldiers, and it was now behind him. He decided he would answer her question honestly. "There was only one woman, and she is the daughter of the tavern owner."

Resi had not expected that he had given all his opportune time to just one mistress, and a common serving woman at that. "Do you like her?" she asked jealously.

Mauro tried to soothe his wife's hurt feelings. "Resi, is this really important?"

"Yes, it is," she whispered.

He took a deep breath and released it. "I honestly never thought of it as liking her or not. I paid her to be with me, if you must know, so I suppose that changes things. It makes it a business transaction and not a love affair. I do not love her, Resi. There is nothing to be jealous of, and I promise I will never take her to bed again." Mauro snuggled under the cover to signify the subject was closed.

But Resi prodded, "And the other women?"

He saw in her expression that she was not going to let him sleep until she had all her questions answered. "I did encounter many willing women in the past," he admitted unashamedly.

"And did you pay for them?" she asked softly.

"There were times I paid, but I did not seek out whores, like some men do," he explained quietly. "I was in line to become a baron. When it is known that you possess wealth, then there is no lack of willing escorts to a dinner party or an outing. Sometimes things became intimate."

"Even though you were betrothed to marry me?" she asked rigidly.

"Yes, Resi. I was still considered an eligible man until I married," he said bluntly. She sighed, accepting the reality of her world, but was glad to hear the truth from him.

She had one important question she had always wanted to ask a soldier, and dared to ask it now. "Mauro, I don't want to make you talk about unpleasant things," she began reluctantly.

"Has this topic not been unpleasant enough for you? You may ask me anything you like, and I will answer you honestly," he insisted.

"Well, you were a soldier for many years. I was told that soldiers rape the women they find when they conquer a village."

He had not expected this serious turn, but after a thoughtful moment, he answered, "Battle changes a man, Resi, and not in a good way. There is a darkness that comes over you when you kill, when you face death." He thought about how he might best explain this to his gentle wife. "Some men cannot stop the rage of battle; some cannot get away quickly enough. I have seen good men do terrible things. I have done terrible things, Resi," he admitted, looking over at her finally. "But I did not rape anyone. I can promise you that."

She looked relieved at his confession, but regretted having darkened the tone of their conversation. She tried to change the mood back to something lighter and asked teasingly, "And should I worry that any of your dinner escorts will show up at our doorstep to challenge me?"

He laughed at the new question. "Like a scorned lover? No. I believe my past lovers have all found more suitable mates by now. Perhaps not as wealthy, but I was not the ideal, romantic partner that women stayed devoted to."

It was Resi's turn to laugh at her husband's admission. "Thank you for telling me of your shortcomings," she said teasingly.

They were quiet again in their own thoughts. One of the last remaining flames flickered out. As much as Resi was curious about Mauro's past lovers, Mauro had the same curiosity. "And do you have any confessions to reveal?"

"You know I came to you pure," she cooed, not wanting to have the tables turned now.

"That does not mean you had no lovers," Mauro stated lightly. Although he was jealous of the possibility, he wanted to know her answer.

"No, I suppose it doesn't. But there was no one of consequence. I was quite sheltered because of you, Mauro," she confided to him. "My father took our betrothal very seriously, even if you did not. Since we didn't hear from you for so long, I thought the arrangement might have been forgotten on the Barics' side."

He was compelled to ask, "Would you have liked that it had been forgotten?"

He had been open and direct with his answers, and she would be, too. "Yes. I secretly hoped that it had."

He had guessed correctly, and Resi saw his disappointment in the dim light. "What would you expect?" she continued quietly. "That I wanted to be married to a stranger? That I wanted to leave my home and family behind forever?"

He pulled her in close to him. "You are right. I am sorry I made you wait," he finally said. "I am glad you are here, Resi."

The last candle sputtered out, and there was no moon that night to light the room. They lay together in each other's arms in the darkness, each deep in their own thoughts now, until sleep finally took them.

Chapter 26

Mauro dressed and left that morning without waking his wife. He met the men just after dawn near the stables. Their horses were saddled and ready for the long day's ride ahead of them. At the last minute, Mauro had decided to equip Jero and Davor with swords, in case they ran into trouble along the route. He was not sure whether they would be more of a danger to themselves or to the bandits, should they have to use the weapons; but Mauro was confident that his three captains would be able to protect them.

The baron handed Jero a sealed letter of introduction so the merchants would put their purchases on invoices with the delivery. Mauro also gave him a purse of lire for their lodgings and entertainment. Jero cheerfully tucked them into his inside pocket for safekeeping.

Mauro motioned to his officers. "Vilim. Simeon. Hugo. Can I have a word with you?"

They stepped aside from the horses. Mauro discreetly pulled out a small leather pouch. "Here is an extra purse of lire. Next week is Davor's birthday. Make sure he enjoys himself."

"Right, Mauro. And shall we also enjoy ourselves with your money?" Hugo asked hopefully with a grin.

"I have seen you enjoy yourself, Hugo. I doubt there is enough there for his and your tab. I am not so generous," Mauro said good-heartedly. "But keep track of him. The young man will be nineteen and has never been outside Baric lands. The city may be a bit overwhelming for the lad."

"I don't know if Davor will be able to ride any wenches after riding ten hours on a horse," Simeon interjected. "He just told me he has not ridden more than an hour at one outing. He is bound to be bruised by the end of our day today. Are you sure he is up to such a long journey?"

"We all had our first, long horse ride and our bollocks survived the initial shock," Mauro kindly told Simeon. "I want to remind you, though, that the purpose of the excursion is to get fitted for your wardrobe, and then you can visit the other establishments." They nodded their understanding with a chuckle. "I am sending the three of you with Jero and Davor as protection. I do not know if Jero can wield a sword, but I know Davor has had no training at all. So keep that in mind, should you run into trouble."

Simeon looked seriously at Mauro. "Every man should be able to protect himself."

"Yes, I agree, Simeon. But do not forget that we have been away more than we have been here these past two years. I hope to rectify that in the near future."

Mauro tried to shake the serious tone of their farewell. He turned his attention to the entire group. "So, men," Mauro said loudly to the five riders, "this is to be a grand affair at the Baric manor house. Remember that, when you are in the shops. Once your chore is done, enjoy the city. I will see you in four days."

Simeon and Vilim set their hats on their heads and mounted their horses. Davor waved to his baron with a toothy grin, and the company rode out the castle gate. Nestor was just walking out the front door as Mauro returned to the manor house.

"That was kind of you, Mauro, to send the boy with them. You know he did not stop smiling all day yesterday," Nestor said cheerfully.

"Well, he is a good, young man. He is too old to have never seen more of the world than these fields," Mauro replied.

"That is how you lose good, young men from your service," Nestor warned him lightly. "Keep them ignorant, and they do not know what they are missing. Let them out, and they may find that they want to stay out in the world."

"I will take that chance, Nestor," Mauro declared. He gave his advisor a second look. "Why are you up so early this morning? Did you come to see them off, or do you have your own errands?"

"A little of both. I will be heading to the Leopold estate to visit with Lady Eleonora, if there are no objections. She sent a note requesting that we review your party plans." Nestor chuckled and then said, "I think it is her ladyship's party now. I assume you are not going to protest her intervention."

"No, you will get no protest from me. I will leave it in her and your capable hands, Nestor," Mauro agreed.

"I sent a confirmation to Lieutenant D'Alessandro for the arrival time and details of his stay. I thought we would lodge his escorts in the top rooms of the Keep. Since he is your honored guest, would you like the lieutenant to stay in your mother's old room?" Nestor asked flatly. "We can move her trunks to the nursery upstairs."

Mauro had still not dealt with his mother's chamber. He did not like the idea of being forced to confront the memories right now. "No, we have six guest rooms to house those who will be staying on for the night. I think the blue room will be fine for the lieutenant. We will leave my mother's room unoccupied," Mauro decided. "Thank you, Nestor."

"As you wish. If there is nothing further you need from me today, Vik and Daniel have agreed to escort me this morning. I should be back at the end of the day," Nestor reported. He gave the baron a short bow, picked up the small satchel beside him, and then made his way to the stables.

The house was beginning to hum with movement as the servants came into the kitchen for their breakfasts. With no valet to arrange his tray, Mauro stopped in to ask a kitchen maid to bring two meals up to his chamber. He would have breakfast with his wife for once.

The bedroom was stuffy and dim in contrast to the bright, fresh day beginning outside. Mauro walked over to the bed and looked at his wife's pretty face under her flowing hair; she had neglected to tie it back last night. She looked sweet and peaceful. He risked disturbing her and opened the glass and shutters partway to let in a little more light. There was a flash as the sun reflected against something on his wife's grooming table. He went to see what could have made the brilliant light.

He picked up the stone he found there. Mauro knew all of the cave rocks that were in the castle. He had spent hours upon hours examining each crystal that lined his precious cave stones while he lay on his bed mourning his brother. Before he left home at thirteen, he had gifted two of them to his mother and two to Idita. This was not one of them. Jero had taken a few stones from the cave, too. Maybe Jero had given this one to his wife; but why would he do that? Perhaps he had them displayed in his room. But why would she have been in Jero's private quarters?

With these thoughts on his mind, he set it back down just as Brigita came into the room carrying the breakfast tray. She placed it on the table by the cold fireplace, curtsied, then left without a word.

Verica came in with hot water for her mistress and was startled to find her master in the room. "I am sorry, my lord," she whispered. "I thought you had already gone. I will come back later."

"Leave the water. I will wake my wife soon for breakfast. She will not need your help right away," Mauro told her. He wanted to spend some time alone with his wife in the daylight for once and did not want the servants interrupting their morning.

Mauro poured his coffee and ate a bite of ham; the smell was too tempting to wait. He used the hot water Verica had brought to quickly shave. He cleaned the small blade and put it neatly away again on his own grooming table.

He gazed into the looking glass he had been using. He had not cut his hair in several months, and it was beginning to curl around his ears, as it had when he was a boy. Most men who kept their hair short did so because of their preference for wearing fashionable wigs. Mauro began keeping his hair cropped after a siege when he was twenty. The unit he had been commanding had spent several weeks at an abandoned farm waiting for orders to advance. The hay barn where most of the men slept was so infested with fleas and lice, that they all ended up shaving their heads for relief. Mauro had let his hair grow again after that, but he found that shorter hair for soldiering was preferable, especially when there was no chance to bathe for weeks on end. With the recent news of a peace treaty signed between the two fighting Empires, maybe he would let it grow out again.

He heard a movement and was shaken from his thoughts. He looked over at the bed, now cloaked in warm sunlight. His wife was sitting up staring at him. "Good morning, Mauro. This is a pleasant surprise to see you in our room in the early morning," Resi said through a yawn.

"It is not so early, my dear. I have already seen the men off, shaved, and have been looking at our breakfast deciding how long I would let you linger in your dreams. Did you sleep well?" Mauro asked. He was remembering their serious conversation last night.

"I did." She stretched and slid out of bed. "I'll join you for breakfast. I, too, am famished." She put on her dressing robe and sat down at the table. "What do you have planned for the day, Mauro?"

"First, I am going to find Idita to have these stitches taken out. My skin itches something awful." His sleeve was rolled up, and Resi could see the nearly healed scar with black crosses of thread lining the wound.

He thought some more as he helped himself to an egg and added, "Fabian is working with my new soldiers, so I have time to ride out to visit the tenants. Some have sent requests for help with various problems. I wanted to see how the crops are coming along, anyway. It is nearly summer. The rains with the sunshine have been good this spring."

Resi helped herself to coffee and spread honey on a slice of bread. "Mauro, I wish you could take Ruby with you today. She would love to go riding again."

"I am not just riding, Resi. I will be stopping and working. I will be gone most of the day," Mauro said sympathetically. "Anyway, she would need a chaperone. I will be taking several soldiers with me."

"You would be her chaperone," Resi said hopefully. Mauro shook his head as he took another drink.

She took a warm, boiled egg from the basket and cracked the top, dropping the shells onto the plate with Mauro's broken shells. She would not give up asking for her friend and had to think quickly before the opportunity passed. Hugo was a safe escort, she thought, so asked, "Will Hugo be going with you today? If not, then he could go riding with Ruby?"

"Hugo has gone with Jero and the others. Besides, I could not just let Hugo take her out riding. It would not be proper; you understand that."

"We have gone riding with Hugo before, Mauro. He is a perfect gentleman and very good company," Resi said.

"Is he now?" Mauro asked playfully. "Does Ruby like Hugo?"

"Of course she likes him. I like him, too," Resi replied innocently. "He is the only one of your guards who talks to us on the wagon. He tells us stories about his days herding in the hills, and wants to know stories about our lives before we came here. He is also very attractive," she added with a smile.

"Interesting," Mauro said cautiously. "I did not know Hugo had made such an impression. Is there some sort of courting going on between the two?"

"Between Hugo and Ruby? No, Mauro, I don't think so. Although it would be difficult to know when he was just being flirtatious or whether he was seriously courting a girl. Ruby does think he is handsome. He has such an easy way about him. Maybe he likes Ruby's company, too, but he doesn't seem to be pursuing her, if that is what you are asking."

He finished his last bite of ham and shook off his jealous thoughts. "That is more than I was asking, but he still cannot take her out alone. Is there not another girl who can ride with them?" Mauro was trying to be helpful, but he knew before he asked that there was not.

"There are no women in the castle who can ride, Mauro; you know that. Verica and Natalija have never even been on a horse. Elizabeta can ride, but she is pregnant, too."

Mauro shrugged. "I cannot invent a partner to chaperone Ruby. She will have to find something else to do with her time." He changed the subject to what he hoped was a lighter one. "Jero tells me you have bought some new books with your household money," he said kindly.

"Oh. Yes, I did. I sometimes don't have a lot to do here, and there was nothing to read but dusty books on history and philosophy." She drank the glass of the water that Mauro had poured for her.

"You did not have to use your allowance in secret. I would have bought you your books, if you had told me what was lacking."

"When would I have come to you? On the battlefield?" she retorted more harshly than she meant to.

"I am sorry for that, too. I cannot change the past." He took her hand across the table. "What kinds of books do you like to read?" he asked her with a forced cheerfulness.

Resi knew her husband was making an effort to get to know her, and she quickly thought about the many books she had purchased in the past year. "It is hard to pick one genre. I like novels with adventure and romance. I also enjoy poetry very much. The Ovid volumes on seduction were very entertaining," she told him playfully.

"Ovid. I have heard talk of his works. I have not read any of them, though," Mauro commented innocently.

Resi laughed good-naturedly. "I didn't think you had." Mauro caught her joke and could laugh too, having already admitted that he was not a romantic man by nature.

"Maybe I will read them. Although I have already captured you, my dear, so I do not need to learn how to seduce you," Mauro teased her.

"You won't find the books on the shelf, if you wanted to begin reading now. I noticed yesterday that the volumes are no longer there. Someone has taken them to their room," she said slyly. He raised his eyebrows, knowing there could only be a handful of people at the castle able to read the complicated Latin.

"Well, I am glad your library is getting used. Tell me, Resi, what book is that by the bed? Is it an English book? You never cease to surprise me."

"Oh, yes, um, I am reading a book of poems by the Englishman William Shakespeare, but my copy is a translation. It is beautiful reading. Do you like poems, Mauro?"

"No. I mean, yes, but . . . I have not often read poems myself," Mauro confessed. He was quiet for a moment, then added, "I like to hear them read, though. You have a lovely voice, Resi. I would be pleased to hear you read to me sometime."

"I would like that, Mauro," she answered sweetly. The poems in the book were sensual and passionate.

He looked around the table at their empty dishes. He had never spent so long over breakfast without discussing war plans. This had been a pleasant change, but Mauro felt the urge to begin his duties for the day. "Before I call in your maid for you, I wanted to ask your opinion on something," he said.

"Of course, Mauro."

"I was thinking Jero should marry. I wanted to ask your advice on a match I am considering for him."

She was surprised he would ask her about Jero's future bride. Secretly, Resi was hopeful for Ruby's chances. "Jero will make someone a wonderful husband, I am sure."

Mauro told her, "I thought Franja might make him a good wife."

Resi was caught off guard. "Franja?"

Mauro was puzzled by her stunned expression. "Do you not like Franja?"

She covered her reaction quickly. "Oh, no, I didn't mean that. I was just surprised you would want your best cook to leave. All the men would be so disappointed."

"Does she have so many admirers?" Mauro had not considered this.

"For her pastries and breads? Yes!" Resi tried to play down his choice. "Franja is a very pleasant woman, and she and Jero seem to like each other well enough. But I don't see any love between them. I don't think she likes Jero more than she likes, say, Hugo."

Mauro was confused by this complication. "She likes Hugo? He is too young for her. He is only twenty-one," Mauro reasoned out loud.

"That is not too young to marry. I was nineteen when I married you."

"No, he is not too young to marry, but Franja is older than Hugo. I think she is twenty-four already, and that would not make a good match," Mauro clarified.

"The man must be older? Is that how it works, Mauro? There are age rules?" Resi thought this was a ridiculous argument.

"Yes, Resi, that is how it works," Mauro told her.

"Well, she doesn't seem to want to marry Hugo, either. So you don't have to worry for Hugo."

Resi liked Jero too much to not argue his cause. "Have you spoken to Jero about your choice for him? You should include him in your decision, don't you think?"

"I will, but I wanted to ask you first what you thought of this match."

"And must he marry one of the castle servants? Could he not choose another woman?"

"That is a good point. I had not considered that he may already have an admirer in the village that he is sweet on."

Mauro would think more on it later. "You have given me good advice, Resi. I will talk to him directly." Mauro collected his jacket and hat.

"Mauro?" Resi stopped him.

"Yes, my dear."

Mauro stood in front of his rumpled wife, still in her sleeping robe with her tangled hair around her shoulders. He found her suddenly irresistible and bent to kiss the charming creature. It was a tender kiss, lingering and long. He had not thought to start anything with it, but now that he held her closely, he had second thoughts about hurrying off.

"You wanted to ask me something?" he prompted quietly when he stepped back from her again.

She had lost her nerve to tell him about Ruby as a choice for a wife. "Oh, never mind. I forgot what I was going to ask."

"Oh, but I just remembered one more important thing I wanted to ask you." This was as good a time as any, he decided.

"Yes, Mauro," she said.

He hesitated; she looked so sweet. "It is about the dogs."

Resi's happy expression fell away, but Mauro went on with his planned speech. "Roko came to me when I was in the stables the other day. You must understand that my hounds are working dogs and are not to be taken without permission. I was told that you were asked several times not to take them out, and you still did." He was sorry to have to reprimand her, but it had to be said.

She hung her head. "I am sorry, Mauro. I know they are yours, and I am not to bother Roko about them. The brown dog is so very sweet, and sometimes I enjoy the company when I walk. I think she enjoys it, too. He has her locked up in the kennels for so long. It won't happen again," she promised.

He lifted her chin. "Good. That is all I wanted to say. Is there anything else I should know about, Resi, before I hear it from the servants?" His expression was still serious.

"Are you angry, Mauro?"

"No. It is your home now, too, but there are some set rules that must be followed, even by you, and I may not have made that clear." He had not forgotten about the crystal rock he saw earlier on her dressing table, but he would let that go unanswered for now. He turned to finally leave.

"Wait, Mauro," Resi called out before he shut the door. "You didn't say when Stephan is leaving. We will miss him at the castle, and we all wanted to say goodbye before he goes."

"He said he would wait for Jero and the others to come back," Mauro explained. "Do not worry; we will have a nice farewell for him in a few days." He took her hand and kissed it goodbye and added, "I will see you tonight at dinner, all right?"

"All right," she agreed at the open door.

Verica was waiting patiently just outside their room, and Mauro nodded to her that she was free to go in.

Ruby came out of her room just as Mauro disappeared down the staircase. She went into her friend's room. "Good morning, Resi. I saw your husband on the stairs. He isn't usually in the house this late in the morning." Ruby noticed the numerous dishes on the breakfast table and the two cups. "Did you have breakfast together?" she asked. Verica noticed the cluttered table, too, and began sorting the used dishes onto the empty tray.

"It was his idea, actually. Mauro is a mystery to me; I suppose any husband would be. But I think I am happier with each day that passes."

"And I am happy for you," Ruby told her.

Resi felt a pang of anguish for Ruby. Resi was not about to tell her that there would still be no horse riding, or unchaperoned visits to the village, or that Mauro wanted Jero to marry Franja.

Ruby did not sense her friend's apprehension and went on to say, "I was trying to decide what we could do today, but I have not come up with anything that would fill the hours. It will be too early in the week to make up the flower arrangements for the ball. I asked Cook if I could help her with any of the preparations. She has all the kitchen maids polishing platters and goblets today, but she insisted that it is not work for ladies," Ruby reported with a sigh.

"Cook is right. We would be in the way for them," Resi replied. She hated to waste such a pleasant day just reading indoors, and thought more about their options.

Verica had been listening to their exchange and informed her mistress, "I heard that Elizabeta Radic is in confinement since Sunday, my lady. Natalija's mother came to the castle with the delivery yesterday. She said poor Elizabeta is already a nervous wreck, and she still has several weeks to go. I am sure she would enjoy a visit while she is bedridden."

"Promise me, Ruby, that you will not let them lock me in confinement. She must be bored to tears stuck in bed on such a lovely day."

Resi eyed the poetry book that Mauro had suggested she read aloud to him, and she decided Elizabeta would enjoy the entertainment as well. "Verica, you have come up with the perfect idea."

"Have I, madam?"

"We will have Nela pack a nice food basket and have lunch with Elizabeta Radic. I am sure Mauro won't mind if we visit her. There must be a few soldiers still on the grounds who can escort us with the wagon."

"Could Natalija and I come in the wagon, too, my lady?" Verica timidly asked. "We wanted to visit Natalija's mother in the village."

Ruby looked at her suspiciously and reminded her, "You said her mother was here just yesterday. Are you so fond of her, Verica? Or is it Natalija's brother that you want to visit?"

Verica turned a deep shade of pink and admitted, "Luka and I are friends, but that is all. What would I want with a tanner's boy? They are smelly and dirty." Verica could not hold Ruby's stare.

"I have seen you with him when we go to market, Verica," Ruby pointed out with a grin. "Dirt and smell washes off, but a handsome face does not. This Luka would be a fine catch, wouldn't you agree, Resi?"

Resi was not so sure. Her maid was only sixteen. Luka was already nineteen and had been working with his father for several years now. He would be thinking about choosing a bride of his own soon. Resi thought Verica was too clever and pretty to settle as a tanner's wife in the village.

"He is a nice young man, yes. But you are far too young to be looking at boys who are ready to marry, Verica," Resi lectured her. She still had not said no, and the two girls looked hopefully at her.

"All right, then! Go watch your Luka soak hides in urine. See if I care!" Both Ruby and Verica giggled at her conclusion. "Ask Cook to fill us a lunch basket, Verica, and find Aron to tell the grooms to hitch the wagon." Verica rushed out the door with enthusiasm.

They soon realized that arranging an escort might not be possible. Nestor and Mauro were gone. Fabian and Stephan were in the training fields with their soldiers. The three other captains had left with Jero and Davor that morning. Eduard and the gatekeepers could not leave their posts.

"Who else can we ask to take us to the village?" Ruby wondered.

"I will find Geoff, and he can look around in the Keep, my lady," Verica offered. "There must be someone left who is not on duty at the castle or in the guardhouse."

Alberto found a solution. The ladies hurried to arrange themselves and their packages for their bed-bound friend, and by midmorning the four were in the wagon being driven by Alberto and Geoff. Mauro would be furious to know his stables had been left unattended, but the two horsemen did not seem to mind an outing with the ladies.

Chapter 27

The baron wanted to have a small, local militia trained that could be called upon should the new Habsburg peace treaty not last. Fabian had been working with Mauro's new recruits for the past week on the shooting fields. His task was to narrow down the group of twenty-five villagers' and farmers' sons to twelve whom he thought would make the best musketeers. Even though Fabian had not used small firearms in battle, he was an excellent archer and was a good judge of potential shooting talent.

Mauro had recently acquired a dozen new flintlock muskets, and he wanted these twelve best recruits trained on them, instead of the matchlock muskets the Baric soldiers currently used. The new muskets were beautiful weapons, purchased from French traders in the roundabout way that firearms were bought in restricted places like Croatia.

Fabian himself had only used the new ignition design a few times while training with Count Toth's army. His expertise in battle was in the heavy artillery, cannons mainly, but he knew all the dangers of working with gunpowder as an army commander. Mauro was not as concerned with target accuracy as he was with the men showing an aptitude for the mechanics of the new muskets. Accuracy would come with practice.

Misfires were the quickest way to lose good soldiers, and prudence was also an asset Mauro looked for in the final group. Fabian took his time working with each inexperienced man. Gunpowder was more dangerous in the summer heat, and there had been several malfunctions during the training this week. They used extra precaution, making sure the muskets were cleaned and cooled after each firing to avoid more mishaps with exploding barrels. Some skin was lightly charred in the accidents, but no body parts had been lost, and none of the expensive weapons had been damaged.

Fabian and Stephan had trained the men on the firing range in the cool dawn hours the first few days, but the castle women complained that the cows and goats would not milk with all the early explosions. For the next few days, they ran other drills in the morning.

Despite the slow pace, Fabian finished making his choices for Mauro's twelve sharpshooters that morning. The baron would work with them beginning tomorrow, and Fabian would focus on battlefield tactics with the remaining thirteen that did not make the elite group.

Stephan and his group of recruits were just walking back from the woods where they had been practicing scouting scenarios among the trees. It was almost high noon, and Fabian decided they'd had enough field work for the day. He instructed the men to pack up the equipment to bring back to the castle.

"Look, there is a carriage coming up the road!" one of the recruits shouted excitedly to his comrades. From where they were standing, there was a good view of the castle road leading down the valley into the village. The road ran next to the training fields for about a quarter mile until it became hidden again by trees.

All the men had stopped what they were doing to watch the stylish contraption. Carriages were a rare sight in this part of the Empire. Mauro's forefathers had never found them to be useful with their limited stable space; they owned only wagons. The Leopolds had a carriage for their matriarch Lady Eleonora, who traveled often, but theirs was small and could be pulled by two horses.

This elegant carriage was larger than anyone from the village had seen, pulled by four strong horses with two drivers on top in front and followed by two guardsmen. The top roof was loaded with trunks and satchels. The blinds were pulled down on the windows, so they were not able to catch a glimpse of the passengers. Fabian squinted in the bright sun to see it better before it went out of sight again and then shook his head in disbelief.

"Shit!" he said too loudly and rushed to mount his horse, tied to a tree at the edge of the training field. He gave no explanation to the men standing near him cleaning their weapons. Stephan had seen the carriage banners and the crest on the side door, as Fabian had. It was the Carrera crest; someone from Fabian's family was visiting unannounced. Without a word to the group, Stephan galloped away after his friend.

Fabian only caught up to the swift-moving carriage after it was through the great gate and had slowed to a halt in the courtyard. Men were running out of the stables and guardhouse to see the magnificent sight. Fabian handed the reins of his steed to Geoff and hurried to the now motionless carriage. The driver had descended and opened the passenger door. He took the hand of a young woman exiting. Her hands were cloaked in black gloves to match the black trim of her billowing, blue skirt, which was twice the size as she was.

Fabian took off his hat and wiped the sweat of his brow on his loose, linen sleeve. He crossed his arms over his chest, hat still in hand, breathing hard from the swift ride back to the castle. Stephan had just dismounted from his horse and stopped a few paces behind him to wait for his reaction. Fabian stayed in his place while the pretty girl walked toward him. She ran the last few steps to Fabian's side and threw her arms around him. She began to shake with frantic, sobbing tears as she held him. Fabian dropped his hat and embraced her in return.

~*~

Mauro had been in his study that morning going over all the purchases and accounts that Jero had managed the past six months without him. He saw the carriage come through the gate from his window and recognized the Carrera banners right away. He hurried outside and saw Fabian ride in after it. Mauro went closer and waited by the well to see what Fabian would do.

Resi had been at the greenhouses and saw Mauro standing in the courtyard. She ran up the path to join him, thinking they would meet the new arrivals together. "Why don't we go greet the visitors?" Resi asked pleasantly, taking his hand to walk with him the rest of the way.

Mauro did not flinch at her tug. "It is Caterina. I think Fabian needs to talk to her alone right now. We will wait," Mauro answered, not looking at his wife, but watching his friend. Resi had seen this hard stare on her husband's face only a few times, and it had always alarmed her. She imagined this was his commander's face, the expression he gave his men before battle.

"Who is Caterina? Is she a scorned lover?" Resi could not think why else the sophisticated, young woman would be crying and holding Fabian so desperately. Mauro said nothing.

Resi became uncomfortable when Fabian released the woman and the couple began to argue. She could not understand the words of their now-heated discussion, so tried to figure out the pantomime playing out in the courtyard in front of the castle residents. Mauro did not seem to notice Resi's distress at waiting, but he continued to hold her hand as he watched for some unspoken signal to intervene.

As Resi regarded them arguing with such familiarity, she came to realize the two opposites were clearly siblings. Caterina was petite; one might have mistaken her for a girl, if they had not seen the swell of her breasts over her low-cut bodice. Her head barely came to Fabian's shoulders. Although Fabian's muscular build dominated her diminutive size, she did not seem overpowered by him. She had fought with her brother before.

She had a pretty face and fine features, with a small, curved nose in contrast to Fabian's slightly crooked, once broken nose. They both had sleek black hair, glossy like a raven's wing. Her thick, long hair was twisted up in a fashionable knot and held with expensive ivory combs. His thick, but shorter hair was pulled back and tied with a red, leather cord. They both had chestnut brown eyes, alluring with long eyelashes and defined brows shading them. Caterina's skin was fair and light, as Fabian's was meant to be, had he not spent so much time with his shirt collar open and his sleeves rolled up outdoors.

Both had earrings dangling against their necks, but his were small and gold and hers were long with black pearls on the ends. Resi had a sense from how they stood their ground that each was used to getting their own way with the other. The girl was no longer crying and seemed to have control of her emotions again.

"What are they saying?" Resi finally asked.

Mauro glanced at her for the first time since the drama began. "I cannot make it all out. They are using their local Venetian dialect, which is different from what we speak here. When they talk too fast, I cannot follow all of it so easily. Something about her refusing to go to Hungary and not being sold like a horse." He chuckled softly, more amused than Resi thought he should be. "It seems she has run away from a marriage arrangement."

There was a second Venetian being helped out of the carriage by the driver. "And who is this woman?" Resi wanted to know.

She was taller and looked older than Caterina. She was exceptionally stylish and attractive for climbing out of a stuffy carriage. She wore a crimson-colored gown and a white lace veil partially covered her flowing brown hair and slender shoulders. The dress was sleeveless for summer, with wide satin ribbons falling across her shoulders connecting the embroidered bodice to the back of the silk dress. She was adorned with several strands of large pearls around her pale neck, and had long, white lace gloves going up her ivory arms.

Mauro seemed stunned at her emergence from the carriage, but did not say anything at all for a moment. Fabian noticed his sister's companion and threw up his arms, saying something in frustration to Caterina. Mauro finally quietly explained, "That is Isabella."

"Do you know her, then?" Resi asked.

Mauro replied calmly, "Yes. I know her quite well."

Resi looked over at his reserved expression. She was now nervous that there could be a story to this visitor that she did not want to know. She put that out of her mind as she watched Fabian walk to Isabella, still standing by the carriage steps. The new woman curtsied low to the ground, confident despite the strained atmosphere. Fabian looked irritated, but took her outstretched, gloved hand and kissed it in a true aristocratic fashion. She looked up at him, unable to completely hide her annoyance under her sweet smile, and then rose from her curtsy and stepped away from the carriage.

The women seemed oblivious to the spectacle they had created. Nestor and Idita were now standing a few feet behind the baron. Ruby and all the servants had come out of the manor house and were watching from the terrace; the soldiers had finally arrived on foot from the fields. Caterina continued to plead something to her brother and now pointed to a young man of her Guard, who stepped forward to her side.

The Carrera guardsman was as young as Hugo, and just as attractive. His tanned face was accented with a narrow beard along his jawline and a thin mustache connecting the groomed beard. He looked fashionable in the brimmed soldier's hat that covered his smoothed, black hair. He wore a tailored officer's uniform that accentuated his lean frame. It was of the same colors as the Carrera banner, pale blue and gold. Despite the heat, a matching blue cape was draped behind his broad shoulders. The man made a stiff bow to Fabian, and then began to talk to him. He seemed confident and calm, and he looked directly at Caterina's brother as he spoke.

Fabian ignored the handsome soldier's speech. Fabian turned to walk away, but then changed his mind. Instead, he strode toward him and planted his fist squarely against the guard's jaw, knocking him to the ground, flat on his back.

Stephan was there to pull Fabian away before he swung his fist again, and the other Carrera guards rushed to the fallen man's side. Mauro finally went to interrupt the chaotic scene.

Caterina was crying again, and Isabella tried to comfort her while yelling unladylike words in Venetian at Fabian. Fabian caressed his damaged hand with his other and ignored the two women completely.

"You, there!" Mauro yelled to the two drivers kneeling by their friend. "Take him away from here. Stephan! Take the Carrera men to the Keep until I say otherwise." Stephan ran to assist the guards as they lifted their unconscious friend into their arms and carried him away.

Mauro looked at the crowd that had gathered at all corners of the courtyard and announced loudly, "The show is over. Everyone go back to your duties."

The servants and onlookers began to leave, speculating quietly to themselves who the visitors might be and what had been said. Nestor took the bewildered baroness' hand and came to stand with Mauro and the others. Idita hurried across to the Keep to ask if her services were needed for the injured guard.

Mauro looked at his best friend and released a frustrated sigh. He took Fabian by the arm and walked him a few feet from the crying women. "What did you do that for?" he asked.

"He was sent to protect my sister, and now he has seduced her away from the marriage my father so painstakingly arranged," Fabian began. "She said she wants to marry the idiot, and she has come here to beg my help to save her from her new husband. Paolo is my father's soldier. He has betrayed my father, so he has betrayed me," Fabian concluded, and Mauro had to agree with his friend's reasoning.

"Caterina is on her way to Hungary for her wedding to Viscount Soltesz, some old-family, Hungarian aristocrat. My family already wrote to me about it." Fabian explained further, "Her new lover, Paolo, is helping her escape instead of assuring her safe arrival. My father will be furious."

Fabian still held the hand he had used to punch Paolo. "I hope I broke his pretty face, because I think his face broke my fucking hand," Fabian groaned.

Stephan returned with Idita. "The man is coming around. He will be in pain for a while and have a nice bruise, but we do not think his jaw is broken."

"Good. Take Fabian to my study, and Idita can look at his hand," Mauro instructed Stephan. He took a deep breath and walked over to the two women. The baron bowed formally, calm and collected, as though no frantic scene had just taken place in his courtyard. "I never expected to see you at my home, ladies. You are very welcome here. These are rather confusing circumstances, and you must be exhausted. Come with me, and I will introduce you to my wife, Terese. She can show you where you can rest."

Resi stood apart from the group with Nestor. She watched her husband take Caterina's hand and walk calmly toward her. There were times when Mauro had frustrated her with his cool aloofness and his unreadable expression. She saw now how this must serve him well in times of stress. She already felt calmer just looking at him.

"You are most generous, Mauritius. I am sorry to have put you in the middle of this. I am at my wit's end, and you are my last hope of refuge until I can convince my father to let me marry Paolo," Caterina told him anxiously before they stopped in front of Resi and Nestor.

Caterina and Isabella each gave the baroness a sweeping curtsy. Resi was speechless at the formality and could not help but curtsy to the two in return.

"Terese, my dear, this is Fabian's sister, Caterina. And this is her companion, Isabella Valli. Will you take them into the sitting room for refreshments, and I will see to their chamber. We will put them in the apartment at the end of the hall."

Resi's eyes gave Mauro a look of surprise, but she remained silent. She took Caterina's small, gloved hand and led the new guests to the manor house.

Nestor looked at Mauro with a questioning expression. Mauro hastily explained, "This may take more than a few days to clear up. I know I told you her chamber was to remain unoccupied, but it is the best room that they can share comfortably. I cannot give up two rooms that we will need for the overnight guests at the end of the week."

Nestor concurred. "I imagine it will take an hour or so for the maids to prepare the chamber," he said. "Lunch was about to be served to the servants, but I will put four of them on the room to ready it with fresh bedding and water for washing. Shall I have your mother's things brought to storage?" Nestor thought quickly of what other details might be needed.

Mauro rattled off his orders. "Bring everything but the black trunk upstairs. Have that carried down to my study. The room is open, and I will be there in a few minutes. Have a tray with lunch sent to the ladies in the sitting room. My wife will want Ruby to join them. And we can have Natalija serve as their lady's maid, since it appears they did not bring one. Oh, and make sure Tin brings the Carrera men some refreshment as well. We will decide where to house them later."

Nestor nodded. "Very good." He went around the back of the manor into the kitchen to organize the maids; Mauro went in through the front door to check on Fabian and Stephan.

~ * ~

Idita examined Fabian's hand and did not find any broken bones. It was swollen, but she thought he had only bruised the knuckles. She suggested that he soak it to help numb the ache. She left to get her bandages to wrap his hand tightly so it would heal better.

Mauro saw her walk up the stairs when he passed through the foyer to his study. Fabian sat across from Stephan at the long table with his hand in a basin of cool water. Mauro asked, "Have you thought of what is to be done?"

Fabian spoke first, looking up at Mauro. "We have. I will write to my father to ask if I should send the girls back home or on to her new husband. They are my responsibility. I will not burden you, Mauro."

Stephan continued, "I can bring Fabian's letter directly to his father. I will leave tomorrow with the Carrera men. We will take a ship with the horses instead of the passenger ferry across to Venice. We will leave the carriage here with you. Either way, the girls will need to return home or travel on to Hungary with it. Perhaps her betrothed does not yet know that she has detoured here. The marriage still might be salvageable."

Fabian added, "If my father sends a message that she is to continue on to Hungary, I shall drive her there myself. Or, I will drag her behind me on my horse! She deserves no better."

Mauro smiled at his friend and calmly advised him, "Caterina is very young, Fabian. How old is she now? Eighteen?" Fabian nodded. "She cannot possibly know how much trouble her decision could cause. We will sort this out," Mauro assured him.

"Isabella should know what trouble it would cause. I am sure she put the idea to run away into my sister's head," Fabian insisted.

Stephan wondered, "Why is Isabella her companion on this journey? Surely she will not remain with her in Hungary? Should I take her back to Venice with me tomorrow?"

"No, she will stay in Hungary with Cat. My mother wrote to me that Isabella was being sent away for one last chance to secure a husband," Fabian answered coolly. "She has a reputation of being difficult, and despite her beauty, she does not have any promising suitors in Venice. What can you expect her father to do but try a new market for her?"

"I do not know what happened between you two, Fabian, but I need your promise that you will be pleasant to her, and to your sister as well. They are guests at my house now, and I will not allow you to upset my wife," Mauro warned his friend. "The ball is in four days, and Jero and the others are not yet back. I do not want any extra strain on the mood of the house, is that understood?"

Fabian nodded; he understood very well the inconvenience this caused Mauro.

Mauro turned to Stephan. "I am sorry you must leave so hastily now, Stephan. The Kokkinos soldiers will be here any day, and I would have been glad for your company when they arrive."

"And I would have liked to witness what Patrik Kokkinos is like around his sister. He is unpredictable," Stephan said.

Idita came into the room with her bandages and a dry towel for Fabian's soaking hand. Two servants carrying Lady Johanna's trunk followed her into the room; they set the chest in an empty corner between the windows. "Thank you," Mauro told them briefly as they bowed and left.

Stephan stood to go and Mauro announced, "I believe I will take lunch with you in the Keep today, Stephan. We can both have a talk with the Carrera men and discuss the details of your return with them tomorrow."

He turned to Fabian and said, "You stay here until I am sure you will not encounter this Paolo again. He can sleep in the guardhouse tonight. Let your father decide his punishment back in Venice." Then Mauro said more kindly, "Thank you, Idita. You always have to put up with our follies."

"For fifty years now, and I hope for many more," she replied with her calming smile.

Chapter 28

"I know you must think us very foolish, Lady Terese. I did not consider what a nuisance we might be for you and your household. I hope you will forgive our intrusion," Caterina said pitifully as she took her place next to Resi on the long sofa. Her skirt took up most of the seat, so Isabella sat on the upholstered chair across from them.

"Of course not, Lady Caterina. Do not worry yourself any further. You were in distress and you wanted to see your brother. It is only natural that you sought him out," Resi said soothingly.

Ruby had not come in through the foyer with Resi and the ladies, but through the kitchen with the servants. She was now standing by the sitting room door. "Come in, Ruby." Resi motioned to her friend, and Ruby took a seat on the chair next to Isabella, who smiled sweetly at her in greeting. "This is my companion and best friend, Ruby Spiros. She came with me on my journey for my wedding, too."

"What a lovely name," Isabella told her. "Ruby is fitting for your lovely, auburn hair. I am sure you turn many heads. Men adore that hair color." Ruby's cheeks bloomed bright pink and Isabella laughed lightly. "Ah, so you do have admirers; I can read it on your face."

"Stop teasing, Isabella. We have barely arrived, and what will our new friends think of us?" Caterina chided sweetly.

Ruby was timid with the elegant women and strained to understand their unaccustomed accent, but she wanted to clarify, "My given name is Rhoda, but I have been called Ruby for so long that I only go by that now."

Resi explained the reason for her name. "It was because Ruby has very fair skin, and growing up in Greece, her skin would become bright pink from the hot sun. The other children would call her Ruby Rhoda, and later just Ruby."

Verica and Natalija entered the sitting room carrying the lunch and tea trays, followed by Nestor, who announced with authority, "I am Silvijo Nestor, Lord Baric's business manager, at your service, my ladies." Nestor bowed crisply to the young women seated across the room. "Your trunks are being brought up to your chamber. Natalija will serve as your lady's maid during your stay here, and she can begin to unpack your things while you lunch, if that is to your liking."

"Thank you, Signor Nestor. That is very generous of the baron," Isabella replied graciously.

"If there is anything that you need, Natalija will know how to assist you. Enjoy your lunch, ladies," he said, and then left the room with Natalija following him.

"I was so distressed to not be able to bring a lady's maid with me," Caterina told Resi as she accepted the cup of tea from Verica. "I asked my mother to send my sister Bianca to help me get settled, along with Isabella. Bianca would not have to stay forever, but she was eager to make an adventure of it. And perhaps she could even have found love there. There must be some handsome men in Hungary."

"Yes, Bianca would have been a good companion," Isabella agreed to the group. "She has quite the witty tongue. She is only sixteen, but already knows how the Court games are played. She was a chaperone for both her sisters, so has been well-educated in what lies ahead of her. She just needs to be introduced, and why not in the Hungarian Court instead of the Venetian."

Verica offered Isabella a plate of biscuits to go with her tea, but she declined. Resi and Ruby held their lunch plates of pheasant in aspic on toast over their laps; both were fascinated by the new visitors as they continued their open conversation.

"My mother would not part with Bianca, not even for my sake. She needs to control everything. I fell in love with Paolo, but she would not hear what I wanted. What I want is irrelevant, I was told. I am to be a prize in some new treaty." Caterina took a bite of her layered toast, then told them, "My other sister, Cristina, was married two years ago and has had her first son. She is lucky; her husband is good to her."

"How many sisters do you have?" Resi had never asked Fabian about his family.

"There are three girls and three boys. The boys came first: Gabriel is thirty, Michele is twenty-eight, then Fabian is twenty-three," Caterina told her.

"Fabian is now twenty-four, because Cristina is twenty-two, and I am between them," Isabella corrected her.

"Yes, you are right. I have not seen Fabian for so long and have lost track."

Caterina set her cup down on the table next to her and looked at her friend fondly. "Isabella is like my third sister. She spent a great deal of time at our house, because she only has one sibling. She and Cristina are nearly the same age, so they came out together. I have known you as long as I can remember."

"Yes, we are like sisters." Isabella smiled at her and added, "I would not make this horrible journey with anyone but you, my dear Cat. They are selling us both off like their prized mares."

Ruby innocently asked, "Who is selling you?"

"Why, our fathers, of course," Caterina explained. "I am to be the third wife of the Viscount Bartal Soltesz in some dark castle in the forests of Hungary; somewhere no one has ever heard of."

"Third wife?" Resi asked with surprise. Verica had stopped serving and listened to the compelling conversation.

"Yes, he crushed the other two," Caterina replied and began sobbing. Resi took her hand to comfort her, not knowing what to say.

"He did not crush them, Caterina. They died in childbirth," Isabella said tenderly to her friend.

"Yes, they died giving him enormously fat babies. I do not know how I will lay with such a large man." Caterina gained her composure again. "And he is so old."

"He is thirty-two, the same age as my brother, Alfonzo. You do not think he is so old," Isabella argued. "And you can be on top," she continued. "He cannot crush you from there. You will have more pleasure from that, anyway, if there is pleasure to be found with his foul breath in your face." Verica and Ruby's eyes were wide with shock.

"I will not survive it!" Caterina cried. She took her handkerchief from her sleeve and dabbed her eyes. "I will die without my beloved Paolo in my life."

"Fabian will sort it out for you, Caterina," Isabella promised. "He will talk to your father."

Resi had never heard such candid discussion between women. She did not have a lot of women friends in Greece, once her childhood friends began to marry and move away with their new husbands. Since coming here, she'd had only formal conversations that did not delve into the realities of married life. She was curious to learn about the man at the center of the controversy. "I think it is incredibly romantic that Paolo is your knight in shining armor," she declared.

Caterina swooned a bit. "Yes, he is. He is my first and will be my only love."

"He is deliciously handsome and was so gallant to try to protect you, Caterina. Fabian was wrong to strike him," Isabella said.

Caterina sighed deeply and acknowledged the truth of her situation. "I know my father will never allow me to marry Paolo. He is from a good Venetian family, but he is the fourth born, and does not inherit much beyond a small villa. My father told me he made a more profitable match with the viscount, and the deal was agreed to. He would not listen to me."

Resi dared to ask, "But if Paolo is your lover and you have already, well, given yourself to him, what will your new husband do when he learns of this?"

Isabella laughed softly and explained, "Caterina may be young and sweet, but she is no fool. She understands how valuable her virtue is to her family. There are many ways to enjoy a lover and keep your virginity."

"Yes, many ways," Caterina agreed with a dreamy look.

"Lady Isabella, I hope you don't mind my asking, but I was curious how you know my husband?" Resi was nervous to hear her answer. Verica tried to keep busy by removing the empty dishes to the tray, but listened intently to the entertaining gossip along with Ruby.

"I know Mauritius from when he lived at the Carrera villa for a few months when we were younger. That must have been six or seven years ago. He was such a serious young man then," Isabella said thoughtfully. "I remember he was more interested in books than balls while he was in Venice."

"Ah, but Isabella, were you even presented yet? How old would you have been?" Caterina inquired.

"I was sixteen and had just come out, so he would have been seventeen," she recalled. "He did make an impression on me. He was handsome enough and already confident then, but you do not have to worry, my dear," she told the baroness. "I was only interested in marrying a Venetian. I did not waste my time with the foreign boys that would take their brides back with them to wherever they came from. I never wanted to be sent away from my beautiful Venice," she mourned. "I did see him with Fabian at the Carrera house after that from time to time. We may have had a flirtation, but nothing of consequence. Mauritius was quite a gentleman."

"Yes, he has the reputation as a gentleman. There were no scandals with your husband, Lady Terese," Caterina assured her.

A memory suddenly came to Isabella. She turned to Caterina and said, "Ah, but I do think Lady Rosella took him as a lover for a short time."

Caterina thought on it a moment. "I believe you are right, Isabella. Yes, he would have been her type. She took most of the new ones at Court as her lovers. She is especially fond of fair-haired men," Caterina explained matter-of-factly.

"Her husband is such a toad, I cannot blame her," Isabella added.

Resi was quite in awe of how bold her visitors were in their commentary. She gave quick glance to Ruby, who was absorbed in the conversation.

"But Isabella, dear, I do not think Lady Terese is interested in our stories about her husband's escapades as a young man," Caterina stated cautiously, and the subject of Mauro was dropped.

After an awkward moment of silence, Caterina ventured to inquire, "I understand that you come from Greece, Lady Terese. The two of you do not look like the Greek women that I have seen."

"Oh, um, perhaps not," Resi agreed. She was used to this comment. "My mother is French. My siblings and I are fairer than most Greeks because of her. My father met her while he was trading there. The Kokkinos family have been merchant traders in Thessaloniki for generations, and they used to travel all of Europe when times were more peaceful."

The ladies looked her over with critical eyes. "I am glad to hear you are French, Lady Terese," Isabella said truthfully. "The French Court is so grand. I had hoped you were not Turkish. That would be such a shame for Mauritius to marry an Ottoman. Is she not exotic, Caterina?"

"She is very intriguing. I like her looks very much," Caterina complimented her as she assessed their hostess with a cock of her head. Resi sat uncomfortably under the stares of the two visitors, being spoken about as though she was not there.

"Did you not tell me once, Caterina, that Terese was your favorite saint?" Isabella asked her companion. She leaned back in her chair, still assessing the baroness.

"Oh, she is indeed. Saint Teresa had such a passion and devotion to God. If God wills me to become a nun after this escapade, I hope he sends an angel to penetrate me the way Saint Teresa was enlightened," Caterina dreamily divulged.

"The sculptor Bernini is carving a depiction of her in Rome. We were to go there this summer. His work is always marvelous. I fear I shall never see Rome again to look upon her finished statue," Isabella said with a sad expression. "I shall be stuck in a castle tower somewhere breeding children. My mother told me it would honor my family if I found a good husband. I think I would prefer to be sent to the nunnery. We can live there together."

"Yes, that will be our plan," Caterina agreed through new tears. Their moods had turned so suddenly that Resi was concerned they would both break down again.

"Oh, ladies, we have kept you too long. You are tired from your journey. Your room should be ready for you by now," Resi said hopefully.

They had been sitting the entire hour, and Resi rose uncomfortably from the sofa. She herself was exceptionally drained from the exciting events of the day. "We will show you where you will be staying. The sleeping chambers are upstairs." Verica opened the door to the foyer for them.

They walked silently together to the staircase, looking around at the ornate foyer. "That is a beautiful clock, but surely it cannot be so late already?" Isabella asked her hostess as they passed the long table across from the marble stairs.

Resi had to laugh, because when she first arrived, she had asked a similar question. "The clock is lovely to look at, yes. But the Barics don't like the noise the chimes make, so it is never wound. Time here is approximate, Lady Isabella. There is a sundial in the courtyard, but it is rarely mentioned." Both ladies raised their brows in surprise. "I would say it is around two o'clock now. That will give you plenty of time to rest before dinner," she told them as they walked up the staircase.

Verica and Ruby stepped off to the side of the hallway, and Resi led them into her mother-in-law's former room. She was pleased to see the furniture had been freshly dusted and extra touches had been added for the guests. Flowers were in a vase on the round breakfast table, and the windows had been opened to exchange the stale air in the unused room. Natalija had already unpacked many of their things from the trunks and had set the important items on the grooming table. "You will be sharing a bed, but it is large and I think you will sleep comfortably here."

The ladies looked around their new quarters. "Yes, this is a lovely room, Lady Terese. We will be very comfortable here," Caterina assured her.

Resi introduced their new lady's maid again. "This is Natalija. She can help you get settled and will be of service to you in the mornings." Natalija made a nervous curtsy. "We generally eat the evening meal together in the great hall near sundown. Shall I send someone when I plan to go down for dinner?"

"That will be perfect, Lady Terese. We will rest in our room until then," Isabella agreed.

"Very well, then. I will see you later," Resi said cheerfully. She and Ruby left with Verica back to her own room.

~*~

The two Venetians removed their gloves as they assessed their new home. They began to tell each other in their city dialect that they hoped it did not take too long for Caterina's father to answer Fabian. They did not want to spend more time than necessary in the dusty backwoods of the Empire.

"Will that be all, my ladies?" Natalija asked them in their same dialect. Both ladies blushed at the unexpected intrusion on their private conversation.

"You are a clever girl, Natalija," Isabella told her in her modern Venetian again. "Are you a linguist? You speak old Venetian and Croatian, as well, I am sure."

"Well, yes, my lady," Natalija began to explain. "My father and uncles are tradespeople in the village, but they do a lot of business with the Venetians. My father says I am like a sponge for tongues, but I promise I will not listen to what you say from now on. The baroness had always told me that I should not listen to her conversations."

The two women exchanged uncomfortable glances at having taken Lady Terese's servant from her. Isabella asked, "Are you the baroness' lady's maid, then?"

"No, madam. Well, not for the current baroness. Verica is her lady's maid. I was Lady Johanna Baric's maid before she died. She was his lordship's mother. This was her room."

"Oh dear. When did she die? I hope it was not recently." Caterina was superstitious about such things.

"Oh no, my lady. It has been a little over a year now, just before the new baroness arrived to marry his lordship," Natalija told them politely. "I was with her when she died; it was quite tragic."

"Tragic?" Isabella asked. "Was she in an accident?"

"No, my lady, she went mad," Natalija stated. Both women looked stricken.

Natalija continued to tell the stunned ladies, "At first she circled the room for an entire day. I thought I would die of exhaustion just watching her walk around and around. She would take no food or drink. His lordship was gone at the time, and we didn't know what to do with her ladyship," Natalija recalled the odd events to them. "Then the screaming began. Nestor stayed with me, and we tried to calm her down, but she was frantically pulling her hair out. The whole time she was yelling something about not wanting to do it. We never learned what she meant by that."

The two women silently stared at the maid in shock of the details of her mistress' death. "She died in that same chair you are sitting in, my lady. She just stopped screaming, and her face sort of, well, contorted. Then she was dead. No one has been in the room since."

Caterina screamed now as her companion went white and slumped over in the dead baroness' chair.

"Help, Lady Baric, help!" Natalija shouted as she ran out the door and down the hallway.

Resi was in her room with Ruby, and they both came running out at her call. "She is dead, my lady. The visitor dropped over dead, just like Lady Johanna did. There is a demon in the room that took her, just like the baroness!"

Natalija was sobbing nonsense as they reached the room to find Caterina fanning her very much alive friend. Resi ran to her side. "What has happened, Lady Caterina? Is Lady Isabella unwell?"

Ruby poured a glass of water and held it to Isabella's lips. She took a drink and opened her eyes. "What is that?" Isabella was able to ask.

"It is only water. Would you like some more?" She held the glass up for her to sip at it again.

"Water? Will you also poison me?" Isabella groaned as she slumped to the floor. Resi and Ruby helped her back to her feet and led her to the bed to sit more comfortably.

Caterina was calmer now that she knew her friend was not dying. "Please forgive her, Lady Ruby. We do not drink the water in Venice," she explained. Caterina sat on the bed next to Isabella and held her hand to comfort her.

"Should I call for Idita? She is a healing woman here and may have something that will make you feel better," Ruby offered.

"I think she is coming around," Caterina said.

"Are you, perhaps, ill from the heat?" Resi asked. She was feeling uncomfortably warm herself today.

Natalija brought her a damp towel, and Isabella accepted it with a cross look. Isabella finally spoke. "The maid was just describing how this room belonged to your dead mother-in-law. It seems she died a terrible death here."

Ruby quickly invented an explanation. "Oh, Natalija. What sorts of stories have you been sharing?" Ruby asked her with a false smile. "You will have to forgive her, Lady Isabella. She gets confused sometimes. Natalija's grandmother just died recently, and she may have mixed that story up with the baroness'."

"She told us the baroness died demented in that chair, where I was just sitting. And no one has come into the room since. Are there ghosts in here?" Isabella demanded to know.

"My mother-in-law did die a little over a year ago. I did not have the pleasure of knowing her, but she was not crazy. Have no worries, Lady Isabella. She was a very devout lady. The priest presided over her funeral, and we do not have any ghosts from her or anyone else to worry about in the manor house. Isn't that right, Natalija?" Resi asked her servant directly and held her stern stare.

Natalija understood what was expected of her. "Oh, I am sorry, Baroness Baric. I do get confused, and I must still be missing my granny terribly to have told such a story. My grandmother was loony, to be sure, but not Lady Johanna. I will open the windows again for some fresh air, madam," she said.

Natalija stood with her back to the women and crossed herself discreetly. She said a silent prayer for the ghost of Lady Johanna to hurry and fly out the open window. No one noticed that the maid lingered there a little too long.

"I think it was the carriage ride and the heat of the day that made me swoon. I am recovering already," Isabella assured her worried hostess.

"I will send Verica to help you undress," Resi insisted.

Natalija came back to the group and stared down at her feet, ashamed of the trouble she had caused. Caterina was feeling more generous than Isabella and said, "There is no need to call for your maid, Lady Terese. I will help Isabella out of her gown. Natalija can return when it is time for dinner." Natalija looked up and smiled brightly, having been forgiven momentarily.

Resi was about to say something when she felt an awkward twinge in the pit of her stomach, and then once more. The women noticed her unusual expression, and they waited for her to recover. "Ruby! I just felt the baby."

Ruby came to her side and instinctively put her hand on Resi's middle. The ladies looked puzzled.

"Are you with child, Lady Terese?" Caterina asked, suddenly realizing what her announcement had meant. Ruby nodded to her, smiling happily.

"And here we have caused you such stress today," Isabella blurted out, her own feebleness forgotten. Both she and Caterina came to her side to comfort her.

"You must go to your chamber and rest at once," Caterina insisted.

"Yes, Lady Terese. We have worn you out. You must rest," Isabella agreed.

Isabella took her arm and walked her out the door. They all went to Resi's chamber at the end of the hall. Ruby closed the shutters while the ladies led her to her canopied bed.

"I am fine, really," Resi insisted, feeling silly to have the three women doting over her.

Ruby untied Resi's voluminous overskirt and let it drop to the floor. They removed her shoes, garters, and stockings before she lay down. They covered her with the top coverlet, and she settled back onto the pillow. "Maybe I will rest just a little," Resi told the concerned women.

"I overheard the baron tell Cook that we will have Stephan's farewell dinner tonight. I will come wake you when it is time to go down," Ruby told her before they shut the door to her darkened room.

~ * ~

Mauro lit only a single candle while he quietly finished his washing up that night. He undressed and put a fresh shirt on for sleeping. He was exhausted from the strain of the day and the numerous toasts at Stephan's farewell party that evening.

He looked at the bed and his wife sprawled across the middle of it, still in her bodice and layered underskirt. He decided if she had already slept so long in the uncomfortable clothes, then she might be alright until the morning. He blew out the candle and slid onto the sliver of free space next to Resi under the blanket.

"Mauro," she said sleepily, "is it nighttime already? Why didn't you wake me?"

"I tried."

"I was so tired," she whispered.

"Go back to sleep," he whispered back, and then nuzzled and kissed her neck.

"Mauro?"

"Shhh," he replied.

"How long will they stay?"

"I do not know."

"Mauro." She was barely audible.

"Resi." He was, too.

"I like them" was the last thing she said.

He put his arm around her waist and slid in closer to her. "I am glad." He breathed the words out as he drifted to sleep.

Chapter 29

Mauro sat up in bed and stretched in the dim, dawning light. He looked with surprise over at his wife. "You are up early," he declared. He was always the first one awake.

"That was more than enough sleep, even for me," she replied sweetly.

Resi had lit a candle while she waited in the dark for him to wake. She was at her grooming table plaiting her long, brown curls. She looped her favorite blue ribbon several times around the end of the long braid to secure it. She could not help but smile at him sitting on the side of the bed in his crumpled shirt. She had imagined that he sprang energetically out of bed each morning, but he looked very sleepy today.

"May I come with you to say goodbye to Stephan this morning, since I missed dinner last night? He has always been so friendly to me. I think he will make a wonderful husband."

Mauro unconsciously frowned.

"What is it, Mauro? Do you not think so?" she asked, puzzled by his expression.

"Yes, of course he will," he agreed quickly. He forced his doubtful expression into a smile for her. He had no reason to be jealous of her admiration for Stephan. Stephan was friendly to everyone, and he only had eyes for his Mira. "You always have such good opinions of my friends. I hope you talk as kindly about me, is all."

He went to Resi's side and leaned in behind her, looking into her mirror. He ran his fingers through his short hair in place of a comb.

"If I do ever talk about you, I can usually find something pleasant to say," she answered teasingly at his reflection. He kissed her cheek as a reward for her cleverness and went behind the screen to fill the chamber pot.

"Caterina and Isabella had kind words to say about you. They called you a gentleman," she told him when he had joined her again.

"I am surprised by that. I would expect them to be more critical of me," he said from across the room. He looked around the floor for his breeches, forgetting he had laid them over the chairback last night. He pulled them on and tucked in his long shirt, leaving the ruffled opening unbuttoned. He rolled up his billowing sleeves before he poured the last of the clean water into the basin to shave.

Resi was still at her table, but turned to look at him now. She wondered how much he really knew about their visitors, since it had been so long ago that he had lived in Venice with the Carreras. "Why would you say they would be critical of you? The ladies seem to like you very much, Mauro."

"I have my reasons," he answered simply. He saw from her expression that it was not enough. "All right, maybe because they generally had quite a lot to say about everything and everyone, and their opinions were not always good."

He splashed water on his face and sat down with his own small looking glass. He unsheathed the shaving blade, then dipped his fingers into the soap pot.

"Well, I think they are fascinating," Resi continued thoughtfully. "They did share a variety of opinions on many subjects. The ladies have lived quite a different sort of life than I have."

"I suppose they have," Mauro agreed casually, not in the mood to gossip himself, and he quickly went about his efficient morning routine. He finished his shaving and wiped his face dry with the linen cloth.

Standing close behind him now, she ventured, "I wanted to ask you about someone that the ladies happened to talk about."

"Of course, Resi. What is his name?"

"Her name is Lady Rosella," she said cautiously. She stepped back from his chair, sensing her question might have been a mistake.

Mauro walked to the window and threw the basin of dirty water out. He lingered there and briefly watched the red sun rising through the crack between the pine-dotted cliffs. "Lady Rosella? That is a name I have not heard in a while," was his quiet reply. He shut the glass again and came back to his grooming table. He put the items he was using back in their places.

Her husband had not completely dismissed the topic, so she boldly asked, "So, you do know her?"

He turned to her with an unreadable expression. "Yes, I know her. The ladies told you so. It is just odd that you are with Caterina and Isabella less than two hours, and of all the subjects to talk about, they tell you about Lady Rosella," Mauro replied, showing his irritation now. "I am sure they took pleasure in explaining the whole affair, so there is nothing to discuss."

Mauro turned his attention back to his grooming. He put on the clean stockings he had retrieved from his trunk and selected two ribbons to hold them up.

Resi did not give up on having her curiosity sated. "They only mentioned her when we talked about how you came to meet Lady Isabella. We are husband and wife, Mauro, so they expect that I know some things about your past. I don't think that they thought they were saying anything, well, secretive—if it is secretive. I just found it curious, is all," Resi tempted him.

He decided to indulge her. "What do you find curious, my dear?" He searched for the leather shoes he wanted to wear in the field and put them on.

"Well, Mauro, you were jealous of men looking at me in my new gown; but as a young man, you had a love affair with a married woman. Is that not hypocritical?" she said confidently.

While Resi waited for an answer, she pulled her voluminous skirt over her head; it had been left on the floor before her nap yesterday. Mauro noticed Resi fiddling to find the right loops to attach her bodice, and he came over to the bedside to assist her.

"Are you going to answer me? Is it true, then? Were you a married woman's lover?" she asked.

Mauro found the ties and began securing the dress. "Yes, it is true," he admitted. "But it is not what you think. And it is not hypocritical."

"They said her husband is a toad. I suppose if he were handsome, it would be wrong for her to flirt with other men." Resi smiled at the image in her mind of a handsome toad.

Mauro chuckled, wondering if she had chosen the wrong word. "What did they call him?"

He gave her a small pat on her bottom to signal he had finished his task, and then reached down to pick up her stockings from the floor. She took them from him, examined that they were still fit to wear, then sat down and lifted her full skirts to her thighs to roll one over her foot. Mauro openly watched her.

"A 'toad' is how they described her husband's appearance," she clarified, wondering if he was even listening now. Despite how annoyingly contrary he was at that moment, she liked that she could hold his attention with such a small act.

"It is not kind to describe a man in such terms," she continued to say cheerfully, "but that was their reasoning for Lady Rosella's romantic affairs at Court."

She took the second stocking and rolled it over the other foot, pulled it high above her knee, then secured it with the garter. She slipped on her shoes, and he responded to her theory.

"That could be one good reason for her exploits, yes. Her husband was fat and unattractive, as I recall. It could also be that Rosella was bored with the same powdered faces to flirt with. She challenged herself to seduce the young arrivals like me, who were newly introduced and did not yet know how the game was played in Venetian society. I was quite young then, only seventeen, I think." He stood in front of his wardrobe and chose a sleeveless, leather doublet to wear over his airy, linen shirt. He would not wear a cravat in the heat today.

Resi continued to be amazed at her husband's casual remarks. "And that was tolerated?" she wanted to know. She poured herself a cup of water from the crock and waited for his answer.

He buttoned his doublet. "Was seducing young men tolerated? Yes, of course it was. If you were at Court, then you were of age for romantic encounters. I was naïve, but I was not unaware of what was going on all around me. Everyone flirted with everyone, especially the young and unmarried; but the married enjoyed the game, too. Sometimes it was just coy conversation, but other times it led to more private dalliances. Seduction was their favorite sport, but at seventeen, I was not so at ease playing it. Rosella was quite persuasive, though. She knew she was attractive and toyed with all the possible admirers. She found a way to put me at ease, and I became her favorite for the month."

Now dressed, he walked to the window again and opened the shutters fully. The bright morning sun illuminated the room. Resi watched him from the bed. He did not look at ease to her now. "You don't regret being an older woman's toy, Mauro?"

"I try not to have regrets." He smiled to himself, remembering the fleeting affair. Staring out at the Baric mountain, he went on to confide, "After Rosella taught me what she thought I should know, I began to have some ideas of my own. She ended it then, and she went on to the next boy. That was how she played her game."

"Like your friend, the lieutenant. That is his game, too, isn't it?" Resi reminded him.

He turned back around to look at her. The sunlight was shining on the bed where she sat dressed and ready for the day. "I had not thought of it that way, but I suppose so."

She asked him, "Were you not humiliated?"

"Why would I be humiliated? It was a lesson I willingly learned from a willing teacher. There was no shame attached to it," Mauro declared honestly. "I did not fall in love with her. It was just a little sport." He hoped this was the end of the topic.

Resi thought his reasoning was too one-sided to be satisfied with his conclusion and asked, "If you were a girl, Mauro, would there not be shame in such a game?"

He was eager to leave for breakfast; the men would be waiting. Mauro stood in front of his troubled wife and tilted her chin up, looking down into her alluring eyes. "Yes," he answered firmly. "If I were a girl, it would have changed everything for me and my future prospects. I might have become pregnant and had a bastard child. And where would that have left me at seventeen?" He walked away from her and grabbed his hat from the peg.

Resi followed him to the door. "And Lady Rosella? Did she not have any bastard children from all her affairs?"

He did not have to think long about it. "I believe she does have several children now, but she was a married woman, remember. I suppose she would lay with her husband every once in a while and claim they were his." He tried to smile at her again.

"That seems rather complicated."

"Or rather simple. It worked for her."

He wanted to go now, but not without a proper closure to their conversation. He bent and kissed her slowly on her lips, and she relaxed in his arms. He released her, satisfied that he would have the last word and added, "Either way, I hope it does not give you any ideas." He opened the chamber door.

Her eyes twinkled mischievously when she said, "It is a little late for that warning."

"Is it? Do you have something to confess?" he asked with a flash of jealousy.

"I am only teasing you! Your men will hardly hold my hand to help me down from the wagon. I think you have trained them too well to not touch their commander's wife."

"That is good to know. Come; let us go have breakfast with my timid soldiers."

She took one last glance into her long looking glass before he led her out the door. "Do you mind if I go back to wearing my robes?" she asked. "I am having a hard time feeling comfortable in these tight bodices and the stiff skirts."

"Maybe if you did not sleep in them, they would be more bearable." She frowned at his comment, so he conceded, "Do whatever you like, Resi. Your other dresses are very becoming, and they cover you more." Mauro winked at her as he took her hand and led her down the quiet corridor.

"Don't you like to see more of me, Mauro?" she asked playfully.

"I can see more of you every night. I do not want the castle to see more of you, though." He stopped at the top of the staircase and touched his finger along the edge of her bodice where the top half of her breasts spilled over. "Did you not say there was some lace that came with this dress?"

"Yes, there was some included. How far up would you like me to tuck the lace? Up to my neck?"

He laughed softly as he visualized it. "Yes, that would be fine," he said.

Resi sighed. "I will have Verica help me dress more modestly for you after my bath. Do you think our visitors would like to join me in the bathhouse?"

"I am not sure they have had the pleasure of a Turkish bath."

"Don't they have bathhouses in Venice?"

"They do, but not for respectable ladies. The Carreras' home did not have a bathing pool that I knew of. They wash privately in their rooms, like most people. But I am sure they would enjoy your bathhouse."

"I will invite them," she decided cheerfully.

They crossed the foyer and went through the doors into the great hall. Resi was famished. The maids had already brought trays of breakfast food to the large table. Stephan and Fabian were seated beside the Carrera soldiers and Baric officers. She guessed that Paolo and Fabian had come to some sort of a truce, because the young guard did not seem distressed to be at the table with his assailant. His face was badly bruised on the left from his bearded jawline to his swollen eye, but Caterina's lover smiled at her as the men greeted the Barics.

Stephan rose to meet the baroness. He bowed and formally kissed her hand. He always made a special effort to greet her, unfazed by Mauro's jealousy. "Ah, dear Lady Terese. I am glad to see that you are well. We missed you last night."

"Thank you, Stephan. I was not ill, just very tired." The Barics took their seats next to Stephan and Fabian. The group began helping themselves to the platters of food laid out on the table. "When can we expect to see you next?" she asked Stephan.

"At my wedding in September," he beamed.

"September? But that is several months away. Why will you wait?" she asked as she added a fresh strawberry tart to her own plate.

"Mira's mother is from Rome and travels there every summer. She had just left for her visit when our fathers finalized the arrangement. I am happy Mira did not travel with her this year. Otherwise, there would be no reason to go to Venice right now. It will take several weeks for her mother to return."

"And Mira is waiting for you in Venice?" Resi asked. She liked that this was a marriage of romantic love, even though permission from the families had to be granted.

"Yes, I will see her by the end of the week. I plan to organize our household during the next few months to be ready for September. I will be joining my father's business and will live their city villa for the time being."

The others hastily ate their meal and conversed among themselves. Stephan had already told them the same news at dinner last night, but the baroness listened with interest while he finished his story.

"You are the first nobleman I have met who is marrying the woman of his choice," she dared to say. "I know you will be very happy with Mira. I look forward to meeting her," Resi said kindly.

"Sometimes you get lucky. Even if she had been chosen for me, I would still want Mira. I see it has worked out well for you and Mauritius. I think we can agree that we have all been lucky." He smiled at her in his boyish way.

This was the first time someone close to Mauro had mentioned what her husband felt about her. "Has my husband told you it has worked out well for him?" she asked.

Stephan was puzzled that she needed his confirmation. "Yes, my lady; he has said so himself. I know Mauritius does not wear his emotions on his sleeve like I do, but he does feel them." Her hand had been resting on the table, and he gave it a friendly pat and smiled brightly at her. "I think we are ready to leave, Lady Terese. I look forward to seeing you again soon in Venice."

The travelers were eager to get an early start. After having eaten their fill, Stephan and the Carrera soldiers said their farewells to the Barics. Resi and Mauro remained at the table in the great hall and watched them through the window as they scattered across the courtyard to gather their gear and horses.

"Resi, my dear, Fabian tells me his sister and Isabella went to bed quite late last night. You may not even see them until this afternoon. You should go about your normal plans until then," Mauro suggested. "I will be leaving now for the training fields. I will come find you later today, all right?" He put on his hat to leave, and she followed him to the terrace door.

"Mauro, I have something to tell you," she said urgently. "You may already have heard it last night from one of the ladies," she began.

He became concerned at the serious tone of her declaration.

She told him, "You asked me before if I had felt the baby. I finally did yesterday, and this morning again too. Just a little flutter, but enough to know it is there."

A wide smile spread over his worried face. "I can tell you that no one has said a word about it. I am glad to hear it from your lips first. Now we know you are truly with child." He kissed her tenderly on her lips, then advised her, "But you must take care to rest more, for the baby's sake. Will you promise to do that for me?"

She wanted to promise him, but was not sure if she could keep it. The party was in three days, and the preparations would begin in earnest today. Her brother and his company were expected to arrive any day as well. "Yes, I promise."

She watched him as he left to the stables, strutting happily with long strides across the courtyard. Verica had been waiting in the shadows of the foyer door and now came across the expansive room to her mistress.

"I think I will take my bath now, Verica. I will need your help to unfasten this gown, but I will wear my old robes when I am done." Resi strolled out the terrace door, through the colorful flower garden, to her sanctuary.

Chapter 30

Caterina and Isabella had just finished their morning meal on the grand terrace when Resi came back from her soaking. She had changed into her comfortable layers of coarse silk and linen robes. Her light waistcoat was held closed with a pretty, embroidered sash tied high on her waist. Her hair was still damp from washing, but Verica had combed the tangled locks and had loosely braided it again before they left for the house. She was quite a different sight from the corseted baroness of yesterday when she walked up the steps to greet the two Venetians.

"Lady Terese, I am glad you are well," Isabella greeted her first.

Caterina smiled broadly and agreed, "Yes, you look very well today." She continued to openly stare with a smile. "Lady Terese, I have to say, I would not have recognized you as the same lady we met yesterday. This is such a change in your appearance."

Resi looked down at the flowing, gauzy sleeves of her summer tunic and long overgown. The first layer was a pale green and was just short enough to reveal that the tunic beneath was of blue silk, with purple and red thread sewn in an intricate design along the exposed hem. The sleeveless waistcoat was a vibrant pink, belted to show her feminine figure. It was indeed a world apart from the full skirt and low-cut bodice of her fashionable gown yesterday.

Suddenly bashful, Resi explained, "I suppose I am not used to company and the appropriate dress. I have just come from my bathhouse, and it is a pleasure to wear something soft and loose after the warmth of the water. I was just on my way to change."

"I envy you, Lady Terese," Isabella told her boldly. "You come fresh from your bath, and still you are enchanting. Please do not change on our account."

Caterina added, "Yes, this is your home, Lady Terese. There is no need to change from your customary dress. Your robes are so very beautiful. I admired Lady Ruby's yesterday."

Resi remembered her promise to Ruby to clarify with the Venetians. "Thank you, Lady Caterina. There is something, though, that Ruby has asked that I explain. You may have gotten the impression from the servants, but she is not a lady, in that sense."

They looked puzzled at her unexpected statement. Resi confided quietly, "The servants found it awkward to call her by her first name alone, as I do, since she is my equal and not my handmaiden. They began calling her Lady Ruby, and once they began addressing her so, my husband insisted that they continue. He found no fault in it, but she is quite nervous that you may find she is being pretentious."

"Of course these titles are complicated for servants to understand. We will think nothing of it and shall call her Lady Ruby as well. She is a gentlewoman, and it suits her," Caterina said sweetly.

"Yes, it suits her well," Isabella agreed.

Resi saw that the terrace table was littered with half-empty dishes and was pleased that her guests had been taken care of. "Did you enjoy your breakfast?" she asked. "I am glad you could have it here on the terrace."

"Indeed. The maid brought the tray to our room, but Isabella and I decided to take some air before it begins to rain." Resi had not noticed the black clouds forming along the mountains. It had been such a bright morning during her own breakfast a few hours ago.

Resi ventured to ask, "Is Natalija to your liking? She can be a bit nervous at times, but she is a very good maid." Resi was hopeful that Natalija had redeemed herself, because she would not so willingly switch Verica's services for Natalija's.

"Yes, she is a bit nervous, but she will do," Caterina said kindly.

"I think we were all a little nervous yesterday, Lady Terese. We were quite an unexpected arrival, and we do not want to be a burden to your household," Isabella politely told her.

"Oh, well, we are glad for your company, even if the circumstances are unfortunate for you. Fabian is a dear friend to my husband. You are welcome to stay as long as you like. As a matter of fact," Resi sat down on a chair with excitement and said, "I am very happy to have two more ladies here. We are to host a ball in three days' time, and we are severely overpopulated by men. Two more dance partners will be very much appreciated by the guests." Resi waited for what she hoped would be a positive reaction, and it was.

"This is surprising news. A real ball? In the territories? That will be a wonderful diversion. I am sure we will enjoy that very much, will we not, Isabella?" Caterina exclaimed.

"Yes, it will be a delightful diversion. Very encouraging. We do so love a ball," Isabella added with a matched enthusiasm.

Resi was heartened to have the women's approval. "It is all very exciting for us. We will begin the final preparations tomorrow. It is to be a grand evening. Ruby and I have just received new gowns from my husband's aunt that we will wear for the first time. The men have gone to the city for new gentlemen's wardrobes. I am sure our party can't compare to the elegant festivities in Venice, but the noblemen and gentry of the region will be attending, as will several of the Venetian Naval officers."

"Well, if the men outnumber the ladies, it will be very agreeable. Will there be an orchestra for dancing?" Isabella asked.

"There will be music, but we do not know how to dance any formal dances. We do dance a jig for our own entertainment often enough, but not with steps and turns like real partner-dancing," Resi admitted.

Caterina smiled at Isabella, who smiled knowingly back. "Then our arrival has been fortunate. We will take you under our wings, Lady Terese, and show you all the dances we love," Isabella replied.

"They are really very simple. Once you learn a few steps, they repeat themselves. Within a few hours, you will be an expert," Caterina assured her cheerfully.

Resi was overjoyed by their offer. "The men should learn the steps as well, if they are to be good partners. We can practice after dinner tonight. I will talk to my husband later," Resi suggested excitedly.

"What do Fabian and Mauritius do all day?" Caterina asked. "I have not seen them about."

"They are usually away from the castle during the day. This week his officers are training new soldiers. Mauro doesn't believe that the peace treaty will hold. If he is correct, then he and his men will be called away again," Resi explained.

"Called away? And what do you do when you are here all alone?" Isabella inquired with concern.

"Ruby and I find things to do together. Before I was pregnant, we were allowed to go riding through the fields and mountain trails. We like to visit the village on market day. I have quite a collection of new books that I enjoy reading. I also sew, when I am feeling patient." Resi laughed lightly at her own statement, since she had not come very far with her embroidery project. "My mother-in-law created a lovely garden within the walls; we take walks through it, or help the gardener tend the spent blossoms to make soaps and scented oils."

"Then we shall have a lot to keep ourselves occupied while we are here," Isabella said pleasantly. "May I look through your library this morning? I would perhaps like to read one of your books today."

Since they had finished their meal, Resi took them directly to the sitting room where she kept her book collection. She left her guests to look through the titles for something that appealed to them while she went upstairs to finish dressing.

Verica had gone up to the room earlier from the bathhouse and had already cleaned and arranged the room for the Barics. "I didn't pack away the gown from yesterday, my lady, in case you have changed your mind. Did you want to wear it again?" she asked.

"No, I will wear what I have on. But I would like something special done with my hair. Maybe you can use the jeweled combs again."

Verica was happy for her choice, and she knew which style she would create to make her mistress beautiful. Verica went to work curling the long locks and pinning her hair with the precious combs while Resi daydreamed about the dance lessons.

Chapter 31

The soldiers had been at the target range for most of the morning, and the training had gone well. Mauro was pleased with the young militia recruits Fabian had selected. He considered offering some of them a place in his permanent Castle Guard. Mauro had just called them in to pack up for the day when a group of horses rode onto the field. Mauro walked toward the riders as they dismounted.

"I was hoping you would be back today. Did everything go as planned?" Mauro asked Simeon, who was the first to meet him. The others were dusting off their breeches and slowly making their way across the field.

"No complaints, Mauro. We made it to Rijeka late the first night and found good lodgings. We set about completing your errand the next morning. Jero was serious about outfitting us all from head to foot." Simeon smirked at Jero, who had overheard his loud comment as he approached the two. "It took us all day, but as a reward for the hard work, we took our time relaxing in the evening." Simeon winked in a friendly fashion to Jero this time, and Mauro noticed his steward blush.

"You will not be disappointed, my lord," Jero told him, ignoring Simeon's teasing. "The merchants agreed to send all the items by wagon to be here in time for the party. We could have waited another day to bring some of the things on our horses, but we decided to leave early and take two days for the return journey. It was a long twelve hours to get there. Davor and I are not used to so much time in a saddle."

Vilim and Hugo now joined the group and reported, "We camped on Dubovic's land by the seashore last night to do some fishing for our supper. His scouts came to give us a warning, but his captain Marko recognized us, and they gave us leave to stay the night on their land."

Simeon took something from his shoulder bag and handed it to Mauro with a playful smile. Mauro took his full money pouch back and asked, "Did it not work out for Davor?" Mauro could not hide his disappointment, but Vilim and Hugo chuckled with amusement.

Davor was still making his way across the field, so Simeon quickly explained to Mauro, "Oh, it worked out alright. When we walked into the brothel, the girls went wild for him. They don't see many golden-haired um, what was their word exactly?" he asked the others, pausing for a bit of drama in his storytelling.

Vilim was happy to pick up the story. "'Cherub', was what they called him. We had to get him good and drunk when he realized where we had brought him and what all the fuss over him was about. The girls offered their services for free for a first-time lad. They took him upstairs and were gone a while. We were beginning to wonder what they had done with the poor man. When we finally wanted to leave, Hugo went looking for him."

Hugo finished the story. "I guess they couldn't decide who would get the honors of being his first, because I found him in bed with two of the women, both very pretty and both very naked. They did not request a payment, so we are returning your purse."

Mauro looked over to Jero for commentary. He only shrugged his shoulders with a grin, but did not admit to being accessory to the corruption of Mauro's valet.

Davor finally reached the group, looking a little worse for the wear from the horse ride. "Well, Davor, did the trip make a horseman out of you? You are walking a bit stiffly," Mauro said with a straight expression.

Davor smiled and told him politely, "I believe it did, sir. I had no troubles with the mare, my lord. She was a good ride. It was all quite an adventure for me. Thank you, sir."

Simeon and Hugo tried to cover their laughter at the innocent double entendre. Mauro shot them a sharp look. "Good," Mauro replied, trying to remain dignified, even if his captains could not.

Davor took off his cap and continued to stand in front of the baron. "Was there something else?" Mauro asked. Davor looked from the baron to the men, and then back to the baron. Mauro understood his silent request and walked away from the group; Davor followed him.

Davor faced his master and cleared his dry throat. "I would like leave to go to the village before I resume my duties today, my lord," he said gravely.

"What do you need in the village?" Mauro wanted to know.

"I have something heavy on my mind, Lord Baric, and I would like to visit Father David."

"Oh? Did you kill a man?" Mauro asked as seriously as he was able, distracted by the four men listening in just a few feet away.

"No, my lord," Davor said emphatically. "At least I don't think so," he added with concern. The memory of the evening at the brothel was somewhat of a blur to him.

"Good, then the priest can wait until Sunday," Mauro told him.

Downcast, Davor replied, "Yes, my lord." He bowed stiffly to the baron and then began to walk back to the horses.

Mauro followed him and put his hand on his shoulder to stop him again. He was close enough for only Davor to hear when he suggested, "You can take a few minutes to say your peace to God in the chapel, but after that, go get cleaned up. We have a lot of work to do before our party." Davor relaxed under his firm hold. "One question, though."

"Yes, my lord?" Davor replied dutifully.

"Was it such a bad experience these last few days that you must talk to the priest?"

Davor grinned at him unexpectedly. "No, Lord Baric. I never imagined such an experience. I must repent because I enjoyed it so much."

Mauro had to laugh at his honesty, and he patted him on the back to scoot him on his way.

The others came to the baron's side again. "I am going to head back with Davor," Jero told Mauro, who nodded his approval.

Vilim, Simeon, and Hugo lingered a moment. Mauro asked, "Was there something else?"

Vilim took the lead and said, "We crossed paths with Stephan along the route this morning. He stopped with the Carrera men to have a drink with us. He told us we have visitors."

"Yes, we do. Did he explain who and why, as well?" Mauro asked them.

"He told us about Fabian's sister and her companion seeking a way out of her marriage in Hungary. What are you going to do about them?" Simeon asked.

"I am not going to do anything. It is Fabian's decision, and he wants to wait for instructions from his father. He should hear within a week. If they are to go on to Hungary, Fabian said he will take them himself. In the meantime, they will be our special guests here."

The men looked at each other optimistically. Mauro understood now what the conversation was really about. "Not so fast, gentlemen," Mauro cautioned. "They are both under Fabian's protection. Caterina is still betrothed, and Isabella is, well, complicated. She is off limits, is that understood?" All three grinned at Mauro's warning, but nodded their agreement to heed it. "I am going to finish up here with the men. I will meet you in an hour for lunch in the manor house, and I will introduce you to our pretty houseguests."

~ * ~

Jero shut the door to his room with a loud click just as Resi came out of her own chamber down the hall. The upstairs servant boy, Aron, was coming from the wooden stairwell with two pails of water. Aron was Alberto's youngest son. He had helped his father with small jobs in the stables for years. He was twelve now.

At Alberto's request, Mauro had moved him into the manor house earlier in the year to train as a house groom. Alberto's oldest son, Josip, was being taught the skills of a stable master. Alberto did not want his two sons to compete against each other for his job when he was finally too old to fulfill it. Jero had made Aron the hall servant as his starting position, bringing water and running simple errands for the residents.

Resi stopped the boy and asked, "Tell me, Aron; has Jero returned?"

He set down his burden and lowered his eyes to his mistress, as Jero had taught him. He was a small boy for twelve, but strong enough for the duty at hand. He had a mop of black hair tucked under his velvet servant's cap that matched his fitted, green waistcoat. Looking down, he saw that his shoes were dirty from visiting the stables earlier, and he hoped his mistress had not noticed. "Yes, my lady," he answered her. "I am bringing washing-up water to Jero's room right now."

"Thank you, Aron. That is all I needed to know."

She patted him on his cap and went along her way down the marble stairs. Aron waited until she was almost out of sight and then sneaked a look at his pretty mistress over the banister as she disappeared on the staircase.

Mauro was just coming through the front door when she reached the bottom steps. She stopped and waited for him. "Have you come in for lunch, Mauro?" she asked.

"Yes, I have. The men are back from their trip, and they will join us for lunch in the great hall. I wanted to introduce Caterina and Isabella to them," Mauro told her. He noticed now that she had made a special effort with her appearance and remarked, "You look very pretty, Resi. What have you been up to this morning?"

"I have been talking to Lady Caterina and Lady Isabella about dancing lessons. They would like to teach us all some dance steps." Resi was not discouraged by his sudden frown and reminded him, "You said that you wanted to practice."

"Yes, I wanted to practice, but I had not thought to make such a public spectacle of it," Mauro replied earnestly.

"And what do you think the Barics will look like at the ball when the music begins and no one can dance properly? That will be a sorry spectacle, wouldn't you agree?"

Mauro looked at his wife's hopeful glare and could not refuse her. "When did you want to have this dance lesson?"

She smiled at her victory and suggested, "Tonight, after dinner, might be a good time; or perhaps tomorrow morning, when the light is better. We will need a lot of space, but the great hall is so dark after sunset."

"We can light all the torches and try some steps after dinner. If it is raining tomorrow, we can go over the dance steps once more in the morning," he offered. "We cannot practice our shooting drills in the rain."

She stood on her toes to kiss him quickly on the lips. "I hope it rains! Thank you, Mauro."

"You are welcome, Resi. I will see you shortly. I have something I need to take care of before lunch." She nodded happily and walked down the hall to the sitting room to find their guests.

Chapter 32

Jero had not planned to linger long in his room. He washed with the warm water Aron had brought him and changed into a clean, starched shirt and his favorite breeches for his duties. He was very tired, not used to long horse rides and evenings of drinking and flirtation. He lay down on his bed for a few minutes to rest his weary muscles. And then he was out.

The table was being set in the great hall, and Mauro went back to his study to work until lunch was called. He wanted to go over a few personal things with Jero before they all met for the noon meal. He had expected him to come down to the study at any time. He had not considered it urgent, but now that Jero was home, Mauro wanted to talk to him.

While waiting, Mauro pulled the customer logs that he had questions about from the shelves. He set those aside. The shipping documents for July needed to be revised, and he laid those next to the log books. He looked over the banking ledger, and that was in good order. He paced the room twice, still waiting, and then decided to go find his steward. Mauro asked the kitchen servants if they had seen Jero come downstairs. No one had seen him since he had gone up to his room close to an hour ago.

Mauro climbed the stairs. He looked into Jero's room, but saw no one there at first glance. He stepped inside and shut the door quietly behind him. Mauro had only been in Jero's room once before, and that was when Jero had first been given his new living quarters almost two years ago.

This middle room was meant to be a guest chamber, and it was larger than the ones Ruby and Idita lived in across the hallway from it. It was spacious enough for a double canopied bed, a grooming table, a wardrobe, a breakfast table with four chairs, and a large floor trunk. Apart from the furnishings, it was sparsely decorated. The dusty clothes he had changed out of earlier had been left on the floor, but otherwise the room was impeccably tidy. The east window had been left wide open to the shadows of the mountains, and the air in the room was cool from the breeze that foretold a change in the weather was coming.

Mauro noticed Jero stretched out on his stomach, faced away from the room, sleeping soundly on the bed. He was wearing his new linen shirt and his blue breeches with red velvet stripping that Jero had chosen from Lord Lorenc's collection. He had not yet put on stockings, and his hair was still damp from washing it. He looked vulnerable, like Resi had seemed last night when Mauro went to wake her. He had let her sleep. But Mauro needed his steward and decided to wake him.

He leaned over Jero's long, relaxed body and tapped his shoulder. There was no movement. He sat on the edge of his bed and shook him a little more. "Jero," he said, "can you wake up?"

Jero stirred, then turned over to his side and sat up with surprise to see Mauro sitting there.

"I did not mean to startle you," Mauro apologized.

"Oh, I am sorry, Mauro. I just sat down for a moment, and I must have fallen asleep."

Mauro smiled at the drowsy look on his face. Jero was always unfaltering. Mauro was glad to know the man became tired. "You have had quite a journey in four days, and you are not used to so much riding and fresh air. I am the same when I have been home too long and then begin traveling again," Mauro told him quietly.

"I will just finish dressing and can meet you downstairs, Mauro. What time is it?"

Mauro stood up from the bed, giving Jero space to sit up. "Lunch is being served in a few minutes. You have been asleep for only a short time."

Jero stretched his long arms, then went to his trunk to retrieve the rest of his missing wardrobe while Mauro lingered near the bed. "I had a few personal things I wanted to discuss, so maybe I could talk to you about them right now, while I am here?" Mauro suggested.

"Of course, Mauro; whatever you want."

Jero's wavy hair fell into his face while he leaned over his belongings, and he tucked it behind his ears with annoyance. He set the chosen stockings and cravat on the bed momentarily, and then went to his grooming table for his brush and a blue cord to tie his thick hair back with. Mauro watched his smooth movements. This was Jero's private space, and Mauro suddenly felt like an intruder.

Mauro leaned against the bedpost, his arms crossed, deciding where he should start. "We already discussed my wife and the trouble she can sometimes cause while I am away," Mauro began.

"I would not say she has caused any real trouble," Jero replied pleasantly while he looked into his looking glass on the table and finished binding his hair. He tucked the last, loose strand and turned his full attention to the baron.

"I spoke to her about Roko and the dogs, and there should not be any further problems."

Jero nodded, but said nothing. He knew this could not be the reason for seeking him out.

"On the same day," Mauro continued, "I found something on her table, and I decided it would be too harsh of me to question her about it. She is usually honest with me, but I sense that she is also protective of the servants. I did not want to make her point anyone out."

Jero was not quite sure what Mauro meant by this. "So you will question me about what you found instead?" Jero asked lightly.

"I think it could be *you* that she would be protecting."

A flash of guilt crossed Jero's face and Mauro saw it plainly. "I found a stone, Jero. And you know what sort of stone I am talking about."

He took a deep breath and calmly said, "A cave stone."

Mauro sat down on a chair at the table across from the bed. "Did you give it to her?"

Jero sat down on the other seat across from him. He had not expected to have this conversation so soon. He shut his eyes for a moment to clear his panicked thoughts. Jero finally asked, "And do I get to protect anyone?"

Mauro could not imagine who he could need to protect. "Yourself, perhaps?"

"I did not give your wife the stone you found. I still have my pieces, and I also have three more that Geoff turned over to me."

He stared hard at Jero, who stared unflinching back. "Geoff had stones from the cave?"

"Yes, and he has been punished," Jero said simply.

"You punished him for having the stones?"

"No."

Mauro struggled to keep his anger in check. "Then why was he punished?"

"Because I did not want him punished by you, so I settled it myself," Jero daringly admitted. "Geoff is like a little brother to me, Mauro. I have watched him grow up. Promise me you will not punish him further." Jero looked him in the eye with a clear challenge. He had never stood his ground with Mauro over anything, and it did not go unnoticed.

"What did he do?" Mauro asked sternly.

Jero stood up from his seat and looked down at Mauro in his chair. "He took Lady Terese and Ruby through the passage. The stone you found on her table, she brought back in her own pocket."

Mauro stood now and faced him at equal height. "Jero! How could you let this happen?"

"How could *I* let this happen?" Jero shouted in a voice that startled even Jero. Mauro had struck a raw nerve. "There is a lot that goes on every minute of the day at the castle, and I cannot know all of it all of the time. I certainly would not have allowed it, if I had."

Mauro tried not to yell to meet Jero's own pitch. "I should hope not."

Mauro paced to the window and looked out, his hands on his hips, disturbed with the new circumstances and what urgent actions would be required. Jero poured a glass from the water crock and sat back down to drink it while he waited for Mauro to calm himself.

"The tunnel is off limits to servants, Jero. How would Geoff know about it anyway?" Mauro asked with a strained self-control.

Jero had regained his composure, too, and declared, "It is not his fault, Mauro. Let me explain." Jero then told Mauro the story from start to finish. "What is done is done, Mauro. He knows it was wrong. Geoff has been avoiding your wife and Ruby ever since."

Mauro sat back down at the table. "And no one saw them?" he asked calmly now.

"Franja saw them come and go from the kitchen, but she would not know about the passageway," Jero said in a quieter voice.

Mauro sighed in frustration. "I will have to move things around, find a better place."

Jero nodded his agreement. "When I was looking for them through the doorway, I could see that they did not linger along the path. They would not have noticed the alcove. I can help you with the move, if you think there is a risk."

"I will have to think of a safe place first. I want to talk to Geoff, too." Mauro was no longer angry at Geoff, but he was still cross that Jero had kept this from him.

Jero leaned against his arms on the table with his head bowed. The boy would be sent away after all. "He has been here his whole life, you know. Must you punish him, Mauro?" he said into his folded arms.

"Yes, but I will let him stay."

Jero lifted his head and softly said, "Thank you."

Mauro raised his voice again to clarify. "I want Geoff to understand he has broken the rules, and that my rules must be followed, without question."

Jero nodded his agreement. He stood up and hastily continued to dress. He found his favorite house shoes and brought them to where his wool stockings were. Mauro watched him in silence. Jero tried to hide his annoyance. "Is there something else you wanted to discuss?" he asked.

Mauro found it awkward to bring up the subject now, but he was determined to share his idea with his steward. He cleared his throat and put on his practiced smile. "Yes, I still have not told you the reason I sought you out in private."

"No, I suppose you have not." Jero forced a smile in return and gave him his attention.

"Well, you met up with Stephan and heard the story about Caterina and Isabella."

"Yes, that Fabian's sister was betrothed, but does not want this Hungarian husband. Lady Isabella was also along to be unwillingly married. But here they are, seeking sanctuary from it all," Jero replied.

Mauro chuckled at his retelling. "Yes, that is the long and short of it. But it got me thinking that you might want to choose a bride as well, Jero."

Jero was stunned by the change in subject. "You mean *I* should marry?"

Mauro smiled at him encouragingly. "Yes, why not?"

"I hope you are not suggesting that I should marry one of the Carrera ladies," Jero said cautiously as he finished tying his gray stockings and buckled his worn, polished shoes.

Mauro laughed at the misunderstanding. "No! That is complicated enough already." Jero looked relieved. "I was just thinking that you are twenty-five, and that is a good age to marry. I do not want you to feel you have an obligation to me, is all."

"Marriage would change a lot of things for me as your steward."

Mauro had not expected Jero to take his suggestion so gravely. He tried to sound encouraging when he said, "I have thought about that, too. You have been very dedicated to my house—too dedicated, Jero. I am grateful to you, but I want you to have a full life."

"I am content, Mauro. I like my situation here; but I will admit, I would not mind marrying, either."

"I am glad to hear that. If you did take a wife, I would want you to live nearby, of course. Perhaps in the last cottage."

Jero listened intently from where he sat on the bed. "Yes, that would be nice."

Mauro finally revealed, "I was thinking you and Franja might make a good match."

Jero was the one who laughed suddenly now. "I am not so sure Franja would agree."

Mauro was surprised at his outburst. He had thought it was the perfect solution. "Why not? You would make an exceptional husband for her. You hold a good position, are somewhat handsome, thoughtful, educated." Mauro grinned as he complimented his steward, and Jero matched his smile. "Franja is near your age, she is pretty, and she seems to like you well enough." Mauro raised his eyebrows, daring him to find fault in his reasoning.

"Yes, and I like her well enough, too. But not well enough to marry; nor on her part, either." Mauro frowned hearing this. Jero went on to explain, "It is just, well, we had a bit of an awkward setback when she first came here. It took some time for us to become friends again. We are friends, though, but we do not love each other."

Mauro felt relaxed again in his steward's company. "Were you and Franja once together? I am curious to know what kind of a tainted past you had here."

"I would not call it tainted; barely smudged, actually. It is a bit embarrassing for me to explain."

"Now you have to tell me," Mauro egged him on.

"All right, I will tell you." Jero blushed as he thought about it. "When Franja first came to the castle, all the young soldiers were seeking her attention. She was quite pretty back then and flirted with the men when they came into the kitchen. She could have had her choice to court any of them in the beginning. I guess I was just sixteen or so, but I thought she could be sweet on me as well. She finally agreed to come out with me after dark one night. We met in the hay barn, but it ended quite awkwardly."

"Let me guess. You deflowered her, but did not confess your love," Mauro teased him.

"No!" Jero said a little too loudly, then laughed. "I mean, we did not get that far. I think she might have been willing, but, you know." By his puzzled look, Jero could see that Mauro did not know. He explained, "A girl has so many layers of skirts that by the time I got through all of them, well, it just sort of happened. The whole thing was over before we really got started. I felt so embarrassed, and, well, I guess I panicked and left as quickly as I could."

"You just left her in the haystack?"

"I did," Jero confessed, still blushing. "We never talked about it, but we never met alone again, either," he said with a little regret.

Mauro laughed in sympathy. "Well, I am sure she can forgive your adolescent failings. You are hopefully a more experienced man and can show her that you can perform better at twenty-five."

"I do not think I will have the opportunity. I would have to fight Simeon for the chance, and I do not love her enough to risk that."

Mauro leaned back in his chair, surprised at the revelation. "Simeon fancies Franja? How could I have missed that?"

Jero did not intend to sound unkind, but told him, "You miss quite a lot, Mauro. He talked about her during our long horse ride. Why else would he eat his meals in the kitchen instead of with the soldiers in the Keep, except for her company?"

Mauro had good instincts for reading people, but his long absences had left him out of touch with the goings-on at the castle. He brightened at the new information. "Simeon is a good man, and he needs a good wife, too. Thank you, Jero, I will ask him about her. But this does not solve a match for you. Is there someone you admire?" Mauro was serious again.

There was someone, but Jero could never be matched with her. "The trouble is, I have known most of the girls at the castle for so long that they are like my sisters. I only go to the village for Mass now, so I have not gotten to know the young women there well enough to choose one over the other. Is this so urgent, Mauro?"

"No, of course it is not urgent. I just wanted you to think about it; to let you know that you are a free man to marry at any time. It can be your choice to pick your bride."

Mauro stood up from the table and walked over to where Jero still sat on the bed. He put his hand on Jero's shoulder and said, "It does not have to be a difficult decision you make alone. Come to me if you need to talk it through. I will leave you to finish dressing now."

They held their stares, and Jero nodded, although he was conflicted about Mauro's offer. They had once been friends, the best of friends. Jero thought he knew why Mauro had forsaken their friendship, and he wanted Mauro to finally forgive him. He wanted desperately to talk that through with him instead.

Mauro went to the door to leave, and Jero seized the chance. "I tried to visit you, Mauro, but they would not let me."

Mauro stopped, but did not turn around. He held the door handle and tried to breathe again. "When?" Mauro asked, knowing the answer already.

"Right after Mateo's accident."

Jero watched Mauro to be sure he could continue. When Mauro did not react, Jero went on to explain, "I asked Alberto if I could visit you in your room. He told me you needed time alone. Then I asked Idita if I could go to you, and she said the same."

Mauro still did not turn around, but he did not leave, either. Jero felt suddenly miserable when he said, "I had to do what I was told, Mauro. They said no, and I stopped asking. I am sorry I did not try harder."

Mauro still held the handle to go, his head bent in thought. He breathed deeply and then stood tall again. "Thank you for telling me, Jero. Lunch is ready. I will see you downstairs." Mauro opened the door and walked out without looking back.

Chapter 33

The sky had been growing dark all day despite the approaching summer solstice. They could see there was a settlement not far up the valley. The mercenaries decided they and their horses should take cover before the storm hit. The men also wanted to be sure they were not off track on their quest to visit Patrik's sister and needed to confirm their route.

They usually sent Cyro in alone to ask about sleeping quarters when staying outside the main cities. Cyro had a nonthreatening charm to him, being a smaller man with well-bred manners and an elegant speech. He was Italian, Genoese to be specific, but could converse in several languages with little difficulty. The language of travelers in this region was Latin, since German and Hungarian were not as well known by foreigners.

They were still in Habsburg territory. Soren was fluent in German, having learned it as a boy in his native Denmark. He could have arranged the room with the Austrian innkeeper. But Soren was an imposing figure, taller than most men, and muscular from years of working on ships before soldiering as a pike man in war. His light blond hair and ice-blue eyes garnered a lot of attention from the locals, where brown eyes and dark hair were dominant. Soren did not want the attention; he had grown distant and withdrawn as the years of war and the death of his brother Niels weighed down on him. Cyro blended in better with his capped brunette hair, deep-brown eyes, and unassuming dress. He stood at the bar and paid for their night's lodgings.

Soren and the others were waiting with their horses outside the stable yard when Cyro came to tell them there was one room left. They had camped each night since leaving Vienna. Not because they did not enjoy a roof over their heads, but because they were fully laden with all their possessions on their powerful warhorses. Theft was a constant consideration in the ruined areas of the Habsburg Empire. They did not want to tempt any destitute man who they would have to later kill because of his poor judgment in trying to steal from them at a crowded inn.

"I have taken their last room," Cyro reported. "The mistress told me the bed would sleep all of us, but I paid extra to have two straw pallets brought in for the floor. We won't have much room for our gear. The bigger rooms are rented, and the commons is full for the night. That is the best we can do."

"And the stables?" Bem asked, stroking his faithful horse next to him. "Is there room for our seven?"

"Yes, most of the travelers have come on foot. She said to speak with the stable keeper directly for his fees," Cyro confirmed.

The five men had brought two extra horses to lighten the load for their own steeds. They carried little in the way of personal items: a few changes of clothes, a warm coat, a cape, and extra boots. But each man had a bedroll, shield, mail armor, several swords, muskets, powder kegs, and Soren had the makings for two pikes and spears. They had purchased some food supplies, knowing it would be scarce along the route, and they packed communal cooking gear and a cup and plate for each man. They had traveled this way for two years as mercenary soldiers—nomads, living off their services for hire. After they fulfilled Patrik's request to check on his sister, they would head south again and unpack for good to finally spend their hard-earned profits.

This was not the type of place they liked to stay longer than one night. Cities were better; they did not stand out in a crowd as much. This was just an outpost with a few dwellings along the trade route at the edge of the mountain pass. There were no towns within days, and the sizable inn catered to weary travelers looking for a soft bed and maybe a washing. The main street had few people milling about, perhaps because of the impending downpour, or possibly because half the population was already drinking within the walls of the inn. Music was playing and drunken voices could be heard through the open windows.

"Well, let us get to it, then," Salar Nassim said to Cyro. "Patrik and Soren can help carry the packs and weapons, and Bem and I will settle in the horses."

They had learned not to enter as one group into a new establishment, but to come in alone or in pairs. Patrik, with his light olive skin, long bound hair, and dusty-blue eyes, could have blended into a crowd well enough with his average height, had he not chosen to wear the brightly colored, loose tunics and trousers of his Oriental friend, Salar Nassim. Patrik was once told by a man that he looked like an Ottoman warrior. The Ottomans were Patrik's sworn enemy, and he had broken the man's arm while explaining his misguided ignorance. Salar Nassim was a Persian, not an Ottoman. Nassim moved around too often to be tied to them, although he housed his two wives in Ottoman lands in Athens and on the island of Rhodes.

Salar Nassim, even if he had dressed in the customary garments of the Habsburg region, would always look foreign in these parts. Not because of his tan skin; many in this region of Europe were of mixed blood from centuries of Ottoman domination. But because of his piercing, dark eyes of the deepest shade of brown, highlighted with long, black lashes and a prominent, smooth brow above his straight nôse. He wore a turban instead of a hat, and his trimmed black mustache and small beard over his chin added to the mystique of his features. The women he met found him hypnotic, but most men could not hold a stare to the average-sized man.

The stable keeper accepted Bem's silver payment, and he let him have his pick of the open stalls for their horses. Bem was used to people being curious about him, but at the same time not ask any questions of him. He was an Ethiopian, or at least once was. He had been away from his native land for eight years and had no plans to return.

His father was Portuguese, married to his African mother. Bem had sailed to Portugal at age sixteen to look for his missing father. He learned there that he was seen differently by the Europeans than he saw himself. Bem was mulatto—neither a white man like his father, nor a black man like his mother's ancestors. His light cocoa skin, narrow nose, and fine corkscrew curls were enough to keep him safe from being captured and sold into slavery. But he was not white enough to keep him regularly employed.

Bem left Portugal and was a horse trainer for an Ottoman general before he became a soldier, a mercenary fighting against the Ottoman Empire. Horses were the one thing that gave him true pleasure since becoming a soldier, and he volunteered each day to brush down his friends' fine but tired beasts. He took pride that they were fed and watered properly to keep them fit for the demands their owners placed on them.

He and Salar Nassim unbridled the horses and removed the saddles, which were their most valuable possessions next to their swords. The other three would be back to carry them up to their room. Salar Nassim asked him, "Do you think Patrik will finally be satisfied when he meets his sister again?"

Bem began to rub down the horse's damp hide where the saddle had been. "Even if she is unhappy, like she wrote to him, it will depend more on our welcome from Mauritius Baric to determine Patrik's satisfaction with his sister's situation."

"That is my exact concern," Salar Nassim said.

"Do you not think we will be welcomed by Baron Baric?" Bem asked uneasily as he briskly finished his task.

"If Mauritius Baric loves his wife, then for her sake we will be welcomed. But her letter did not give me the impression that he does. I am still against going there."

Bem stopped his work. It had been thoroughly discussed in Vienna and agreed to by all four. They would accompany Patrik, and no one would go back on their word, especially not their leader. "So, what are you saying, Nassim? Are you not going?"

"Yes, I am going. I am saying, though, that this is not about visiting his sister, but about meeting his brother-in-law again. I am worried for Patrik. We will need to protect him."

Bem regarded him curiously and asked, "Protect him from Baron Baric?"

Their three companions were coming back for the saddles. Bem watched Patrik take a saddle and then leave again with the others.

Salar Nassim finally answered, "We must protect Patrik from himself."

"I do not think he will do anything stupid, but I will keep an eye on him with you," Bem agreed. He patted the horse and went on to the next one.

When they had finished settling the horses in the stables, they met Cyro, Soren, and Patrik in the common room of the tavern. The two were oblivious to the usual stares of the local patrons to their foreign garb and brightly sheathed swords as they crossed the room.

"The ale here is excellent, Salar Nassim. I have ordered you one," Patrik told his friend in Greek.

"Yes, you may pass me my mug of bread and water," he replied cheerfully. When clean water and proper food had been lacking, the Persian had been persuaded to drink the ale, despite his aversion to alcohol.

Salar Nassim was a Muslim, and he followed the doctrine when convenient. He kept his prayer schedule as best he could when they were not in battle. Despite his entrenched faith, he had another vice—he was an avid card player. The money he would win in the tavern that night would pay for their room and meals, and he took pride in his ability to be charitable to his companions.

Salar Nassim finished his mug and turned to Cyro. "If we can get back on the road tomorrow, how far did the innkeeper say it was to the Baric Castle?" he asked in his melodic Latin.

"The Barics are known in this region already, so directions were easy. The innkeeper warned not to take the main trade route after the storm, though. It will be clogged with carts stuck in the fresh mud. We will have a longer but easier ride through the low passage along the mountain range in Habsburg territory. We can cross over directly into Baron Baric's land from there. It will take us two days to reach the pass, and another day to his castle, once through the mountains. Only if the weather clears, of course," Cyro thoughtfully concluded.

"Here's to fair weather." Salar Nassim said. He raised his mug, and the others rowdily followed suit.

~ * ~

Resi was thinking about the earlier dancing lesson when Mauro finally slid into bed and blew out the candle. He had shut the glass because of the driving rain, but left the shutters open as he preferred, so the first rays of sunlight would wake him. Every now and then, a bolt of lightning lit up the room as the storm lingered into the night.

"Do you like storms?" she asked him, as he settled in under the covers. The bed was cold on his side, and he moved in closer, seeking out her heat.

"Only when I am under a roof, and especially in a warm bed with you," he answered. She turned to him and found her favorite spot on his firm chest.

"I think we will need more practice, Mauro. Lady Isabella seemed a bit frustrated with our effort after dinner," she told him quietly.

"Well, I think the men got the idea of the dances. I have decided we will not train tomorrow. The storm is not letting up, and it will be too wet for the powder. We can try dancing again in the morning, as you wished." He shut his eyes. It had been another long day for him, and he wanted to sleep now.

"What I wish is that we had music and more women to practice with tomorrow. Lady Isabella was tired of clapping to the songs and being everyone's partner at the same time. She was losing her patience."

"Do not be worried about her, Resi. She has little patience to lose." He sighed softly, knowing that she was right, though. He offered a solution. "I do know that Alberto can play a nice beat on his drum. If you like, I will bring him in to be Isabella's music in the morning."

"And can we bring in a few more girls to partner with your men, and then they can know if they are twirling and stepping correctly in line?"

"We only have two days, and the servant girls will be busy with the preparations tomorrow," Mauro argued softly.

"Cook is used to preparing food for more than a hundred at a time, and her menu for the ball will be even smaller than most of the banquets. Nela told me everything is coming along, and Brigita told me Cook hasn't yelled at all." Mauro chuckled to himself at this bit of news. "I talked to Natalija," Resi continued, "and the rooms have all been cleaned and are ready for the guests." She looked up at him in the dark. "Please, Mauro. If the girls cannot dance on Friday, then at least let them partner with the soldiers and pretend a little tomorrow."

Mauro thought about it for a moment, then answered, "Do you not think it will be distracting to pull in more dancers? I am not sure the dancing is as important to them as it is to you."

"I am certain everyone will enjoy the distraction. To get to hold a man's hand in public will be a treat for the maids. I don't think the soldiers will object to that."

His laugh rattled her softly as she lay against his chest. "All right, but I will do the pairing up."

"Thank you, Mauro." She slid her hand through the front opening of his sleep shirt and stroked the soft hairs there. "Mauro?"

"I thought we were going to sleep now?" he whispered, his eyes still closed, but enjoying her touch.

"I was just thinking of distractions, and it made me remember to ask you whether something happened on the way to the city?" She moved her hand absently around the curve of his lean ribs.

"No," he told her with certainty. "It all went as well as could be expected. They could be sleeping outside in this storm tonight, for one." Her touch was lulling him to sleep.

"Didn't Jero seem distracted today, though? He was so quiet and unlike himself." Mauro was quiet, too. "Mauro, are you awake?" she whispered.

"Yes," he replied halfheartedly. "That could be my fault. Remember I asked you about a wife for Jero? Well, I mentioned it to him today." She stopped her stroking and looked up at him.

"And you suggested Franja?"

"I did. But it seems Simeon is sweet on her. Did you know that?"

She lay back down on his ribs with a thud.

"Now that you say it, yes, I believe he is. I don't know if Franja returns the affection. I have not had a meal with them to see how they are together, but he has been in the kitchen often in the evenings. You should pair Franja with Simeon for dance practice tomorrow."

He could feel her smiling on his chest, and he had to laugh again.

"And who would we pair with Jero?"

"Ruby," she said too quickly, and he felt her tense up next to him.

He sat up on his elbow and let her slide off to her own side of the bed. "Are you playing matchmaker, or have I already missed more courtships while I was away?"

"It was only a suggestion. Jero and Ruby would be nice dance partners. There has been no courting going on yet, but I will say this: they would make a good match. She enjoys his company, and he seems to like being with her."

He lay back down, and she took her place against him again. He stroked the loose strands of hair that fell across her cheek, then finally said, "Jero is one of the few men who gets to decide who he marries, but her family still has to agree to it. I do not know if Ruby's family would agree to a Venetian husband. They never planned for her to stay here permanently. She is to go back home after our first baby is born. We have to respect that request. Her father may have already made a marriage match for her."

"Ruby has not been told of any plans. She gets a letter once a month, and there has been no mention of a future husband when she returns."

"I have not written to Angelos Spiros this whole year. Should I write to him about Jero?"

Resi was silent for a moment. "If Jero has free choice in a marriage, then you should ask him, not me. But it wouldn't be fair to give him false hope either," she decided. "Yes, write to Ruby's father. Tell him about Jero as a match, and then Ruby can know once and for all what she is to do."

The lightning lit up the room again, and she saw her husband's face in that split second. His expression was strained. "What is troubling you, Mauro?"

He hesitated, not knowing why this talk of Jero brought these thoughts to the surface. "It is hard to explain," he said quietly. "I rebelled against the life I was given for many years, and now I am not sure why I was so against it. I am still not sure I deserve it."

Resi whispered, "That is my rebellion you just described, Mauro. That is why we are a good match."

He wrapped his arms around her and pulled her close again. He had never said the words, but Resi felt loved at that moment and hoped that he did, too.

Chapter 34

In preparation for the ball, the banquet tables had been arranged along the far wall under the Baric family portraits, leaving the middle of the great hall free for dancing. Several of the noblemen would be bringing their eligible daughters to the party tomorrow night, and the bachelors Mauro had singled out were looking forward to one more chance to practice their newly learned gracefulness.

Resi and Ruby joined the Venetian ladies downstairs for round two of lessons after breakfast. Mauro had allowed Resi to bring Verica, Natalija, and Franja to partner with the invited soldiers for the special rehearsal. The men arrived with Mauro and Fabian in the hall after their morning duties had been fulfilled, and they looked to Mauro for instruction when they saw the added women in the room. Nestor and Idita had also arrived to watch the amusing show. They took their seats on the cushioned chairs by the fireplace.

"I brought you in because the baroness asked that we practice one last time, but with partners," Mauro told them. Resi noticed there were no visible objections from the smiling soldiers. "I will partner you off, and then Lady Isabella can walk you through each dance again." Isabella came forward to Mauro's side, ready to take charge.

Mauro announced the pairing he had chosen in his mind earlier that morning. "Lady Caterina will dance with Vilim. Lady Isabella shall be partnered with Jero. Fabian shall dance with Ruby. Simeon will partner with Franja. Davor will practice with Natalija, and Hugo with Verica. And I shall dance with my wife," he said with a smile. "Alberto is familiar with most of the dance music, and he will be here in a moment with his drum." They all looked to their new partners and lined up, like Isabella had instructed them yesterday.

Isabella came over to Mauro and quietly said, "Mauritius, I would not second-guess your choices, but since Fabian knows the steps to all the dances, he would be a better partner for me to demonstrate with in the front of the line." Mauro knew she was right, but he had been protecting his friend from an uncomfortable arrangement. She waited with her cool, confident stare for his agreement.

"Very well, you shall be partnered with Fabian and Jero will practice with Ruby," he said loudly enough for the others to hear. He looked over to his wife and saw that she was pleased with the new pairing, as well.

A soggy Alberto came in through the servants' entrance, shaking off the rain, followed by Geoff, who stayed in the doorway to watch his friends. Isabella gave the stable master instructions for the first sets of music and organized her students, fixing postures and foot positions before the music began. She thought it improbable that the soldiers would remember the intricate moves of the court dances she had taught them yesterday, but they did not disappoint her. The maids focused on their new roles and were quickly following their partners down the line and through the circles of dancers with confidence. Mauro allowed them one more round of each dance, and the group took advantage of their situation to make small conversation with their temporary mates.

Isabella set aside her displeasure with him and told Fabian, "You have not forgotten your dance steps since you left. You were always such a good partner."

"I was a faithful partner, while others were not," he pointed out, as they mingled through the other chatting couples.

"That is not fair, Fabian," she replied quietly while they moved gracefully down the line.

"You made your choice, Isabella, and I no longer care," he declared bluntly.

"Can we still be friends?" she asked expectantly.

They moved away from each other and through the circle with the other dance couples. He regarded only his new dance partner until he and Isabella were paired back together in the line of dancers.

He looked at her hopeful smile and decided, "No, Isabella. I do not think we can be."

The music came to a conclusion and the dance was over. He bowed gallantly, and then walked away from her and out the terrace door and into the drizzle.

Mauro watched Fabian leave, and Isabella's stunned expression told him the session had gone on long enough. "Thank you, Lady Isabella, for making dancers out of my soldiers. But that will have to do for the lessons. You may go back to your duties, everyone."

He took Resi's hand and led her to the side. "Well, Madam Matchmaker, I shall leave you to your afternoon. I will take my lunch with the men in the Keep and then will be gone for the day. I will see you this evening." He bowed, raising her hand to his lowered head and formally kissed it.

"I would have liked to have seen you at Court, Mauritius Baric."

"Yes, but you would not have approved. They dressed me in far prettier clothes than you wore back then. Remember, you would have only been thirteen and playing swords with your brother's friends." He playfully brushed an imaginary smudge off her nose.

"What happens if your new clothes do not arrive in time tomorrow?" Resi tried not to sound worried.

"Then we shall dress in our military uniforms, which always impresses the ladies," he told her with a charming smile.

The soldiers kept their uniforms stored and ready in the Keep. The group was a spectacular sight when they rode out together in full dress. The knee-length, wool Baric jackets were a deep green, with brass button closures trimmed in gold satin to the waist, open in the front and back for protecting their legs while riding. The baron had spared no expense to clothe his Guard in tough deerskin breeches for riding through rough terrain, with tall leather boots, long woolen capes, and fur-trimmed hats in the winter to help fend off the harsh weather. All in black, except the green of their jackets and the gold of their brass trim, they wore their traditional Croatian neck scarves in the red Venetian color to show their allegiance to the Republic. That was all that distinguished them until they were in battle, and then his Guard carried the Venetian flag along with his own green and gold banners. In battle, his soldiers also donned the armor they carried with them for war. Resi was glad they would not need their armor so soon again.

"One more thing, Resi," Mauro told her. "I received a note that the Leopold ladies are expected this afternoon. Lady Eleonora does not trust we have enough crystal goblets and punch bowls to quench everyone's thirst." Mauro suspected she was probably right. "Neven will arrive tomorrow, along with the other guests."

"This is very exciting, Mauro. I don't think I will be able to find enough to do today to make the time go by."

"I am sure you ladies will find something. Play some cards, or have a nice soak in your bathhouse. I must go now," he said distractedly, thinking of all that must still be organized. With those worries in mind, he walked out the terrace door and into the receding storm.

Chapter 35

Resi found Ruby and the guests in the sitting room after the dance lesson. Brigita had just left them a tray of tea and honey cakes. She passed her mistress at the door with a small curtsy and shut it behind her. Resi joined them at the round table near the window; the rain no longer splattered against the glass.

"That was lovely of you to have the servants filling in as partners," Isabella complimented her when the baroness took the seat next to Caterina. "I think the men have the steps down well enough that they will not be tripping on any dresses tomorrow."

"Yes, I think everyone enjoyed it immensely. I did, at least," Caterina proclaimed. "I did not remember meeting Vilim when he came to Venice with Mauritius all those years ago. What a handsome man he has grown into."

"The castle is swarming with handsome men. Perhaps I can find a husband here before I leave," Isabella declared. "Lady Ruby, you have surely narrowed down your selection."

Ruby blushed at the daring comment, but Resi came to her rescue and explained, "Ruby will not be staying long enough to find a husband here."

"I am sure the castle's bachelors are greatly disappointed, your steward especially. He could not keep his eyes off Lady Ruby," Isabella said playfully.

Ruby defended herself this time. "We were partners, so he had to look at me while we danced."

Isabella mischievously looked at Ruby over her steaming teacup and declared, "Not in that way, my dear."

Resi was helping herself to Franja's delicious cake and knew she must intervene. The lovesick Ruby would slowly come unglued if the conversation continued about Jero. She offered the teapot in Caterina's direction and suggested, "Why don't we play a game of Ombre while we wait for the rain to clear?"

The topic was quickly switched as Caterina jumped on the offer of a card game. "That is a wonderful idea, Lady Terese. I have several decks of playing cards in my luggage."

The Barics had various games stored in the cabinets along the wall, but Caterina had answered so eagerly. "Shall I ring for the maid to fetch them for you?" Resi asked, amused at her guest's enthusiasm.

"No, I will go myself. I am not exactly sure where I put them. I will return momentarily." Caterina left the three to finish their refreshments.

After a long moment of silence drinking their tea, Isabella remarked pleasantly, "I have noticed that you are very fond of your lady's maid. Will she also be allowed to dress for the ball, or will she be serving?"

"Neither," Resi said a little too curtly.

"Oh?" Isabella found her answer lacking. "Will she be away?"

"No, I am sorry to say it is rather complicated," Resi began cautiously to explain. "Mauro is not allowing any of the unmarried girls downstairs except for Ruby. He has been informed that his guest of honor has a bit of a—what would be a good word, Ruby?" Resi looked hopefully to her friend.

"'Fetish' is the word that comes to my mind," Ruby replied, and Isabella burst into laughter.

"Well, that is quite a descriptive word. I thought your guest of honor was a young naval commander of some rank." Isabella leaned across the table and insisted, "Do tell, ladies. I always enjoy a bit of a scandal."

Resi looked to Ruby, who shrugged her agreement, and Resi began to tell the Venetian what she knew of the stranger making all this trouble for them. "He is a lieutenant in charge of the port brigade based a bit south of here. My husband says he has the reputation as an exceptional commander, but also the reputation as an avid gambler. His most recent win was a gentleman's maid," Resi told her. "He seems to have an inclination for the art of seduction, too. He is a newly married man, but only has an appetite for young virgins."

Isabella was not as shocked as the Greek women had been. "Ah, well, that is not what I would call a fetish as much as a compulsion. If the man is such a nuisance, then why is he Mauritius' honored guest?"

"This is how it becomes complicated," Resi continued with seriousness. "He has confiscated a Baric ship, and my husband is charged with a few petty crimes along with it. Mauro is hoping to persuade the lieutenant to release the ship and let him continue with his trading, as the family has been doing for years before the commander put him under his, um, special watch."

"Oh, I see," she replied, unfazed by this news. "Then Mauritius is looking to charm and flatter him by inviting him to an important gathering?" Isabella asked, knowing already that this was the angle Mauro had chosen.

"Yes, I suppose so."

"What he should be doing is exploiting the lieutenant's weak points of gambling and young women," Isabella offered.

"It had crossed his mind, but that is a risky bet to put a girl's maidenhood on the card table. I think he expects the commander's desire to be included with the aristocracy here reward enough to gain his cooperation," Resi explained.

"I do know of a situation that was very similar to yours. There was an aristocrat who spent a season in Venice. He was fully out of control until— Ah, Caterina. Tell me, what was the name of the baron two years past whom they played that trick on?" Isabella asked when she returned to the table with her deck of cards.

"I am not sure who you are talking about, Isabella," Caterina replied thoughtfully. She took her seat again and began shuffling the deck.

Resi and Ruby continued to be astonished by Caterina. She was the epitome of well-bred politeness. She had a delicate, petite stature that made one feel the need to show her special consideration. But the baroness would soon learn that she played cards with a determined talent to match the best gamblers of the region.

"Yes you do, Cat, my dear. He was the handsome baron who was staying with the duke and duchess that one time. He had ginger hair and the elaborate mustache."

Isabella turned back to Resi and Ruby to continue the story. "He was a nobleman of no great importance really, and I do not know what he was doing there, but he was extremely charming and very seductive."

"I remember now," Caterina interjected. "Lord Marcellis was his name, Isabella."

"Yes, thank you, Caterina. Lord Marcellis was a friend to the Court and had seduced most of the duchess' maids within a matter of weeks. The duchess was furious, but her husband did not see it in the same light. As Baron Marcellis' visit continued, the duchess learned he had his eye on her daughter, who was pledged to marry later that summer, but only if she was untouched, of course."

Isabella paused for their agreement, and the three nodded they understood the seriousness of his new objective. "Her maids helped the duchess formulate a plan, because they now knew his game. They let Lord Marcellis seduce the duchess' daughter, but she did not show up when the time came to meet in secret. The duke came to the predetermined meeting spot himself and caught the scoundrel with his breeches down." Resi and Ruby could not hide their shock at such an outcome, but Caterina had not been paying attention; she was busy dealing the cards to her victims.

"And what became of the baron?" Ruby asked Isabella.

"He did not admit why he was caught in such an awkward position, but he quickly fell out of favor because of it and has never returned," Isabella concluded with satisfaction.

"Shall I begin?" Caterina suggested abruptly when Isabella's story was done. The others looked down at the cards dealt out in front of them and nodded for her to start the game.

Resi thought again about the scheme the duchess had used. "Are you suggesting, Lady Isabella, that this trick could be replayed tomorrow night to gain the advantage Mauro might need?"

"It is not complicated, really. And if it does not work as planned, our maiden would not have to make an appearance. No harm is done to anyone if it fails. But we would need a pretty, young girl to entice him."

"It is your turn, Lady Ruby," Caterina pointed out, after she had played her card. Isabella looked to Ruby for more than her play at the card game.

"You said that you have a new fashionable gown, Lady Ruby. Is that right?" Isabella asked her, and Ruby nodded nervously that she did. "If we did something with your hair, but did not adorn you with too much jewelry, you might just do."

Caterina stopped her shuffling and assessed Ruby, contemplating Isabella's suggestion. She finally declared, "She has such a fresh, pretty face. You are like an auburn fawn, with your wide, brown eyes and light freckles." She continued to stare at Ruby across the table. "Yes, Isabella. I think if we tempted the commander with a story of her not having a proper protector. Maybe we should lure him with the idea of a seduction before he saw her. She should arrive late to the party, and he would already be wildly anticipating her entrance." A broad smile grew across Isabella's rouged lips. She was fully in agreement with Caterina's assessment.

"She will not be at risk of actually being, um, seduced, will she?" Resi wanted to know before she approved the plan.

"No," the Venetians both said together.

"You are sweet to look at, but can you play false, Lady Ruby? Can you outright lie without it being known?" Caterina asked her frankly.

Resi tried to suppress her grin to not give her friend away. Resi had gotten out of many difficult situations over the years because of Ruby's ability to invent a quick fib. "What do you say, Ruby, will you try this for me?" Resi did not want to outright beg, but she needed her to say yes.

Ruby was pale with apprehension at this monumental role. "Yes, I will try," she told her friend bravely.

Resi let out the breath that she had held in, and the women congratulated themselves at their own clever plotting. "It will be easy, my dear," Isabella told Ruby confidently. "The man will try to seduce the woman, like a dance is danced: he bends, you sway; he moves forward, you pull back. Then you pick the right moment to twirl in delight of his charms, and he bows to yours. At the end of the dance, a decision is taken to continue to the next level or not. We will be sure he believes you will go to that next level. And that is where you will betray him, and he will be caught."

"You learned the dances earlier quite quickly. We will explain how this one goes, as well," Caterina added encouragingly. The four finished their card game and formulated their plan.

~ * ~

The rain had stopped just after lunch, and Resi introduced the Venetians to her favorite place at the castle. Seeing Ruby nude in the bathhouse convinced the two women that she had the seductive curves needed to pull off her part in the scheme to trap the lieutenant. They reproached her for hiding behind such modest layers of clothing, and overtly formulated a new plan to bring her back with them to Venice to match her with a rich husband there. Resi found the women's bold plotting entertaining, even though she knew Ruby would never agree to go.

The clouds had blown over the mountains, and the long June day had warmed again into a muggy evening. Resi was in her chamber dressing for dinner when Ruby came to tell her the Leopold carriage had just arrived. She had managed to fill the day after all, and was excited to see the Leopolds again.

Verica finished brushing her mistress' drying hair and twisted it into a neat, soft pile, leaving a few strands to curl around her face. Verica added a peacock feather comb to the back of the twist for color, but Resi protested at too much ornamentation.

The showy comb had been included in the chest from the countess. Verica held the small mirror up for Resi to see into the larger looking glass behind her. "See, my lady, how beautiful that looks." Resi had to agree with Verica's instincts. She loved the effect.

"You have a knack for dressing me, Verica. I suppose I should not doubt your opinion any longer." Verica just smiled to her in the mirror. She teased the last curl into place by her mistress's smooth cheek, and then stepped back so the baroness could be on her way.

"I will put you in charge of styling Lady Ruby tomorrow. She is to look exceptionally, um, seductive." Verica giggled at her mistress' joke, not realizing the reality of it.

~*~

When Resi arrived downstairs, the great hall was full of commotion as servants carried boxes of accessories through the front door from the loaded Leopold wagon that had accompanied the carriage. Resi could not imagine what the dowager could have brought to add to their decorations of flowers and fine table cloths already laid out in the great hall. She saw Mauro had arrived to greet their first guests; he was standing with Ladies Eleonora and Nikolina near the portrait wall.

"Lady Terese!" Nikolina met her halfway in the center of the grand room. "You look so well," she added, after a friendly embrace and peck on the cheek.

Resi stepped back and smiled warmly, "As do you, Lady Nikolina. How was your journey?"

"Oh, we should have been here hours ago. The carriage lost a wheel along the route, and the poor drivers are covered with mud from repairing it."

She locked arms with Nikolina and walked her to the refreshment table that had been laid out near the terrace. "You must be exhausted from the rough ride." Resi poured her a glass of wine; Nikolina wearily accepted it and took a drink.

"I would like to lie down for a few minutes before dinner, if you would not mind. My midwife thinks I may be further along than I calculated, and the baby is feeling a bit heavy this past week."

"Of course, Lady Nikolina. I will take you up to your room myself. And when you have rested, I will introduce you to our guests from Venice. The sister of Fabian Carrera and her companion arrived just this week. They have been helping us with our dance steps. They are quite elegant ladies and are very enjoyable company."

Lady Nikolina set her glass back on the table and took her friend's arm again. "I will be delighted to meet them."

Resi looked over her shoulder to catch Mauro's eye, and he gave a slight nod when he saw her walking toward the foyer door. He had hoped for her help in entertaining Lady Eleonora while he supervised the delivery of decorations, but he was alone with the task now.

"It is so good of you to take such an interest in the success of our ball," Mauro praised her.

"We have not hosted a party in so many years, but I have boxes of silk ribbons and rosettes we used in the past that will make the evening festive. I brought you several candelabras to add to your tables."

"It is the summer solstice, and we shall have a long evening before dark, as well as torches on the terrace," he mentioned kindly.

"Yes, but torches in the hall will be a smoky annoyance for the dancing, dear Mauritius. Candles will set a special mood."

He had not considered that the baroness would have such a romantic streak. "You are right, Lady Eleonora, and I am grateful for your forethought on our behalf."

"Neven told me you only fly one Venetian flag on your ramparts. You know you are supposed to fly two. I have brought you one more," she said with a scowl.

"I could fly twenty, and it would not change my opinion of the Republic," he said with a practiced smile. "But I thank you for your attention to those details, and for saving me another penalty." Mauro gently took her arm in his to guide her to the refreshment table. "You must be thirsty after your long carriage ride. Shall we have a drink on the terrace?"

She stood her ground, looking up at the framed portraits of the Baric ancestors before he could direct her away. "Mauritius, my dear, I am looking for the portrait of your new wife and it seems to be missing."

"I have not had the opportunity to have her painted. There have been many complications that have interfered with my duties at home this first year."

"Well, it is bad luck to not have one done at once. Better still, a portrait of the two of you would be advised. You make such a handsome pair." She was no longer scowling at him, but gave him a maternal smile.

She then turned back to look at the other portraits. "I have not visited your castle since your father died," she commented.

Mauro continued the polite conversation, still hoping she would come away with him to the refreshment table. "Did you know my father well?"

"Yes, your father was a bit younger than my late husband, but of course they had grown up as neighbors together. Before my Karloff went missing, we would have wonderful dinner parties once a month here or at our manor house. Old Cedomir did not approve of your grandfather, but he had nothing against Lorenc," she told him.

"There were dinner parties here?" He found her statement curious; he had thought his father incapable of entertaining for the pleasure of it.

"Oh, yes, my dear. I suppose you know your father was married to Margaret before he married your mother. In those days, your father was a different man."

He hesitated before acknowledging, "My cousins told me about Mateo's mother. Did you know Margaret well?"

"Yes, she was a dear friend to me. Those were the days just before the long war. Although she was Austrian, everyone was very fond of Margaret." Mauro nodded politely at this, but was uncomfortable hearing the details of his father's first wife. "She was a gentlewoman, but had such a wicked sense of humor." Lady Eleonora smiled to herself at a memory she did not share. "She loved a good gathering and lively conversation. Your brother was very much like her, God rest both their souls."

"And did you know my own mother well?"

Her expression lost its brightness. "Ah, my dear, your mother was a beautiful lady; we all said so. She was quite elegant as the daughter of a count. But it is difficult for some to be the second spouse, which is why I never remarried."

Mauro looked again at the portrait of Margaret, searching for the wicked sense of humor painted in her lovely face. "I have looked for portraits of the other children, in case you are wondering why they are not included on the wall." He motioned to Margaret's painting. "I put this one back up recently, to honor the Baric ancestors."

"That is good of you, Mauritius. Her other children all died in the plague that swept the land. I recall it was a terrible spring, and we lost many, many friends during the sickness. Your brother was just a babe, but he somehow survived." She walked farther down the collection and stopped in front of Lorenc Baric's portrait. "I believe your father was away on some siege or something. He had no idea his family had taken ill. He did not even get to say goodbye."

"I had not heard that story," Mauro said solemnly, looking at his father's happy appearance in the painting.

"Yes, they had called in a wet nurse for Mateo, a woman who had lost her own husband and baby in the plague. Your father never recovered his bright spirit after their passing, and he kept to the castle for a time. Then he suddenly married your mother."

"I did not know it was so sudden," Mauro said, almost to himself.

Lady Eleonora was silent for a moment. "Speaking of sudden, we are fortunate the storm has passed so quickly, Mauritius. I expect we shall have fine weather to sit outdoors on your lovely terrace tomorrow."

He turned from the paintings, puzzled she had switched the conversation to the weather after being so free in her commentary earlier. "Yes," he agreed, the way he did when there was nothing else to say. "It will be a fine evening."

Jero came toward them, bowed, and then cleared his throat to say, "My lord, if I may interrupt you for your assistance?"

"Please forgive me, Lady Eleonora. I believe I am wanted in the wine cellar for some last-minute choices. I shall send Idita to show you upstairs for you to refresh yourself before dinner." He bowed formally, and she gestured her wigged head in return.

He made a quick stop to talk to his faithful servant, who had been put in charge of the room arrangements for the ladies and their lady's maids. He then followed Jero out through the servants' entrance, glad to have something new to think about instead of his dead, unhappy parents.

The kitchen was busy with preparations for the evening meal. "You already brought the wines up, Jero," he said as they stood by the doorway to the cellar.

"I am sorry, Mauro, but I had the sense that you needed to be rescued." Mauro hoped it had not appeared that way to anyone else but Jero. "I did mean to remind you, though, that the new clothing for the party has not yet arrived."

Mauro motioned for Jero to follow him away from the noise of the kitchen and out the back door. "I have been thinking about that, too. For all the trouble we went to, it would be a shame if the garments arrived too late."

They continued down the path to the fountain below the terrace steps. Mauro pensively watched the servants efficiently set the table for dinner while Jero waited. He finally decided, "I will send some riders to see if they can find our delivery wagon along the route. There are still a few hours of daylight left. The Leopolds' carriage had a hard time rolling in the muddy tracks. If the delivery has gone missing, at least we will know to go with our second plan tomorrow. But I am hopeful my men can find them tonight."

Chapter 36

Daniel and Eduard rode out with two of Mauro's new trainees before dinner. The baron was insistent that they cover as much ground as they could in the last remaining hours of daylight. They found the right delivery wagon outside Baric lands before darkness set in completely. The driver and his companion had already unharnessed their horse to settle in for the night along the clogged route. The four Baric men shared a fire and meal with them at their camp and waited for first light to ride back to the castle.

When dawn broke, it was clear to all of them that without force and persuasion, the baron would not have his wardrobe for the ball that day. The long lineup of other merchant wagons and carts that had waited out the heavy storm now attempted the rutted trade route. As it was, they were a full day's ride from Solgrad at the delivery wagon's pace.

Eduard was not opposed to using the influence of a sword and musket to clear a path for the urgent cargo, and Daniel and his young soldiers-in-training proved to be just as capable in persuading the other travelers to give way to the one-horsed wagon. By noon, the delivery had arrived at Baric Castle.

Mauro greeted Eduard and Daniel as they gave their horses over to the stable grooms. "To be honest, I was not counting on you finding them," Mauro declared with obvious relief to see his soldiers back so soon.

"We found them easily enough, but getting the other stuck carts and wagons out of the way was another thing," Eduard replied.

"And are you sure you do not want to be relieved from gate duty tonight to try a little dancing?" Mauro tempted the officers again as a reward.

Eduard had already made it clear days ago that dressing up for a grand gala was not to his liking. He was glad to give another man a chance to dance tonight, and he would happily take the reward of an extra day off duty later.

Daniel was a young officer from Mauro's father's Guard who had proven his capabilities time and again to his new baron. He was an attractive man, but he had only begun to come out of his mute shyness. He could speak to his baron directly now without stumbling too much over his words. Dancing and conversing with pretty girls would be too big of a hurdle for him, and Daniel turned down the baron's offer as well. "N-n-no, my lord. I am g-g-good g-guarding the g-g-gate," he stuttered his thanks without embarrassment.

"As you like," Mauro agreed. It saved the other soldiers from having to draw straws to take his guard-duty shift.

Mauro instructed the young recruits, "Bring the trunks to the second-floor common room. Jero can sort out the delivery better from there." He walked with the wagon driver into the manor house to pay the invoices due, and then directed him and his companion to the Keep for a hot meal before they drove back out to fend for themselves along the route home.

Mauro had not seen his wife that morning, but he thought she would be busy with her own preparations. Jero was just coming down the stairs when Mauro locked up his study again.

"Good news, Jero. The trunks have made it on time. I am having lunch in the Keep, if you want to come with me?"

"Yes, I'll join you. Everything is readied upstairs, but I hope the overnight guests do not arrive too early. Verica is already running back and forth between the Carreras' and your room, and they are not even dressing for the party yet."

Mauro looked up the flight of stairs with a grin. "It is best to leave them to their pageantry undisturbed. Come on. There is still much to do."

The Keep's massive, arched doorway was across from the stables and was left open for easy access day or night. The windowless ground-floor entrance led directly to the armory, where the weapons, armor, and battle provisions were stored. It was also the most convenient entrance for deliveries of other basic staples that met the needs of the men living there. The wide corridors beyond the armory led to the root cellar, an ale cellar, and a pantry for preserved meats, dried cheeses, and pickled vegetables meant to feed the soldiers daily. Should the manor residents and servants need to take defensive shelter in the tower, there were enough supplies stored to feed the entire compound for weeks.

Before the manor house had been built, the Keep had been the Baric family residence for hundreds of years, as well as their defensive fortress. Three of the four cornerstone towers had spiral staircases leading from the armory, up to the common rooms of the first floor, then directly to the third-floor landing and onto the roof, where the guardsmen were originally housed. The second floor could only be accessed by one of the four corner staircases. That floor had been the private residence of the Baric family. It was split into four grand rooms: a large meeting hall, the baron's sleeping chamber, the children's chamber, and the family sitting room.

After the new manor had been built, and the Barics moved their living space there, the tower had been renovated to better house the baron's expanding Castle Guard when it became clear that there was no letting up in the fighting between the Empires.

Just twenty-five years ago, the internal walls on the second floor had been removed and new walls constructed for eight small apartments, each with its own entrance off a central common area. Lord Lorenc had retained one locked apartment as his treasury, and the other seven chambers had been given to his officers. The original sleeping chamber for the baron and his wife had been preserved, and it was now kept ready for the baron's own family in the outside chance of an attack against the castle.

The Keep was self-contained. There was constant water for drinking and washing from the Roman plumbing that tapped into the natural spring running under the Baric compound. The occupants of each floor shared a common privy room near the stairwell. The communal toilets emptied along a graded stone chute between the floors, down underground pipes, then to the cesspools outside the walls. For security, the windows on the top three floors were small and could be shuttered both outside and inside. The thick, defensive walls kept the tower temperature cool but never cold, even in the deepest winter. When needed, small brazier furnaces lit in the individual rooms could be vented out inconspicuous slits in the stonework. There were no vulnerable chimneys on the tower, except the one for the kitchen's fireplace.

The old kitchen, dining hall, and common sleeping quarters for the unmarried soldiers were above the armory and pantries. Lord Lorenc had added a separate outside stairway on the south side of the tower for convenience. It was a tall flight of wide, stone steps that opened directly into the dining hall. Mauro and Jero climbed these steps together now to have their lunch.

The room was filled with men seated on benches with platters of fresh, crusty bread covered with sliced, roasted meat. Fresh apricots and cherries had been set out in baskets on each of the plank tables. Some sort of pickled vegetable was always offered in a crock to flavor their simple meal. Today it held cabbage.

There were three men in charge of feeding the hungry soldiers. Drazen, Andro, and Milan took turns cooking offerings of hearty stews and roasted meats in the ancient fireplace to feed the variable shifts of guardsmen. These three carried on a tradition of bachelor soldiers who, by age or injury, were unable to manage another grueling horse ride into battle or wield a heavy weapon. It was considered a role of honor, doing their duty to feed the ranks and showing their loyalty to Baron Baric in the efficient running of his Keep Tower.

The tower's cooks provided the hot main dishes around the clock to the hungry soldiers, but the necessary supply of baked bread and any supplemental delicacies, like the spiced beets set out for the men that day, were made by the servant women in the house kitchen and were brought over by the two young grooms who served the Keep. No women had been allowed in the tower since the new manor house had been built over fifty years ago.

The Keep's two servants were not under Jero's authority but Eduard's. Martin, or Tin, as he went by, was the main errand boy for the soldiers. The second servant boy was his younger brother, Lazar. Their father was Milan. When the boys' mother died three winters ago, and they had no one to take care of them in their cottage, Lord Lorenc allowed Milan to move his sons into the Keep. The boys had managed fine being raised with the uncouth soldiers.

Tin and Lazar were now fourteen and twelve. Tin was a responsible and serious boy, and Mauro planned to train him for his Baric Guard when he came of age. Lazar was not so reliable, and mostly helped bring supplies from the storage rooms below, or firewood for the fireplace that was kept burning in the kitchen. Running water did not flow up beyond the first floor of the tower, so the boys would help carry pails of water to the officers there when needed. Both boys saw to it that the piles of laundry were delivered to the washing women of the castle, and then brought back to their proper owners.

There were fifty or so men bunking in the common quarters. It was a noisy mix of camaraderie at the sacrifice of privacy, but they seemed to enjoy the fellowship. Along with their regular scouting duties, each soldier served a weekly rotation in the guard house and on the ramparts.

The handful of married guardsmen, who lived with their families in the Baric cottages outside the walls, would usually eat their morning and noon meals with the bachelors of the Keep. Mauro, too, enjoyed having meals in the tower with his soldiers and ate with them once a day. It was an opportune time for him to casually discuss training, security, and the general needs of his small army.

Jero knew all the guards who served Lord Baric by name and rank, but he had little reason to go into the Keep. It was under the officers' authority and managed with a different sort of military efficiency. They made and accepted their own supply orders separate from the manor house. As steward, Jero arranged their delivery payments and recorded all their costs, but he did nothing further for the baron's Guard than that. He was not included in their world.

Jero ate his delicious meal and listened to the officers tell Mauro about their plans. The low grunts and booming replies of the soldiers were a stark contrast to the feminine manor house voices. After they helped themselves to seconds, Jero and the baron went upstairs to unpack the newly arrived wardrobes.

The trunks had been carried up to the second-floor meeting room, with its three walls of doors that were the officers' chamber entrances. Light came in through the deeply cut windows of the fourth wall that faced south. The openings in the stone gave enough daylight so they would not need to light torches. The open space was furnished with only one large, solid table similar to the ancient one in Mauro's study. It would normally have twelve chairs surrounding it, but several had been moved aside, and the trunks set down in their places. Jero opened them and laid out the contents of the two chests to pair the garments for their new owners.

"I am pleased, Jero," Mauro congratulated him. "I paid the invoice, and I have to thank you for your thriftiness. I was expecting less than this for the cost, but you have chosen well."

"We arranged a deal, since we purchased all our items at the one shop. I am pleased that it was worth the long ride and they arrived on time. These are for you, Mauro." Jero pointed to the stack laid out at the end of the table.

Jero watched the baron hold up the petticoat breeches and matching waistcoat. Mauro ran his hand over the smooth, pale green taffeta, with its contrasting satin ribbons along the edges of the breeches. He held up the elegant jacket against his worn leather doublet. The long jacket's front panels were embroidered with gold thread and small crystals that would catch the light of the torches. Mauro grinned. "You think highly of me, Jero. So much sparkle and ribbons; is it not too much?" He laughed nervously, not sure if he was pleased with the ornate styling.

"No, according to Signor Donati, this is perfect for a respectable nobleman. And you said it must match your wife's gown. Mine has less embroidered touches, but my sleeves are all lace. I rather like yours," Jero admitted.

"But your breeches are velvet. That is more to my liking." Mauro held up his green, taffeta bottoms.

"The shopkeeper said this was the newest fashion that is being worn at the Venetian Court. The men all agreed you should look, well, courtly." The baron preferred his wool and doeskin to silks and velvet. "It is only one night, Mauro."

"There is no changing it now," Mauro conceded. "Let us get Milan's boys up here to distribute these to the proper rooms so the officers will know what they are to put on. I will leave mine here to change into after the initial welcome on the terrace. We'll dress while we will give everyone an hour or so to rest and primp in their rooms before the gala begins near sundown."

"Then I shall leave mine here, too," Jero said. "I will find Tin and Lazar, and then see you later."

Chapter 37

The noblemen and their entourages began arriving a few hours later, in a trickle at first, and then in a flood of wagons, carriages, and horsemen. Several brought grooms and maids to serve their individual masters and mistresses. Those servants were greeted and sorted to the proper housing by Nestor and Idita.

Mauro and Jero directed the dignitaries to the terrace, where refreshments had been laid out under the shadow of large awnings. The Baric women had been excused from the initial welcoming festivities. Mauro was especially worried for his wife, who seemed to fade easily each evening. He had asked her to stay in their room to rest for the long night ahead. Resi waited instead in Ruby's room, which had a view of the entrance gate and courtyard. Together they watched the richly dressed aristocrats ride in and be greeted by Mauro.

"I've counted thirty so far. How many will come tonight?" Ruby asked.

"I cannot be sure, but this must be about half already. Mauro has reserved the rooms at the village inn and tavern for those who cannot be housed here." Ruby and Resi continued their surveillance of the new arrivals. "Look how beautifully the women are dressed. Some look familiar, but I have not met all of them. I am glad to see so many daughters with them."

"I hope the visiting girls will not distract the lieutenant from our trap," Ruby said with a worried look. She would bear the brunt of the responsibility if the plan failed. "Will you go down to meet them now, Resi?"

"No, Mauro insists I stay here until he comes for me. He wants me to take a long nap, as if I could do that with so much going on outside my walls," Resi replied. "Verica is fixing Lady Caterina and Lady Isabella's hair in their chamber, and then she will come to style mine. I suppose if I am to rest, I should do it now."

"Will she do my hair, as well?" As the pawn in this game, Ruby knew she would be carefully attended to. In her nervousness, though, she was feeling unsure of the plan.

"You will be the last one dressed, Ruby. Verica and Natalija will wait with you once we have gone down to the party. The Venetians must be sure the lieutenant is fully tempted to meet you, and then we will bring you to the dance. You must be patient and keep to the plan."

Ruby went over to the gown hanging in her open armoire and touched the pale pink silk of the skirt. It was soft and billowy like a cloud; she loved the feel of it and could not wait to wear it tonight. "I know the plan. I only hope I can play my role after such a long wait. I am already nervous."

"I am having some brandy sent to you with your dinner. Drink it, but not too much. I might help with your nerves. I will leave you now, Ruby." Resi kissed her friend goodbye on her cheek and went to her quiet chamber.

~ * ~

Caterina was seated at the large table as Verica brushed out her long, black hair. "Isabella, you are making me nervous with your pacing," Caterina told her. "Come sit down and talk to me."

Isabella was watching the gathered gentry. She could see the corner of the terrace from their bedroom window. She went to her friend's side and smoothed her own hair in the looking glass. "I am going downstairs to enjoy some fresh air and have a look around. Maybe I can meet our adversary as well."

"You mean the lieutenant?" Caterina asked her, and Verica stopped her brushing to listen. She had not been told about the plot, and Isabella did not wish to share it with her now. It was better that the maid was able to honestly say she had played no part, should it all go wrong for the women.

Isabella bent and whispered, "Shhh, Caterina. You cannot give it away already. I will be back in a few minutes." And with that, she left the room.

~ * ~

Mauro was talking to Barons Raneri and Leopold on the terrace when he saw the naval officers arrive. Lieutenant D'Alessandro was greeted by Jero, and his horses were led away by the Baric stable grooms. Nestor showed the lieutenant's two escorts to the Keep. The two officers, along with other valets and groomsmen, would be housed on the third floor in the small, unused guard quarters there. D'Alessandro would sleep in one of the Baric guest rooms in the manor house, but he followed Nestor and his men up the outside staircase and disappeared into the Keep. Mauro would have a few minutes before he would need to greet his guest of honor.

There was already a sizable gathering of men and women sampling the light buffet offerings and enjoying cool beverages on the terrace. Despite the sea of hats and wigs, Mauro noticed Isabella standing at the double doors of the great hall. She was taller than most women, even in the flat, velvet slippers that she wore in the house. She had not yet seen him, but he excused himself from Neven and Baron Raneri and made his way toward her.

She was dressed demurely in a simple, cream-colored gown. The loose lace of her contrasting pale blue bodice modestly covered her narrow waist and full, corseted figure. Even with her long, dark hair tied unadorned down the center of her straight back, she commanded attention when entering the crowd. Her lips were already stained pink from the rouge she wore most of the time, but her smooth, feminine features were not yet enhanced with powder and liner. Mauro thought she purposely chose to meet the arriving guests in this fashion so her change later would make for a more dramatic entrance. She did nothing without a motive.

Mauro had once been enticed by Isabella's courtly charms and beauty. Mauro had met her briefly when he first stayed at the Carrera villa at seventeen. It wasn't until he went with Fabian to visit the Carrera family during their first home leave as army captains that he took a romantic interest in her.

Count Toth would give his officers leave once a year. Mauro went with Fabian to Venice, instead of making the trip alone to his parents in Croatia. Mauro had known about Fabian's earlier failed attachment to Isabella, but as a naïve nineteen-year-old Mauro thought she might be attracted to him, as well. He was not interested in finding true love; he was betrothed already. But to have a lover for his time in the city would be a relaxing diversion before going back to war.

Maybe Isabella had been bored with the choices of suitors that winter, but she had flattered him by reciprocating his attention in their innocent game of seduction. He knew few men who could ignore her natural beauty and her way of making a man feel he was in control. Mauro had been equally drawn to her youthful wit and had enjoyed her exclusive companionship, for a few weeks at least.

Eventually, she had told him she was still pining for Filippo, who was soldiering with another Venetian regiment, and Mauro had backed away from his pursuit of a more intimate courtship. Fabian had been unsympathetic to Mauro's disappointment. Fabian knew she had only been playing with him, and that Mauro had no chance acquiring the desirable Isabella. Nobody did in those first years at Court—not even Fabian, who had known her for most of his life.

Mauro thought about the brief romance and smiled at her with no regrets. Isabella now saw him coming toward her and smiled back. "It is a pleasure to have you join us, Isabella. I was not expecting to see you this afternoon," Mauro said in a friendly tone before he kissed her outstretched hand.

"You know it is not in my nature to sit by and miss the chance to be social, Mauritius," she said truthfully, then flicked open her fan to help her ward off the radiating heat on the terrace.

"I will bring you a drink. What would you like?" He stood patiently by, like a waiting servant. Isabella had that effect on people.

"I will walk with you to the table. Is that your guest of honor coming across the courtyard?"

Mauro looked over the heads of the mingling visitors and saw she had guessed correctly. The lieutenant stood out boldly in his red naval commander's jacket. He was with Jero, who had been assigned to show him to his room upstairs. Before the men reached them, Mauro answered her in a low voice, "Yes, Isabella. He is the reason for this occasion." Mauro turned then and said more loudly to the men approaching, "Ah, Lieutenant D'Alessandro, I am glad to see you again, sir."

"And you, sir," he said as he bowed crisply to his host. "Thank you for the opportunity to visit your estate." He looked around at the lords and ladies on the terrace, and then fixed his stare on Isabella at Mauro's side.

"I see Jero will be showing you to your room. Can I offer you some refreshment first?" Mauro handed him a glass of the wine punch he had also offered Isabella. The lieutenant took the glass and nodded to Isabella, who stood next to Mauro, appraising him behind her lace fan. Mauro did his duty and announced, "May I introduce you to our special guest from Venice. This is Lady Isabella Valli. She is the companion of Fabian Carrera's sister, whom you will meet later this evening. They are on their way to Hungary to marry."

"I am enchanted to meet you, Signorina Valli. Alas, another Venetian loss to the Habsburgs," he said with a mischievous smile. "Have you been here long?" he asked her gallantly.

"I have not, Lieutenant. We only arrived a few days ago, but it seems we came at an opportune time. I do so love a ball," she purred, hiding coyly behind her fan. "I was just heading back up upstairs to rest a bit before the festivities. I want to dance all night. Do you dance, Lieutenant?" she asked sweetly.

"I do indeed. Especially now that I know what a charming dance partner might be available. I would be immensely honored if you were to save a dance for me. Immensely," he repeated with emphasis.

She knew now what her play would be. She dropped her fan and snapped it shut to let him have the full effect of her engaging smile. The officer gave her a flirtatious grin and said to the baron, "If you will excuse me, Lord Baric, I should also like to be shown to my room now. Is it in the same direction as Signorina Valli?"

"Please, call me Isabella," she said softly in her melodic Venetian dialect, and offered him her hand to lead her away.

"Um, Jero, will escort you, Lieutenant," Mauro answered the brazen guest. He wondered whether Isabella understood the risk of flirting with the lieutenant so shamelessly. But he had other things to worry about than her lack of self-control.

Jero walked ahead of them through the doors into the great hall. He had been watching the interaction with a silent interest. The lieutenant was said to be a newly married man, and Lady Isabella was on her way to be married, but yet they openly lured each other. Ovid's volume on seduction had seemed complicated while he had read it. Maybe it wasn't so complicated after all. Jero secretly hoped he would get the chance to practice with a certain lady tonight, too.

~ * ~

Verica stood behind Caterina's chair in front of the looking glass at the grooming table. "Do you know what I think, my lady? I think you would be exceptionally beautiful with your hair piled in the center, and spirals coming down at a slant to the side. I have the iron heating on the brazier. Would you like me to curl your hair like that?"

Caterina contemplated her image in the reflection. "I am not sure, Verica. I would like to have it curled down the sides, but not all on top, too."

"I think it would make you look taller, my lady. Not that you need to be taller, but it would be very becoming." The maid lifted her hair in contemplation. "Especially if you had some feathers or ribbons added. Shall I give it a try?"

Verica was only a servant girl, but she could be very persuasive. Caterina nodded and watched in awe as Verica turned her silky, black hair into perfect ringlets spiraling down one side of her fair face. Verica took some of Caterina's hair pins and held the curls back at an angle. It made the young woman look sophisticated and elegant. Caterina approved of the final addition of ribbons, and then Verica began to help her into her lavender gown.

Isabella came hurriedly back into the room, interrupting their quiet struggle to fasten the gown's bodice. "He can be won over," she announced as she took a seat on the bed near the two women.

"Are you sure?" Caterina asked breathlessly as Verica tightened the laces of her dress.

"Yes, I walked with him upstairs, and he would have followed me into this room had Jero not accompanied him. He is quite in heat, and it is not from the sun, either."

"Is he at least handsome? I mean, it is always more amusing when you enjoy looking at the man's face, too."

"I was surprised, but I did find him quite attractive. He seems overly confident, but that will play to our advantage. At least he is young and well-groomed. He has wide, dark eyes; you know I like that. I already mentioned that you and Ruby were also unmarried and would be coming down later. Jero gave me quite the shocked look," Isabella told her.

"Will Jero give you away?"

"Jero? No, he is a servant and will not repeat what was spoken between me and the lieutenant," Isabella told Caterina, forgetting at the moment that Verica was also listening in on the conversation not intended for her ears.

Caterina examined her finished look in the mirror. "What do you think, Isabella?"

Isabella had been so preoccupied with her mission that she had not noticed her friend's appearance. She stood and walked around her with a genuine smile. "Perfect, Caterina! I love the new hairstyle. You look stunning." She turned to Resi's maid. "You have a special talent, Verica. I will have to steal you away from the baroness when we leave."

Verica beamed in appreciation. "If you are ready, my lady, I can style your hair now."

"Yes." She thought about it for a moment, and then added, "The curls are perfect on Caterina, but I would like something smoother."

The maid gave Isabella a serious look, touching her hair and lifting it off her face. She smiled confidently at Isabella and said, "I know what to do, my lady."

~ * ~

Natalija woke the baroness up an hour later for her tea and the final preparations for her own hair and costume.

"Verica will be here in a few minutes, madam. She is taking a quick meal in the kitchen, since she has been helping the Venetian ladies this whole time. There is quite a lot of commotion in the corridor with all the visitors. I have never been in the manor house when all the guest rooms were filled."

"Is it nearly time now?" Resi looked out the window. It was still daylight, but the sun was fading in the west.

"Some of the people are dressed in their finery and are down in the great hall already, but there is still plenty of time for you to have a small meal, my lady. I asked in the kitchen, and his lordship is in the Keep with the other officers. I will make sure Verica knows you are awake now." She left the baroness and her tray of food.

Resi was too nervous to eat, but she thought she might be too busy greeting the guests to enjoy any food offered later. She took a bite of the hearty soup Natalija had ladled for her.

"I am sorry to take so much time, my lady," Verica apologized when she rushed into the room a few moments later. She had a glow of excitement from sharing the corridor filled with the descending nobility dressed in their elegant attire. "The great hall is all ready for the ball, and I took a quick peek. The silk ribbons they hung from the chandeliers this morning are fluttering in the breeze from the open doors. They have lit all the candles, and it looks magical."

"I am sorry you cannot come, Verica. But there will be another opportunity in the future, if the baron finds this ball to be a success," Resi told her with encouragement. The young maid nodded. She looked at her mistress' full dish of stew with disappointment. "Do not worry, Verica. I have eaten a few spoons of it," Resi defended herself to her maid. "Now I just want to dress and join the others."

"The Venetian ladies are beautiful, but I have saved my most special idea for you, Lady Baric," Verica announced enthusiastically. "I took some of the smaller silk roses from those that Baroness Leopold brought for decorations. I hope she will not mind, but they match the roses embroidered on your gown perfectly and will look very special accenting your hair." She took the borrowed silk flowers from her pocket and set them on the grooming table. "Should we get started, my lady?"

While Verica went about her plan for her mistress' hair, the baroness asked her to describe what the other ladies had chosen to wear.

"Lady Caterina is in lavender, with a train of white down the middle of the back, flowing to the floor," Verica began. "The gown is a heavy satin. I don't know how such a small lady can wear all of that fabric, but she looked very fashionable and quite lovely, my lady. And Lady Isabella is wearing a pale yellow skirt with a dark blue bodice. The stomacher has yellow flowers stitched into the blue silk, and a wisp of yellow sleeves tapering down her arms," Verica explained with admiration. "She has matching yellow gloves to her elbows and is wearing jeweled rings over them. I am embarrassed to say that she stuck little crystals along the top of her bosom, so you are drawn to look there. I think it is for the gentlemen, but that is where I looked, too," Verica admitted shyly.

"Don't be embarrassed, Verica. Lady Isabella has a sense for dressing for this kind of evening, and she will be leaving you some crystals to put on Lady Ruby in the same manner." Verica nodded dutifully that she would.

After hearing about how beautifully dressed the Venetians were, Resi now had doubts about herself, despite the expensive costume Mauro's aunt had given her. She confided her worries to Verica. "Do you think you can make me look like I, too, belong with the nobility tonight?"

Verica regarded her mistress with an odd expression, but finally said with a smile, "Do not fret, Lady Baric. You will be the most glamorous noble lady at the ball."

It took less than an hour for Verica to work her magic with her mistress' hair and help her into her new gown. The dress was one piece, but was a perfect lightweight satin for the summer heat. The maids had already let some of the stitching out along the waist to compensate for the baroness's growing middle, but she still wore her new corset to be able to fasten the closures along the sides. The bodice of the emerald gown was unadorned, except for a covering of delicate green lace that had been stretched over the rich fabric of the stomacher. The capped sleeves were of sheer, green silk with intermittent patches of embroidered roses. The sheer material was trimmed in the same green satin to close the cuffs against her upper arms. The hem of the skirt was decorated with small, white roses stitched among embroidered, darker green vines. The underlayers of skirts lifted the flowing gown's fabric to expose the toes of her new shoes of crushed red velvet, with mother-of-pearl heels.

"How do women walk in such shoes, Verica?" Resi was just practicing when the bedroom door opened and an elegantly dressed man entered. Resi cried out in surprise and told him, "You have the wrong room, sir. I must ask you to leave."

"I will not leave," the wigged man answered, "until you grant me a kiss." Verica giggled at the stunned look of her mistress's face.

"Mauro! You have given me a shock!" She studied her chalked husband in his long, brown locks that curled down around his shoulder. "You look, well, different. How was I to recognize you?"

"I have not seen myself. Fabian powdered my face, but I told him only a little. May I?" He walked around his wife's voluminous gown and peered into her looking glass on the grooming table. "Oh, I *am* rather changed," he said laughing. "Should I wipe it off?"

"No, you look very handsome. Really, you do. Once I knew it was you," Resi assured him. "Verica, what do you think?"

With both the baron and the baroness looking to her for an answer, Verica was suddenly speechless. "I, um . . ." They waited for her to find her words. "May I fix the curls, your lordship?" She went to him and slid her fingers through the tresses of her baron's wig. She reached for the baroness' comb and teased the locks loose, arranging them neatly over his shoulder. "The wig is splendid," she said in seriousness. "You look regal, my lord." She lowered her eyes at being so forthright.

"There, Resi. I am satisfied now with Verica's confirmation. She has exquisite taste." He winked at the blushing maid. "Let me see your gown." Mauro stepped back, and Resi turned for him. "If I am regal, then this is my queen. Do you not agree, Verica?" he asked the servant.

"I do, my lord," Verica told him with a bright smile.

"If you are ready, they are waiting for us downstairs. May I escort you to the ball, Baroness Baric?" he asked with a flourishing bow that sent the lace of his cuffs sweeping the floor.

"Yes, my lord, with pleasure. But you will have to hold me tight until I can walk properly in these shoes," she confessed, and he happily took her arm in his.

They met Fabian, his sister, and Isabella waiting for them at the top of the stairs. Looking at them together there, Resi imagined they were a portrait of the best-dressed, young aristocrats in Venice.

Fabian had a dashing sense of style in his normal wardrobe, but she had never seen him in his element. He had chosen not to wear a wig, but had left his thick hair unbound, curled at the ends and resting neatly on his shoulders. His tanned face was lightly chalked, and he had the slightest tint of rouge on his high cheeks and his curved lips. His fine white shirt had a low, laced collar; a long strip of the same lace had been wrapped and pinned against his throat with an elegant, red jade broach. His usual hooped earrings had been replaced with jade balls to match his tie pin.

His family traded silk fabric, and his garments reflected the best that was sold in the Empire. The long waistcoat under his fitted jacket was of a fine, Oriental patterned weave of pale blue, with splashes of black and red that were strikingly masculine. The light orange brocade silk of his silver-buttoned jacket, which he wore open, contrasted with the pale blue of the full, pleated breeches that stopped at his knees. Orange ribbons held his white stockings at the top of his shapely calves. The shoes were the final touch of extravagant excess, adding unnecessary height to his already tall frame. They were one more splash of orange silk, tied closed with soft blue ribbons.

Resi had not seen the ladies that afternoon. Verica had already described their gowns to her mistress when she was dressing her, but the maid's words had not captured their true beauty. Next to her brother, Caterina was an exquisite blossom of a woman in her fine, flowing purple dress. Her high shoes and high hair made the petite woman fully grown—although, next to her brother, she was still delicate and feminine. Her friend stood by her side as a taller, bolder version of a Venetian courtier. The soft, pale yellow seemed bold in contrast to the added rich blue touches. She had powdered and rouged her lovely face. It only added to the message that Isabella was the porcelain doll to be admired most among the other beauties. She would be noticed in the crowd. Men would want to touch her, dance with her. That was her desired effect.

The three watched Mauro and Resi approach with genuine smiles on their faces, and Resi was pleased to be sharing this special event with her new friends. They greeted each other with flattery and pleasant compliments at the top of stairs. Fabian made a sweeping bow to the two and said, "After you, Baron and Baroness Baric." The five descended into the changed but familiar great hall.

Chapter 38

Resi knew their efforts to decorate the great hall would make a special setting to their festive evening. But she could not have begun to imagine how the addition of the colorfully adorned guests could transform the ambiance of the room. Verica had been right. It was magical.

The Carrera siblings and Isabella left their host and hostess at the entrance to the great hall. The onlookers strained to catch a glimpse of the new baroness as Mauro paraded her across the room to make the obligatory introductions. Mauro made most of the small talk while receiving their guests together, while Resi stood decoratively by his side, curtsying and nodding as she welcomed the partygoers. With their duty nearly done, Mauro turned suddenly to Resi with a troubled look. "You have forgotten Ruby upstairs. Shall I send Jero to escort her down?"

"Oh." Resi had to think quickly. "I did not say earlier, but Ruby has overslept and will need some time to dress. May she come down by herself when she is ready?"

Satisfied that Resi's friend had not been neglected, Mauro agreed, "Yes, I suppose she knows her way." Then he asked a more important question. "Are you ready to dance, Resi? They are waiting for us to open the ball."

There was a large, open space for the dancing, and Mauro had hired Venetian musicians to play for the party. Resi had not considered she would be spotlighted on the dance floor, and she anxiously followed him to the center of the room as the others gave way to the couple. "This is all too new to me. I don't think I can remember my steps," she whispered, as he held her at arm's length for the spectators to admire.

Mauro did not want to prolong her worry and confidently nodded to the seven-man band to begin. The musicians played a song that sounded familiar to her, and she focused on her husband for courage. Mauro held her close for a moment, breathing in her irresistible scent before he began gliding her through the steps they had practiced just a few days ago. She was still trying to filter out the extravagant clothing and curled wig of the man holding her, searching for her husband there beneath the powder and the rouge. She guessed it would not be too difficult to enjoy this companion tonight, though. Her full skirt forced a space between them, and she suddenly yearned to hold him closer. They'd had no time together today, and she longed for a private moment to tell him how special this was to her.

Her partner smiled and twirled her as the dance required. Her nerves were settled, and she enjoyed every moment of it now. After the first minute of the dance, other couples joined them in a cascade of colorful fabrics gliding over the polished stone dance floor.

The song ended and Mauro bowed graciously to his wife. "I will leave you to mingle with the ladies. There are a few gentlemen I promised to speak to sooner than later." Resi gave him a disagreeable look, but Mauro explained, "Later they will be too drunk to remember what I am to tell them. I shall find you in a little while for another dance." He took her face gently in his hands and kissed her softly on her lips. "You did wonderfully," he said, and then walked across the crowded room.

Including the Baric residents, there must have been eighty people in attendance. Resi surveyed the faces. The Leopolds were prancing along the row of laughing partners in one of the line dances she had enjoyed during her practice. Lady Nikolina looked refreshed from her difficult trip yesterday. She had donned a wig instead of bringing a lady's maid to help her with her hair. Natalija had been given to the Leopold women earlier to help them dress for the evening. Resi spotted Lady Eleonora near the punch table with Nestor. The two of them seemed to be enjoying a light conversation. Resi had not seen Nestor look livelier in the year she had known him. She wondered what history they shared and memories they would talk of.

She scanned the room and saw Jero and Vilim near the open terrace doors drinking horns of ale. She was glad the two had become friends since their trip together last week. She looked to where their eyes were facing, and it was toward the group of young women Resi had just been introduced to. She hoped the two would gather their courage and ask the debutants to dance the next song.

She smiled to see the stylish siblings, Fabian and Caterina, dancing along the line in the center of the hall. Watching them made her think of the brother she longed to see again in just a few days.

Across the floor, in the calculated yellow gown, Isabella flirted with the attentive Lieutenant D'Alessandro. Bravo, Resi thought; Lady Isabella was not wasting any time to put her trick into motion. Ruby should be coming down soon, and she hoped Lady Isabella could safely sell their pretty friend's virtue to the corruptible naval officer.

The music ended and the room came into motion again as spectators and dancers exchanged roles on the dance floor. A man she had not met earlier in the receiving line was suddenly at her side and bowed formally.

"May I introduce myself, Baroness Baric? I am your neighbor, Sebastijan Dubovic."

"Lord Dubovic," Resi said and countered with a practiced curtsy in reply. "I have heard your name often, as a neighbor to my husband. I am delighted to finally meet you, sir."

"I had hoped to honor your invitation to your last banquet, but I, like your husband, am called away unexpectedly sometimes. The Venetians can be so tedious for us Croatian landlords," he told her.

"So I understand. But tonight our guest of honor represents the Venetian Navy, so we celebrate them as well," she replied, hoping she was not being too contradictory to her guest.

"Under the right circumstances, yes, we do," he conceded. The older baron gave her a sly but charming smile, like they had shared a joke together. Was this the unlikable neighbor that Mauro avoided? He seemed pleasant and elegant. She wanted to like the fatherly gentleman in his powdered wig and overly perfumed costume.

"May I tell you, Lady Baric, that you look exquisite tonight? Did your husband choose his Baric green for you? It suits you superbly." He looked into her bright eyes and held his glance.

Resi laughed softly, but could not hold his stare. "My husband has little say in my wardrobe. It was the Countess of Toth, actually, who picked my gown for me. Have you met her, my lord?"

"She is Lady Johanna's sister. Yes, I have met her. She is a woman of impeccable taste. You are lucky to have her in your family."

Resi was feeling warm now in the stuffy corner of the great hall, away from the draft of the terrace doors. She opened her fan, then told the engaging stranger, "I have not met the countess myself, nor did I meet Lady Johanna. You may already know, my mother-in-law passed away just before I arrived."

"Of course, Lady Baric. What a pity to have missed out on that relationship. I was a friend to your husband's parents. It was a tragic year for him to lose both of them so closely together," he said solemnly, and then his expression changed. "Lady Baric, I could not help but notice the ring you are wearing. May I?" She folded her fan again, and he took her hand gently in his to admire it. "The gem is flawless. That is quite a stone."

"It matches my husband's," she told him, then immediately regretted discussing the Baric treasures, even with an old family friend.

"How extraordinary." He let her hand gently loose again and leaned on his walking stick, his own hand disappearing under the long lace of his cuff dangling over it. "I am curious, though," he added. "I knew Lady Johanna for many years, being that we were neighbors all this time, of course. We became well acquainted, but I do not recall her wearing such a ring. I am compelled to ask: where did the ring come from?"

"I am at a loss to say whether she had worn the ring before me. My husband tells me it was originally his grandmother's. That is all I know of its ownership." She hoped that would satisfy his curiosity.

"Exquisite. Lovely," he said, admiring her hand again, but finally sensing her discomfort in the attention.

The baron motioned toward the open doors and changed the subject to other gems in the room. "I was trying to learn who the two ladies near the terrace are. I have not seen them before."

"No, sir, you would not have had the opportunity. They have only been here a few days. The lady in lavender is Caterina Carrera, my husband's captain's sister. The woman next to her is Lady Isabella Valli, of Venice."

"Carrera and Valli from Venice," the baron repeated smoothly. "I did not realize your husband had such a link to the ruling government in the capital, Lady Baric."

"How do you mean, Lord Dubovic?" Resi had never heard Mauro talk politics, and she could not imagine why Lord Dubovic would infer such a connection.

"The patriarchs of the Carrera and Valli families are long-standing councilmen of the Empire. They are very influential in how we are served here, Lady Baric."

"I am not sure how influential their daughters are, Lord Dubovic, but they make for entertaining guests. They are here for pleasure, and not for politics, I assure you." She flicked her fan open again, and Dubovic understood the topic was concluded. "Are you enjoying the ball, sir?"

"I am. I have not been to a ball since my wife passed away fifteen years ago. I had forgotten how delightful it is to be around so many young people."

"You must have a lot of young people come and go at your home. You have two daughters, I understand." Resi thought this would be a safe subject.

"Yes, but they are both married now. My first daughter married a gentleman in Venice three years ago. My second married just last year, about the same time you arrived. She lives with her husband in Split."

"That must be a comfort for you, that they are well situated not too far from home. And you did not remarry after your wife passed, my lord?" He looked at her with an odd smile, and she regretted her question. "Oh, I am sorry if that is too personal."

"Not at all, madam. After fifteen years, most men do remarry. I will confide that I did think about it and was nearly successful. I actually became quite close to Lady Johanna after the tragic passing of Lord Lorenc." He did not seem to notice Resi's shock at this casual statement. "It was a difficult time for her, especially with your husband still away most of the year. She was in great need of consoling after such a loss."

Mauro had said nothing about Lord Dubovic visiting his mother. Maybe that accounted for Mauro's distrust of the baron. "Well, that was kind of you, sir, to be there for her. She was a fragile woman in the end, I understand." Resi gave him an uncomfortable smile, but he was too distracted by his own thoughts to notice.

"Do you enjoy dancing, Lady Baric?" he asked, suddenly changing the subject.

She read too much into his question and worried that perhaps she had not looked like she had enjoyed dancing when she opened the ball. "Yes, I do enjoy dancing," she politely confirmed.

"This next dance is an old favorite of mine. Shall we join in?"

She was the hostess and was expected to dance with the gentlemen guests, so answered dutifully, "With pleasure, Lord Dubovic." He offered his arm and escorted her out onto the dance floor.

Mauro had been watching his wife and Dubovic conversing across the room. Jero was standing nearby; Mauro walked over to his steward and asked him, "What do you think of Lord Dubovic, Jero?"

"I have never had a conversation with the man," Jero diplomatically answered.

"Yes, I suppose you would not have had the opportunity. But what do you know of him?" Mauro asked in the way he did when he wanted information and not casual conversation.

Jero reflected as he watched the baroness with the neighbor on the dance floor. The older baron held her hand as they went down the line, smiling together at the amusement of the twirling dance steps. Jero finally answered, "From the stories I have heard, you do not have to worry about him seducing your wife."

"Yes, that is what I thought. Which is why it is odd he would ask her to dance, would you not agree?"

"He may be a deviant man who prefers boys over women, but he is an aristocrat with a lifetime of manners and training. He may also just enjoy dancing," Jero offered.

Mauro accepted this as fact and turned again to Jero with a happier expression. "You seem to be enjoying your evening, Jero. I saw you dancing earlier."

Jero smiled. "I am, Mauro. So far it has been quite enjoyable. I have even gotten used to my wig." They both smiled at that.

"Promise me you will not become too accustomed to one and turn into a Silvijo Nestor."

Jero laughed loudly at this and then pointed out, "I see Nestor is also enjoying himself this evening." Jero motioned to the other side of the room, where Nestor sat conversing closely again with Lady Eleonora.

"Well, you know he was married once before," Mauro explained offhandedly.

"No, I did not know that," Jero said with genuine surprise.

"Yes, before he became my father's steward. I think that was the reason my father offered him the position; he had just lost his wife."

"Oh. How did she die, Mauro?" Jero asked with sincere interest.

"I do not know anything more than that. My uncle was the one who told me, and he is not one to expand on stories of love and loss."

They were quiet for a moment, and then Jero dared to ask, "Have you seen Ruby? I thought she was to attend the ball as well?"

Mauro looked around the great hall. He had not paid attention to whether she had joined the party or not. "My wife said she had overslept from a nap and would be arriving late. But you are right, maybe someone should check on her. Do you want to go see if something has gone amiss? I see D'Alessandro is still in the room, so at least we can be confident that he has not abducted Ruby."

"I was just wondering, Mauro," Jero replied. "I do not want to disturb her, if she is not ready."

The music ended and Mauro did not comment further on the subject of Ruby. "Excuse me, Jero. I am going to rescue my wife."

~ * ~

Lieutenant D'Alessandro and Isabella were mingling at the portrait wall with several other over-danced couples. The buffet tables there had just been set with a variety of trays and dishes offered as a casual dinner for the guests. The song had finished, and Caterina and Fabian were coming from the dance floor toward the buffet tables. Neither of the Carreras had eaten lunch that day. They decided they would sit out the next few songs and enjoy some of Cook's special dishes out on the cooler terrace instead.

"Signorina Isabella, will you introduce me to your friend?" the lieutenant asked her.

"With delight, Lieutenant," Isabella cooed.

"Caterina. Fabian. May I introduce Lieutenant D'Alessandro?" Isabella asked the two as they walked by within earshot.

Fabian was not eager to stop. He had met the irritating man already under strained circumstances, but Caterina hooked her arm through her brother's and pulled him the few steps to where Isabella and the lieutenant stood.

"It is a pleasure to make your acquaintance, I assure you, Lieutenant," Caterina said in her soft Venetian. "You may have already met my brother."

Fabian tried his best to smile pleasantly to the naval officer who had caused so much trouble for his best friend. For Mauro's sake, he would make an effort in winning over the lieutenant. "Yes, of course. We have had the pleasure."

The lieutenant bowed slightly to Fabian and said formally, "Captain Carrera," but did not acknowledge him further. He turned instead to Caterina and said, "I saw you on the dance floor earlier. You dance beautifully, Signorina Carrera. If you would do me the honor, the music is starting again." He held out his crooked arm for her to take. She shot a quick glance toward Isabella, who nodded, then took the lieutenant's offered arm to be led away without another word.

"You and Caterina are taking this welcome to heart, it seems. What are you up to?" Fabian asked Isabella as they contemplated the busy buffet table together, assessing their choices.

"Up to? That is a bit harsh, Fabian. Why should we be up to anything?" She put a slice of roasted pork on her plate next to some grilled prawns.

"Because there are thirty eligible men lined up ready to dance with each of you, and you danced the first three songs only with the lieutenant. He is not really your type. He is married, you know."

She knew from the start she would need Fabian's help in the next part of her plan, and there was no delaying it any longer. She set her plate down on the serving table, took Fabian's hand, and led him to a dim corner of the room before he could protest. She took a deep breath and said without interruption, "Fabian, we will need your assistance. We are helping the baroness with something important. Do not ask me for the details. But after this dance, Caterina and I will play a game of cards with the lieutenant, and you will join the three of us in the sitting room. You will nod your head, smile, and let me and Caterina do the talking. There is a good reason for it. Can I count on you?"

Fabian had listened intently. "Are you out of your fucking mind, Isabella?" He tried to contain his anger so they would not attract attention, but he was furious. He was done with Isabella and her schemes. Done! "Whatever game you are playing, you are playing it with the wrong man. And I am not talking about cards." He held her arm and angrily looked down into her mesmerizing brown eyes. "Stop whatever you are doing, now. If you cause Mauritius more trouble, I swear I will carry you both to the sea and throw you in. Do you understand?"

She shook her arm free of Fabian and hissed, "You are not the only one who can defeat a foe, Captain Carrera. This will work, if I can get your cooperation. Do *you* understand?"

"I should lock you in your room right now." He ran his hand through his long locks. They each held their stares for a moment before he backed down. "Very well, Isabella, but you must promise me that you cannot make more of a mess than Mauritius already has."

She nodded earnestly, looking so appealing with her powdered cheeks and red lips. Fabian had avoided her all week, and here he was agreeing to help her with her foolish game. He was the fool, he thought, a stupid, idiotic fool. He told her, "I do not want to know the details, so do not try to explain what you have planned."

He took her hand and led her back into the crowd of partiers mingling at the laden food table. He leaned in to whisper to her, "Let us get something to eat and take it to your card game, all right? I will play my role to nod and smile, but this had better be good."

She picked up her abandoned plate and said, "No questions, then." He nodded. "We need someone to escort Ruby downstairs to the dance. Can you do that on our way to the sitting room?"

The music had quieted, and Caterina and D'Alessandro were walking toward them again. Fabian skillfully erased the doubtful expression on his face, changing it to a smile as the two approached.

"Fabian, the lieutenant does not believe that I have never lost a card game. I told him you could tell him it is true," Caterina said merrily when they joined the two at the food tables.

"Yes, Lieutenant," he confirmed eagerly, "my sister has a remarkable talent. Do not wager against her unless you do not mind going home with an empty purse."

"I told you that on principle I never gamble with a lady, but now I am tempted to test your luck, Signorina Carrera. You see, I, too, never lose," D'Alessandro bragged.

"Well then, we have a challenge," Isabella chimed in with a broad smile. "Let us fill our plates with this tempting food, and then we can find the cards in the sitting room. We will not be disturbed there. Fabian and I are terrible card players, so we will make it a fair game: the gentlemen against the ladies."

"Agreed," said Fabian, pretending to be happy with the arrangement. "I will already take my plate and meet you there in a few minutes." He went to follow his instructions to find Ruby and escort her to the party first.

The torches and several candles had all been lit in the bright, empty foyer. It was cooler there than in the great hall and the thrum of the music was dampened. He took his meal and a candle from the table into the dark sitting room and lit the two candelabras and the wall sconces. It would be bright enough to play cards by, he decided. He took a big bite of a meat pie before leaving his plate on the table and hurried upstairs. He did not like this already.

Fabian wasn't sure which room was Ruby's, but he was sure it was on this side of the corridor. He saw a light glowing under the middle room and knocked on that door. He was not prepared for the sight of the woman who opened it. His sister and Isabella were up to some courtly trick, and Ruby's beautiful makeover had confirmed it. "Lady Ruby, I was asked to accompany you downstairs," he said to her at the threshold.

Verica and Natalija were with Ruby in the room, and they both hopped to their feet from their place on her bed and curtsied to the unexpected escort. He then spoke to the maids, "Please leave us now, ladies."

Both girls gave Ruby a nod of encouragement, and then hurried out the door, past Fabian, and down the hall to Verica's small chamber. He waited for Verica to shut her door.

Fabian took a few steps into Ruby's room so his voice would not echo in the empty corridor. He knew this would be considered inappropriate in the Baric household, so he left the door open.

She looked both innocent and alluring. The new gown was sleeveless, with just a twist of dark red velvet at each shoulder, drooping seductively onto her slender, pale arms. The low, straight bodice was fashioned as a triangle ending where her navel would be. At this point, soft pleats made the layers of light skirting lift around her feminine hips. The only adornment of lace was what showed along the trim above her tight corset. Crystals were pasted along the edge of Ruby's swelling cleavage. Ruby had practiced her breathing, because with each large breath, her breasts would expand indecently.

He took in her changed appearance, and surprised himself when he could not take his eyes off her for a moment. "You are very becoming in your new gown, Ruby," Fabian said sincerely. "May I say, I have never seen you look so beautiful."

"Thank you," was all the blushing girl could answer. Fabian's size and handsome masculinity was overwhelmingly intimidating, and she unconsciously took a step away from him. She looked down at his pale orange shoes.

He wanted to test her; he needed to be sure she was a willing participant. Fabian reached out and gently tilted her chin to meet his eyes again. "It is just me. Fabian. If you are afraid of me, Ruby, then you cannot go through with whatever my sister and Isabella have asked you to do."

She smiled at him and took a step forward again. Her exhaled breath was audible, but it helped her to gain her composure. "I would never be afraid of you, Fabian. It is just, well, I have been waiting for hours to be taken downstairs. Now that the time has come, I am a little nervous. The ladies have asked me to do something important, but it will not take much time. I did not think they had told you."

"I have asked not to be told, and I do not want to hear any more. But I must ask you one thing."

"Yes, Fabian?" she replied with a new calmness.

"Do you have a looking glass?" he asked as serenely as he could manage the odd question.

"What? Yes, why? Is there a smudge?" She had a worried look on her powdered face again.

Fabian chuckled and offered her his arm to leave. "No, there is nothing wrong. I just wanted to be sure you know what you look like tonight. I will remind you that the castle men have only seen you in your traditional robes, never dressed in a gown like this. Many male eyes will be upon you when you arrive downstairs, and they will all want to dance with you. Are you prepared for that?"

"Yes, that is the idea, Fabian. But I will say no more. Thank you, though." He smiled at her and nodded. She shut her door behind them and let him lead her down the stairs in her floating, gauze gown.

Fabian walked Ruby into the great hall filled with the chatter of voices and clattering of utensils on plates. The heads of the partiers slowly turned one by one toward her and Fabian at the entrance. She stood before the wide double doors and Fabian whispered into her ear, "Good luck, my dear." He left her to join his card game.

Resi saw her standing alone at the edge of the room. Ruby's appearance was transformed in the flaming light that surrounded her. Her pale skin and auburn hair were complemented by the pink rouge Verica had put on her lips and on the curves of her cheeks. Caterina had been right about keeping her hair simple. Verica had loosely pinned wisps of strands from her temples with Resi's jeweled combs. She had curled the bottom half of her waist-length tresses to make soft spirals that floated over the layers of pink fabric down her back. Isabella had also been right. Ruby had been hiding behind her tunics and robes. Resi hoped her friend knew that after her emergence from them tonight, there was no turning back.

Mauro had been standing near his wife talking to some of the gentlemen, and she asked to excuse him from their conversation for a moment. "Ruby has arrived. Can you come with me?"

Mauro looked across the room and could not conceal his dissatisfaction. His one maiden had come to the party looking like a seductress. "I shall have to write a letter to my aunt asking if her seamstress works for a bordello," Mauro quietly told Resi before they met her. Resi secretly agreed, but gave him a stern look anyway.

Mauro corrected his frown before they arrived by Ruby's side. Resi spoke up before Mauro could spoil the moment. "Ruby, I am glad you have come to the ball. You look enchanting. It has been a wonderful evening so far," Resi told her encouragingly. "Mauro, would you like to get Ruby a glass of punch?"

He was going to ask why they did not walk over together to each get a glass, but he thought better of it. "Yes, of course."

Once Mauro had left them, Resi updated her on their progress. "Lady Caterina and Lady Isabella have been dancing with the lieutenant all evening. They have gone with him to play cards with the purpose of complimenting your virtues. When they come back, it will be your play, Ruby. Are you ready?"

"Yes, but I have to tell you that Fabian knows something is going on. He said he doesn't want to be told the details, but this may not be good. I am worried, Resi."

"Don't be worried. If anyone can be trusted to protect us, it is Fabian. It might be a good thing that he is in on it," she decided. She could explain nothing further. "Here comes Mauro again."

"Here you are." Mauro handed her the glass of fruited wine and she drank it gladly. "The music is starting up again. Would you like to dance this first dance with me, Ruby? I expect I will be interrupted before it is over, if you will not mind." He gave her a brotherly smile, and she appreciated his honest effort to initiate her to the party that was already in full swing. He escorted her to the center of the dance floor.

The elegantly dressed Baric men were gathered at the end of the buffet table looking toward the dance floor. Resi boldly walked over and stood in front of her husband's soldiers and servants. They each bowed to their baroness; she nodded and smiled broadly at them. Before any of them could get a polite word out, she bluntly said, "Yes, gentlemen, that is Ruby dancing with my husband. I anticipate she will have the pleasure to dance with each one of you tonight. The baron expects someone to cut in on his dance at any time." The men looked at each other speechlessly as she left them and walked away toward Lady Nikolina, standing near the open terrace doors.

Nikolina had seen the baroness and the group of soldiers react to what she had said. She could not contain her curiosity when Resi arrived at her side. "What did you say to them, Lady Terese?" Nikolina had flicked open her ornate fan and was only half-visible behind it. She continued to watch the men with amusement.

"I suggested that they should all have a dance with Ruby. Why?" Resi turned back to look at the animated group of men. "Are they already drawing straws for the first dance?" she asked.

"They are practically crawling over each other. She will be married by the end of the summer, I guarantee you," Nikolina said with satisfaction.

"I wish it were that easy," Resi leaned in to tell her over the loud music. "My husband has written to her father to ask if she may marry here. I would be happy for her to settle near me, but I am afraid her father may have other plans for her."

"Do not underestimate fathers and how they can or cannot be persuaded, Lady Terese. My own father was against my marriage to Neven. But when he thought about how efficient it would be to let me marry someone I wanted instead of having to work to find me a match, he quickly gave in. But then Neven was heir to a barony. That did help, I suppose."

"There are no heirs to anything among that group, but they are all fine men. Oh, look, Lady Nikolina. Hugo drew the long straw for the first dance." They watched with delight as he tapped Mauro on the shoulder and took his place on the dance floor holding Ruby. She genuinely smiled at Hugo. Jero was her favorite, but Hugo was not a bad second choice, Resi thought.

Not far from the two baronesses were Nestor and Lady Eleonora. "Oh, but to be young again, Silvijo. Is it fair that such pleasure is wasted on the young people?" she asked him lightly.

"What pleasures are you referring to, Lady Eleonora? Flirtation is not wasted on the young; it nourishes them. You reach our age, and we know too much to fall for false words of admiration. It has no effect on us."

"Oh, come, come, Silvijo. Do you not want to hear false words of admiration? Or must they all be true?" she provoked him with her leading question. She had been flirting with him all evening.

"I would not expect a lady to tell me *true* words of admiration, but I would wish it. I cannot help that I am a man of honesty and desire the truth," he answered her with a slight smile. "But perhaps I digress, and the pleasure you spoke of was dancing. That is not wasted on anyone. May I offer you my hand, so we might enjoy that pleasure together tonight?" Nestor cocked his wigged head and waited for her reply.

"Well said, Silvijo. It has been a long time, but I will gladly dance this next dance with you." He stood, bowed gracefully, and offered his arm. She hooked her sleeved elbow into it and was led to the edge of the dance floor as the song ended.

Chapter 39

"You are right, Signorina Caterina, our partners are utterly hopeless." Lieutenant D'Alessandro leaned in to her and added playfully, "But tell me, madam, where did you learn to cheat at cards? Oh, I mean play."

"Lieutenant! Just because you have lost over and over, it does not mean that I have cheated. I told you I know how to play. You are good, sir, but I learned from the best," Caterina teased him, and he bathed in the attention.

Fabian could just barely tolerate the company. He had done his best to play a good hand while the lieutenant cheated to win against Fabian's cheating sister. "Shall I tell you how she got so good, Lieutenant?" Fabian began to explain without waiting for a reply. "She was very petite as a girl, but my parents gave her the grown-up task of chaperoning her older sister, Cristina."

"And chaperoning me," Isabella interrupted.

"And Isabella, too," Fabian agreed, trying to smile at her. "If Caterina were honest, she would admit she was a very poor chaperone. Cristina got into endless trouble. Caterina did not watch out for her or Isabella at all."

Caterina continued where Fabian left off. "It was boring to sit with my sister at parties with her lovers, so I watched the men play their table games instead. I was not so young really; I was just small for my age. To the players, I was an innocent little girl. But I could understand how the strategy was decided, and who was playing the better hand. I stood by their sides, watched the cards in their hands, and took note of when they played them."

"They let you stand by their sides and look at their cards?" the lieutenant asked with skepticism. Fabian poured him another full glass of Mauro's best brandy he had found in the cabinet, and the lieutenant drank it down in one, smooth gulp.

"Yes, they let me linger as I pleased. I was like their little pet. I would bring them wine or food, if they asked. And then one day, some of them let me play." A wicked smile curled over her pretty, rouged lips. "And, as I said earlier, I have not lost yet."

"And you are to waste your talent with some Hungarian blue blood who probably does not even know how to shuffle a deck of cards?" he sympathized. She had told him earlier the story of how she came to visit here.

"Yes, both Isabella and I must go soon. Our new husbands are waiting for us. But alas, our companion, Lady Ruby, is allowed to stay behind. Her intended husband is no longer with us," Caterina lied smoothly to the lieutenant.

"God rest his soul," Isabella finished her sentence. "Poor Lady Ruby. She has been so sheltered waiting years for this marriage, and the old man died on her. We have only just found out."

"He was an old man? How old is your companion?" D'Alessandro asked selfishly.

"Lady Ruby is only nineteen, and she is so pretty, too—like a little auburn fawn. What a waste. Such a beautiful and voluptuous maiden, and now there are no plans for her." Isabella put all the important words plainly out there for the hungry D'Alessandro to eat up. "She is a cousin of mine from Greece, and they do not want her back. I am hopeful that she may come with us anyway and make do with any husband we can find for her," Isabella said mournfully. She did not dare look over at Fabian, who stared open-mouthed at her tale in silent disbelief.

"I would enjoy meeting your cousin. Why is she not here tonight?" D'Alessandro asked.

He had been drinking glass after glass of brandy since they began their game, and he no longer noticed the quiet Fabian at the table. His focus was on the enticing Venetian women. He had thought he could take one to bed tonight, but perhaps he would first have a look at the third girl.

"She overslept earlier, but I believe she is here now. She is probably dancing with all the eligible men in the great hall. Since she was denied male company for so many years, men are irresistible to her now. Shall we play another game, or would you like to dance again, Lieutenant?" Caterina asked, setting her deck of cards back down on the table.

"I would only lose to you again, Signorina. But I believe I can still dance." He stood up clumsily, and Fabian was not so sure the drunken sailor would be able to succeed at that or anything now.

"Then let us rejoin the party, shall we?" Caterina suggested sweetly. She took his arm and confidently led him out without a glance back at her conspirators.

Fabian was about to blow out the half-used candles, but Isabella stopped him. She let the others go ahead and out the door, then said, "Leave them burning, we will need this room shortly."

"I know what you have planned, and I do not like it," he told her firmly. "It may have worked once for the duchess, but you cannot be sure it will work again."

"If you play the duke, it will work, Fabian," she answered just as firmly. "I need you to find a reason to bring several of the important noblemen to this room in thirty minutes. That is all the time Lady Ruby should need."

"What pretense shall I use? Come watch the lieutenant take his virgin?" Fabian unpleasantly reminded her why this was risky.

"She will not be in here," Isabella said determinedly, standing directly in front of him. She could not have Fabian back out now; she needed him.

She glided her hands on the front of his waistcoat and slowly touched each silver button of his jacket while she spoke. "He will be in here alone, waiting. If he is the arrogant degenerate that I expect he is, he will be impatient for her. If not, we will have failed and he will just be passed out on the couch." She looked up at him and tried one last, practiced, innocent plea, "Will you help me?"

He removed her hands from his chest. "Mauritius is my friend, and I am not going to let you fuck this up for him."

His vulgar choice of words never surprised her, and she did not waver. "Am I no longer your friend?" she asked softly.

"We have been friends for a long time, Isabella. But you are toxic to me."

She hesitated a moment, then formulated her play. "You used to say I was intoxicating, that you could not be without me." She took his warm hand from his side and brought it to her cheek, moving it gently for him to caress her. She shut her eyes. He kept it there for a moment, looking at her, deciding, and then let his hand drop.

"Yes, well, I know the difference now," he replied, recovering from the temptation. He distanced himself by taking a step back and told her, "When this is over tomorrow, I will arrange to send you home. Caterina will be better off without you."

She began to pout and then changed her mind; it was no longer worth the effort. She stood tall and replied, "You do as you please, Fabian. You always do."

"No, Isabella. There you are mistaken. There are people's livelihoods at stake, people I care about. To you, this is just another game." He was annoyed at her for involving him, annoyed that she was getting to him. He was trapped. Fabian sighed and said, "I will do this for you tonight, but ask nothing more of me."

"I won't," she promised. She looked at him earnestly, and he believed her.

"You have thirty minutes. I will start gathering your witnesses. The evening is wearing on, and even the noblemen will begin passing out on the chairs soon. Let us get this over with." He offered her his arm, and they shut the door behind them.

~ * ~

Davor led Ruby away from the dance floor. He was dashing in his new red-and-white ensemble, and had already danced with many eager partners that night. Ruby was Davor's favorite of the eligible girls, and he asked to escort her to the terrace for some refreshment. Jero walked up to the couple and interrupted his plan.

"Ruby, I was wondering if you cared to dance the next song with me?" Jero asked politely. Davor let her arm loose, knowing he should not interfere with the steward's turn to dance with the popular partner. He made a small bow to her of thanks and of regret.

She smiled her thanks to Davor and took Jero's arm. "I could not dance another step," she confided when they neared the waiting dance partners. "I have danced the last five songs. I think I will sit this one out." He was plainly disappointed, so she quickly suggested, "Maybe we could get some punch first and dance together later."

"I would like that," he said, thinking that sharing a drink on the bench under the torchlight would be just as intimate.

Caterina approached the pair with the lieutenant at her side. "There you are, Lady Ruby," she said above the noise of the great hall. "I have been looking for you. I wanted to introduce you to Lieutenant D'Alessandro." Caterina turned to the naval officer and said, "Lieutenant, this is Lady Ruby Spiros."

Ruby put out her hand, like the ladies had taught her, and the lieutenant took it in his and kissed it gently, watching her with a gleam in his drunken eyes.

"I am happy to make your acquaintance, Lieutenant. Are you enjoying your evening?" Ruby asked him with Jero still on her other arm, ready to escort her to the terrace for that quiet drink.

"Indeed, I am having the most wonderful evening with your cousin and Lady Caterina. It has been a pleasure to talk with my countrymen, and especially such beautiful ones." He looked to Caterina, who mimicked his charming smile. "But the music has started again, and I wanted to ask you if you cared to dance with me, Signorina Ruby."

Ruby tried her best to ignore Jero's insulted expression when she accepted. Jero released his hold on her arm and abruptly turned to walk away. She would explain to him later; she would make him understand. She tried to put him out of her mind and followed the lieutenant to join the other dancing couples. It was the perfect slow song; they would be able to talk while following the simple steps.

Ruby had not seen the lieutenant before, but was glad he was more pleasant to dance with than she had expected. He was only slightly taller than her in her new heeled shoes, but he was trim, perhaps even slender, under the full pleated breeches. Ruby was slender, too, so they matched well in size while dancing. He wore his full naval uniform, and his lapel was covered in patches and metals of merit. He was ornately accessorized, wearing a long, curled wig and a laced shirt under his stiff, wool military jacket. He smelled musky from the hours in his warm attire, but she caught the lingering scent of fragrant soap on his skin when he pulled her close as the dance required. If she had not known that he had dishonorable intentions tonight, she might have enjoyed her time with him. She was there to seduce him, though, and she understood the ladies had given her two dances to accomplish it.

Ruby began her game with the flattery they had practiced. "You must dance often, Lieutenant; you have such a natural smoothness to your movements. I feel very drawn to you, like we have been partners all night."

"Yes, I feel drawn to you, too. That is a beautiful gown for dancing, the way it lightly sways to the music." Without the bulk of layered underskirts, the lieutenant was able to hold her close for many of the dance segments.

"I have not been to any balls. My marriage arrangement was made a long time ago, so I did not need to be introduced to any suitors. But alas, my future husband is no more. I find dancing very comforting in overcoming my melancholy." She leaned into him and sighed deeply, her hot breath lingering on his neck.

"Oh, of course. Such sadness you must still be feeling. Holding another's hand is always comforting. Touching another person brings relief to your pain, I am sure." He managed to slide his hand down the small of her back.

"You speak as though you know this need, Lieutenant. I have been dancing all night, touching the other men, twirling in their arms; but with you, I already feel some release." She leaned into him, pressing her hips to him more than the dance called for, like the ladies had instructed.

"That is what we all are craving when we are in such a state, dear Lady Ruby: release." His breath was heavy now on her neck. Ruby felt nauseated with the closeness, but the floor was filled with a dozen other couples, and she knew no harm could come to her in this public setting.

Resi was on the dance floor with Mauro at the same time, and she watched the seduction with discomfort as well. Especially since she knew Mauro was also watching the inappropriateness of their closeness. "Resi, I think I will cut in on Ruby with D'Alessandro," he whispered in her ear. "She may not know how to reject his advances, and I do not want her in a compromising situation."

"I don't think she is being compromised any more than Lady Isabella or Lady Caterina were. You can let her have her dance, Mauro." Resi said the words, but did not mean them.

"I was concerned about Isabella dancing so long with him at first, but then I decided she is on her own to make her fateful choices. I hate to say this, Resi, but if Isabella bedded him tonight, then he may find her a worthy reward. She is not the virgin he seeks, but she is usually unattainable," Mauro explained.

"Mauro," Resi whispered, "that is terrible to say. Besides, how do you know she isn't a virgin?"

"I am friends with Fabian, for one. Second, she has never kept it a secret. I am not saying she was a loose woman at Court; quite the opposite for a long time, really. She played hard to get for many years. But then I think she just sort of gave up. She was engaged twice already." He held her close for the turn in the dance.

"My goodness, Mauro. You are the gossipy one tonight. How much have you had to drink?" He smelled heavy of the brandied punch.

"Quite a lot," he said, "but I am fine. I am enjoying our ball. I now see the amusement of it all." He guided her across the line of other dance partners, in step with the music.

"So will we have another next month, like your grandfather preferred?" she joked.

He laughed a bit too loudly. "No, no. Maybe next spring, though, as a christening party for the baby." He kissed his wife quickly before they twirled away from each other.

The music ended, and they bowed and curtsied as the dance finished. Mauro led her through the crowd of other couples that came and went for the next dance. He walked her to the refreshment table while she searched the sea of people for one of her fellow schemers.

"I have had enough dancing for a while, Mauro. I needed to ask Lady Caterina something," Resi announced suddenly, then excused herself to meet up with the Venetian. Mauro was alone with his cool drink when Jero came up to him.

"Mauro, may I speak to you for a moment?" Jero asked quietly.

"How has your evening been, Jero?" He put his arm around his steward's shoulder, ignoring his question.

268

Jero did not seem to notice the unaccustomed embrace. He had pressing concerns that clouded his thoughts. "Splendid, I suppose. But I wanted to talk to you about the lieutenant," Jero said urgently.

Mauro released his hold on Jero, but still stood shoulder to shoulder next to him. "Oh, he looks to be enjoying his evening, too. That was the goal, was it not?"

Jero quietly complained, "Yes, but he has danced two dances with Ruby, and I thought we were to keep her away from him tonight?"

"Ah, I see your point. You should rescue her when the song is over. You are allowed to cut in, you know." Jero had already had plenty to drink as well, but Mauro noticed that his steward's mood was not as light as his own.

"Yes, I would, but here is the curious thing: she does not want to dance any longer," Jero explained. "She told me she was too tired. We were on our way to have a drink together on the terrace, and then the lieutenant was introduced to her. The music started, and she left right away to dance with him without complaint."

"And you feel jilted, Jero?" Mauro was sympathetic and concerned for the man's pride.

"No. Well, yes, I do. But why would she be so anxious to dance with him, especially after you warned her about his immoral character?" Jero could not understand her reasoning at all. He wanted some confirmation from Mauro.

Mauro had listened to Jero despite his drunken disposition and agreed that what he had observed made sense. It was very uncharacteristic of Resi's gentle friend to put herself on such public display; first the dress, and then the close dancing. Something was going on. He looked around for Resi. "Excuse me, Jero, but I must find my wife." He began to walk away.

"Mauro!" Fabian came to his side before he could cross the room to interrupt his wife and Caterina. "Can I talk to you privately?"

The two walked to the corner by the double foyer doors. Fabian had a serious expression that did not fit the mood of the evening. Something was very wrong. "I do not like your look, Fabian. What is going on in my house tonight?"

"Do not ask me for the specifics, Mauro. You need to trust me when I say it will all soon be clear enough. I have to ask a favor of you. It is important, and you will need to follow my lead."

Mauro looked him in the eyes. Fabian was stone sober, and Mauro was puzzled. "Now I am nervous, very nervous. Why are you not drunk and flirting with all these eligible women, Fabian? What can be so important that you cannot enjoy my party?"

He had not kept track of the baron tonight, and Mauro was drunker than Fabian had seen him in years. "I have been talking to Lord Leopold and Lord Marquis. They are still halfway sober at least. I have told them that you have an urgent matter to discuss in your study tonight. But Mauro, you will have forgotten your study door key, and so we will go to the sitting room instead," Fabian told him emphatically, hoping his instructions would sink in.

"You know I always have my key with me," Mauro told him, annoyed at the accusation.

"I know that, but they do not. Please, Mauro, just be agreeable and it will all become clear later."

Mauro took a deep breath and tried to shake off the brandy's effect. "All right, Fabian, you will have my cooperation. Where are the barons then?"

"The barons are dancing this dance with their wives. When the next song begins, but not before, we will approach them. After five minutes, we can make our way to the sitting room. Not before."

"Do not do this to me, Fabian. You know I am not one for games." Mauro was becoming sober quickly.

"I am sorry, Mauro. I truly am. It is not my fucking game, but if you win, then you win big. Remember, you have to follow my lead. You will know what to do when the time comes, but please do not ask me to explain anymore." The two stood silently in the dim corner and waited for the music to change.

~ * ~

"I would like to help you with your situation, Signorina Ruby. Will you meet me in my room?" The second dance with him had ended, and Lieutenant D'Alessandro and Ruby were still together on the dance floor.

"No, Lieutenant. It would be too risky," Ruby whispered. "All the doors open to the same corridor, and there are too many people coming and going. But I know of a place that is closed off tonight."

"Where is this place?" D'Alessandro asked softly, almost caressing her with his accented Latin.

"It is the baron's sitting room. It is at the end of the foyer. No one will come in there."

"I know this room. I played cards there tonight with your companions. I will meet you in ten minutes," he reassured her.

"No, meet me now. Or I may lose my nerve. I feel a connection to you, Lieutenant, and I want to know you better. But I am worried that if I don't come now, then I will be too afraid." Ruby hoped she sounded like she wanted him.

"Oh, my darling Ruby, do not be afraid. I know just what to do to help you through your difficult time. I will go now, and you follow me in a few minutes."

They had been talking face to face, and he took her hand from her side and moved it to the space between them. Ruby was startled when she felt his hard arousal through the fabric of his long jacket, but she willed herself to continue.

"Be ready for me," she choked out the words. "It will be noticed if I am missing, and we may not have enough time to thoroughly, um, release my feelings."

"Yes, yes. I will be ready for you, sweet Lady Ruby." He brought her held hand away from him, kissed it gallantly, and then walked out the double doors into the foyer.

Ruby stood alone now on the edge of the dance floor, and Resi and Caterina came to her side. They escorted her outside before she fainted from her anxiety. She was near tears, now that her role was over and her part fulfilled.

Jero had been talking with a young, future baroness and watched with concern as the ladies escorted the distressed Ruby outside. He bowed to the pretty girl and excused himself from her company. The ladies were lost to the shadows of the garden, but he needed a few minutes alone in the night air. He headed for the courtyard to have a cool drink from the well. He could not pretend to enjoy himself after seeing Ruby leave the party. After a sobering drink of cold water, he made his way to his room through the back entrance and the servant's stairwell unnoticed.

Fabian had also watched the scene between Ruby and the lieutenant from Mauro's side. He could not tell from Ruby's body language if she had succeeded or failed, but D'Alessandro looked pleased with himself as he left the great hall.

The musicians began to play another dance song. "Our game has started, Mauro. We must find the barons now."

Chapter 40

Barons Marquis and Leopold followed Mauro and Fabian out the double doors of the great hall and across the foyer to the study. "I am sorry to have taken you from your entertainment, gentlemen, but I have already forgotten once to share this important information. It occurred to me that we may not meet up again in the morning," Mauro repeated the charade that Fabian had suggested.

"Not to worry, Lord Baric, a break from my wife is not the worst you could ask of me tonight," Lord Marquis joked.

He had been a friend of Mauro's father and owned land at the southernmost end of the Croatian coastline. He was heavily invested in sea trading with the Venetians as well as the Republic of Ragusa, which bordered his landholdings. Baron Marquis had a loyal relationship with the commanding lieutenant at his own busy port and with the governing admiral overseeing the entire fleet of Venetian warships anchored in Croatian waters. Mauro had taken the opportunity earlier to ask him about Lieutenant D'Alessandro, but Lord Marquis had never had any dealings with him.

Mauro searched his pockets and repeated his scripted declaration, "It seems I have left my key in my other jacket in the tower. That is inconvenient, gentlemen, but I suppose we can go over this business in the quiet of the sitting room. I keep a good bottle of brandy in there. We can all enjoy a glass while I tell you this, um, urgent news."

"Your father always had the finest imported brandy. The Barics have some special connection, I recall," Lord Marquis said as they went together down the corridor to the sitting room.

"Their secret is to have a count in the family. He is Mauritius' source of everything contraband," Lord Leopold told Lord Marquis, and they all laughed at the truth of it.

Fabian caught a glance of Davor's red jacket coming from the privy room door, heading in the direction of the kitchen. He had a sudden idea to add to the scheme. "I have forgotten something important, gentlemen. I will join you in just a moment." Fabian's near-run toward the kitchen was not noticed by the guests. Mauro wondered whether this would affect the outcome of his game, or if it was even a part of it. Mauro continued on without him, and he opened the door to the sitting room for the others to enter.

"Good God, man! What are you doing?" Baron Marquis shouted as they entered the candlelit room to find Lieutenant D'Alessandro lounging on the couch in full military dress, minus his breeches and boots.

The lieutenant was on his feet, suddenly alert and sober. "It is not what you think."

"You will put your cock away, if you are to speak to us, sir," Lord Marquis demanded, clearly upset that he had borne the brunt of the vision. "This is a rather shocking position for any man to find another man in, especially as a guest of Lord Baric. Do you not have your own private chamber to pleasure yourself in?"

Lieutenant D'Alessandro hastily pulled his breeches on and buttoned the closure. "You are mistaken, Lord Marquis, sir. I was meeting someone. I arrived too early and, well . . ."

"Which lady will be joining you, lieutenant? Unless you have brought your own, all the young women are either married or under the protection of their guardians here tonight," Lord Leopold reprimanded him. "I cannot imagine whose ward you have persuaded to join you in your objectionable state. Or do you always take your breeches off when meeting someone alone, Lieutenant?"

The curtain of the open terrace door moved back and caught the attention of the barons. A fair-haired man's face peered in, and then just as quickly left with a flash of red fabric in the doorway. D'Alessandro turned to look at what the barons were watching and then said, "No. This is a mistake. I was waiting for a young woman to join me." He had managed to pull on his boots.

"I see all too well now, sir," Lord Marquis warned him. "I am not a man to publicly criticize another man's preferences, but you are commander of almost a thousand sailors, Lieutenant D'Alessandro. Should your superiors learn of your preoccupation with one here tonight, I am afraid they will not see this in such a favorable way. What do you say, Lord Baric?"

"I do not know what to say, Lord Marquis. I invited the lieutenant to my home to enjoy an evening of dancing and festivities. I welcomed him as my guest of honor, only to walk in on this, well, unacceptable circumstance. It is indeed a revelation, sir. I am as confused as you are. I do not know what to think at all," Mauro spoke truthfully.

"Well, I think we must report this incident, Lord Marquis," Lord Leopold offered. "The lieutenant's character has come into light tonight, and the admiral should be made aware of what sort of moral fiber is holding his navy together."

"Your lordships, there is an easy explanation for this entire misunderstanding. There is no need for the admiral to become involved. It is a party, and I have enjoyed too much drink tonight, is all. There was some miscommunication on my part, and I beg your understanding for my indiscretion." D'Alessandro straightened his attire, went toward the door, and humbly stated, "The hour is getting late, sirs, and I would like to bid you a good night and retire to my room. I must be on my way early in the morning."

Mauro turned to the two barons. "Gentlemen, I will escort the lieutenant to his chamber and hear no more about this awkward incident tonight. I think we can have our arranged meeting at another time, if you will permit it." Both agreed that the urgency of their conference was now irrelevant, and the two barons followed Mauro and the lieutenant out of the room, murmuring their conclusions between them.

Mauro and D'Alessandro walked up the stairs in silence. At the guest room door, D'Alessandro finally spoke. "You set me up for this scandal, Lord Baric." He opened the door and walked in. Mauro followed him in with the candle he had taken from the table at the top of the stairs, shutting the door behind him.

"You are wrong, sir. I was just as shocked as the others to find you undressed in my sitting room. *My* sitting room in *my* house! I apologize for not playing more of an active part in your evening, but it seemed to me you were entertaining yourself perfectly without my interference. My only goal tonight was exactly that: for you to enjoy yourself, Lieutenant, not to cause you a scandal. That you were half naked on my chair is not a concern to me. Who you were waiting for is my concern. My servants and the women under my roof are under my protection, and they are not to be used for your pleasure. On your next visit you can lodge at the Green Goose, where you will find plenty of pleasurable opportunities, but not here, sir. I understood you wanted to meet and discuss business with the other noblemen. You took that opportunity before the music began, and I expect you will profit from that. What I demand in return from you is respect for my household and the people under my charge."

The lieutenant had listened attentively to the baron's speech. He decided it was genuine and unrehearsed. Perhaps Ruby had tried to meet him and had seen the barons at the doorway. Perhaps the man at the terrace door was a servant coming to clean the dishes from their card game, and left when he saw the room was occupied. The lieutenant considered all of this for a moment and then told the baron, "Forgive me, Lord Baric. I did seduce one of your young ladies and convinced her to meet me, but I thought she was a

274

willing participant. Had you and your party arrived ten minutes later, you may have found me in an even more delicate position. I will indeed leave early in the morning, but if you could meet with me before my departure, perhaps we could discuss how to resolve Lord Marquis' opinion of me."

Mauro shook off the headache now growing over his temples. "All right, yes; I will meet with you. I am not sure if Lord Marquis is such an early riser, but I will knock on your door at sunrise. A bit of sleep usually helps clarify fact from fiction, anyway. I bid you goodnight, Lieutenant," he said somberly.

Mauro left the candleholder in the room and went back out into the dimly lit hallway. He could see a faint light glowing under Ruby's door and another under Caterina and Isabella's shared room. His own room was dark. He would go find his wife downstairs and learn what had happened here tonight.

Fabian was sitting on the chair in the foyer near the bottom of the stairs. Mauro paused when he saw him, and then continued walking past. "May I explain?" Fabian pleaded. He rose from his seat and caught up to Mauro, opening the door to the great hall. "Mauro, talk to me," he implored.

Mauro paused and turned to Fabian. "Yes, we will talk," he said calmly, with a cold glare the Baric men had perfected in their green eyes. "We have a lot to talk about. First, I will hear from my wife, and then I will hear from you. The stories had better match."

Mauro turned to go through the door and Fabian caught his arm, challenging him. "She had nothing to do with it."

"I believe she did. And you already admitted you did." Mauro spoke in a whisper now, but he was ready to burst with anger. "Do not ever put me in a situation like that again, Fabian."

"No. I never will, Mauro. You can be sure of that." He released his challenge and Mauro's sleeve.

Fabian followed him into the great hall, but stayed by the entrance. It was well past midnight, and the guests were beginning to leave for their sleeping quarters. The band would play until the baron released them, and several young couples were still dancing and laughing in the center of the room. Mauro spotted his wife among those on the dance floor, enjoying a slow dance with Baron Raneri. Mauro stepped in front of the nobleman and said politely, "I am sorry to interrupt your dance, Lord Raneri, but my wife is needed urgently in the other room. Will you please excuse her?"

"Why yes, of course, Lord Baric. Thank you, Lady Baric, for the dance," the baron told her and bowed politely. Mauro took her firmly by the arm and walked her away.

"What am I needed for, Mauro?" she asked him lightly.

He did not answer her, but picked up his pace and walked her toward the servants' entrance and out of the great hall. "Ouch, you are hurting my arm. What is it?" she asked anxiously.

Mauro did not let loose of his grip until they were in the corridor to the kitchen and had stopped along the wall. He raised his free arm and moved a latch; the wall moved. He slid it a few feet, pushed Resi inside, and closed the panel behind him.

Fabian had watched the baron retrieve his wife and pull her along in the direction of the kitchen. He was sure Mauro would not hurt her, but he decided he would intervene and face Mauro's full wrath himself. He opened the door to the corridor connecting the kitchen to the great hall, but it was empty. He walked to the end and into the kitchen. "Where is the baron?" he asked one of the remaining serving maids.

"The baron has not come in here, my lord," she answered with a small curtsy. Fabian walked out the back kitchen door and along the path outside to search for them.

~ * ~

"What is this place?" Resi asked after he had shut the door. It took a moment for her eyes to adjust to the thin light coming in through the small holes in the wall. Mauro released her arm finally, and she instinctively walked over to one of the peepholes and peered through. The view was into the great hall. She could see Davor dancing with a young guest and Lady Eleonora talking with Baron Raneri on the settee. She looked back into the dark and saw Mauro in the shadows, almost forgetting he had brought her there. "Why are we in here?"

"It was the quickest place to take you to be alone. I need some quiet, and I need for you to tell me what you have done." He slid down the wall and sat on the floor, his head bent between his legs.

"Are you drunk, Mauro?"

He looked up at her with a flash of anger, and she immediately regretted asking. He knew what she had done, and she knew she was in trouble for it. She went to his side and eased down onto the floor to sit next to him. Her full skirt filled the entire width of the long, secret corridor that ran the length of the great hall.

"Is it ruined?" she simply asked.

"Ruined? I have no idea," he barely whispered.

He was angry at her, but was drawn to touch her. He took her hand in his as they sat there together. He finally told her, "All I know is, the lieutenant does not think I know what is going on in my own house tonight, and he is right. My wife, my best friend, and two silly women from Venice added a virgin to my bet tonight." He let her hand drop to her side again. "How could you plot something this dangerous?"

Resi was suddenly numb. Dangerous was not a word anyone had spoken of. But she wanted to know, "Did it work, Mauro?"

He moaned softly in disbelief that she really had been involved. He turned to her and said, "I do not know if it worked, but if it had not, then everything could have been ruined. How dare you do this behind my back, Resi? An hour ago I was drunk and enjoying a wonderful evening with my wife and friends. And now my head is splitting, and I have to iron out the remnants of some courtly trap."

He sat brooding in silence until he became aware of the soft sobbing noise next to him. He stood up, offered her his hand, and pulled Resi up to him. Mauro took her in his arms and held her for a long moment as she continued to shake in her effort to suppress her tears.

"I was angry at you, Resi, but I am not any longer." She let the tears come freely now, and he rubbed her back gently to soothe her. "I know you had good intentions. You will also be happy to know that your mad scheme may have actually worked."

She looked up at him and tried to dry her eyes with the back of her hand. He took the lace of his sleeves and wiped the streaks of tears off her wet cheeks. "They told me that this could not fail," she said. "Well, it could fail, but there would be no harm done if it did. Ruby was never going to go into the room. The ladies figured if you didn't catch him waiting indecently, then at least they had fed him so much brandy that he would have passed out and fallen asleep while waiting. He would not have been caught, but he would not have known what we had plotted, either."

Mauro listened to her explanation. There was one part left out. "How did Fabian get involved?" he asked.

"He wasn't involved until just a few hours ago. Lady Isabella needed his help to get you and a few witnesses to the right room at the right time. Don't be upset at him, Mauro. He was against it at first, but he eventually went along with it, because he saw a chance that it would work."

They could hear the music repeat another favorite dance song. "I should put the musicians out of their misery. They are paid to play until I tell them to stop." Mauro rubbed his temples. "Are you as tired as I am, Terese? Shall we go end this ball?"

"I could go to sleep right here, if I had space to lie down. Where have you taken me?"

Mauro smiled for the first time since Fabian told him to trust his plan. "This was one of my favorite rooms to play in as a boy. Jero and I would spy on people from here. Old Grandfather Fredrik had this false wall built into the great room."

"What is its purpose?" Resi asked.

"It was either for his servants to keep out of the way, but to know when to bring in the next course. Or, what we decided long ago was that grandfather used it himself to spy on his guests. The holes are placed near the sconces and are not noticeable from the inside wall, unless you already know that they are there."

Resi walked along the wall and peeked out the various holes again, which gave different views of the great hall. "Do the servants still use this room?"

"No, I am not sure who might know about the false door, except maybe Nela. She has been here the longest. The trick, though, is to leave without anyone noticing you coming out." He took her hand. "Come; let me have a listen at the door first for footsteps along the corridor."

They both paused and listened. Resi felt a surge of excitement, like she was playing a hiding game with a childhood friend. He turned to her; excitement also sparkled in his tired eyes. "I think it is clear." He showed her where the door latch was and opened it. They peeked around the corner, quickly walked out of their hiding place, and latched the door again.

"I do like playing with boys. They get into such trouble," she declared.

"Tonight the girls are the ones who made the trouble," he could say without anger in his voice this time.

They lingered a moment in the empty hallway. Mauro could not resist his spirited playmate, and he leaned down to kiss her. He pulled her to him, his headache forgotten as a new ache came over him, but his tall wig and her layered skirts kept him from pressing more closely. He released her with a tired sigh. "I really want to play some more, but I think here is not the place. Come, let us say goodnight to our guests and continue this upstairs."

Chapter 41

Mauro quietly shut the door of their sun-lit chamber and saw his wife kneeling, crouched on their bed with her arms stretched out low over her head in front of her. He watched her in amusement for a moment and then broke the silence. "Mecca is in that direction, if you have converted to Islam."

She sat up suddenly and looked over her shoulder at him. "Mauro, you startled me."

"I did not expect to find you awake. I wanted to crawl back into bed with you."

He walked across the room and sat next to her on the bed. She hunched over her tucked knees again and stretched with a groan. "What are you doing?" he wanted to know.

She lifted her head and explained, "I woke up because my back was hurting me. I am trying to get some relief, and this seems to be helping."

Mauro rubbed the small of her back as she remained crouched on the bedcovers with her bottom pointed toward him. "Do you think it is the baby? You were on your feet for too long last night."

"No, I think it was the heeled shoes from last night. I should have worn my flat slippers." She moaned as he rubbed the sore knots in her lower back. "I cannot lie on my stomach any longer, either. I have grown too big."

Mauro laughed. "You are barely showing in your clothing. Wait until you are as round as the constable's wife. Has she had her baby yet?"

"We saw her not too long ago. She still has a little time to wait, but they have her in confinement. I do not want to get that big, Mauro. She was so miserable."

"You saw her recently?" Mauro asked, knowing already that she had.

Resi remembered she had not gotten permission to visit Elizabeta Radic, and she had taken Alberto and Geoff from their duties to escort her. "Maybe not so recently," she tried to cover for her misstep.

Mauro frowned at her, disappointed she had chosen not to tell him the truth. Alberto had already told him that same evening about their outing. She had followed his rule that she and her companions were to be escorted by at least two Baric men, but he must not have made it clear the men were to be soldiers. This discussion could wait for a different morning.

"Here, Terese, come stand in front of me and I will knead this out for you." He had strong hands, but gently massaged her back and hips, and then down her legs. It felt heavenly to her.

"I suppose you will go talk to the lieutenant now," she said, relaxing under his touch as she stood in front of him sitting on the bed.

"I have already talked to him. We had an early breakfast together in my study, and we have come to an agreement," Mauro explained, giving nothing away.

"Oh? He was already up?" She looked out the window at the sun just coming over the top of the mountain to the east. "And you have already finished breakfast with him?"

Mauro massaged her shoulders. "Soldiering does that to you—you can no longer sleep into the morning. That does not seem to affect anyone else in this house. Only the servants are moving about. The rest of our houseguests seem to be asleep."

"You said you came to an agreement. Was it to your liking?" She should have been nervous to hear the reply, but Mauro's massaging hands were too comforting.

He turned her around and sat her on his knee. She put her arms around his shoulders to listen to his answer. Mauro tried to keep a straight face, but she was too irresistibly sweet to tease for long.

"Yes, Resi, it is very much in my favor. D'Alessandro decided I could not have been plotting against him. He said the whole seduction with Ruby was a misunderstanding on his part, and he does not blame her for not showing up with us mingling in the foyer."

Resi leaned into him to embrace him closely. She was beyond relieved it had succeeded. Mauro stroked her hair as she rested her head on his chest. "He wants me to protect his reputation with Baron Marquis," Mauro continued to say.

Resi was puzzled. "Was Lord Marquis so shocked that he would rendezvous with a young lady at the party?"

Mauro explained, "I did not tell you, but I think Fabian arranged to have Davor come check the terrace door in the sitting room. He stuck his head in at an inopportune time for the lieutenant, and it looked as though the lieutenant was waiting for Davor, not for Ruby."

"Is that bad?" Resi innocently asked, not making the connection that Davor had been mistaken for a male lover.

"Davor wore a red jacket, the same color as D'Alessandro's escorts. A Naval commander might have a reason to be meeting one of them, but not in the dark with his breeches down."

"Oh, I see," she agreed with a laugh.

"Baron Marquis is friendly with D'Alessandro's commanding admiral. At my request, a report could be filed with the admiral regarding the lieutenant's conduct."

"So, to protect his good name and reputation, you won't file a report?"

"That was our main discussion over breakfast before he left. He was here on official navy business, not just for pleasure. I told him I should follow protocol and have this incident in the sitting room reviewed in Venice. Or, I could forget the entire misunderstanding, and he instead could file new documents with Venice exonerating me of all my charges. He agreed with the latter."

She looked up into his gleaming eyes and was finally convinced he was happy. "That is the best you could have hoped for. You will get your ship back."

"Yes, the lieutenant will not be bothering my ship again. I have convinced him that my diverting a little salt and skins is not worth the Venetian Navy's trouble. We will see if he keeps his word, but that is what we finally shook hands on. It is more than I could have hoped for."

"Oh, Mauro. I am so happy for you."

Mauro could not hide his relief, either. "I did agree to send a different sort of report. I will talk with Baron Marquis later at lunch and ask if we might have a glowing account of his representation sent to Venice instead. Perhaps D'Alessandro will get a promotion and be moved to another part of the Empire." Mauro moved Resi from his lap to sit instead on the bed next to him. He began to remove his shoes and stockings. "There is paperwork that must be signed, so I will have to go to his office myself."

She wrapped the bedcovers around her. She was still in her thin nightshift, and realized she was cold without his warm touch. "When will you go?" she asked when she was settled in again.

"I will leave tomorrow. I do not want to give the lieutenant time to change his mind. But you will come with me, like I promised you. We can make it a true outing and stay at a small inn on the seashore. Would you like that?"

She smiled at him as he unbuttoned his shirt. "I would like that very much. I can see the Adriatic from here, but have not been in its waters the entire year. How long can we stay?" She watched him remove his shirt and breeches. He laid them over the chair for later.

"A few days perhaps. It will be nice to be alone with you, Resi." He took the covers she had wrapped around her and spread them back over the bed. She crawled to one side, and he followed her, covering them both with the blanket. He pulled her close to him and settled into the pillows.

"Mauro, I am wide awake now and don't want to stiffen up again after your wonderful massage," she whispered. "Do you plan to just sleep now?"

"In my mind, I would like to do more than just sleep, Resi, but I am bone-tired. The house will be quiet for a while, and I am going to shut my eyes for a few minutes. Verica can bring you your breakfast. You will not disturb me if you eat in here."

She slid out of bed, leaving the blankets unmoved to preserve her warmth for him. She contemplated their outing as she put on her dressing robe. She leaned over him in bed and asked, "But what about my brother?"

"What about him?" Mauro quietly answered. He had already shut his eyes and sleep was quickly taking him.

"What if he arrives and I am not here?" Resi protested loudly enough to wake him to answer.

He rolled over onto his side and cracked open one eye. "I have scouts who watch our borders, Resi," he explained quietly. "They will know when your brother and his company are on our land, and I will have word sent to us at the seaside. It is only half a day's ride. We will leave tomorrow morning, just you and me." That was the last thing he remembered telling her.

Chapter 42

Resi checked on Ruby after her quiet breakfast beside her sleeping husband. Ruby was awake, but in bed wallowing in her misplaced misery. She did not look up when Resi entered the room and went to her side. Ruby's hair was still pinned with Resi's precious combs and her rouge had smeared off onto her pillows. "What is the matter, Ruby? Are you ill?"

"What am I to do, Resi? I shall never live it down," Ruby moaned. "I danced with the lieutenant like a wanton woman for the entire castle to watch. Jero will never forgive me for rejecting his invitation and dancing with the lieutenant instead. All my chances here are ruined. I might as well go home tomorrow." Ruby lay on her stomach, clutching a small pillow, and sobbed pitifully.

"Do not fret, Ruby. It is already forgotten." Resi stroked her hair. "Why don't you go soak for a while in the bathhouse? You will feel much better afterward."

Ruby stopped crying long enough to whimper, "I would have to pass too many people in the halls. I cannot face their judgment of me."

Resi took the small combs from her tangled hair and let the locks fall. She found Ruby's brush on the bedside table and began to smooth the messy curls. "There is nothing to judge and no need to hide. From what I saw, you and the lieutenant looked like any other couple on the dance floor." Resi wanted to believe her own words. She had been watching closely because Ruby was her friend, but had anyone else really noticed? No, they would not have, she decided.

"You don't think Jero noticed me dancing too closely with him?" Ruby sniffled.

Resi finished brushing out the knots in her hair and went to wet a towel in the basin to wipe the pink stains from Ruby's cheeks. "You said he left the room, right? So he could not have even seen your dance with the lieutenant. By that time of the night, most of the young couples were dancing very closely and were only paying attention to their own partner. Sit up now, Ruby dear, and I will plait your hair."

Ruby did as she was told, and Resi hummed an upbeat song softly to her friend while she fixed her long, auburn locks into a tidy, single braid again. "I will send for some water so you can freshen up and get dressed. You should come down to lunch in the garden," Resi said.

"I will get dressed, but I am not hungry."

Resi accepted the small victory just to get her out of bed. "I will ask the kitchen maids to bring you a tray, Ruby. You need to eat something today. I am going to talk to the ladies now. I will see you later."

Resi first went down the hall and carefully opened the door to her own room. Mauro was still napping. He had restlessly pushed the covers aside in his sleep and was immodestly stretched out across their bed. She pulled the covers up again and tucked the blankets around his bare torso. She had never seen him in bed during the day. He looked peaceful, though, like a small boy sound asleep. She leaned over and kissed his cheek before leaving her room again.

At the other end of the hall she heard chattering through the solid door of Caterina and Isabella's room. She knocked and waited for an answer. Caterina opened it and said, "Oh, thank goodness it is only you, Lady Terese." She motioned for her to enter, and then shut the door behind her.

Both ladies were dressed for the day, but their floor was still littered with their scattered gowns and shoes from last night. Their empty breakfast dishes were stacked on their table. "Let me call for the maids, Lady Caterina. Why don't you two come down for lunch while they arrange your chamber?"

"No, we are quite useless company today, Lady Terese," Isabella told her. "Tell us, did the plan work? We are overwhelmed with curiosity waiting here. What happened after we left the ball?"

Resi was embarrassed at her oversight. "Oh, dear ladies, I am sorry that I did not come to you earlier. Of course you have not heard the good news. It was all a success, thanks to you. The lieutenant did not suspect he was set up, and he apologized to my husband for his indiscretion last night with Ruby. My husband is taking me with him in the morning to arrange the release of his ship. It all ended quite perfectly," Resi reported to the happy women.

"Oh, well, I am relieved then," Caterina told her. She plopped down on the cushioned chair and opened her fan to stir the stale air around her.

"As am I," Isabella agreed happily. "And what did Mauritius say to you, Lady Terese? Was he intolerably angry? I can imagine he was not pleased that this went on in secret."

"You are right. He was not pleased at all. But he did give me a chance to explain it to him. You had the Barics' interest at heart in your plan. He knows that now. He forgave me quickly, and I am sure he will forgive you, too." She smiled broadly at the ladies.

284

"Have you seen Fabian this morning?" Isabella asked apprehensively. "If he is downstairs, I should like to talk to him. He may not forgive me so readily."

"I have been with Ruby most of the morning and have not been downstairs myself. She is not well today after the strain of it all last night. She will come to realize that nobody has a poor opinion of her."

Caterina and Isabella looked worriedly at each other. "We did put her in a difficult role," Caterina admitted.

Isabella declared, "She played it beautifully, though; exactly as we asked her to. No one will fault her for that. Perhaps we should go talk to her."

"I think she will come down for dinner, and we can all have a good laugh then," Resi said hopefully. "The other guests are still in their chambers, but Davor just told me they are setting the tables outside for lunch. Would you like to come with me outside and greet the others before they leave for home? I am certain they have no idea what took place with the lieutenant. They would enjoy visiting with you at lunch."

"We should worry no more about a scandal. Talking with your guest about other topics will surely clear our minds of this," Caterina agreed. She was hungry and was ready to join the baroness.

"I would like to talk to Fabian and Mauritius in private first and not face their anger in a public setting. They will surely be with the others at lunch. I think it is best we take lunch in our chamber," Isabella said, and Caterina sat back down again.

"Can you tell your husband we will be in our room when he has a moment for us, Lady Terese?" Caterina added.

Resi nodded with a sympathetic smile. "I will find Natalija for you now and come again this afternoon. It will all be fine, ladies. Mauro will talk to you later when the other guests have gone. He is very fair, and I am sure he has already forgiven you," Resi assured them. With her friends eating alone in their room, she decided she would keep Ruby company and would take her meal with her.

~ * ~

The room was bright with the midday sun shining in through the unshuttered windows. Mauro opened his eyes and tried to focus. He was alone in his bed, sweating under the too heavy covers despite his nakedness. It took him a moment to clear his groggy memory of why he was in bed so late. He slid his legs out of his cocoon of blankets and looked around for his clothes. The room had already been cleaned, and his clothes from the morning had been tidily put away. Had he slept through all of that?

He went to his wardrobe chest and took out the breeches folded on top. He hoped he had not missed the whole day. He opened the door, and Davor was waiting outside where Mauro had expected to find him. He said nothing to his valet and walked back into his room, leaving the door open for Davor. His servant followed him inside and shut the door.

"How long have I slept?" Mauro asked. He sat back down on the bed to contemplate his plans for the day.

"Most of the morning, sir. The kitchen girls are laying out the lunch buffet shortly. The maids have not finished cleaning the great hall, so Nestor told them to arrange some tables in the shade of the garden, if that is to your liking?"

It did not matter to Mauro where lunch was served, but he answered, "Yes, of course. It will already be hot outside. Tell me, Davor, who has already gone home?"

Davor stood by the closed door with his hands crossed behind his back. He looked at the baron through his droopy, blue eyes. Davor had been up since dawn. He had served breakfast to the baron and the lieutenant, despite his lack of sleep and his throbbing hangover from the festivities last night. Since breakfast, he had been standing by the chamber door watching the goings-on in the corridor, like the baron had asked him to do before he went back to bed.

"No one has left, my lord. Just the naval officer you breakfasted with this morning. The Leopolds just went downstairs a few moments ago, as have Baron and Baroness Raneri. Baroness Baric is with Lady Ruby in her chamber. Lord and Lady Marquis are most likely awake, because Baroness Marquis' maid has already come and gone from their room. The Carrera ladies have not come out of their chamber. Natalija has just gone down to arrange to have their meal brought to their room on a tray."

Mauro listened carefully to Davor's report. He thought he had been a poor host for missing the morning, but it seemed his absence had not been noticed. "Then I have woken right on time," Mauro found himself telling his valet. Davor suppressed his smile.

"May I help you dress this morning? I can have some hot water sent up." Davor did not wait for the baron's reply and opened his garment trunk.

Mauro went to the grooming table. "I will use the rest of the water that is here." Mauro looked at the clothes being laid out. "Choose something appropriate for entertaining. I will spend the day here at the manor house with the remaining guests." Davor nodded cheerfully.

Mauro had a wardrobe full of finery, but rarely found the occasion to wear a complete outfit like the one Davor assembled that morning. Most summer days Mauro worked on horseback with his soldiers, so he wore a practical doublet, a loose linen shirt, and broadcloth or deerskin breeches that were sturdy and comfortable for riding in the summer heat.

The thick-walled, stone manor house remained reasonably cool despite the hot sun shining on it, so the baron could wear a more formal ensemble indoors. Today Davor picked out a blue Venetian silk waistcoat to wear under a cream-colored jacket, delicately embroidered with gold and blue thread to match the golden fabric of the breeches Mauro was already wearing. The finely woven cotton shirt Davor set out had a high collar to accommodate his lace cravat. Mauro was glad to not have to bother with the selection himself. Mauro hastily washed with the cold water and, with his valet's help, was dressed and downstairs for lunch a quarter hour later.

The last dozen of his party guests were seated under the shade of his mother's grape arbor, just outside the small terrace steps. It was cool and quiet in this corner of the garden. Mauro had never sat here as the baron. He found it quite pleasant for entertaining. He thought of all the other pleasures of his own house that he had not yet enjoyed.

He bowed a gracious hello to the group. "Please, gentlemen, do not get up on my account," he said to the men moving in their chairs to stand to greet him. He took a seat at the table with Lord Marquis and his wife. They were dressed in comfortable traveling clothes, and Mauro expected they would not linger long after their meal. The Marquis' landholding was quite far south, three neighbors beyond the Leopold's.

After polite conversation about their restful sleep and the good weather, Mauro told his guest, "I wanted to have a quick word with you in private before you left, Lord Marquis; perhaps in my study after lunch. I think Lord Leopold might join us, as well," Mauro said casually.

"Yes, Lord Baric. I was expecting you would want to discuss a few things after the revelations from last night." Lord Marquis knew better than to discuss such delicate matters in front of the other guests, so did not ask any further questions of Mauro.

"Lady Eleonora was just telling us your mother designed this lovely part of your garden, Lord Baric. What a most remarkable talent she had. I am sure you miss your mother very much," Lady Marquis said sympathetically.

"Yes, she was quite remarkable," Mauro agreed cordially, knowing Baroness Marquis was being polite to offer a compliment to his mother. Lady Johanna did not have many close friends among their neighbors, so it was an uncomfortable conversation point, but one that was expected from mannered aristocrats.

Mauro was not good at small talk and pleasantries with noblewomen, and he wished he had sought out Resi to join him for lunch with the houseguests before coming down. She would be consoling her friend, of course. He was glad, though, to have a bit of time to think about what had happened last night, and especially what he would say to Ruby, Caterina, and Isabella.

~ * ~

Mauro and the two barons met in his study after their leisurely meal in the garden, and he told them now about his meeting with D'Alessandro earlier that morning.

"I believe the lieutenant was quite inebriated," Lord Leopold declared. "Why else would he have been in such a situation?"

"Yes, but the man should have some self-control. It does not sit well with me, knowing he has charge of the middle fleet. I still think this should be reported," Lord Marquis insisted.

"D'Alessandro seemed quite regretful this morning. He feels he was not representing the Venetian Navy after the earlier meeting was adjourned, and was just letting loose a little. Maybe too loose for respectability, but I feel no lasting wrong has been done to me or my household. I accepted his apology and agreed to forget the entire encounter in the sitting room," Mauro told the two noblemen.

"Well, Lord Baric, if you can forget the indiscretion in your own house, then who am I to hold a grudge? Very well, I will not discuss this with the admiral," Lord Marquis agreed.

Mauro poured a glass of brandy for each man and glanced out the window as he set the bottle down. Fabian was riding through the gate toward the stables. Where had he been this morning already? Mauro wondered. He shook off his concern and turned back to his guests with a polite smile to match their own.

"I raise my glass to you, Lord Baric, for hosting a very pleasurable and successful ball. My wife and daughters could not stop talking about how much they enjoyed the evening," Lord Marquis declared. "Lord Leopold, I am glad we had a chance to discuss our mutual concerns. I will visit you in a week's time to finalize our agreement." The elder baron set his glass down and went to the door to leave. "The drivers should be packed by now, and we will need to be on our way if we are to make it to our next lodging before dark." Mauro opened the door for the baron, and they bid him a safe journey home.

He shut the door and the two old friends took their places again at the table. "Well, Neven, I shall go tomorrow to take my ship back. The lieutenant should not be bothering me again in the near future. I appreciate your discretion to not mention my 'crimes against the Empire' to Lord Marquis."

"I know it was a delicate situation, Mauritius, but I am pleased you have reached a compromise. I had a feeling that there was more going on last night than I personally witnessed, but I will not ask."

"Thank you, Neven. Perhaps next time we meet, I will tell you the whole story and we can have a good laugh over it." Mauro finished his drink and said, "I appreciate your help in this success, especially your mother's assistance with the ball. Are you leaving soon? You are welcome to stay on."

"I am afraid we must go back today, but we are in no hurry. It will take another hour or so for the grooms to pack all of the decorations again that my mother sent ahead."

"If you do not mind me leaving you to your organizing, Neven, I have an urgent errand I must attend to. I will be back to see you off."

"Take your time. I will leave you to your affairs." He set his empty glass down, and the two walked out together. Lord Leopold went up the stairs, and Mauro went out the front door to the tower.

~ * ~

Lunch was long over in the common room of the Keep. Those soldiers who were not specifically assigned gate duty had been given the day free. While the party went on into the night for the gentry in the great hall, Mauro had arranged several casks of ale and wine to be tapped for the soldiers and visiting servants. Most of the baron's men were sleeping off the celebration, and the communal hall was empty and quiet. Mauro made his way directly upstairs to Fabian's chamber. The door was closed. He knocked and entered without waiting for an answer.

Fabian's room was one of the largest of the officer's chambers. It was along the west wall of the second floor and had a full view of the Adriatic. The heavy shutters were open and the afternoon light shone in on the carpeted, stone floor. Fabian had furnished the room himself. It was not decorated grandly like his accommodations at his family's villa, but it was stylish for a bachelor. Fabian was a tall man and had brought in a large, canopy bed for his comfort. The Keep's temperature was cool in both the summer and in winter, and his curtained bed had billowy blankets and feather pillows. His own collection of the weapons he used was hung on the wall next to his armoire and storage chests.

Fabian was at his ornate writing desk when Mauro entered. The carved legs were painted and gilded in the renaissance style, and the smooth writing top trimmed with inlaid squares of mother of pearl. He sat leaning over his quill and parchment in front of him. There was a neat stack of scrolls in the top compartment of the desk, and other folded, once-sealed papers arranged below them. Mauro noticed whatever Fabian was writing had filled most of the page already. Fabian had a close relationship with his father despite their distance, and Mauro imagined it was a letter to Roberto Carrera. Now that the war treaty had been signed, Roberto had commissioned his son to observe and report on the regional politics of the outer Venetian Empire.

Fabian set his quill down and put the parchment to the side when he noticed his friend at the door. "I see you have come without your sword, Mauro. So have you forgiven me?"

Mauro shut the door and sat down on one of the two wooden chairs at the small table across from his desk. He gave Fabian a stern look, which Fabian accepted as deserving. "You are lucky I did not have one last night, old friend."

"I did not expect you to understand at the time, but I thought ignorance would work to your advantage. I know you, Mauritius. You think better under pressure. I knew you would say the right thing, and it would be believable." Fabian sat up in his chair and waited for Mauro to have his say.

"You should have told me what you were planning with the girls. It was quite a shock to find the lieutenant on my couch with his pants down waiting for Ruby. I will not get that image out of my head soon enough." Mauro raised his brows in emphasis.

The tension was broken, and Fabian laughed. "Well, D'Alessandro is the eager type Isabella expected him to be. Did Davor make his entrance all right?"

"That was quick thinking on your part to arrange that. Lord Marquis was already appalled our lieutenant had planned a rendezvous in my sitting room, but to be meeting a man was shocking to the good baron."

"I know from experience that morality is graded differently to different gentlemen. I had to bet Davor's appearance would not be approved of by your witnesses."

"Lord Marquis brought two unmarried daughters to the party. I think you would have been safe without Davor's entrance, but it was a nice touch."

Fabian leaned back in his chair and looked at his friend with a smile. "So, if you have not come to challenge me to a duel or kick me out of your castle, am I to hope you have brought good news? What was the final word with your friend, the lieutenant?"

Mauro could not keep the smile from his face any longer. "It is good. I am to get my ship in two days. Tomorrow I will take my wife along with me for a much awaited outing together."

"She makes you happy. That is very plain to see now, Mauritius," Fabian told him lightly.

"I am surprised myself, but she does, Fabian." He had once told Fabian that he could never imagine an arranged marriage would be a happy one for him. He knew he had no clue what to expect when marrying his assigned wife, but he had not expected his prediction to be wrong.

They were quiet for a moment, and then a smile began to curl over Fabian's rugged face. "What are you smiling about?" Mauro asked skeptically.

Fabian began to chuckle as he thought of something Mauro had not. "You get your ship back. That is excellent. But have you thought beyond that?"

Mauro was puzzled. "What do you mean?"

"You will have to sail your ship back to your inlet."

"Yes, I will send word today to have my crew meet me at the naval dock on Monday. They will sail it back for me. What do you find so humorous in that?" Mauro asked confidently.

"The Venetian authorities make it all so tedious for the ship owners. Your crew can sail it back, but your captain does not have authority to sign the cargo manifests after D'Alessandro rejected everything. You will have to sail back with them for the ship to be allowed to unload here." Fabian held back his laughter again.

Mauro leaned back and glared at his friend. "You are not funny, Fabian. You think my problem is a joke? It is not," he warned.

"Here is an idea: your wife could sail back with the ship. She is a sea captain's daughter. I am sure she loves boats, unlike some people I know." Mauro gave him a cross look, but he added, "Or, I suppose your steward has the authority to register the shipment's arrival on your behalf."

"I was just going to suggest that," Mauro said, although he had not thought of it so quickly. "Yes, I will have Jero meet the ship, and then I can stay on a few extra days at the inn with my wife." Fabian nodded and smirked at his own cleverness.

"One thing, though," Mauro said, serious once again. "Terese's brother has been spotted only a few days out. Can you be here when he arrives, if I am not back?"

"Yes, I can be here. I was at the village this morning to arrange an escort for Isabella on the ferry, but there is not a chaperone available for four days. I am sending her back to Venice. I was thinking about escorting her myself tomorrow, but I do not want to spend that much time alone with her."

"Will you not wait for instructions from your father first? I know it has been a week, but you should get word any day." Mauro thought Fabian would regret sending her away, should the letter from Venice instruct otherwise.

"No, I won't wait. She tricked me, Mauro. Four more days is already too long. I was hoping there would be a coach to send her home tomorrow. It would serve her right to make her take the land route alone. The girl is like a poison in my life. I have not seen her for two years, and she has the same effect on me again."

Mauro rarely knew his friend to be so distraught. He had not realized the full situation. Mauro looked at him sympathetically. "I have not yet spoken to Isabella or your sister today. I suppose they are expecting some sort of punishment. I am not looking forward to confronting them. Frankly, I am no longer angry at them."

"You are more forgiving than I am, Mauritius."

"I was very angry last night. They are lucky that I did not come to their room after talking to D'Alessandro."

"And what did you say to your wife?"

Mauro assured him, "I did not lose my temper, if you are wondering what happened when I found her. You could have provoked me, but not Terese. I knew she had no idea of the real trouble this could have brought." Fabian nodded his agreement. "The good news is D'Alessandro did not suspect the girls set him up, and he took the blame for the sitting room incident. I think the best resolution is to let the girls off without a punishment. I will leave it up to you to resolve. Terese and I will be back on Wednesday."

Fabian decided, "I will keep the girls locked in their room if the mercenaries arrive before then. I do not want any more seductions taking place." In a lighter tone, he added, "I thought I would dine at the house with you tonight. We can talk to the girls together after dinner."

Mauro patted his friend on the shoulder and said, "I am no longer angry, but I need a few more days to decide what I will say to them about their prank. How about I have dinner with you and the others in the Keep instead?"

"Yes, let Isabella and Caterina think long and hard about the trouble they caused you," Fabian agreed. "I have a few letters to write and post before the day is done. I will see you at dinner."

Chapter 43

Mauro was at his desk writing when Resi came to his open study door. She called across the room, "May I interrupt you, Mauro?"

He looked up from his papers, smiling. "Hello, Resi. Come in. I have not seen you since this morning," he said cheerfully. "Where have you been hiding? The Leopolds are leaving in a few minutes, and they will want to say goodbye to you."

"I just talked with Lady Nikolina and Lady Eleonora upstairs. That is why I have come looking for you. Shall we go outside together?"

"Just let me seal this message and then I am ready." Mauro removed his signet ring and lit a flame to melt a dot of green sealing wax. He pressed the Baric seal into it on the folded paper.

"After we see the Leopolds off, Isabella and Caterina have asked to speak with you."

"Ah, yes. Well, I have decided I will wait until we return to speak to them," Mauro replied frankly.

"I don't understand. Until we return from what?" Resi asked him.

He rose from the chair behind his desk, took his fine jacket from the chairback, and put it on. He smiled at her and offered his arm to walk her out. "When we return from our outing tomorrow. I will speak to them when we are back," he clarified casually.

"But that is several days away, Mauro," she protested.

"I have many pressing matters to attend to before we leave in the morning, and I did not intend to talk to the ladies today," he stated firmly.

Resi was taken aback. She thought of her conversation with Jero in front of the wall of swords. "Is that how the Barics resolve a problem? Lock it away in a room?" Resi did not stop there. "Is that what they did to you, Mauro, leave you in your room until it suited them?" she concluded boldly.

Mauro shut the study room door and turned back to her. He lost his smile. "We will only be away three days."

"Is it fair to have them waiting in their chamber thinking that you are angry at them? Will three days be long enough for you, Mauro? How about a year?"

"That is enough!" He turned away from her and walked to the window, looking out at the carriage being loaded in the courtyard. "They made their choice to play their game, and I do not agree with how they went about it behind my back. The ladies may stay in my house, but I have nothing to say to them right now. I will speak to them when we return." Mauro turned to her and said, "That is my final decision."

Resi went to his side at the window. "I stood by, Mauro, while the lieutenant took my best friend's hand and held it to his sex so she would know how much he wanted her. Because of her loyalty to you, husband, she did not take her hand away and slap him on the face. For you and your ship, she swallowed her fear and told him to be ready for her."

After her biting words, there was real anger in Mauro's eyes. "Do not blame me for her misuse, Wife. I told you I was going to rescue Ruby from the lecher when I saw him holding her too closely. It was you who said I was to let her enjoy her dance. I would have protected her, if it had not been for you."

She lost her conviction with him looking at her so angrily. "Yes, I deceived you the same as the other ladies. You should leave me to rot in my chamber and go without me tomorrow." She willed herself not to cry when she told him, "Go alone, Mauro. I don't want to come any longer."

Mauro had not intended to begin an argument with her. She looked so pitiful, and his temper lost some of its heat. He took her in his arms and let out a deep sigh, holding her against him. "Why are you saying all of this? I want you to come with me tomorrow. I told you, I have forgiven you."

She stepped away from his warm embrace and answered, "They are truly sorry for what they did, and they want to explain everything. They want to explain *today*. They are our friends, Mauro. You cannot treat them this way. You have forgiven me, and you must forgive them." The tears were too hard to hold back now.

"I have forgiven you because you are my wife, not because we are friends. You want to protect your new friends, but you have not known them long—I have. I have good reason to wait to talk to them later. I do not want to explain it to you any further," he said, standing an arm's length away from his agitated mate.

His logic baffled her. "You say you have known them a long time, and still you do not call them your friends. You do not consider me your friend. I understand now, Husband. You have explained it all well enough."

"That is not what I said, and you know it. They are my friends, but that is irrelevant to my decision. You and I have something different, Resi. We are bound to each other now. That cannot be called a friendship. It is something bigger, set before God."

He had been in such a good mood earlier, and he wanted to have that feeling back. Mauro was ready to concede this victory to his wife. "I will talk to them today, when the guests leave. Does that make you happy?" he asked quietly.

"No, I am not happy," she cried.

Mauro was exasperated by her hasty reply. He had other obligations to attend to; the Leopolds were waiting for them outside. She walked away from him to sit at the long table, in her usual spot with her back to the door.

"It just came to me that I cannot go away now," she said with resolve. "I cannot enjoy myself knowing that Ruby is in her room too humiliated to come out. And the ladies are just waiting for the courier to tell them to go east or go west. Can we all not get away for a few days at the seaside?"

Mauro sat down across from her and thrummed his fingers on the table in frustration. "No," he decided, "now you are being impossible. I cannot escort four ladies by myself, and I won't." He stood and paced again, upset with his wife's new requirement. "I would need at least two more men for protection. No, we cannot all go, so put it out of your mind."

Resi crossed her arms stubbornly over her chest. "Then bring escorts."

"It is a small inn, and there may not be rooms for everyone. It was just planned for us two, Resi."

He contemplated her intently. Where had this willfulness come from? He did not realize that his wife was such an irrational creature. He could not understand why she was being so unreasonable.

"We don't need to stay at the inn. We can sleep on the beach, Mauro. That would be so romantic. We can fish and cook our dinner over a fire. I have not done that for ages." She wiped her wet eyes, feeling better that she had found a solution to the problem so easily.

Mauro was not convinced. "I want to leave tomorrow morning. You are making this too complicated. There is too much to pack and plan. It won't work, Resi."

"What is there to pack and plan? Alberto is readying the wagon for me to ride in already. Cook can put together a basket of supplies by tomorrow. It can be quickly organized," she argued.

He reached across the table to take her hand in his. "You do not understand. The ladies are Fabian's responsibility, and he will not allow it. He is going to send Isabella back to Venice on Thursday," he confided to her. "He is very angry at her for involving him and is not willing to forgive her right now."

Resi put her other hand on top of his and tried to explain. "Fabian has nothing to be angry at. Isabella tricked him, yes, but not to hurt him. She knew he was loyal to you and used that to persuade him to help her."

"Fabian feels he has a duty to keep them safe, and he wants the ladies near him until they are on their way again. He will not allow them to leave for three days." Mauro thought this would end the discussion.

"Then bring him with us." She released her hands from his on the table. "Or I will stay."

Mauro glared at her. Three days alone with his emotional wife no longer felt like a pleasurable outing to him. He shut his eyes and considered what she had asked. He opened them again and declared, "I will ask Fabian what he thinks on the matter. And Vilim can come as a second escort."

She dared to up the ante. "Why don't you ask Jero to escort us instead of Vilim?"

He leaned back in his chair and stared at his wife, a woman he realized he did not know well at all. "I need Jero here to receive the ship," he said sternly.

"Why is that?" she inquired. She was sincerely interested to know why Jero was needed.

"Either my steward or I must meet the authorities at our docks before the ship can be unloaded. The lieutenant will sign the responsibility for the cargo over to me, and then it must be inspected in case we have smuggled other goods back. There is a lot of paperwork to sign, and I need the ship emptied right away for the coming delivery."

"That is all quite aggravating for you to organize, I am sure." Resi tested him further, but Mauro said nothing more to her.

She walked across the room and thought about it a moment, then offered a solution. "Can't Jero sail with your ship from the naval harbor to Solgrad? Is that not what you would have done, had you not planned to stay with me at the seaside for a few more days?"

He did not intend to tell her that he never sailed with his own ships, but he did like her new suggestion. "Jero could do that, yes. But then I still need a third escort," Mauro argued. "Our intimate party is growing too large, Resi."

"We are just crossing into Lord Leopold's land, aren't we? Is it so dangerous for seasoned warriors like you and Fabian?" The words were not meant to be insulting, but they broke Mauro's fragile temper. She had interfered too much. He stood and walked around the table to the door.

Resi could not read his expression. It was his soldier's face. The one that calmed her yet worried her, because it was unpredictable. "Are you quite done now, because I am done with this conversation," he told her quietly. "I will follow your original advice. I will go alone, and you can stay in our room. I will bolt the door from the outside before I leave in the morning," he threatened.

After everything that had been said, he had proved he was pitiless and uncaring. "That is fine with me, Mauro," she replied angrily. She could not stand to be in the room with him another moment.

"Where are you going?" he asked sternly, when she suddenly opened the study door and walked out.

"To my sanctuary. I will see you when you get back," she turned to tell him.

"I will see you after dinner," he said in a normal tone again.

"I will not be coming in for dinner," she answered. She walked away toward the sitting room to go out the small terrace door, the shortest path to the bathhouse.

"You cannot stay in the bathhouse all night," he raised his voice to tell her.

"I can and I will," she shouted. "There is a bolt on the inside of the door, and I will use it." She was gone.

~ * ~

Mauro let her go. He had been warned that pregnant women were unpredictable. Her mood would lighten after she had a bath and time to think about how disrespectful she had been. He locked up his study and went to see the Leopold party off. Lord Raneri's group was also in the courtyard. His driver was readying the small carriage for the baron, his wife, and her lady's maid.

"It was an advantageous party, Lord Baric," Baron Raneri told him. "I will be hosting a council meeting next month at my castle to discuss the new policies coming from Venice, but perhaps I should make it a ball as well."

Mauro had managed to shake off the disappointing conclusion with his wife a few minutes ago and had become the jovial host again. "Why not? Either way, we shall be there, Lord Raneri."

Mauro then turned to the baroness. "It was my pleasure to finally meet you, Lady Raneri. I wish you a safe journey home," Mauro told her in his controlled, aristocrat manner.

Jero had come out into the courtyard a few minutes after Mauro to see the last guests off. When they had all departed, the two turned and walked the path together to the front door. "I have not seen any of the ladies this morning. Are they well?" Jero asked.

"I am not sure if well or unwell would explain their absence. It seems a bit of courtly theatrics took place behind my back last night, and they are waiting for me to hear their apologies." He was unable to hide his annoyance at how the situation had evolved further today.

Jero looked confused. "Apologies?"

"My wife conspired with the ladies yesterday to use Ruby as bait to tempt Lieutenant D'Alessandro to find himself in a most compromising situation that would force him to reverse the crimes against me," he coolly summarized while they made their way to the house.

"Oh. That does sound theatrical. That happened last night?" Jero recalled the scene he had witnessed on the dance floor.

Mauro thought about his explanation and began to chuckle. "Yes, it seems it did. The women are regretful over it and are in hiding until I forgive them."

Jero's expression changed, and he gave Mauro a curious look. "But did you just say the crimes were reversed? Have the charges been dropped, Mauro?"

"Yes, the lieutenant and I came to an agreement at breakfast."

"That is great news. You do not look happy about it."

They were at the door, and he stopped when he explained, "It is great news. And to celebrate, I wanted to take my wife on an outing to get my ship. I was to have the crew sail it into our harbor, and you would meet our captain to sign the cargo documents back in with the authorities here on Monday."

"Yes, I can do that," Jero said dutifully.

"But that is no longer the plan. You will accompany us on our outing." Mauro walked into the house.

Jero was not sure if he had heard correctly. He lingered a moment contemplating what it could mean, then hurried to catch up to Mauro. "Accompany you and Lady Terese? I would not want to impose, Mauro," Jero protested.

"No worries. My wife wants Ruby, Caterina, and Isabella to impose as well. With four women, I will need a few escorts. She has chosen you, Jero." They were in front of the grand staircase. Mauro watched the surprise form in Jero's eyes.

"Me?" Jero asked. "Do you not want to take a soldier with you instead? I would not make a good escort, Mauro."

Mauro crossed his arms defensively. "I happen to agree with you, but she thinks differently."

"If you are accusing me of something, Mauro, you are very wrong. I do not know why Lady Terese would want me to come with you, but . . ."

Mauro interrupted him, "Relax, Jero. I know her reasons, but I am glad you agree with me in her choice of escorts. This time I will follow my wife's request. Instead of meeting the ship in our port, you will sail with the crew and settle the paperwork directly when you arrive. Are you willing to do that?"

Mauro started up the stairs and Jero followed. "Go on the ship? Yes, that would be a rare treat for me." Jero had never been invited to sail on the Barics' cargo ship before.

"Good. I have some other things to attend to. Be ready to leave first thing in the morning. You will sail on Monday. The rest of us will stay on at the seaside another day or two."

Mauro left Jero in front of his chamber door and went into his own room to see if his wife had come back. Verica was sitting on the window seat; she stood and curtsied when she saw him.

"Where is the baroness, Verica?" Mauro inquired.

"She is in the bathhouse and won't open the door to let me come to her. I am worried for her, my lord. Do you think she is in distress?"

"Yes, she is in distress, but of her own making. We had an argument, Verica. She will come out when she is ready."

"But your lordship, dinner will be served shortly. Should I bring her meal to the bathhouse?"

"No. She can come to dinner if she is hungry. That will be all, Verica." She curtsied again and walked quickly out of the room before she began to cry at the cruel instructions the baron had imposed upon her.

Mauro sat down on the chair at his wife's grooming table. This was a fine mess he had made of the day. There was still clean water in her basin, and he splashed his face in it to revive himself. He knew he would have to follow through on Resi's request. He had already invited Jero. He would get Fabian to agree to come, and then he would need to talk to the other ladies. It would do him no good to delay any longer.

~*~

Mauro went in through the armory first. He looked over the weapons and shields neatly hung on pegs, and the oiled mail organized on their hooks. He would not need mail. He went to where he kept his sword case and took out two blades, their sheaths and leather belts. Jero would wear one and Mauro the second. He pulled out two muskets from the storage box, a pouch of balls, and a horn of powder. He told Henrik, the guard on duty in the armory, "I will be taking the wagon tomorrow. Alberto is already hitching it for me. Have these loaded under the seat, along with a pile of hay in the bed. And tell Alberto Jero will ride Janus. Have him ready my wife's gray mare in the morning, as well." The guard bowed and turned to go. "Wait." Mauro had a second thought. "Tell him to only bridle the mare. Have him put the saddle into the wagon bed."

"Yes, right away, Lord Baric," Henrik replied and went directly to carry out the tasks ordered.

From the armory, Mauro took the closest of the tower staircases and stopped on the first landing. The door was thick and solid, blocking out all light and sound. He pushed the heavy door open and released a bombardment of voices and the smell of roasting meat. It was a welcome assault to his senses.

The bustling common room was filled with soldiers sharing their evening meal. He went to the fire to help himself to a plate of the savory venison stew. The cooks had made it hearty with chunks of turnips, carrots, and pasta dumplings. Mauro noticed the kitchen maids had sent over wild cherry tarts for the men tonight after Davor had told them the baron would be eating his supper in the Keep.

He went to join Simeon and Vilim, who were sitting across from Eduard. Three of the people Mauro needed to talk to.

"Always glad to have you join us for a meal, Mauro," Eduard said with a chuckle when the baron approached. "The kitchen girls don't send over their best delicacies unless you are coming to dinner."

"You look like you eat your share of delicacies without the baron's company," Simeon joked. "A few more months of peace, and we will have to find a stronger horse to carry you."

"You have only seen me in times of war and famine. This is how God meant for me to be—well fed and thick in the middle." Eduard patted his bulging belly.

"No one will argue that, would you not agree, Simeon?" Vilim tempted Simeon to get the last word in.

"He made you thick in the middle alright, but thicker in the head, and that is God's truth," Simeon added with a laugh. Vilim laughed heartily with Simeon until Mauro gave both men a sharp look.

When the baron had first arrived, he had given Simeon charge of the gatehouse security and Eduard charge of the Keep. The two had not worked well together in the beginning, and at times had butted heads. Despite their differences, they had become good friends over the two years, and the bantering now was meant to be goodhearted.

Mauro put his platter down and sat next to Eduard at the table. "Speaking of peace," Mauro began in a serious tone, bringing his men to attention. "I have come to talk to you about your special duties this week. I will be leaving in the morning for a few days, and Fabian will be joining me. I have cleared up the dispute with the navy, and my ship is being released. I am going to the naval headquarters to claim it back."

Vilim had gone with Anton to negotiate with the authorities when the ship had first been seized. "Well, this is excellent news!" Vilim declared. "Congratulations! May I come along? I would love to see D'Alessandro's face when he is forced to return your cargo ship."

"You were my first choice, Vilim, but unfortunately my wife has other ideas." Mauro had expected Vilim's look of surprise. After Fabian and Stephan, Vilim was Mauro's most trustworthy officer and traveling companion. "We are turning this into a mixed outing, for both business and pleasure. My wife, the three ladies, Fabian, and Jero will be coming along."

"Jero? Why Jero?" Simeon asked, puzzled that a second soldier would not travel with them.

"Jero is needed to sail back with the crew and deal with the Venetian authorities. We are just going a few hours into Leopold's land. He has his own scouts, and I do not expect any trouble there." Mauro tried to sound confident as he repeated his wife's argument. The men nodded at each other and accepted the baron's reasoning.

"While you are away, you said there were special assignments?" Eduard reminded him between bites of his cherry dessert.

"Yes. No one is to leave the compound. There will be no training outside the walls, and no visits to the village," Mauro declared a bit too seriously, and the men become suddenly concerned.

"Are you locking down the castle? Do you have news of an invasion?" Simeon was the first to ask what they were all wondering.

"No, there is no trouble brewing on the borders. I want my full force to be seen here at the castle, though. My wife's brother and his band of mercenaries will be arriving while I am away. I would delay my departure in order to greet them myself, except I cannot risk the navy changing its mind."

The men began to grumble. Mauro had expected their protest. "The mercenaries will be our guests. My wife has invited them, and they will be welcomed by us to please her. But I want the message to be clear that within my walls, they will be watched."

"Is this a large company of mercenaries?" Eduard asked.

"No, Eduard, there will only be five of them. But they have a reputation of being volatile men. They have made an unfavorable impression on me in the past."

Eduard objected, "Why would you allow dangerous men into the walls as your guests?" Simeon and Vilim looked to Mauro for affirmation.

"My wife seems to think they are not so dangerous. She has only favorable things to say about the mercenaries, so for her sake, they will be treated well and given the best lodgings. But they will be housed with you in the Keep, not in the manor house."

The three men shifted uncomfortably in their seats. "Shall we send the scouts to find you when they cross into your land?" Vilim suggested.

"Yes, I will leave instructions in the morning how to find us. We will return right away if they arrive in the next few days. It may happen that they take a leisurely pace and not reach the castle in that time. I just want you to be prepared. Go about the regular training in the yard, but keep the men together." Mauro concluded his order and began to eat his meal.

The officers mumbled their agreements, and then the topic of conversation shifted to more interesting subjects of firearms and the new barmaid at the Green Goose. Mauro finished his dessert just as Fabian came down the stairs into the dining hall. Mauro excused himself from the table.

"Have you eaten?" Mauro asked Fabian, meeting him by the stairway.

"No, I am just now finished with my correspondence. I thought I would join your table."

"I am finished with my dinner. Get your food and we will talk over there in private." Mauro motioned to a smaller plank and barrel table normally used for cards. It was away from the other diners. Fabian did not question Mauro's reason and went to the fire to fill his platter. He returned to sit on the stool across from Mauro.

Fabian took a long drink from his mug of ale. "What happened to the happy Lord Baric I met this morning? Did bad news arrive in the course of the afternoon?" Fabian asked lightly, then bit into a chunk of bread.

Mauro held his mug of ale and looked down into it, pondering how to tell Fabian about the changes. "My wife is not coming with me tomorrow unless I take the other girls with us."

Fabian was about to eat a bite of his stew, but put his spoon down. "She wants my sister and Isabella to come with you? Is she daft?"

"I am wondering that myself. She has locked herself in her bathhouse," Mauro said with a chuckle, finding the words amusing, even if the reality of it was not.

Fabian was relieved it was only more marital problems and took his bite of food. "What did you do to make her do that?"

"I did not do anything. She wanted me to talk to the girls today and let them apologize to me. We argued, and I told her I would lock her in our chamber. She beat me to it and locked herself in her bathhouse."

"I like her more and more, Mauro, I really do." He stuffed his mouth full of dumplings, then gave Mauro a crooked smile.

Mauro became serious again. "Do not even start, Fabian. When I finish my story, you will not find this funny."

Fabian fixed his expression. "I am sorry. Please tell me the rest."

"Well, there is something that bothers me. During our argument she said some things about me that she could not have known. Am I such an open book to be read so easily?"

Fabian laughed loudly, and the officers at the other table turned toward them grinning, wondering what joke they had missed. "No, Mauro," Fabian confirmed, "you are a closed book with the cover tied shut. But some women have an unworldly perception about men."

Mauro drank the last of his ale and cracked a smile. "Unworldly perception? Are you calling my wife a witch?"

"Ha! That would be interesting for all of us," Fabian said. "You know I do not believe in witches; such a stupid explanation for all the complexities of the female sex. Your problem is that your wife is overeducated, and only you can be blamed for that."

"How can that be my fault? I have only known her a year," Mauro protested.

Fabian leaned in. "If what you told me is true, she has spent years alone with her books waiting for you to claim her. She is far too smart for you now. You should have married her four years earlier, when she came of age."

Mauro looked at his friend, deciding whether he was joking or not. "That is most unhelpful advice," Mauro said. "And what is my remedy today?"

"It is too late to get a simpler wife, so you will have to accept that she may be right sometimes. Maybe today is one of those times," Fabian told him.

"All right," Mauro agreed. "So let us say she is right today. Do you think I should take all of them with me to the seaside?"

"Sure, why not. But you cannot do that alone. You will need—"

A smile curled over Mauro's lips as Fabian became aware of his own part in this solution. "No," Fabian said. "I told you, I do not want to spend any more time with Isabella."

"You told me she is your responsibility. You will have to come." Mauro was now the one holding back his amusement.

"You, me, and who else? Vilim?" Fabian asked, beginning to consider the new assignment.

"I am taking Jero," Mauro quietly told him.

"Jero?" Fabian repeated more loudly than Mauro would have liked.

"Yes, my wife wants Jero," Mauro said with a defeated look. She would win on all points today.

Fabian looked troubled for the first time since their conversation had begun. Mauro knew what he would say, and he said it. "That is not a good sign. You realize, don't you, that she has spent more time with Jero than with you. Is there some romance going on there?" Fabian had been on both sides of adulterous love affairs and always suspected the worst of couples.

Mauro shook his head. "I had wondered the same once, but I do not think there is on either part. She is matching Jero to Ruby."

Fabian laughed loudly again. "This will be a marvelous outing. Your wife is not talking to you, I am not talking to Isabella, and shy Ruby will not be talking to timid Jero. Why don't we just stay here and save ourselves the misery?"

"Because it will not be miserable. It will be enjoyable, and we are leaving at first light." Mauro stood and concluded, "We will be back on Wednesday. Isabella can take the ferry with her escort to Venice on Thursday, as planned."

Fabian looked up and asked, "And will we all stay at the inn?"

"We will camp on the beach," Mauro answered hesitantly, waiting for Fabian's reaction.

"Ah, well, this *will* be an enjoyable outing." Fabian stood now and the two walked toward the stairway. "I do not think my sister has ever slept on a beach. She will be moaning about the sand in her toes, the bugs up her skirts, and worse things than that. This is the worst choice for her."

Mauro wanted Fabian to come willingly. "I know it is an undesirable situation for ladies, but let her moan. You are her brother, not her nursemaid."

"Will you talk to them tonight, then?"

"I will do that right now."

"Very well, Mauro. I suppose you will not give me peace unless I agree."

"I need your support in this."

Fabian patted him on his shoulder in acknowledgement. "If this is what you want, then I will see you at first light." Fabian walked up the stairs, and Mauro took them down.

Chapter 44

Mauro decided to talk to Ruby before the Venetian ladies. He expected Ruby would not try his patience like the others would. It was already dusk, and he hoped she had not gone to bed early. Mauro knocked on Ruby's door.

Ruby answered the door right away, still dressed in her daywear. "Lord Baric," she said with surprise. She had expected him earlier, but had given up on his visit today.

"May I have a word with you, Ruby? I wanted to talk to you in private," he said and shut the door. He motioned to her table, and they both sat down.

He had decided he would do the talking and keep it simple. Mauro and Ruby had never had a conversation without Resi's company, and it was obvious to Mauro that Ruby was still intimidated by the baron. He smiled at her. "I wanted to thank you for helping our cause last night. I hope you were not too upset by your part. You have not come out today, and the others have asked if you are well," Mauro told her in a kind voice. When she did not reply he suggested, "Perhaps you are not?"

"I felt a little unwell earlier, but I am better now," she answered. It was apparent she was trying to keep a smile on her face.

"Good." Mauro regarded her and decided how to continue. "I wanted to tell you something, Ruby."

"Yes."

"I want to grant you a favor," he said soothingly, like speaking to a child.

"Oh? That is very kind of you," she said quietly.

"If you could do something special tomorrow, what would you choose to do?"

The question surprised her, and she thought on it a moment. He knew, though, what answer to expect. "Well, I haven't been riding in a long while. I would choose that," she answered honestly.

He smiled at her again and she smiled back.

Mauro told her, "I am glad you chose that, because it fits very well with our plans. Tomorrow I am taking Resi to the seaside, and she wants you to come." He paused to wait for her response, but she just looked at him with astonishment. He continued, "I would like you to ride her horse instead of riding in the wagon." She finally managed an eager nod, and he explained,

"We are going to the Leopold's coastline. Can you ride for several hours without stopping?"

"Oh, yes. That is no problem. I won't hinder you on the journey," she assured him.

"I know it is short notice, but you will need to be packed and ready to leave in the yard just after sunrise. Do you think you can be ready?" Ruby was now on the edge of her seat, and she nodded that she could. "We will be camping on the beach for two or three nights, so you should pack for that."

"I don't know what to say. Thank you, Lord Baric. I will be ready at sunrise."

He patted her hand resting on the table, and then rose to leave. "Thank you, Ruby, for joining us. Good night." He shut the door behind him and looked to the end of the hallway. He hoped the next visit would be as easy.

The servants had lit the wall sconces, but he could still see a light under the crack of the door of his mother's old room. He felt an odd chill as he knocked. Isabella came to open it when he did not enter.

Isabella gave him an exasperated sigh and opened the door wide for him. "Mauritius, we have been waiting all day to talk to you. Do come in. I thought that was the maid knocking to help us retire for the night," Isabella told him as he followed her into the familiar room. It looked more colorful than he had remembered, and smelled of perfume and flowers. This was a pleasant change that gave him strength to finish his last task in the long day.

"I apologize for keeping you waiting. There have been a lot of people to attend to and guests to see off. I hope you can understand the delay," Mauro said formally.

"Oh, of course, Mauritius," Caterina said as she motioned to him to sit across from her on the empty chair. "We know there are many important duties that fill your day, especially after such a glamorous evening."

"That is, of course, what I am here to talk to you about," Mauro stated flatly.

He would let the women set the direction of the conversation. He knew it would be quicker that way. It would be futile to argue with them. Mauro sat down and waited. They did not disappoint him.

"You must think we are despicable, and you may be right, Mauritius," Isabella began mournfully.

"We had no right to interfere with your guest and your plans," Caterina told him humbly.

"Lady Terese told us you know what trick we played, and we are very sorry to have plotted this in secret," Isabella said with a pleading look on her pretty face.

"We were very wrong to do so, and we are very sorry," Caterina concluded with a sweet smile.

"You know Fabian had nothing to do with this until the moment I begged him to help me. He should not share the blame. It was our own idea. He is angry at me, and I am most distressed that I could not talk to him, too," Isabella said with her head bowed, wringing her hands.

"You must want to punish us, and we do not fault you if you do. It was most insolent of us. We are guests in your house, and it showed extreme disrespect to you," Caterina offered, nearly on the verge of false tears.

Isabella looked up with concern. "Yes, we were grievously wrong. How will you punish us, Mauritius?"

Their stares met. They'd had all day to invent their apologies. He wished he'd had his way and could have convinced his wife that the only way for the Venetian ladies to understand remorse was to be ignored for a while.

"I have thought about what you did and do not agree with your methods," Mauro began. "But the results were very beneficial, and for that I am grateful and thank you both." The women smiled and gracefully acknowledged his thanks with a nod of their prettily coiffed heads. "But you did step far over the line of mannered and respectful guests, and for that you should be punished. I will call in the maid when I leave, and she will help you pack."

Both their smiles fell from their rouged lips.

"You are to be ready at sunrise," he explained further. "You shall join us on a wagon ride to the seaside. We will camp under the stars on the beach and eat our meals from the fire for three days. We will bring no servants or assistance. You will enjoy it, ladies."

"This is a joke. Are you making a joke, Mauritius?" Isabella asked hopefully. Caterina looked stricken.

"It is no joke. That is the sentence I have chosen for your deeds last night. It is getting late, and you will still need to pack."

"You can be severe, Mauritius. Very well, we shall do our best to be ready," Caterina said.

He stood to leave. "You will do more than try, Caterina. You both are to be in the courtyard at first light, or you will be taken from your bed and shall travel in your sleeping garments and bring nothing else," he said in a purposely patronizing manner.

He had gotten their attention. Isabella was visibly shaken by the prospect. They both nodded tearfully, and Mauro left the room before he could no longer keep a straight face. That had gone better than expected.

As his last stop, he knocked on Verica's room and told her about the new circumstances for the visitors, as well as his wife. "Is her ladyship to stay the night in the bathhouse?" Verica dared to ask the baron. She was clearly concerned for her welfare, and he did not take offense at her direct question.

"She will be fine tonight, Verica. There is drinking water, a chamber pot, and plenty of linen sheets to wrap in."

Verica looked down, still not approving of the baron's treatment of her mistress. Mauro held up her chin to look at him and assured her, "I am not angry at the baroness, Verica, if that is what you are thinking. We were both being quite stubborn today, is all. Remember, she can let herself out at any time." He smiled kindly at her, and she could see he meant it.

Verica promised to be back early in the morning to pack a satchel with the baroness' personal effects needed for the trip, and then she went down the hallway to help the Venetians pack their bags.

Verica usually readied the room for bed, but he could see that Davor had been there as well. Mauro's travel saddlebag was near the door, and his riding clothes had been laid out for the morning. Satisfied that he had done all that was needed, he sat down on his bed and took off his shoes and stockings. He undressed completely and thought about his obstinate wife while he washed away the day's stress.

Feeling refreshed from the cool water and his comforting routine, he climbed into their big bed alone. He leaned over to her pillow and breathed her scent, missing her presence already. He noticed the sewing basket on her side table, and he reached over to get it. She may want to do her needlepoint while relaxing on the seashore. He got up and set it near his own bag, then slid under the cool bedcovers again.

Under the basket was the book that she had been reading this week, Shakespeare's collection of poems. He reached for it and looked at where the page marker lay. He brought the candle closer and read the marked poem called Sonnet CXVI. He skimmed the words. Is this what your mind is filled with, Terese Baric, he wondered after reading the love poem.

He held her book for a moment in contemplation, and then set it down to light the second candle in the holder. He said to the empty pillow next to him, "You are going to make this hard for me, aren't you?" He opened the book again, turned the page, and continued reading well into the night.

Chapter 45

Mauro pounded on the door for a second time. "Open the door, Resi!" He heard the bolt slide, and she stood sleepily in front of him, dressed only in her light summer shift with a linen towel draped over her shoulders. He handed her the stack of clothes in his arms; she took them and turned to walk back inside. He shut the door quietly behind him and followed her in past the screen and into the large bathing room. It was still steamy in the domed chamber, and he wondered how well she had slept on the hard marble in the moist air. He saw the folded linen towels spread along the far bench and knew it could not have been a good night's rest.

"Get dressed, my dear. We will leave when you are ready," he told her, walking along the edge of the pool, pretending to be interested in the murals. "Verica has packed an extra change of clothes in a satchel for you already. You must be hungry. You can eat your breakfast in the wagon."

"I told you, I am not going," Resi said firmly.

She had taken a long bath after leaving Mauro yesterday, but it had not helped to change her mind. After her soak, she had found a comb to unsnarl her wet hair while she paced alone in the quiet, vaulted room. She had not plaited it again, and her soft curls fell partly against her face, flowing around her shoulders and down her back under the linen shawl. She'd had no flame last night to light the wall sconces, so had fallen asleep when the bathhouse became too dark to see.

Now the morning sunrise was still too dim to light the room completely. She sat down on the closest bench near the entrance and set the crisply folded garments next to her. She pulled her unkempt hair back out of her face to get a better look at what Mauro had brought. They were her favorite traveling clothes, which she had not worn since last summer. She wanted to put them on.

Mauro watched her indecision. "You are a stubborn woman, Terese Baric. Definitely more stubborn than I am." He sat down on the bench next to her. "I cannot have you disobeying me and locking yourself away like this. Verica was very concerned for you last night when you did not come in."

Her head was bent, looking at the traveling clothes. She wanted to go with him; she had asked to go. But now she would remain firm in her decision. "And you weren't concerned for me?" she wanted to know.

"No. That was your own doing. I did not lock you in, and you had the means to come back out. It was very childish of you." Mauro tried to gain back some authority over her.

"But you were going to lock me in our chamber, like a child," she reminded him.

"I did say that, and I am sorry. If you had thought about it, though, you know there is no way to bolt the door from the outside." She looked up at him, and he smiled back at her. "I lost my temper, Resi."

A long moment passed, and then Mauro reasoned, "We do not know each other very well yet. That will come with time. But there are things in my past that I would like to leave in my past, all right?"

"All right," she agreed. "But you can still go without me. I will be staying at the castle."

If they were to be on the road soon, he would have to tell her that she had gotten her way; that he did as she required. He decided to take the softer approach again and took her hand in his and said, "When you did not come in for dinner, I did go talk to the ladies. I listened to each of them and their apologies, like you asked. I have told them I do not agree with going behind my back, but I think their motives were commendable. They are coming to the seaside with you and me today."

She leaned her head against his shoulder in relief, and he put his arm around her. "I was wrong to say those things to you, Mauro. I thought about it all night. You did not deserve to have me speak to you that way. I am sorry if I hurt your feelings," she said quietly.

He pulled her close and kissed the top of her head lightly, then released her. "I think we can all agree that we are a very sorry group. And now we will forget the entire affair and enjoy some time away from the castle. I have arranged a tent for the ladies to sleep in, and Cook has the baskets almost filled. I told everyone to be ready at full light. You are the last one we are waiting on."

On hearing this, she stood eagerly and rummaged through the stack of clothes on the bench, looking for her tunic. She let the linen draped over her shoulders fall to the ground and began to dress.

She had slept in the new summer shift in the muggy air last night. "Is this also from my aunt?" Mauro pointed to the pink, sleeveless undergarment she was wearing. It had satin strings for straps, and wider ribbon was tied under her breasts to lift and accentuate their fullness. "It is very pretty," he said, unable to stop looking at her. He leaned back and watched her in the emerging daylight of the bathhouse.

"Yes, she sent it with the other bordello garments," Resi remarked, wondering if he remembered his own comment about Ruby's dress at the ball. He raised his eyebrows, acknowledging with a nod. "It is nice and light in the summer heat," she told him. "I thought I would wear it again." She slipped her tunic over her head and put her arms through the gauzy sleeves, and then stopped to look at him. "Are you staying?"

Mauro chuckled. "I have no ulterior motives. I just thought I would keep you company while you dress."

"Of course, if it pleases you, Mauro. It's just, well, I have yet to relieve myself this morning, and there is no screen here, so . . ." she said awkwardly.

"Then I will leave you to finish in private," he told her agreeably. "The others will be in the courtyard. I do need to talk to Nestor before we go, so I will be with him, if you cannot find me." He stood and kissed her gently on the lips. "I will see you shortly," he said, and left the bathhouse.

Mauro strode along the path and went in through the kitchen's back door. The maids had readied two large baskets for the grooms to carry out. Mauro peeked into each to see what they had filled them with. Resi was right to suggest they could fish for their dinner, but in case they failed at that, it seemed there were plenty of cured sausages, smoked ham, meat pies, hard cheese, pickled eggs, fresh fruit, dried pasta, and black bread to feed all seven of them for three days. He had seen that a cask of cider and small keg of ale had been loaded into the back of the wagon already.

Nela came over to him as he closed up the top again. "My lord, you know your wife is eating for two. Why didn't you let us make up a tray for her?" She had her hands on her round hips, waiting for a reasonable answer.

Mauro was not offended by her brazenness; he had expected to be scolded by her. "My wife was being childish, and she knows where the kitchen is. She could have come in on her own if she was hungry enough."

Nela was much shorter than Mauro, but she still knew how to make him feel like a little boy, and he loved her for it. "She is hungry now, Nela. Can you make her up a small meal to take in the wagon?"

She handed him the tied linen sack that held two boiled eggs, several freshly fried plum dumplings, a few dried apricots, and a small stoneware jug of apple cider. "Don't you go eating it yourself, my lord!" Nela warned. "The baroness doesn't eat enough as it is."

Mauro promised he wouldn't, and then leaned down and kissed Cook on the top of her starched, white cap. "Thank you, Nela," he said sincerely, and she grinned back at him with satisfaction.

He left with the breakfast parcel through the servants' door into the foyer. Mauro walked up the stairs two at a time to Nestor's apartment. Now that Jero had taken over the role of steward, Nestor enjoyed leisurely mornings in his room before he came downstairs to see what was needed of him that day. Mauro knocked on his chamber door and entered.

"Good morning, Nestor. Have I disturbed you?" Mauro asked. Nestor was still in bed and reached for his spectacles on the little side table.

"No, no. I am awake, but had not yet decided to get up. I guess you have decided that for me," he said as he pulled himself up and sat on the edge of the bed in his long night shirt. Nestor looked smaller without the customary wig that covered his thinning hair.

Mauro took a seat on the chair across from his bed. "We will be leaving in a few minutes. There is a bit of a problem I just heard about, and I will need you to handle it for me." Nestor was all business once fully awake, and he looked intently at Mauro for his instructions. "The scouts rode in a half hour ago, and they reported the five mercenaries have crossed into Venetian territory in the east, not far from our border."

Nestor looked suddenly concerned. "If they crossed through the pass yesterday, they will be here at the castle tomorrow at the latest. Do you not want to postpone your trip and wait for them yourself?"

"I have considered it, but I am determined to get my ship back on its way Monday."

Nestor was in agreement that his ship took priority. He had concurred yesterday that Mauro should leave directly to settle the affair. "What do you need me to do?"

"You know that both Fabian and Jero are coming with me, so it will be up to you to welcome the Kokkinos clan. I have already instructed Eduard that all the guards are to remain at the castle. I do not expect the mercenaries will cause any trouble, but I want the grounds fully guarded. There will be no training and no leave while I am gone. Send word to me at Leopold's lagoon when they arrive, but otherwise you are to give them a proper, friendly welcome."

"I will do my part to welcome them," Nestor said, nodding still, but thinking of other details that might have been missed. "Where should they be housed? In the Keep, or should the servants ready some rooms here?"

"I think they will be better off in the tower. They are soldiers, and they can live and eat with mine. Give them the Barics' family chamber."

"The Barics' chamber? Next to your officers? What if they do not get along? Should we not house them in the sleeping cubicles on the third floor?" Nestor did not like the idea of housing them at all. He thought they should sleep in a tent outside the walls, and he had told the baron that originally.

"If they do not get along, then they can leave. Ready the room with a few more cots so they can sleep comfortably. There is more than enough space for all of them. Those are my instructions." Mauro stood to leave.

Nestor looked up at him with a frown. "As you wish, Mauro. But what I wish is that you would not leave this to me."

Mauro put his hand on the older man's shoulder. "I am sorry, but you are the only one I can leave it to. Thank you, Nestor. I will see you soon."

Mauro left his reliable advisor sitting on the edge of his bed and went back to his own chamber to collect his bag and Resi's sewing basket. He hurried out of the house to join the others.

The three young women were talking quietly among themselves, already waiting near the wagon. He saw his wife coming toward them along the bathhouse path; she was looking beyond him, toward her friends. The sun had just emerged fully over the eastern mountains, and Mauro smiled to himself that the day was beginning better than he had expected. He waited a moment for Resi to catch up to him. She looked pleased with herself, and he agreed that she should be.

The others were waiting for instructions from the baron. "Good morning," Mauro said cheerfully to the group. "Fabian, if you could help the ladies into the back of the wagon. My wife will ride on the bench with me, and Ruby will ride her mare."

"But there is no seat," Isabella protested when she looked into the wagon bed.

"You can sit on the hay here in the back," Fabian told her pleasantly. "It will be plenty comfortable on the ride there, before the horses eat it all. Or would you prefer to ride like Lady Ruby? I can have a horse saddled for you." He kept his expression blank, but he was enjoying their distress too much to keep his amusement masked for long.

"I do not ride, and you know it," Isabella spitefully replied, doing her best to maintain her composure.

Caterina had already taken Fabian's outstretched hand and struggled to climb into the back of the wagon with her skirts tucked around her. Fabian finally took her by the waist and easily lifted her in. Isabella glanced to her friend for courage, but Caterina looked like she would cry at any moment.

Isabella gave Fabian a cold glare under the brim of her large, feathered hat. She offered him her gloved hand, ready to be loaded into the back with Caterina. She did not want to be picked up by him. "Do not manhandle me," she warned.

"You will have no help from me," he replied stubbornly.

Fabian managed not to laugh as she clambered in with her billowing skirts and heeled shoes to sit as best she could on the hay in the back of the wagon. The others were busy readying their own departures, so at least she did not have an audience witnessing her clumsiness. He secured the end board of the wagon bed, gave her a wink to annoy her more, and then mounted his own waiting horse.

Alberto helped Ruby up onto Resi's gentle mare, which Mauro had given her on her last birthday. Ruby rode astride without a saddle, even though it was unladylike. She was dressed comfortably for riding in ivory-colored trousers, similar to what Ottoman soldiers wore riding. She had modestly covered the leggings with a long, blue linen tunic and wore a pale red, broadcloth jacket over that. The tunic and riding jacket were split in the front and back to flow over her legs and down to her short boots while sitting on the horse. The baron had reluctantly allowed Resi to wear the same unconventional garments when she rode, but only after persuasive debating on her part when she had first arrived.

Ruby did not care for the large hats that were the fashion for Venetian women, but had donned a smaller one to simply shade her eyes. Her hair was tied carefully with a sapphire blue scarf under the hat, with the end of her long, auburn braid showing out the bottom of the flowing silk.

Jero was on Mauro's chestnut stallion behind her. He could not stop glancing over at Ruby. She looked like she belonged in a painting of Persian warriors he remembered seeing in a gallery in Florence many years ago; only Ruby was naturally more feminine and far too beautiful to be mistaken for a soldier. She and the baroness had ridden often when they had first arrived at the castle, but Jero had never escorted them. He was glad to be riding with her today. He had not spoken to Ruby since their separation on the dance floor, and he was anxious to smooth out the misunderstanding.

Mauro helped his wife step up and onto the bench seat. He had cushions placed there for her comfort, although he knew this would bring only a little benefit. The trip would be bumpy as the wagon was bound to follow the rutted tracks. He hoped she could tolerate the discomfort it would cause her. He brought her saddle, in case it would be easier on her to ride the horse after all.

Josip handed the reins of the two hitched horses into the baron's gloved hands when he was settled. Mauro looked around to his companions. They were all mounted and ready. "Off we go," he said to Resi, and she held onto the bench as Mauro put the horses into motion. She stared ahead of them with a happy smile on her face.

The gate was opened for them, and they rode at a steady pace down the castle road to the main north-south trade route. The Baric party would enjoy limited company on the usually well-traveled road south. It was a Sunday morning, and most of the good Catholics of the region would soon be attending Mass.

Resi looked behind her at the Venetians huddled next to each other chatting quietly and was satisfied. She opened her small bundle and began to eat her packed breakfast. She offered Mauro one of her dumplings, but he declined despite the temptation, thinking of his promise to Cook. Resi finished the food and drank down her cider as they quietly journeyed along. She felt much revived.

"The next time we stop, can I sit in back with the ladies?" Resi asked Mauro.

"No, I like it better if you stay here with me," he replied cheerfully.

"And don't you care what I would like?"

He looked at her, surprised, and laughed softly. "I do care, but there is something you do not understand. You thought you were doing the ladies a favor by inviting them to a grand time at the beach, to swim and lounge on the seashore for three days. Fabian told me this would be the least enjoyable excursion that I could have offered. Which is why he agreed to it, as long as I make them stew alone for a little while," he explained with a playful look in his brilliant green eyes.

She was not pleased that Mauro and Fabian had taken advantage of the new circumstances. "So this is a punishment to them?"

"It seems it is, but it was you who insisted," Mauro reminded her.

"That was not my intention. I don't like this at all, Mauro," she told him firmly.

"Fabian is my friend, Resi, and he thought they should somehow pay for their misdeed. I am honoring his request. They are spoiled young ladies, and they cannot do whatever they please, whenever they please. There is no real harm done by making them sit in back, or do you disagree?"

He looked only forward, watching the road ahead of them as he drove the horses at a brisk pace on this good stretch of road. Resi looked back at the two heaps of billowing fabric among the other satchels and baskets. Isabella was holding the brim of her hat, which threatened to fly free. She turned back and agreed, "I suppose they are fine sitting in the hay. And do you think I am spoiled, Mauro, for being so contrary yesterday?"

He patted her on the leg. "In a different way, maybe, but I do not find you as bothersome as they are." She frowned at his answer, and he told her, "Do not be offended, Resi. All aristocrats are spoiled to some extent. You have now joined our rank."

They were silent for a moment and then Mauro said, "You did not mention that I am honoring another of your requests." He looked at her, waiting for her acknowledgment.

She turned around again. The three horses were several paces behind them. She smiled and gave in to his need to be praised. "You have allowed Ruby to ride today. I know she is very pleased, and so am I. Thank you, Mauro."

There were several ruts in the road that could not be avoided, and Resi grabbed the side bar of the bench and clung to Mauro's thigh to keep steady on her seat. "You should lock your arm in mine until the road smoothes out again," he suggested, and offered his arm. She threaded her elbow through his, and he took the reins back with both hands again, holding her against him, his wide-brimmed hat shading her a bit more. They rode quietly this way for a little while. The chatter of the two women in back died down, and he noticed Resi leaned heavily against him. She had fallen asleep.

Fabian had noticed, too, and rode ahead to talk to Mauro in the driver's seat. "You have a wagon full of sleeping women. Napping seems like a good way to ride. I should have left my horse back at the castle and joined them."

"You can nap all you like after we get camp set up. There will not be much else to do for a few days," Mauro said. That was what he was looking forward to, as well.

"I would like to do a bit of bow hunting when we are unpacked. Would it be alright to leave Caterina and Isabella to you and Jero?"

"Of course. I am glad you thought to pack your bow. I will be counting on you now for our dinner. Perhaps squirrel and rat stew?" Fabian was not offended by his teasing. With Fabian's skill and patience, Mauro knew they would more likely have a nice meal of venison or wild goat tonight.

"I did see the two baskets from the kitchen, so Nela must not have confidence in our survival skills. I overheard Ruby talking to Jero about going fishing, so between the three of us, we should have plenty to eat."

"Ruby talked of going fishing? You know, Fabian, sometimes I wonder if Demetrius Kokkinos sent me boys instead of girls. I never hear them talk of needlepoint and paintings; just swimming, sailing, and riding." Mauro did not think he had ever known such peculiar women who were interested in these sorts of activities.

"From what I saw at the party, I am confident that they are both girls," Fabian said with a cheeky smile. "Speaking of boys and girls, I think you are right, though. There is a bit of a courtship blooming back there."

Mauro looked over his shoulder. Jero and Ruby were now falling farther behind the wagon, talking as they rode next to each other. "Well, one can hardly stop it, Fabian."

"Do you not think you should, Mauro?" Fabian asked a bit too seriously.

Mauro was surprised by his concern. "Who are you protecting, Ruby or Jero?"

"Both, I suppose. Will she be staying here?" Fabian asked casually.

"Are you interested in her, Fabian?" Mauro would not put it past the charmer who needed little enticement beyond a pretty feminine figure to choose as his next conquest.

He thought about it a moment. "She is quite lovely uncovered, but she is too young and tenderhearted for me. You know I like my women to be a bit more experienced and agonizing."

Mauro looked over at the pitiful Fabian, reminiscing about his failed romances. "Why do you doom yourself to be a brokenhearted bachelor, going from one bitter love affair to another? Why do you not allow yourself tender devotion from a young woman like Ruby?"

"That sounds almost poetic, Mauritius. What a remarkable thing to say. I am impressed by your wisdom," he said and chuckled.

Mauro laughed quietly with him, trying not to wake Resi. "I stayed up last night and read from my wife's book of sonnets. I may have read one too many. They were all quite dramatic, full of heartbreak and lost love."

"I am sure her poems confirmed that you do not have to be a bachelor to be heartbroken. Did you make up with your wife this morning?"

Mauro shrugged. "I truly do not know. I think we have made up, but I am probably wrong."

Fabian looked again at Resi rocking softly, still fast asleep against Mauro's shoulder. "Well, we will give you two enough space today for you to be sure. If there is a time to rekindle love, it is on the beach on a day like this."

"You are a romantic, Fabian. Why not try to rekindle love yourself, instead of wasting such a day shooting at big-eyed does?"

He looked over at Isabella crumpled next to his sister. "The four-legged or the two-legged kind?" Mauro understood his friend's point.

Mauro slowed the horses. "This turnoff leads to a nice sandy cove. It is up ahead about ten minutes, if I remember correctly."

Mauro turned onto the narrow track from the main roadway they had been following. "This is Neven's favorite beach, but I do not expect he will be using it in the next few days. I did not have time to get his permission, but his scouts will recognize us, if they come by. We can park the wagon between the pines up ahead. There should be a place to camp and small dock just below that. There is a nice stream through the trees that way for our fresh water."

"And how far is it from here to the port?" Fabian asked as Mauro guided the horses on the soft dirt that was little more than wide pathway.

"It is only a thirty-minute ride, but still far enough that nobody will be bothering us here."

~*~

The change of pace woke the sleeping women, and Jero and Ruby caught up to the wagon. Most of the two-lane road until now had been densely lined with hardy pines, low scrubby oak, and wild olive trees. Ahead of them was a full view of the Adriatic Sea. Its azure expanses sparkled with the late-morning light streaming down. The gentle tide was a lighter blue, almost green, against the pebbly sand shore of the sheltered lagoon. It was a calm day with only a light wind, and they could hear the hungry cries of seabirds still fishing for their morning meals. Resi sat up and broke the silence of the group. "That was not so far, Mauro. Have I been sleeping long?"

"I would say you were sleeping almost two hours. My arm is about numb from you leaning on it." She sat up completely, now self-conscious. He reassured her, "I will be your pillow any day, Resi. You were tired and needed the nap, so I dared not move you."

He maneuvered the wagon through the narrow path between the overgrown tree bows. He stopped at the end of the track just moments later and hopped down, holding the reins to tie to one of the long overhangs.

The women sat up in the back of the wagon and looked out at the view onto the sea. Fabian pulled alongside them and dismounted, loosely tying his horse to a narrow tree trunk. "Oh, Mauro, this is a beautiful spot. Where are we?" Resi asked.

"This is Neven Leopold's beach. He does not have the fields for crops on his land that I do, but he has a very accessible coastline. This is where his family spends their leisure time; at least they did when I was younger," Mauro explained.

He took his wife by the waist and lifted her down from her seat. She walked in front of the two horses, admiring the view. She saw the path leading down to the beach and small dock, and without a word, she disappeared over the low hill to the water like a happy child. From the beach she shouted back, "There is a small sailboat, Mauro. This will be a perfect outing." He did not feel the same joy for sailing that she did, but he smiled at her genuine delight.

Fabian took charge of unloading the quiet cargo from the back of the wagon. The women were stiff from their uncomfortable sleeping positions.

They crouched awkwardly now while they waited to be lowered onto the soft, sandy ground.

"Are you pleased with yourself?" Isabella asked Fabian after he set her down. She had allowed him to lift her this time, since her long skirts made it too hard to find her footing.

Fabian still held her by the waist, but was not smiling this time. He told her in a quiet voice, "You should try to enjoy the excursion offered you, Isabella. The sun is shining, there is good food packed for our lunch, and you will have shelter to sleep under. It is not the opera, but Lady Terese finds this outing to be a luxury. Do not insult her with your negative opinions today." Then he released her and turned to help his sister down.

Isabella straightened her skirts and waited in brooding silence for Caterina to be on her feet again. When she was, Isabella took her friend's hand and the two walked away from their assistant. Fabian brushed off the cold looks and proceeded to unsaddle his horse.

Ruby had stopped her horse a few feet behind the wagon and watched the others depart. Jero dismounted next to her, smiled kindly, and then walked his horse to the open space near Fabian's steed to unsaddle Janus. Ruby waited on Resi's mare.

Alberto had told Ruby when she first went riding at Baric Castle what he knew to be proper horse etiquette for a woman. A lady was allowed to ride only if she maintained herself in a ladylike manner. Ruby did not know what Alberto had meant by that and had told him so. She was not a "lady" in the aristocratic sense, and most common women did not have a horse of their own to ride anyway.

He had explained that a proper lady did not mount and dismount without assistance, and Ruby had agreed it would have been impossible for her to get onto the side saddle by herself. Because of that, she refused to use the cumbersome thing to ride on. She argued with the horse master that she would not be able to ride over the rocky terrain sitting on such a saddle any faster than walking her horse, and walking would be preferable to sitting on the strange, box contraption. Alberto had then offered her a normal riding saddle, and she protested that bareback would suit her just fine. Alberto had not agreed.

Ruby had stubbornly shown him how she could mount and dismount alone fairly elegantly without a saddle on the small mare. Alberto was personally sympathetic to her previous training, but had told her that he would have to ask permission from the baron for her to ride in that manner. Without the stirrups of the saddle to help guide her up, the stable master had decided that sliding on and off the horse was too unrefined for any lady. Alberto had brought all his concerns to the baron at the time.

Fortunately, Mauro had been at the castle during the first month of Resi and Ruby's arrival to be consulted about Ruby's unusual preferences. The baron had decided that Ruby could be allowed to ride bareback, if she had been so trained in Greece, but would be assisted by Alberto with a stepping stool to mount and dismount. The women would be allowed to ride astride only if their legs were decently covered. Mauro insisted, though, that his wife was to ride with a proper saddle, which he picked out himself. Both of the Greek women had agreed to these terms from the start.

Ruby sat impatiently now, waiting to be helped off her horse. "Jero," Ruby called out to him. He came to her side with a pleasant smile. "Can you help me down, please?"

He blushed slightly and told her, "I am sorry, Ruby. I would willingly, but I have been advised not to. I am not a married man, and it would be improper for me to hold you. Only the baron can assist you."

Ruby grumbled in frustration. She would never understand the baron's rules of propriety between men and women. "But you could hold my waist dancing with me. There is not a lot of difference, is there?" she protested sweetly.

Jero looked up at her on her horse. Despite wanting to hold her, he knew there was only one answer. "Yes, I agree with your reasoning. But as a gentleman, I am not allowed." He shrugged and walked away to find Mauro for her while she waited.

Mauro was unhitching the two horses from the wagon when Jero reminded him, "Lady Ruby is waiting to dismount."

"Oh, I forgot about her. Can you finish this?" He turned the task of unbridling the second horse over to Jero.

Ruby stroked the neck of sweet Ophelia while waiting. She liked this mare. She had only ridden the tempo the wagon could travel on the uneven road today, but Ruby knew Resi's horse could gallop like the wind and climb trails smoothly.

Ruby was lost in her thoughts when she noticed the baron by her side, with his arms outstretched for her. "I am sorry to keep you waiting, Ruby." She delicately swung her right leg in front of her across the mare's back to meet her other, and Mauro lifted her down by her waist and into his arms. He set her on the ground.

"Thank you," she said.

Mauro bowed politely; the years of training made it second nature to him.

"Lord Baric," she added quietly.

"Yes, Ruby?"

"I can dismount unassisted," she simply said.

He considered what seemed to be a request before stubbornly replying, "I compliment you. You have been well-trained in horsemanship; I can easily see that. Whoever trained you would also have instructed you how to get on and off your horse alone."

"Yes, but—" she impatiently interrupted.

He continued to state kindly, "But you do me the great honor, as your guardian, to assure your safety until your feet are properly back on the ground. I am at your service, Ruby." He bowed again elegantly and walked away.

She watched him with her mouth still open. She would never understand his reasoning, but she did feel protected when she was with the baron.

~*~

Resi was already on the dock when Caterina and Isabella made it to the beach. The rocky points of the far ends of the sandy beach wrapped around to make a protective lagoon that would be calm for bathing. Beyond the opening of their cove were two islands in the open sea. The closest island to them looked small and rocky; the second beyond it was somewhat larger, with trees and a visible shoreline. Ruby ran from where she had left her horse in the care of the men and arrived breathless next to the Venetians.

"This will be marvelous," she told them, panting to catch her breath. "It is not too hot today. I am going to take off my shoes to see if the sand can be walked on." She sat down where she stood and unbuckled her riding boots.

"Yes, marvelous," Caterina replied unenergetically, looking at Isabella for reassurance.

Ruby was busy peeling off her stockings when Isabella quietly said, "Well, Caterina, maybe Fabian is right. We should try to make the best of the difficult situation." She, too, sat down in the sand, her full skirt ballooning around her, and began to remove her heeled slippers and stockings. The unaffected Caterina remained standing, staring blankly out into the distance beyond Resi on the dock.

Resi was examining the little boat tied securely to the end of the small pier. The water was only shoulder deep by the boat, but it became a darker blue beyond the wooden dock planks as the shore dropped off into the deeper sea. They should be able to fish just fine from here, she imagined.

Resi had removed her shoes and stockings earlier on the beach, and now carefully put a bare foot onto the bench of the boat's interior and stepped in. It was obvious by the accumulation of rainwater in the bottom of the small vessel that it had not been used in a long time. There was a bailing pail tied to the mast, and she used this to empty the water from the floor. The sail had been wrapped securely, and she hoped there were no tears in it. The rudder seemed to be in good working order, as well. Either way, she was going to sail it.

She looked up for the first time from her task and saw the women crouched on the sand removing their shoes; above them was Mauro, with his hands on his hips looking out at her in the untested sailboat. She should probably ask his permission, she realized. She waved to him, then made her way carefully out of the boat and walked back up the dock to meet the others.

"What do you think, Resi?" Ruby asked. She stood and brushed the sand off her garments, leaving her stocking-filled boots on a rock.

"I think Lady Nikolina is very lucky. This is the perfect spot, and the boat looks sailable," Resi replied.

Caterina asked with a worried look, "Do you intend to go out onto the sea, Lady Terese? Is the boat not too small?"

"We can sail it here in this cove to be sure it is seaworthy. But if it is, I think I can still remember all that my two brothers taught me," Resi answered.

"I have three brothers, and the only thing they taught me about boats was that it was meant for getting to the next party, not for a lady to sail," Caterina declared. She did not intend to be judgmental, and Resi understood her own experience was unusual for a woman.

"My family owns boats and ships, so I was taught how to manage safely on the water, the same as my brothers. I suppose in a place like Venice, where it requires strength to move the boats, a woman is not able to do anything but travel in one. But in sailing, the wind is the strength. All you need is the skill to understand how to manipulate the wind's power," Resi explained.

Isabella looked at Resi with honest admiration. "I applaud your fortitude, Lady Terese," she said. "But will your husband allow you to use those skills?"

"Well, I suppose I will have to ask him. Excuse me, ladies; I will go find him now." She hurried along the loose sand and climbed the short path to where the wagon was.

The men had already quickly unpacked the gear and were setting up the canvas tent that would house the women for their stay. They had found a flat spot on the edge of the sand, not too far from where the wagon was parked, and pitched the tent there.

It seemed that this camping beach had indeed been used many times before. There was already a large fire pit built in the sand between the tent and the water. Massive stones had been placed around the pit for fireside seating, and there were solid planks resting on two even stones nearby as a makeshift kitchen sideboard. That is where Fabian had brought the baskets of supplies and casks of drinks.

"I think we should eat first," Mauro said to Resi when she found him on the beach. If he was famished, then the others would be, too. "Do you want to call the ladies over to have a meal?"

Fabian had already taken the cloth off the first basket and had laid it out on the dusty boards. He took out the crocks and linen bundles one by one, swatting at the insects that were also interested in the offerings. Resi had not thought that Fabian and Mauro could be so domestic, but then remembered they spent months fending for themselves when they were not waited upon at the castle.

The others did not need to be called; they walked slowly toward them on their own. "After lunch, Mauro, may I—" Resi began to ask, but Mauro put his finger up to her lips.

Mauro took his wife into his arms and said, "Yes, you may!" She reached up and planted a lingering kiss on his mouth. "But," he continued, after he took a needed breath, "I want to look the boat over first. It has probably not been used in a while, and I do not want you sinking in the middle of the sea."

"I looked it over, and it is sound," she assured him. "I could not judge the sail, but perhaps Ruby and I will sail it around the lagoon to test it. If it passes your inspection, then we can go visit the island." She pointed out to the open sea, beyond the stony points of the shore.

"One thing at a time," he answered before she hurried off to meet her friends again.

~*~

Jero had just finished putting the three women's bags and sleeping blankets into their canvas shelter. He left the Baric couple's supplies and blankets out on a boulder nearby for Mauro to decide on a sleeping location. "I think that is everything," he told Mauro. "If you do not mind, I will sleep in the wagon. I left some of the horse's hay in the back for a bed for tonight. I can also watch the horses better from there."

"I do not think anyone or anything will bother us here, but it is good to keep guard. You might have the best rest of all of us in your hay bed," Mauro agreed quietly.

The two walked to the sideboard, where Fabian was unpacking their lunch. Mauro grabbed the wooden pail that had been used to hold some of their packed food. "I will be right back. I know where to fetch some water to go with our meal," he announced.

Fabian came over to talk to Jero once Mauro had left. "I have already told Mauro I am going to do a little hunting after we eat. There are plenty of woods to explore, and I saw some deer on our ride through the trees just over there. Do you mind keeping close to the ladies? I think Mauro wanted to spend some time alone with his wife."

"I have no plans," Jero said. "If all I have to do is sit with my feet in the water and watch three ladies amuse themselves, I am very willing."

"I thought so." Fabian smiled.

He turned toward the colorful mass of dresses coming slowly along the beach. "What is taking so long?" Fabian said to himself. They had found some shells near the shoreline, and were looking for more. He then called over, "Do you ladies not hunger? The food is laid out. Come, let us eat!"

Chapter 46

Before Fabian left with his bow on his solo quest, he made his best attempt to ensure Isabella and Caterina would be no trouble for Jero that afternoon. Fabian had brought the cushions the baroness had used on the wagon down to the beach. He leaned them against some large rocks near the shore to make impromptu chairs for the girls to sit against. He securely propped their parasols near the cushions to shade their faces, allowing them to have both hands free for the idle work he had unpacked for them to fill their time.

His sister had not thought to bring any activities beyond her favorite card games. When Fabian heard the baroness had offered Caterina her sewing basket to occupy her on the beach, he was impressed by her generosity. He knew women were particular about their embroidery projects, taking pride in their own workmanship, and scrutinizing that of others. What he didn't know was that the baroness had been working on the same tiny gown for two months with no progress. Resi had never practiced embroidery growing up, and only made an effort now because it was expected of a pregnant lady to decorate her own child's baby gown. Caterina's eager acceptance to forge ahead decorating the little dress had been more of a relief to Resi than a sacrifice.

In their haste last night, Isabella had the forethought to pack a few things to amuse herself, along with her several changes of clothing. She had emerged from their tent after lunch wearing a light, gauzy gown to replace the layered, satin one she had worn for the wagon ride. It had long, loose sleeves and a high collar to protect her from the sun's harsh rays. She carried the book she had borrowed from the baroness' library, along with a binder of blank paper and several pencils. She would have no need to write to anyone back in Venice, Fabian thought when he saw what she was carrying. A letter would not arrive home any quicker than she would. He had forgotten she had an unrealized talent for drawing the world around her.

Thanks to Fabian's careful organization, the ladies proceeded to make themselves comfortable on the blanketed sand. Mauro had earlier secured the casks of ale and cider in the water under the shadows of the dock to keep them cool. Fabian poured each of them a mug of the refreshing cider, and then quickly drank one himself. Despite the heat of the afternoon, he had not changed out of his sturdy riding clothes. His thick leather jacket would protect him from the thorny underbrush and would help camouflage him while he hunted. Deciding he could do no more for them than that, he finally bid the girls a pleasant afternoon. He was excited to finally begin his own leisure pursuit in the woods. Caterina and Isabella watched him walk away up the path, past the wagon, and into the trees with his bow and quiver of arrows.

~*~

Mauro was at the end of the dock tying the fishing line onto the flexible poles that Alberto had thoughtfully packed for them. He had not gone fishing since joining his uncle's army six years ago. As a foster son, he had fished in the streams around his uncle's estate often enough with Vilim and his cousins, but the poles had always been readied for them, packed with the hooks and lines in place.

Stream fishing in the mountains was different from fishing in deep waters, and Mauro and Jero had just figured out that they were missing some components. Jero rummaged through their kitchen supplies to improvise extra cork to keep his hook afloat and some bait to attract the bigger fish. Resi and Ruby could have offered helpful advice before they left on the sailboat for a tour around the shallow cove, but it had not occurred to the men to ask them.

Jero came back with his hands full of potential solutions. He sat down on the edge of the dock next to Mauro. Both had earlier removed their stockings and shoes, along with their jackets and waistcoats. They looked like overgrown boys in their billowing, tucked shirts and trim-fitting leather breeches, sorting their pile of treasures between their bare legs.

"I had to open the bottle of wine to get a cork, but I figured we would drink it tonight anyway," Jero began to explain. "I know that bright cheese can be good bait, if it does not get nibbled off." He set the small wedge down. "I thought the fish might smell the sausage and be attracted to that." He had cut a handful of bite-sized pieces and put that small pile on the dock next to the chunk of cheese. Then he set down a mug of water with silver swimming in it. "I scooped up some little fish from under the dock. We could hook them live, and the larger fish might want to eat those." He grinned at Mauro, who grinned back, excited at the options Jero had brought.

"Well, if we cannot attract our dinner with all of this," Mauro declared, "then we can still eat Nela's ham tonight."

Jero neatly organized the bait out of the way temporarily and took up the other pole to fix the hooks Mauro had found packed for them. They had been secured in a piece of cork, and Mauro would use this for his line float.

With all of the distractions of the bait choices and tying the lines, Mauro had not been watching his wife and Ruby sail out to the edge of the rocky shore that protected their little lagoon and beach from the open sea.

~*~

"We have the wind again," Resi called over to Ruby, who happily knelt on the floor of the bow, her dangling fingers skimming the surface of the clear water as they glided along. "I thought we would be stuck longer. It is very unpredictable in this sheltered area. I am going to sail us back and ask if we can go out into the open waters," Resi said, letting out the canvas sail to gain the full wind.

"Don't you want to sail with the baron instead of me? He has been very attentive to you today. He is probably trying to make up for yesterday. You should enjoy some time alone with him," Ruby suggested.

"You don't mind staying behind?" Resi asked. "He did intend for the outing to be for just the two of us, so we can get to know each other better."

As their little boat sped across the cove, Resi could see the other four at their camp clearly now. "I know why you are so concerned about my time alone with my husband, Ruby Spiros," she declared laughing. "I can see the ladies are occupied on the beach, and you will have Jero alone to yourself." Ruby grinned at her friend, delighted with this pivotal arrangement.

Ruby leaned back and let the sun kiss her already sunburned face. Both of them had left their hats at camp so they would not have the misfortune of losing them to the wind. Their scarves covered their long, braided hair and flapped like banners as Resi tacked the little wooden sailboat across the lagoon and then back again, progressing toward the men on the dock.

~*~

Mauro and Jero had sunk their lines in the water for a half hour now with nothing more than a few tugs and nibbles on their hooks. "It looks like my wife is sailing back to shore," he announced to the dozing Jero. He watched the boat's sail flutter and fill again. "I have been bound to her for thirteen years, and yet everything she does is new to me," he remarked out of the blue. "I do not know when she was taught to sail a boat, or learned to read Latin, or who taught her to play the lute."

Jero had his hat down over his eyes, lounging up against the end beam of the dock. Mauro looked over and said, "I have known you since my first memories, Jero, and yet I do not know what happened to you in the last years, either."

Mauro was not so sure Jero was awake to hear him, but it really didn't matter. He had finally said out loud what he had been thinking for almost two years.

"I have been exactly where I was when you left us," a voice answered from under the hat. Mauro took his line out of the water and turned to sit in front of Jero.

"I have wondered what it would have been like to have grown up under my father's roof. What was he like, Jero? Did he treat you well?" Mauro sincerely wanted to know.

Jero pulled his line out of the water, too, and crossed his stretched legs. He looked out at the boat tacking across the middle of the lagoon, and he looked back at the Venetian women talking to each other as they sat against their cushions under the shade of their parasols. Jero would have a few uninterrupted minutes, so he truthfully explained, "He did treat me well, Mauro, as well as any orphaned boy could have expected to be treated, and probably better. He was a good employer, a good baron, and ran his affairs well. But despite his wealth and the respect he was given, in private your father seemed to be a broken man. I always wondered what had happened to make him that way."

"Maybe I broke him," Mauro said softly.

Jero had never heard Mauro sound so insecure. "You did not break him. You should not think his unhappiness was your fault. I am certain you were the one piece that kept him together."

Mauro absently picked at the drying cheese among the pile of bait they had been using. "Did he ever talk about me?" he asked without looking up.

"Not to me, no; but he did wish you well. I was with him once or twice when he received a letter from your uncle, and I know he was relieved when he heard you were safe. He would have been happy for you to return, you know?"

"So I could sire Baric children to continue in his footsteps? He did not want me. He just needed a son to make more sons." Mauro's words were meant for his dead father, not for Jero.

Jero reasoned, "And is that not what all fathers want, to see their children come full circle in life? He was not a callous man, Mauro. He knew he had everything to offer you, but he did not care about those things himself. He cared about the future of the House of Baric, but he denied himself much of the rewards of being a baron. I do not know how to explain him."

"You were his valet for two years. You must have gotten to know him very well during that time."

"When I became his valet, sometimes I would go everywhere with him and hardly leave his side. And then, for no reason, as though he could not stand the sight of me, he would send me away and not want my help for days. He immersed himself in the war and his business. He had so much around him that could have made him happy, yet he only focused on the problems." Jero saw that Mauro scowled at hearing this. "I do not mean to say it was wrong, Mauro. Those were troubled times. He had a lot of responsibilities, and we both know he was good at what he did."

Mauro listened as Jero continued to tell him, "Lord Lorenc was a generous man, though. I will never be able to repay your family for his kindness to me. He educated me, and I was his companion on wondrous excursions. But he also kept me at a distance, like he did you. I never knew if I would be in or out of favor from day to day."

Mauro finally looked up at him again. "I am surprised you ended up with such a pleasant disposition after all those years in my house," he said thoughtfully. "My father had his moods, but my mother was practically mad. It could not have been tolerable to be around her. Or perhaps living with him had made her crazy. I have always wondered whether both my parents could have led happier lives without each other."

Jero was not sure how much he should say, but he told Mauro, "Lady Johanna did not like me. Lord Lorenc never told me why, except to advise me to keep my distance from her. I know she was your mother and you loved her, but she was the one who was not easy to live with."

"She was my mother, but I did not miss her all those years. She wrote to me about my father and how terribly she thought he treated her. I wanted to have pity on her life with him, but she had treated me with the same temperamental disdain."

He threw some of the cheese into the water, and several fish came to the surface to steal it. Both Mauro and Jero watched the fish until the cheese was gone. "I should have burned her letters and not read them, but I hoped one day there would be happy news in one of them. There never was," Mauro admitted. "I did not think I loved her until she was dead. I should not have let so much time pass before coming back. And now they are both dead."

Jero reached out and put his hand on Mauro's left shoulder. But Mauro said nothing, gave nothing away as their eyes met, and Jero released his touch. Mauro got to his feet and looked out onto the water, his arms crossed in front of him. His wife waved at him, and he lifted his hand to wave back. She only needed a few more minutes to get to the docks, but he needed a moment to himself first.

"I am going for a cool drink," he told Jero. "Can you manage the docking? I will be right back."

"Yes, I will help them land and secure the boat," he replied, and Mauro walked away.

~*~

Jero moved the fishing poles out of the way and stood to be ready to stop the boat as it glided to the dock. The women were sunburned and windblown, and he joined in their laughter as he helped them with the boat.

He offered the baroness his hand and helped her step out. "Are you done for the day then, my lady?" Jero asked.

"I plan to go out again soon," Resi declared. "I just brought Ruby back to help you catch our dinner."

Resi gave Ruby her hand as she gingerly climbed out, and Jero tied the boat's line to the post. "Where are your fish, Jero?" Ruby teased him. "We saw so many through the water, we were betting you would have already caught too many to eat today."

"We all have our weaknesses, Lady Ruby, and now you know mine. If you can show me how to do better, I will gladly keep you company."

"I will take your challenge," Ruby replied with a charming grin.

Mauro came toward them with his hands full with drinking horns. He could greet his wife with a smile now. He had splashed his face in the cold stream to shake his mood and had filled four horns with water. The women happily accepted the offered drinks, and he handed the last off to Jero. "How does the boat sail?" Mauro asked. He leaned over the small vessel, examining the inside for any leaks.

"The sails are different from what I am used to, and we lost our wind once, but we had a nice tour of the cove. I would like to go out to the island and explore a little. Once you are at the opening by the rocks, it is not so far to the first island."

"No, Resi, I do not think that is a good idea. If something happened, we would not have a way to help you," Mauro explained.

Jero and Ruby were listening to the Barics' conversation. Jero interjected, "Lady Ruby wanted to try her luck at fishing. She could stay here with me and the two ladies, and you could take the baroness out to the island.

Besides, we are having no success fishing ourselves; maybe Lady Ruby can catch us our dinner."

"Yes," Resi quickly agreed. "I will go get some more water and freshen up a minute, and then we can leave again." She took the two leather water pouches from the boat's bench and hurried up the dock. Ruby followed her, carrying the empty drinking vessels from Mauro and Jero.

Mauro had no way out. He could think of no plausible excuse at the moment to avoid it. He would have to go on the boat to the island.

"Was that wrong of me to suggest that, Mauro?" Jero asked. "I thought you liked sailing, and Fabian told me to give you some privacy with your wife today."

Mauro shrugged it off and tried to smile. "No, no. You are right. I sailed a lot when I was a boy. It is just these islands are not very interesting. But if that is what she wants to do, then I will oblige her."

He stretched his arms and rested them on the top of his head, as though he had to hold his thoughts still. He began pacing. Jero waited uneasily.

Mauro made his choice. He lowered his arms again and turned back to Jero. "We will probably be gone a few hours, Jero. Will you be all right with the three ladies?"

"Absolutely. Go enjoy yourself. Do not worry about us. Anyway, Fabian should return at any time," Jero assured him cheerfully. "We will have dinner roasting for you when you come back."

Chapter 47

The afternoon sun had made the beach hot to walk on, but the Greek women did not seem to be bothered by it. They had sacrificed the sandals they had packed so the ladies would have something to wear in the sand. They had planned to be in and out of the water, so were happy to go barefooted. On her way to the stream, Resi stopped by where the women had been lounging the past hour. She crouched down in front of them so they could see her through their parasols and brimmed hats. "Hello, ladies. Have you been enjoying the sunshine?" Resi asked, catching her breath after hurrying up the sandy beach. Ruby came up behind her.

"Ah, you are back," Isabella exclaimed. "I did not imagine I would be saying this, but I am having a lovely afternoon, Lady Terese."

Caterina set her sewing down. "And I am enjoying working with the needle again. But Lady Terese, I do have a confession to make."

"Oh?" Resi had no idea what to expect her confession to be.

"I took your stitches out of your little dress and redid them all. I am sorry, dear Lady Terese, but I could not match your unusual spacing," Caterina confided.

Isabella explained with a smile, "Caterina is a bit of a perfectionist. She can be very tedious at times because of it. I am sure it was meant well."

Resi was not offended. "May I see?"

Caterina handed the baby gown to Resi, and she examined the work. Ruby looked over her shoulder. "I have a confession to make, too," the baroness admitted. "Those stitches that you removed—I redid them twice already. I am so grateful to you, Lady Caterina. It is beautiful now."

"The baroness never learned to sew," Ruby told them bluntly.

Caterina took the gown back and assured the baroness, "Sewing takes time and practice. You are good at so many other things. I would be surprised that you would have ever had time for stitching. If you like, I can work on it while I am here. It will be my gift to your baby."

"Thank you, Lady Caterina. I will treasure it," Resi said happily.

"Are you done with your sailing tour?" Isabella asked pleasantly.

Ruby explained their new plans for the afternoon, "The baron and baroness are going out on the sailboat, and I am going to fish with Jero. You can join us on the dock and dip your feet into the water. It is very refreshing."

Resi held up the water pouches. "We have just come back for more supplies. Can we bring you anything?"

"Fabian left us drinks earlier. But I think we will get up in a few minutes to stretch our legs. We will join you then, Lady Ruby. I am going to finish this one detail first," Isabella told her.

They had not noticed that she wasn't writing words on her paper, but was sketching a picture of the dock and the sailboat in the lagoon in front of her. She had captured all four of them in her realistic drawing.

"I am impressed, Lady Isabella. I didn't know you were an artist," Ruby said in awe, looking over her work.

"I am not the only perfectionist," Caterina said, cocking her head toward her companion. "She has been erasing and redrawing the corner of those stones for ten minutes now." The two Venetians smiled at each other. Isabella knew her friend did not find fault in that.

"Have you drawn anything else?" Resi asked.

"Not today, but I will show you some other sketches when we return to the castle. I have left my recent drawings there. I drew a picture of our friend Lieutenant D'Alessandro from memory, and a few of your garden out our bedroom window and from the terrace. I have been sketching as long as I can remember."

"I look forward to seeing them when we return," Resi told Isabella warmly. She looked out to see what Mauro was doing and suddenly cried, "Oh, I had better hurry. Mauro is already in the boat. We are going out to the island for a few hours."

Isabella winked at her. "Oh, that should be very private." Resi had not thought of their excursion as being a romantic one, but she liked the idea.

"I thought Mauritius did not like boats," Caterina said to Isabella. "Remember that one time?" She began to laugh.

"Let us not retell that story now, Caterina." Isabella cut her off with a warning glare. She smiled sweetly to the baroness. "Enjoy your excursion, Lady Terese. We will love to hear all about it later."

Ruby and Resi followed the well-worn path through the woods to the stream to fill their water pouches. On the way back, Resi stopped at the food baskets near the fire pit and packed a smaller basket with the water containers, a cloth bag of almonds, a pouch of raisins, the rest of the bread loaf, and two stoneware jugs of ale. She grabbed her hat to spare her face from becoming too brown, and made her way back to the boat dock, where Ruby was already adjusting the fishing line and cork on Mauro's pole, which she would use.

Mauro was in the boat, and Resi handed him the little picnic basket. She tied her scarf over her hat and took his offered hand. "Shall I sail, or do you want to?" she asked cheerfully. Jero pushed them away from the dock and waved goodbye.

"It will give me pleasure to let you steer. Maybe I will just shut my eyes for a while, if that is all right. Just let me know if I am in the way of the sail," he said, and leaned back on the bench next to her.

"Of course, you must be tired, Mauro. You have had no rest today. Take a nap, if you like. I will take us out to the second island," she told him, concentrating on finding the best path in the wind.

They sailed like that for a quarter hour, tacking back and forth, until they were out on the open sea. They approached the first island. There was no beach there; its rocky shore came straight out of the water to become bleached cliffs. Birds were nesting in the cracks of the rock face and in the courageous pine trees that weathered the elements on its jagged peak. Resi looked up and down the coast at the numerous islands that dotted the sapphire blue surface of the Adriatic. "Who owns all the islands?" she asked.

"The Venetian Empire claims them, of course. We are their colony, and they have rights over even the rocks jetting out of the sea. The navy has holdings on the larger ones," Mauro answered with clear spite in his voice.

"Do the Leopolds claim these islands, like you do the islands in front of Solgrad?" she asked with curiosity.

He opened his eyes enough to look at her. "Yes, but my islands and these along the coast here are uninhabited and are quite useless. Fishermen will sometimes set up a temporary shelter in the summer months. There is no fresh water on any of them and no refuge from the winter storms," he explained. "But, if you look farther south, you can see those four islands in the distance. Baron Raneri claims those as his landholdings. There is a port and a small town on the larger one, and fishing villages on the other three. I will probably visit the largest one when he holds the council meeting later next month."

She wanted to hear about this council he was on, but could not ask for any further details while she maneuvered their way around the first island in the stiff wind. At her request, Mauro moved to the front of the boat so the boom could swing freely until they were on a straight course again. He then moved back from the bow to the middle seat and lay down on the short bench.

"Mauro, are you ill?" she asked with concern, observing how pale his tanned face had become.

"No. I am fine," he insisted. He pulled his hat over his eyes.

"Are you seasick?" she leaned over to ask without shouting in the wind. "If you don't like boats, Mauro, you should have told me."

"It is not the boat, and I am not seasick," he assured her and himself. She watched him for a few more moments and his coloring returned to normal.

"Mauro, can I ask you about something?" He murmured that she could. "Lord Dubovic talked to me at the ball before we danced, and he said something curious about the Carreras."

Mauro had wondered what his neighbor and wife had talked about. "Did he? What did Dubovic say about them?"

"Nothing scandalous. He said that Fabian's and Lady Isabella's fathers are important government officials; they are councilmen. He was impressed that you somehow were friendly enough with them to host their daughters."

Talking would help to keep his mind off his misery. He gladly explained, "My uncle knows Roberto Carrera, Fabian's father. Since Fabian and I are the same age, my uncle asked if I could stay with them in Venice. Lord Carrera *is* an important councilman, and so was Fabian's grandfather. That is how Isabella is a friend of the family. Her father has been in politics with Roberto Carrera for years."

"Are you saying your uncle sent you to the Carreras so you could rub elbows with the Venetian lawmakers?"

He opened his eyes and looked at her with amusement. "Everything is political with my uncle. I did not realize it then, but yes, I was sent there to make an impression on the Carrera family. I was to become the next Baron Baric, and my uncle wanted me to become socially tied to them, in case I should need some favor from the government in the future."

"And did they know your uncle was using them?"

"No one was using anyone. It was a mutual agreement. The council wants to know firsthand what is going on in the territories, and they need eyes in all parts of the Venetian Republic. I could help them with that."

"Are you spying for the council, Mauro?"

"Me? No, I try to keep a low profile with the Empire. I go about my business without talking to the officials in the capital too much, but I have made my house available to them."

She thought about this for a moment. "So that is your link to Fabian? I thought he was your best friend?"

"He is my best friend; a true friend to me, and me to him. I did not think we would ever be so close when we first met. I did not even like him at first." Mauro laughed at the memory.

Resi was surprised. "How could that be? You get along so well."

"Fabian has always been somewhat arrogant and self-assured. The seventeen-year-old version of Fabian was almost intolerable at first. I think he was so self-absorbed that he did not notice I was annoyed by his cockiness."

"Mauro, what would Fabian say if he knew you described him so harshly?"

"He would say it was true," Mauro said with a laugh. "He was once like his sister and Isabella; maybe even more so. He did not mind my own arrogant manners, and led me around during my first visit like his new pet. I did not like the Venetians in the capital even back then, and that was our common thread. He did not mind the lifestyle there, but he wanted to get away. He wanted out of his future obligations."

"Did you convince him to join your uncle's army?"

"He convinced me, really. He had already been taught to shoot and ride; the rest came naturally to him. My uncle offered to train him along with me to see if he was officer material. Roberto Carrera still had other plans for Fabian, but he thought the experience was good for a young man, so he agreed to it. My uncle promised that he would not hold Fabian to a career in his army, if Lord Carrera had another professional position lined up for his son. Men who join the army are generally bound to stay for their lifetime, unless your father is a councilman."

"And your friendship with Fabian grew after that?"

"It did. I suppose we balance each other out, and we formed a lasting bond. He is my closest friend."

"And the political alliance of your friendship was forgotten?"

"Politics will always interfere, Resi. I will admit, this alliance has helped the Barics and the Toths a few times in the past. Fabian may be a third son, but he is very close to his father and very much like him. Fabian has used his ties to the Barics to keep a distance from his future responsibilities. As a friend, I have been happy to accommodate him."

Resi worked to keep the boat on course with the changing wind. She turned the tiller again, and the sails flapped and filled. "And Stephan—is he a political friend?"

"Stephan is a friend because I genuinely like him," Mauro admitted with a chuckle. "He is the balance between Fabian and me. I can count on Stephan to be an agreeable and predictable man. I cannot always count on Fabian to be that." He laughed again at an unshared memory. "I will miss Stephan's company."

"But you still have Jero," she pointed out. "He is also your friend."

How could he explain his relationship with Jero? He tried to open his eyes to look at her without looking at the water. "It is different with Jero. I think I trust Jero more than I have ever trusted another man. But I am a baron, and he is my servant, Resi. He is where he is because of my wishes. I do not think we can ever be true friends because of that. I would like it to be otherwise, but that is the only way we know each other."

"I am here because of your wishes, too. You sent for me," she reminded him.

"That is also different." He reached over and took her free hand in his.

She squeezed it to acknowledge his simple gesture. "Because you have made me your baroness and not your servant?"

Mauro chuckled and put it in plainer words. "You were sent to be my wedded wife. I have already explained how that is different from a friendship." She was about to argue the point again, but thought better of it. They fell into an awkward silence.

Mauro looked out to the island that was their destination. "Why are we not moving?"

"The wind has not been reliable. I think the first island is blocking what little there is right now. I have been trying, but I cannot seem to catch it again. It seems we are in a bit of a dead zone. Maybe you could use the oars to row us in."

Mauro sat up and found the handles of the two, rotting oars along the bottom of the boat. He pulled one out and put it into the water, only to have the flat of the paddle break off on the second stroke. The next oar did not fare well, either. "I will have to give Neven a lesson in taking his equipment out of the water during the rainy season. These oars look ancient anyway." He threw the handles into the sea. "May I have a try?"

Mauro took the tiller and held the sail out. His wife was right; there was no wind to catch here. The little boat drifted slowly toward their destination, but not fast enough for Mauro.

Resi reached for the small basket next to her. "I packed a little snack. Would you like some?" She pulled out the pouch of almonds and handed it to him, noticing her husband's distress. "Oh, Mauro, you do not look well!"

"I am sure I do not, but it will pass." Resi watched Mauro attempt to calm himself. He fought back the building panic. She quietly ate several handfuls of the sweet nuts and drank from the water bladder while he sat on the bench with his eyes closed.

Resi broke the silence. "I have an idea. The water is not so deep anymore, and the current is in our favor. If you are well enough, you could pull us to shore from here. The boat should not be that heavy."

"Jump in and swim the boat to shore?" Mauro asked a little too abrasively.

She was surprised he was being so unhelpful. "Yes, you can swim, can't you?"

"Yes, I can swim," he mumbled back. He did not want to argue. There was no telling how long they would be floating until they could land the boat under wind power again.

"Only if you are well enough," she cautiously added.

"I am well enough," he said without looking at her.

He pulled off his shirt and unfastened his breeches. He folded them carefully and put them into the basket. He noticed that she was staring curiously at him. "I only brought one change of clothes, and I will want to put these back on later," he said, defending his neatness.

"I have just never seen you wear smallclothes, is all."

Under his riding breeches he wore tight cotton leggings that came to the middle of his thighs. Their edges were elegantly embroidered with golden thread. "Then you have always slept through the mornings when I dressed in my riding garments. I mentioned that all of us are spoiled in some way. Well, my uncle is to blame for these," he explained quietly, smoothing the fabric against his legs. "He took me and his other foster sons to his favorite Turkish tailor before we left for our first expedition to the Ottoman Territory. Leather breeches are hot and uncomfortable in the summer, especially traveling farther south, so he instructed that we wear these under them."

"They are beautifully done." She ran her hand along the ornate stitching of the thin, woven fabric. "They are so soft. Oh, I am making you uncomfortable," she said with a chuckle. She found it amusing that even in his misery, her husband could be affected by her caress. She moved her hand away from his thigh.

"I admit they are a bit fanciful, but I cannot wear my leather leggings without them now. I still buy them from the same tailor my uncle introduced me to, and I have new ones sent from time to time." The luxuries of his upper-class lifestyle no longer surprised her, and she said nothing more about it.

"I will swim in them," he concluded, and slid over the side of the boat and into the dark sea, coming up to the surface again near the rudder.

They were still in deep water, but the depths were clearer as he pushed from the back of the boat, kicking them to shore. He concentrated on the movements above the water and not below.

Resi tried to help by moving the sail for any chance of filling it with the flat breeze. After several minutes of swimming, despite the barely contained anxiety rushing over him, Mauro's feet touched the stony shore. He grabbed the tie line and pulled the boat the rest of the way onto the narrow beach. He found a large stone, secured the line around it to keep the boat out of the tide and, without a word, hurried on toward the dense shrubs of juniper and oleander near the middle of the island.

Resi secured the sail; her back was toward the shore as she tried to convince him, "That wasn't so bad." She turned around to be helped out of the boat and saw him disappearing into the underbrush. "Where are you going? Come back here!" she called out. "What is the matter with him?" she asked the boat quietly.

She easily climbed out herself and took the basket and his dry clothes with her. The bottoms of her robes were wet from the tide, and she suddenly felt the heat of the day as she stood on the sunbaked shore of the island. The beach was not sandy like the one at their camp, but the water was clear and inviting.

She lost track of where her husband had disappeared into the trees. He would not be going far on the small island. He would see her in the water and perhaps join her when he was finished with what he needed to relieve himself of. Resi took off her hat and scarf; she put it and a stone into her hat to keep them safe from blowing away. She unbelted her light robe and tugged it off. She left it nicely spread across a boulder to let the bottom half dry; she did the same for her tunic. She knotted the hem on each side of her new summer shift to make it short and tight around her thighs, and then waded into the shimmering water. It felt refreshing in the hot summer sun. She plunged under its surface and swam away.

Chapter 48

Jero and Ruby watched the boat as it made its way across the glistening water. It was midafternoon now, and Ruby said the fish were probably sleeping and would not be biting again until near sundown. Jero suggested they try anyway. Ruby liked the idea of sitting next to him on the dock and agreed to the futile activity. She felt at ease with Jero. They had already talked about their abrupt separation at the dance while riding this morning. That was the first time they had ever talked without others around within earshot. She yearned to spend more time with him, to talk to him, and to know him without his servant's armor.

Jero was happy to have her all to himself too, but was still not sure she shared his admiration. The first few minutes alone they talked about the weather and the filling lunch the group had enjoyed earlier. They checked the bait on their line every so often to keep themselves occupied when they had nothing to say. Both were using the live fish as bait now, and Ruby had moved their cork floats higher on the line so the hooks would sink into deeper water. They sat on the planks at the end of the dock with their feet dangling in the dazzling sea. They were not close, but close enough to converse quietly. Ruby was content.

"Do you like it here?" Jero finally ventured to ask something beyond polite conversation.

"Do you mean here at the sea?" she asked hesitantly. Ruby had diligently learned Croatian this year, and the two were practicing it together now, mixed with the usual Venetian-flavored Latin they spoke at the castle.

"I mean here in general, at the Barics' castle and in Croatia," he clarified kindly. "I know it must be hard for you to be so far from home." He wanted to ask more, but this was a start.

She knew her answer, but she wanted to get the new words right. "I do like it here. I think I surprise myself even telling you that right now. I never dreamed I would want to stay, but I do."

He smiled. Now he could ask her the real question he wanted answered. "Will you stay here, Ruby?"

She moved her line in the water, trying to lure a catch that was probably too far down to notice her bait. "I wish I could definitely say that I will stay, but it is not my choice. I have already stayed beyond my planned year. Now that Resi is pregnant, I may get to stay until her baby is born. I do not know for sure."

He did not realize he was frowning. She went on to explain, "My father was doing Demetrius Kokkinos a favor; they are good friends. Resi required a companion for the journey here. Her other friends are married and starting families. I was free, in a sense."

"Was it your choice to join her?" Jero asked.

"It had been discussed years ago that I would chaperone her. My father did not ask me directly, but Resi did. The last year I was in Greece, I was staying at my uncle's horse ranch in the mountains, helping his wife with their small children. Resi came to visit me twice while I was there, and we talked a lot about it."

He was interested to hear more about her family. "That is where you learned to ride, isn't it?"

"Yes, and Resi learned to ride during her visits, too. Life was quite different for me there compared to here. My grandfather was my teacher, and he did not have rules for riding that the ladies here must follow. Saddles are expensive, and there was not one to spare for me, so I rode without it. My cousins and uncles all had chores to do on the ranch. They did not have time to be chaperoning me. Besides, there was only extended family for miles, so they trusted that I would not come to harm. That was very freeing—like riding is to me."

She had not recently thought about the extended family she missed back in Greece. She had tried to live in the present, not to think of the past or what was to come. But now she could not help it, and it made her homesick. She stared out at the water, not trusting to look in Jero's direction just then.

Jero looked out at water, too, thinking about her story. He felt compelled to admit, "When you first arrived, you and Lady Terese were a surprise to me in many ways. For one, it had not occurred to me that women might want to ride a horse for pleasure. The other noblewomen come in carriages because they can afford it. Aristocratic ladies are different. I am not an aristocrat," Jero continued, "but I have spent my whole life following their formalities and protocol. Not that there is anything strange about how you ride as a lady, but it is, well, enlightening that you can ride like a man." Her puzzled expression told him he had been misunderstood. "I am not explaining myself very well," he concluded.

Ruby's emotions were in check again. "I know what you are trying to say," she reassured him kindly. "It is the same where I come from. Women do not ride horses for pleasure in Greece, either. My uncles breed horses, so I had an unusual opportunity. There are complicated rules in Ottoman lands about riding a horse at all." She did not know the right words to explain what she wanted to. "In the back of my mind, I know I must give it all up again going back to Thessaloniki—the horse riding, the leisure time, the independence. Maybe that is why I want to stay."

She looked at his disappointed face; he had hoped Ruby wanted to stay for a different reason. She tugged on her line again, tempting the fish to bite.

"I suppose being at the sea makes you feel at home," Jero offered as a new topic.

"I am glad to be at the sea," she said to him. "You live on the edge of the Adriatic, so you must feel the same way."

"I have lived within shouting distance of the Adriatic my entire life, so it is a part of me, I suppose. But I have never really spent time like this on its shore before. Living next to something does not entitle you to have it." He would be honest about his station in life. "I have been a servant since I was a little boy. Did you know that?"

"No, I didn't," she replied sympathetically.

"I was indentured to the Barics until the elder baron's death. I was granted little choice in how I used my time until I began working for the new baron." He searched her eyes for disappointment in him, but he found none. He was relieved.

To Ruby, it seemed Jero had free roam of the castle and he would often be gone to the village. It had never occurred to her that he had grown up with none of those chances. "Were you never allowed to swim in the sea as a boy?"

"The Barics' seashore is hard to access, except for the salt flats and the baron's shipping port, but those are off limits to anyone but the Baric soldiers. There are well-used paths down to the sea here and there at the village, but there are no beaches like this. The river is not so far from the castle walls. In the summer, the servant boys were allowed to walk to the swimming hole there to bathe."

Ruby was about to tell him that she was glad he was here with her on this beach today, but her line began to tug violently. She had an angry fish on the other end, and it was fighting to be unhooked.

Jero jumped to his feet to help her hold the flexing pole. She tried to stand up as well, but her foot slipped over the edge. Jero caught her by the waist as she almost tipped into the water. "You hooked a big one, Ruby! Do not drop your pole!"

She found her footing on the dock again. "I will hold the pole, and you pull in the line!" she ordered excitedly. "If we don't hurry, the line will snap. I can see the fish now. I wish we had a net to scoop it up in."

She held the pole steady, and Jero gathered the line bit by bit in his wet hands, losing some to the advantage of the fish every third or fourth pull. Finally, the thrashing catch was hovering above the water, and they both instinctively yanked it onto the dock together. Jero and Ruby fell backward with a thud, and the fish flopped furiously on the wooden planks next to them.

Ruby's screech during the fall, and their laughter that followed, caught the attention of the Venetian women, still comfortably amusing themselves in their makeshift chairs. Fabian walked up to them, streaked with dust and blood on his clothes and cheek. "What is going on over there?" he asked without a greeting.

"What happened to you?" Isabella asked just as informally, with a shocked look.

"I have caught our dinner," he announced proudly, unaware of his appearance.

"And so have they," Caterina added. "It seems Lady Ruby is going to lose her catch. Look, the fish is jumping and twitching all around, and they do not seem to be retrieving it."

Isabella laughed as she watched the couple on the pier. "Lady Ruby has her catch in hand, all right. This is most entertaining; do you not think so, Fabian?" Isabella smiled up at him.

"Hmm," was all Fabian could think to say to her smirk, and then strode off toward the dock.

Ruby and Jero were earnestly trying to save their supper, but the big fish fought for its life, still hooked on the line. Jero tried to hold it down, but the flapping, wet tail was hard to grip, and he had no experience knocking out a fish.

"You have to hit it over the head," Ruby told him, looking for something to use to stun it. Jero looked around, too, thinking there had been a stone on the dock earlier. During their frantic search, they heard a whoosh and a thrum vibrate near them, and Jero turned to see the fish motionless on the dock.

"Fabian! You could have killed one of us," Jero yelled at him, shocked that he had thrown his dagger so close to where they were moving about.

"You insult me, Jero. I have an excellent aim and always hit my target. I could not stand to see you lose our dinner over the side. I thought I was helping out," he explained with an innocent grin on his face.

"Well." Jero tried to compose himself. "Your help was not needed. I had this under control." He held up the newly found stone. Fabian took the stone from Jero's hand and knocked the fish in the head. Then he pulled his dagger from the dock to cut the line and lifted the sizable fish into his arms.

"Excellent fishing, Lady Ruby," Fabian congratulated her. "Do you clean your own catch, or should Jero do the honors?"

Ruby was speechless. She began straightening her appearance; her scarf was cocked and her tunic twisted at her knees.

Fabian explained to Jero, "I came to get your help to carry the buck I shot. We can clean the fish as well." Fabian then said directly to Ruby, "Please excuse us for now, dear Lady Ruby. We will be in the woods just beyond the wagon, should you need us." Fabian tipped his hat, and Jero understood that it was his cue to follow. He picked up his own hat from the dock planks and tipped it also, smiling broadly at his darling Ruby.

Fabian was all business now. He walked directly to the wagon and looked around for a rope to tie the legs of his catch. Jero caught up to him after he grabbed his stockings and shoes from the boulder. "I am sorry, Jero. That was bad timing on my part. I really did not intend to spoil your fun," Fabian assured him.

"Well, you did," Jero simply said. He leaned against the wagon and dusted off his toes. He slipped on his shoes without taking time for his stockings.

Fabian found his rope and a small ax to cut a strong pole to carry their burden, and they began to walk away. "Where did Mauro go off to?" Fabian casually asked. Jero pointed behind them to the first island. Fabian could see the small sail going around the side of the rocky cliffs in the sea. He burst out laughing. "Mauro is sailing on the open waters? Well, this should be good. The man has more pride than I gave him credit for."

Jero was confused. "What should be good? The baron can sail them out of any trouble."

"Then why are you accompanying the ship tomorrow instead of the baron?"

"He wants to spend time with his wife."

"Do you not think his wife would be happy to sail on that cargo ship with him—a sea captain's daughter, who has been around ships her whole life?" Jero did not understand his point, so Fabian spelled it out for him. "Mauro is afraid of the water, Jero. That is the reason you are here."

Jero shook his head; he knew Fabian was wrong. "I swam with the baron his whole childhood. I know he sailed with the other boys growing up. He is not afraid of the water."

"He is fine bathing along the shoreline or on the edge of the river, but he cannot be over deep water. He panics, you know?"

"How do you know that? Count Toth's castle is inland."

"Mauro came to live with my family in Venice. Our villa is accessible only by boat or small walkways and bridges between the buildings. The water is murky, and you cannot see the depths. He was petrified of falling in. His fear practically paralyzed him at times."

"Now it all makes sense," Jero replied. "He was pacing on the dock just before they left, like he does when he has to make a difficult decision. I guess he was deciding to go or not."

"Well, when he does panic out on the water, I hope he comes clean and tells his wife the truth. The man cannot admit to any weakness."

Jero looked out at the small vision of their boat as it rounded the first island and disappeared out of sight. "They are almost to the second island, so he must be all right," Jero said quietly.

"He has to get back, though," Fabian said, still amused at Mauro's predicament. Jero stared out again at the distance, and Fabian interrupted his thoughts. "Come, Jero, let us see if I can find my deer again to go with Ruby's fish for dinner."

~ * ~

Caterina and Isabella put away their work, got up from their cushioned seats, and ventured down to the dock to comfort their new friend. Poor Lady Ruby. They had watched the scene and saw how Fabian had spoiled her chance to get closer to the attentive Jero. Fabian never let others have fun, Isabella thought. They lifted their dragging skirts and hurried to Ruby, who dejectedly busied herself taking the second fishing line out of the water and collecting the scattered bait.

"Leave that, Lady Ruby. Come with us to the tent, and you can change into some dry clothes," Caterina suggested as they met her at the end of the dock.

"You have been in the sun all day, and that cannot be good for you," Isabella scolded gently. "You are pink like a sweet little prawn. I think I brought some soothing cream I can put on your face."

"Yes, I think I might need some. I feel quite hot on my skin," she agreed. "I would like to wash up a bit at the stream first."

"We will come with you, Lady Ruby," Caterina said, and Isabella nodded her agreement. The three walked arm in arm past the camp and into the woods. They would console each other on the obvious shortcomings of men.

Chapter 49

Mauro stepped into the clear water and washed his face, then took a handful of the salty sea to rinse the taste of vomit from his mouth. He would be fine now, and tried not to already think about the trip back. He had not been able to shake the nightmarish vision from his thoughts on the boat. The logical side of him knew there was no danger of being dragged under, but a small corner of his mind told him otherwise. Sailing the boat himself might keep his mind occupied on the journey home. He would have to try that, since there was no avoiding the return trip.

But that was still a few hours away. For now, he would finally enjoy some time alone with his wife. He looked around for Resi and saw her swimming in the shallow waters off the island's shore. A new panic set in, and he fought back the urge to call out to her, to tell her to hurry back. He breathed deeply. She was not out in the deep; she would be all right, he told himself.

He walked up the rocky beach to where she had spread her clothes, and he sat down to wait for her. Mauro looked in the basket Resi had brought on shore. He was pleased that she had thought to pack the jugs of ale, and he opened one and drank it slowly while he watched her swim. His stomach was settled now, and he tore a piece of bread off the loaf stuffed in the basket.

She leisurely floated over the rocks and silvery fish. She had always loved to swim as a girl but was surprisingly exhausted by it, now that she had not been in the water all year. She noticed Mauro had come back to the beach and was looking in her direction. She waved to him sitting on the tall boulder. She saw him smile and wave back. They had sailed to the island to spend time together, and that is what she wanted more than anything. Resi swam back toward the shore.

Mauro watched her come out of the water. He saw that she had fastened her shift to be able to move her legs freely as she swam. She was shockingly seductive; the thin fabric clung to the curves of her feminine body. "You look like Aphrodite herself coming from the water. You would be less exposed if you went naked," he playfully told her when she was back at his side.

"I will not go naked in the open sea. A boat might be going by," she replied earnestly. Mauro's expression was cheerful once again, and she was glad he was over whatever illness he had experienced.

He chuckled and shook his head. "I imagine it would make no difference to a random sailor. You are beautiful either way."

He could not tell if she was blushing or sunburned when she said, "Thank you, Mauro."

She stood next to the boulder where he sat contemplating the view. Threads of water still ran down her legs from her swim. "I love the heat when you can be by the sea to cool off," she said.

He opened the second bottle of ale. "You should drink something in this heat. Would you like this?" He offered her a chunk of the fresh bread as well, and ate another piece himself.

"I see you have your appetite back."

"I never lost my appetite," he told her lightly, finishing his bite.

"You know there is no shame in being seasick. Many strong men are," she declared kindly.

He didn't know why he was so stubborn with her, why he didn't just tell her the truth, but he couldn't come clean. "I was not feeling myself today. Maybe it is the heat. I was wrong to walk away from you like that." He gazed at her, hoping that would end the discussion. She held his gaze sympathetically. She believed him.

"You should put on your shirt, Mauro, if the heat is bothering you. You don't have my Greek skin to protect you from burning."

"I can be in the sun for a little while. It feels nice after the water."

"Yes, it does," she agreed quietly.

He made room for her to sit on the boulder next to him and handed her the pouch of almonds from the basket next. She gladly took a few. He leaned back, stretched out his legs in front of him, and closed his eyes. They sat quietly for a few minutes enjoying the unusual solitude of the island.

She took the opportunity, while he was unaware, to study his peaceful face and admire his body. She had seen him without his shirt on in their bedroom, of course, but the light was often dim—or he was taking one shirt off to put another one on. Seeing him exposed in the stark daylight made her realize just how much he had suffered in war. "When did you get all of these scars?"

The question woke him from his trance, and he unconsciously looked at the numerous, familiar marks on his fair skin. "I have been wounded a few times, I guess."

She touched his knee at the edge of his cotton leggings. "What happened here?" she began her inquiry.

"Here was just a small cut. There, that was a slice from a blade, too." He lifted the embroidered hem to show the thin line that went up his leg a few more inches.

"And this?" She stroked the side of his ribs.

"I was shot there, but it only grazed the skin. I broke a few ribs on this same side another time when I was shoved in a sword fight. That was more painful than the time a horse broke my foot," he said nonchalantly.

"Goodness, Mauro. How did a horse break your foot?"

"I got in its way," he told her frankly, which made her smile.

He uncomfortably let her continue her inspection. "Those were just a few cuts while fighting," he explained as she slowly moved her fingers over the marks on his hand. "I consider myself lucky, though. Many of my friends have had much worse happen."

She stroked the neat stitching that made a jagged cross on the firm flesh above his heart on his left shoulder. "This looks serious, Mauro. What happened here?"

"I was shot when we were attacked coming back from surveying the estate," he told her flatly.

She shook her head in disbelief. "You were attacked on your own land?"

"Yes. We can never be truly safe anywhere, except inside our walls. That is why I am so protective of you, my dear. You are unscarred, and I intend to make sure you stay that way."

Still intrigued, she walked around the boulder and stopped behind him. She traced her finger from the cross-shaped scar in front, over the top of his shoulder, to his shoulder blade in back. She had seen the strange tattoo on her husband's shoulder before, but had never found the right opportunity to ask about it. "The shot didn't go out the other side. It seems the hand blocked the musket ball."

Mauro touched the smooth scar carefully. He thought about how long the recovery had set him back. "It would have been better if the hand had not interfered and the musket ball had gone through. Idita had a hard time finding it in the wound. She gave me one of her famous sleeping draughts to get me through the pain after she did successfully dig it out. I was asleep for two days, and then could not move my arm for a month."

"Does it trouble you now?" She was still touching his smooth shoulder, distracting him.

"It healed well enough to use it normally when we were called back out a month later. I am right-handed anyway, so I could give it some rest."

She put her fingers one by one onto the outline of the tattooed fingers on his back as she listened to him. "What are you doing?" he asked protectively.

"I'm seeing if my hand fits." He did not stop her. "You have never told me the story of how you got this. I have seen sailors with marks and pictures on their arms and chests, but I did not know barons did such things."

He sat tensely, her hand still on his shoulder. She hoped she had not offended him, comparing him to common sailors. "No, it is not something barons normally do. But I was not a baron when this was made."

"It fits my own hand perfectly," she declared contentedly. He put his own larger one up to meet her fingers and left it there holding hers.

"The hand was smaller when Idita marked me with it," he told her, which only fueled her curiosity.

"Idita gave you this?" she asked louder than she intended, astounded the gentle nurse would be allowed to tattoo her ward. She leaned over his shoulder to see his face and asked softly, "Will you tell me the story of how it was made?"

He thought about it a moment. He had never told anyone about that day, not even Fabian or Stephan. But they had never asked, either. "It is not a very interesting story," he remarked.

Resi came around to stand in front of him. Her shift was nearly dry, no longer clinging to her skin. He draped his hands around her narrow hips as she stood in front of him. "How old were you, Mauro?"

He shook his head. What he knew for certain about his wife was her need for details. What surprised him, sitting there looking into her eyes, was that he wanted to tell her everything. "I was just a boy still. It was my thirteenth birthday present."

"Oh." She had not imagined Idita would offer such a torturous gift. "Why would you ask for such a marking? It must have hurt."

She touched his face gently as she gazed at him. It was hot from the sun. He found it distracting, but he answered her lightheartedly, "It was very painful, I remember, and unexpected. I did not ask Idita for the marking, but it was the right gift to give to me. I have not minded having it all these years. I have grown since then, and the hand has grown with me. I never looked at it really, but I always knew it was there."

"Is the 'M' in the center for Mauritius?"

Mauro had not planned to have this conversation now, but there would never be a good time to talk about his brother. "Idita never said, and I never asked. To me, the 'M' was for my brother. He died when I was younger," Mauro answered. He began to fidget, having sat on the hot boulder for so long. He released his wife's waist and stood to stretch his arms.

Resi tried to match his informality. "Your brother's name was Mateo, is that right? And he drowned in the sea?"

She waited, unable to read his blank expression. Mauro thought it was strange hearing this from her. He was certain he had never spoken to her about Mateo, and yet she already knew his name and how he had died. Who had told her? It really didn't matter anymore.

"That is right," he answered her faintly. "It sounds ridiculous now, but Idita told me this would pass his strength on to me."

She didn't think it was ridiculous. "It worked," she reassured him calmly.

He was content to have told her all of this. At least he could talk openly about his brother without becoming melancholy. But Mauro needed to move around. He packed the jugs into the basket and covered them with the cloth. He had come to the island to enjoy some pleasure with his wife, not to relive difficult memories. He knew what he wanted to do.

"I would like to explore the island a little with you, and I will tell you a story about my childhood," he said unexpectedly after he had finished his busy work.

He did not wait for an answer, but grabbed his wife's hand and walked away toward the trees. She jogged the few steps to match his pace. The movement made him animated, and he began the story he had promised. She did not interrupt him as they walked along the shore where the beach met the woods, searching for a path through the scrubby trees and bushes.

"Mateo was friends with Neven," he began in an upbeat voice. Mauro surprised her that his previously undisclosed brother was the subject of his story, but Resi listened with interest.

"Mateo was three years older than I, and Neven was two years older than Mateo. Mateo and Neven were matched better in age, but sometimes I was allowed to come with him to stay at the Leopolds. We never came to this particular island, but we went to one not far from here, with scattered trees and hardy brush across most of it."

He quickly contemplated how he would weave his tale to his best advantage. He smiled playfully at her and continued his true story while they walked across the island. "We were sometimes with a group of other boys when they brought us to the island. Once there, we would do childish things, like play pirates and pretend-fight each other. My favorite game was one in which we imagined that we arrived on two opposing ships, both looking for the same buried treasure. We would chase and capture the other ship's crew to keep them from finding it first," he recounted with exuberance, assured that this island was theirs alone. "We would have our wooden swords, and we brought old rope with us to tie the captured sailors to a tree. The last pirate not tied was the winner."

As Mauro had concluded his story, they found themselves on the far side of the small island with only the Adriatic open in front of them. The mainland and their waiting friends were in a forgotten world behind the woods now. He reached down and picked up a small, pink shell he had spotted at his feet. Without a second thought, he handed it to Resi to admire, like he would have shared with a boyhood friend on the beach. While looking at the interesting shell, she lightheartedly continued where he had left off.

"That is not so different from the games we would play as children. My favorite one was when the girls and the boys played together."

"Ah, that sounds like fun. How was that game played?"

His lively mood had lifted hers, and she matched his enthusiasm. "The girls were marooned on a deserted island, waiting to be rescued. We pretended a sea captain came with his ship of sailors to our island and discovered us alone there." Resi raised her brows to tempt him into her story.

Mauro gladly took the bait. "The girls must have hidden when they saw the sailors," Mauro reasoned. "Sailors can be an ugly, smelly lot after months crowded on a ship at sea. The captain is usually not much better."

"No, no; there you are wrong. The captain had been to the Spice Islands and had a cargo of cloves and cinnamon under deck. It permeated his skin, and he smelled delicious." She put her arms around Mauro's waist to pull him closer and took a deep breath of his bare skin. She gave him a feigned look of longing, and he laughed at her comical expression.

Recovered from her dreamy state, she told him, "Of course, in real life, the marooned girls probably smelled of fish themselves. They would have had chapped lips and matted hair with twigs and shells stuck in it. But we pretended we were still beautiful after all that time alone on the island."

She offered his shell back, and he put it through her braid. "I think I like your game better than mine. Can we play it?" he asked shamelessly. "I don't think we will need these, though."

He gently lifted her shift up and over her head. She watched him put it neatly on some rocks. He took off his cotton leggings and laid those next to her garment. He turned back to his stunned wife and declared, "We still have to wait until we have our wind again to sail back. Our clothes will need some time to dry." His nude body was only an arm's length from hers when he asked, "Now, how did your game go? Was there any talking involved?"

She cleared her dry throat. "No," she decided right then, "they did not speak the same language."

"Ah, so when the spice captain found one of the fishy maidens, did he pick her up like this?" She let out a weak cry when Mauro took her suddenly into his arms. "And then did he seek out a secluded place to ravage his captive maiden?"

"Um, no," she said with a laugh, still suspended in his strong arms. "Our game did not end that way; not at all. We were just boys and girls being silly. There was no ravaging." She looked into his mesmerizing eyes. "Usually the boys just chased the girls and pretended to kill us, so they could have the game to themselves again."

He set her back down on her feet near the shade of the wind-whipped pines. "That is too bad, but I think I would have done the same when I was a boy," he acknowledged.

She thought he was done with their playtime, but he stood close by her and declared, "But I am no longer a boy, and you are definitely not a girl. There is a different version of your pirate story in your grown-up storybooks, is there not?"

She stared up at him and nodded hopefully. He smiled at her sweetness. In a quiet voice he described to her, "It is written that the sea captain looked deep into the eyes of the beautiful maiden, and they knew they were meant to be together. Is this the right story?" She nodded again, caught up in the game.

He looked quickly at where they had ended up, and saw that the patch of dirt below them was smooth. He guided her to the ground. "If I remember the story right, the captain begins to kiss her, starting with her lips, even though they are cracked and sunburned from the years on the island." She giggled at his description with a sudden nervousness, but was silenced as he began to thoroughly explore her soft, smooth lips with a growing anticipation.

He stopped his exploration of her mouth and continued his tale with a new passion in his voice. "The cinnamon captain craved the taste of the sea. He found it on the maiden." He paused in his story once more in order to kiss his way down her neck to her ample breasts, stroking and tasting each one gently. She closed her eyes, breathing shallowly as he took his time exploring her. She dared not disturb his tale. This wasn't ravaging. It was ecstasy, and she wanted more.

Mauro sat up again to kneel by her side. He stroked the taut skin over her curved belly. It was fuller than he had remembered, and the curve now began at her navel. He lovingly kissed her protruding middle, then continued on with the fantasy. "The spice captain was overcome by her beauty, especially her feminine curves."

He stroked and nuzzled his way down her hips to the soft hair before her thighs. He spread her legs with care and tasted the folds of her inviting sex. She was not accustomed to such lengthy attention from her husband, but she submitted to his exploration without protest.

He rose from his pleasurable work and sat close by. "This sea captain brought something quite dangerous with him," he whispered near her ear. "He was daring, and he asked the maiden if she would like to see his weapon. She told him she would."

He brought her hand to his own hips, and Resi opened her eyes again. She firmly took hold of his hard erection, and he let out a hushed sigh that told her he approved of her improvising.

With closed eyes, still being caressed by her, he concluded quietly, "And the spice captain and his salty maiden lived happily ever after—the end." She laughed at his sudden ending and released her grip.

But he was not laughing, and he was not done. He looked at her with such a compelling mix of tenderness and longing that everything else suddenly fell out of focus for Resi. The anticipation of what he would say next was aching.

He did not disappoint her when he said, "I believe this is what really happens between the man and the woman in the story. It is the inevitable ending that they do not tell you in your books," he whispered, then straddled her lounging body.

She knew what scene came next in his tale and she could hardly contain her desire for him. "Yes, I think you are right. This is really what happens," she repeated as he lifted her hips to meet him.

Resi willingly surrendered to her spice captain, and Mauro took possession of his young wife—careful and lovingly, hungry and wantingly. She was all he needed at that moment. They forgot about the rest of the world. In this moment he would say with his body all the things he could not tell her with words, and she was sure he was saying he loved her.

Chapter 50

The three ladies had given up on their gossip about Fabian and Jero and now chatted casually about themselves. Ruby had taken off her outer layers of clothing and knelt in the swift, shallow stream, dressed only in her airy shift. She washed the sand out of her tunic and robe in the current. They had talked about Ruby's life in Thessaloniki, and now Ruby asked Caterina about her life in Venice. "I thought you might go to the seashore all the time living in Venice?"

Caterina crouched next to her and splashed her face with the cold water. The bottom of her summer skirt dragged in the watery bank of shiny stones. "We are surrounded by water at our villa in Venice. Sitting in the sun looking at more water is not so important to me. There is so many ways to entertain oneself indoors, anyway. There are museums and art galleries, there are operas and theaters, long lunches and parties."

"Were you ever schooled growing up?" Ruby was curious to know.

"My sisters and I had a tutor, Signora Francesca, who came every day for a few hours to teach us all the important things young ladies should know. We all learned to read and write Latin and Venetian, of course. Our tutor taught us a little about adding numbers for general household requirements. She took us to the museums to discuss the famous artists and their works. We were taught to converse in French, Spanish, and German for the odd chance of being paired with foreign nobility."

Isabella added, "It is helpful at the opera to know a few of the European languages."

"That is quite a lot of learning," Ruby remarked.

Caterina nodded her agreement. "We were educated in all the essential subjects, but we were not required to learn tedious topics like history and philosophy."

"Those dull studies are best left to the young men," Isabella interjected.

Caterina agreed thoughtfully. "Mostly," she added, "we were taught how to conduct ourselves like ladies."

"I can imagine there was much to learn to become a true lady," Ruby said. "When we arrived here, it was thought that Resi already knew what was expected of her. We are still surprised by what is required of a baroness."

She finished her washing and wrung out the wet fabric of her tunic; beads of water rained back down onto the rocks. She looked around the edge of the flowing stream shadowed by the woods. "These will dry best spread out in the sun on the beach. I should have brought my clean clothes from the tent to put on," she said regretfully. "I hate to put these wet clothes on over my shift."

Isabella dried her hands and face on the folds of her gauze gown. The slippery rocks were difficult to walk across in her borrowed sandals, and she teetered back to where Ruby was standing on solid ground. "I think we are quite alone, Lady Ruby, so no one will see you wander back into our tent in your undergarment. The men have all but abandoned us," Isabella said.

"Where do you think they have gone off to?" Caterina asked.

"Fabian said he caught our dinner. You saw how filthy he was. I am sure he shot a boar or something heroic, and the two will carry it back on their shoulders, dripping blood everywhere," Isabella said.

"Why do you dislike Fabian so much?" Ruby reluctantly asked.

Caterina crossed her arms and waited for Isabella to admit she didn't dislike him at all. The romantic side of her wished Isabella would stop claiming that her past affection for him was gone.

"Is that the impression I have given you?" Ruby nodded that it was. "Well then, I suppose I dislike him because his is very disagreeable," Isabella answered vaguely.

Ruby pondered her remark. "I have only known him the year I have been here, but I think he is very agreeable. He is kind and good-humored."

"And attractive?" Isabella finished her thought for her. Ruby blushed through her pink sunburn. "One year is not a long time, Lady Ruby. I have known him since we were children. About two years ago we had a misunderstanding that ended our friendship for good. I had not thought about him in all that time until we arrived here last week. And I am sorry that I must encounter him still."

They gathered their things and walked back through the trees toward their camp. "People change, Isabella," Caterina said sympathetically. "Lady Ruby has a point. Fabian can be very agreeable. Maybe you should give him a chance to show you that again."

"I think he does not want another chance. He already told me he is sending me home on Thursday," Isabella reminded her. Caterina had already heard the upsetting news that Ruby was just now learning. The group's merry mood had shifted back again.

Isabella tried to brighten the conversation once more. "I was teasing you earlier, Lady Ruby. I do not believe it is Fabian who catches your eye.

How long have you been in love with Jero?" she asked, skillfully transitioning the conversation back to Ruby.

"Yes, that is what I was wondering, too," Caterina added coyly.

Ruby fretted she had been caught being too bold. "Is it so obvious to you that I like him?"

"To us, yes. But it is not obvious to Jero, or he would not be trying so hard to get your attention," Caterina declared.

Isabella studied Ruby's puzzled reaction. "Oh, I see the problem, Caterina," Isabella said confidently. "Lady Ruby does not see the obvious, either. Well, I saw it on Jero's face before Fabian dragged him away from you. The man is smitten. He is head over heels."

"Do you mean in love? With me?" Ruby could not dare to believe that.

"Yes, Lady Ruby, of course with you," Isabella said.

Caterina nodded that it was true. "We can see he is practically lovesick," she added.

Ruby began to panic at this new revelation.

"But what to do about it, that is the real question," Isabella pondered mischievously.

They came out of the woods and went to the food table to pick through the choices packed away in the baskets. It was late in the afternoon, but it would still be a while until their dinner would be roasted and ready. Isabella took some apricots from a woven basket and gave two to Caterina, who put one into her mouth.

Ruby stood nearby with her dripping clothes in her arms. "If what you say is true, ladies, then I do not know what to do now," she admitted.

"Do you want him to court you, or do you want to play coy and reject his advances?" Isabella asked plainly.

Ruby was not sure herself. "I don't want to reject him, but I should not lead him on, either. That would not be right, since nothing can come from it. I would like to just be Jero's friend and enjoy his company while I am here. That would satisfy me."

"No, no, no, Lady Ruby. You are beyond that point," Isabella warned. "A man and an unmarried woman cannot just be friends, anyway. There is always some romantic tension that interferes."

Ruby thought about the many men she considered her friends and asked, "That cannot be the rule for all men, can it? You are friends with the baron. Surely you do not feel romantic tension from him?"

Isabella conceded the flaw in her theory. "There are exceptions to the rule here and there, and the baron is one of them. Mauritius has a lovely new bride, so his focus is securely rested on her for now. Fabian is the perfect example, though. Just when I think we can dance and have a few laughs in a social setting, he corners me. It is always the same tired question—will you choose me tonight? It is all about the conquest, Lady Ruby, no matter the man. I do not even know why they ask. As if I had a choice," she said sullenly.

Ruby frowned at the new insight. Caterina came to her side and added more upbeat advice. "It does not have to be as dramatic as Isabella's love affairs are," Caterina said. "Make Jero do the worrying about where it will go from here. At least you have his attention, and that is most of the struggle in finding love. If he is devoted to you, he will fight to keep you."

Isabella listened to Caterina with pity. Would her beloved Paolo fight for her? Perhaps the answer would be waiting for them when they returned to the Baric Castle.

Ruby was overwhelmed and needed some time to think on all of this love advice from these experienced ladies. She walked beyond the camp and found a clean place to drape her soggy clothes. Caterina had already gone into the tent while Ruby finished hanging her washing and Isabella snacked from the baskets. Caterina opened the canvas flap with her deck of cards in her hands. She smiled at her two companions and declared, "Hurry and get dressed, Lady Ruby. I have brought something to help us forget our troubles. How about a nice game of cards?"

~ * ~

While the women were at the stream discussing the men, Fabian and Jero were in the woods fetching their evening meal. Fabian picked out a sturdy sapling among the young trees to use to carry the deer carcass back to camp with. They only had the one ax, but Fabian quickly downed the small tree and cut the branches away to make a stiff pole. Jero distractedly picked at the leaves of a bush while Fabian worked. "What is on your mind, Jero?" Fabian finally turned to ask him.

"You have been the baron's trusted friend a long time," Jero began.

Fabian set the ax blade down on the ground and leaned on the handle. He and Jero were not friends, but he answered him as an equal, "Yes, I suppose so. The baron and I have been through a lot together."

Jero nodded. "You know that I grew up at the castle with the baron. I have known him since we were little boys."

"I do know that."

Jero threw down the last of the leaves in his hands. "Did he ever tell you about his brother, Mateo?"

"He did many years ago, yes. I know that his brother drowned before Mauro went to the count's castle," Fabian said. "He did not tell me much beyond that. I suppose I did not ask, either."

Jero was silent for a moment.

"What would you like to tell me, Jero? I am sure you will not be breaking any confidences. Mauritius and I have very few secrets from each other."

Jero took Fabian's reply as fact. "It sounds silly now, but as boys we both believed in the tales of the underworld and the gods who ruled the depths of the sea. The baron was alone with Mateo when he died. His brother did drown, but he was taken by the sea. His body never surfaced to be recovered and buried. He just seemed to have vanished."

"Vanished? How did it happen? Where were they?"

"They were just playing at the seaside where they had been many times before. No one knows what really happened. The baron never talked about it to anyone. He actually did not talk at all for an entire year—not to his father, not even to me. That twelve-year-old boy is still in there, Fabian, and has convinced the grown man that they will come for him, too."

"They?"

"The underworld gods," Jero said uncomfortably, realizing it sounded childish.

"Jesus Christ." Fabian unconsciously crossed himself. "Is that what you think his fear of murky water is all about?"

Jero nodded.

Fabian thought about Jero's theory. "What a thing to happen to a boy. To be swimming with your brother, and he just disappears into the depths. And you believe Mauro panics in the boat, because he fears Neptune himself is going to grab him and drag him under, like his brother?"

Jero resolutely nodded yes again.

"Shit," Fabian said under his breath. "I am glad you told me, Jero. This is good to know."

Fabian carried the ax back to the nearby wagon and put the freshly cut pole over his shoulder. "I do not love my brothers half as much as I should, but that would be hard to bear, very hard indeed." He shook his head and thought more about his friend's irrational fear. Fabian walked into the trees and Jero followed, carrying their pole between them.

"I would not say anything to him, at least not today," Jero added.

"No, not today," Fabian agreed.

There was a narrow deer path worn in the underbrush, and the two marched along it. "Well, maybe this little sailing expedition will help the baron realize that there are worse things for a wife to learn about a man than that," Fabian said. "His wife has been good a match for him. She is breaking his hard shell," Fabian asserted.

The deer was up ahead, dead on the forest floor with the feathers from an arrow showing from its neck. Fabian made one final remark on the subject. "It will not be a pleasant trip for him, thinking he is doomed at any time. He should have just told her here on the dock. Stubborn man."

Fabian bent over the deer and slowly pulled the arrow's shaft out with his gloved hand. "We have an hour or so until they come floating back," Fabian reasoned. "If you can help me hang this deer, we can skin it and take some pieces for roasting. The weather is too warm to keep the meat, but if we roast the haunches and tenderloins, we can have a good meal tonight and fry some for breakfast, too." Fabian looked over at the baron's steward. "What is the matter, Jero?"

Jero had a big grin across his face while listening to the nobleman. "I am sorry, Fabian. I do not know what has come over me." He began to laugh nervously. "I just, um, you surprise me, is all. This is somehow unexpected."

Fabian stood tall and stretched his back. He smiled good-humoredly. "Even a self-indulgent Venetian aristocrat can learn to feed himself, Jero. I have known how to shoot a bow since I was a boy, but one of the first things General Toth taught us was how to feed our troops when the food supply was gone. I learned to kill, skin, and prepare everything from birds to dogs. I can set traps for rabbits and butcher a deer. These skills have served me well in my six years of soldiering, and I am quite good at them. There is never enough food to eat in the army," Fabian said frankly. "I do prefer a table graced with ornate platters prepared by servants in crisp aprons. You know I like to eat well, but I can feed myself in a pinch."

Jero had been told what war was like, but he had not directly been affected by it. They had never known hunger at Baric Castle. He had always thought of Fabian as Mauro's captain, under his command, following the baron's orders. But Fabian was used to taking charge and giving orders; Jero could see that clearly for the first time. "I apologize. Tell me what you need me to do," Jero said with a straight expression again.

Fabian went on as though the conversation had not happened. "We will sling the carcass on the pole to carry back to camp and rope it up to skin it. I hope someone thought to pack a crock of Mauro's salt. With that, we could preserve the hide to take back to the castle."

"There is a sack of salt and more rope in the supply box in the wagon. I know how to skin a deer," Jero added. "But that is about all."

Fabian patted him on the back. "Good. That is already helpful." He proceeded to tie the deer's hooves front and back, and then slid the pole through its legs. Each man took an end, and they headed back to camp carrying their load on their shoulders.

As they trudged along, Fabian remarked, "Once we get the fire going, I will teach you to shoot my bow. That is if Ruby knows how to tend a roast. I know my sister and Isabella will be of little assistance."

Jero smiled to himself. "I think Ruby is quite accomplished in many things. I believe we can count on her."

Chapter 51

Mauro knew it did not matter, since they were alone, but his wife looked sinfully scandalous. Her face glowed from the sun and the salt water and the sex. She had retrieved her sleeveless shift and slipped it over her head, then untied the knots that had made the flowing length swimmable. Mauro was dressed in his smallclothes again and went behind her to pick the bits of twig and grass out of her braided hair. He could not resist wrapping his arms around her middle to stroke the subtle roundness that was the baby they had made together, asleep in his mother's depths.

"Are you not doing too much, Resi? Is he all right with all of this moving about?" Mauro asked with a fatherly concern.

"Babies don't mind normal activities. He is active himself. If you wait a minute, you might feel him." She had been feeling the flutters within her for a week now, and had just noticed she could feel them on the surface of her trim belly, too. She put his hand on the spot where she last felt movement and they waited. There was a small ripple under her skin.

She could not see his face behind her, but it was a mix of surprise, fear, and wonder. "That is remarkable. Is that really the baby? Does it hurt you?"

She laughed. "No, it does not hurt me, but it is a strange sensation. At first I thought it was just my meal not settling right, but now I am sure it is the baby. I am almost five months along."

"When we get back, promise me you will rest in the tent before dinner?"

She was always promising something to her husband, but she did feel tired and would look forward to shutting her eyes. "I promise," she said.

They walked back to the other side of their island hand in hand. The wind whipped at Resi's shift when they came out of the shelter of the inner island and back onto the beach. Resi broke their silence. "We have been gone quite a while, haven't we? They will think our little boat has sunk."

"We will not be missed so quickly. They know it takes time to get here, and we have only been gone a few hours." He bravely suggested, "I would like to sail the boat back for you."

"Then I can be the one who shuts my eyes this time," she said. It would be preferable that she closed her eyes, he thought, in case he panicked again out on the water.

They were back near the boat when Resi surprised him by saying, "I am glad to know that you can be romantic when you try."

"Was I trying?" he asked as innocently as he could manage.

"Weren't you?"

"I guess I prefer direct actions over poetic overtures," he said. He reached for his shirt near the basket and slipped it over his head. "Did you enjoy the story, though?"

She looked almost bashful when she told him, "I did, very much. The ending was especially nice."

He pulled on his leather breeches over the cotton ones and tucked in his long shirt. He continued to smile at her when he brought the dry tunic and she slipped it on. "So I am not hopeless?"

She reflected a moment. "Did I call you hopeless before?"

He laughed. "Maybe those are my own words. You made it easy for me today, especially when you looked so much the part of the marooned maiden." He handed her the last garment draped over the boulder and prepared the boat for their departure.

They drank the last of their water, and then Mauro secured the basket in the boat and helped his wife settle onto the bench. Resi efficiently tied her long scarf over her hat to keep from losing it in the wind. He freed the boat from the island's grip and jumped in before the shallow shore dropped off into the sea again. The tide and new wind did the rest of the work, and within a few minutes their small boat had pulled away into the open water. Mauro set the sail. He could do this, he thought.

The wind was behind them, and they made good speed with little effort on Mauro's part. His wife's talkative mood helped distract him from looking down at the rudder and into the depths of the azure water.

Their conversation came back around to the ball. "You were very insightful at the party, Mauro. I have never talked to you when you have drunk so much," Resi said merrily.

"I rarely have the occasion to be drunk," he said. His memory was spotty, at best, from the first dance with his wife to when Fabian ruined his evening at the sitting room door. He was curious what she was referring to and asked, "What insight did I share?"

"You had some opinions about Lady Isabella, for one."

"I suppose I do. What did I divulge in my drunken state?"

She had been lounging with her eyes closed, and now opened them to watch his reaction. "You seemed to know quite a bit about her virtue."

He laughed, not remembering any comments about that. "I can promise you, I have not tampered with Isabella's virtue. I do not know why I would have said that."

She gave him a sharp, scolding look. "Something about letting the lieutenant take her to his bed as his prize."

He just shrugged guiltily. "That could have been plan B."

"How could such a plan B be any different from what you were originally avoiding, Mauro? Besides, I thought a marriage contract between nobility required the wife to be a virgin. Lady Isabella could never marry a gentleman, if she had slept with the lieutenant."

Mauro focused on the boat's course and thought about her remark. "That is the beauty of a contract, Resi; it says whatever you want it to say," Mauro assured her. "It is better for the man if his wife is a maiden when they marry, but it is not necessarily unacceptable if she is not. An untouched bride won't give him syphilis or be pregnant with some other man's child when he marries her. Some men insist, though, because they want the pleasure of being the first and only lover."

"Maybe so the bride doesn't know the difference, if the man turns out to be a terrible lover," Resi suggested mischievously.

"I had not thought of it that way," Mauro conceded with an agreeable grin.

He continued talking to keep his mind occupied on something besides the sea rushing along the side of the boat. "I have met men who really do not care how inexperienced the bride is on their wedding night. They care more about the dowry she brings into the marriage," he explained. "And then there are men who will court a beautiful woman for the sport of it. They want to steal her from their challengers, like a trophy won at the end of a game. Isabella has the advantage that she has a large dowry *and* she was a prized beauty."

Resi considered his words and asked, "Was a prized beauty? Don't you think she's beautiful now?"

He answered honestly, "Yes, I think she is still very beautiful, and most men would agree. But she will turn twenty-three soon, and she is competing against newly introduced beauties for a good marriage contract. That is why her father is not giving her any more time to secure a husband."

Resi leaned back. "It is more complicated than I realized."

"Marriage *is* complicated, Resi."

"Only when men make it so," she countered boldly.

Before he could protest, she asked, "And did I bring a dowry into our marriage? My father did not tell me any details."

Mauro wondered why any of this should matter to her, now that they were already married. But he liked that she had an inquisitive nature, and their arrangement had been fairly straightforward. "No, there were no monetary exchanges that I know of. I suppose that was only fair, since this was forced upon your family. Other women marrying a baron would need to bring wealth or land into a marriage."

"So my father got a bargain from the Barics?" she asked, a little too harshly.

Mauro disregarded her bitter tone. "It was not in our contract that you provide a dowry."

"So we had a written marriage contract?"

"Yes, of course," Mauro continued to tell her truthfully.

The wind was varied and unpredictable as they circled the smaller island. Mauro tacked several times to steer toward their cove, and Resi had to keep out of the way of the sail. When they were no longer distracted by Mauro's maneuvering, Resi dared to ask, "What did our marriage contract say exactly?"

Mauro had to think for a moment. "I do not know exactly," he said.

"How could you not know? Did you never read it?" she asked in disbelief.

He laughed. It was a fair question. His wife might have made a good business advisor, had she been a man. He was enjoying this conversation, after all. "Why would I need to read it? I was told all the important points, and I had no choice in the matter, just like you. I figured your father must have read it and would fulfill his end. Nestor read it, and would fulfill ours. It was already decided without me."

Her scowl told him she did not believe her meticulous husband would not have read a contract that he thought would ruin his life. "I did glance through it once," he admitted, "but that was over a year ago. Is it so important to you?"

"It is," she said earnestly.

"All right then, let me think. Just offhand, I do know you were to provide your own lady's maid for the first year, which is why they sent Ruby with you."

"But Ruby isn't my lady's maid."

"Well then, you have broken the contract," Mauro teased her playfully.

She was not amused. "What else was required?"

"Well," he began slowly, "your father was required to give you a clothing allowance for the first year, which we agreed to match. But you spent that on the library."

He hoped that would satisfy her curiosity, and he looked ahead to the approaching lagoon.

"Nothing else?" she asked when he became silent again.

He clearly remembered this next detail. "If you insist," he said. "It was written that you are to give me an heir within the first five years."

"Give you an heir? What does that mean?" She thought she had misunderstood.

He managed to keep a straight expression. "It means, if you birth only daughters, I could send you back."

"What sort of a restriction is that to impose on a wife?"

She looked genuinely troubled, and he was immediately sorry he had played with her emotions. He could have picked one of the many other requirements to disclose instead of that one. "I do not know why it was written in the contract, Resi," he said sympathetically. "The Catholic Church does not grant divorces anyway. Maybe it is to keep you coming to my bed until we have a son, or perhaps two or three." He winked at her, but she did not find the humor in it that he did. "My mother left my father's chamber after I was born. That may have been a sore point with him, and he wanted better for me."

"But your mother gave him an heir," Resi reminded him.

He did not have to be reminded. "Yes, she did."

"Mauro," Resi began warily, "why was I was not contracted to marry Mateo? He was alive when our arrangement was made."

Mauro had asked Nestor this same question. He explained to her what Nestor had told him. "Mateo was the firstborn son and heir to the barony. He had to marry within the aristocracy. They would not waste the chance to increase his wealth by marrying him to a commoner."

"Is that what I am called?"

"Well, you are not a commoner in the sense of being a servant or a barmaid. But when you do not have a title for your husband to claim and no particular wealth to give to him, then yes, that is the term used."

"And they could sacrifice your noble bloodline to mix with my common one?"

Her description was accurate, and he acknowledged, "I was not as important as the second son. Unless something happened to Mateo, which it did, I would not inherit the title or any of the family fortune."

"Mateo would have gotten everything, and you would be put out with nothing?"

"I would have been given a profession, or continued as an army officer on my yearly allowance. My father gave me the old villa house and the land surrounding it. It could be profitable enough to live off nicely, and you would have been comfortably taken care of, too."

"Who was Mateo betrothed to?"

The topic of Mateo was becoming difficult. Mauro had already talked more about him in the last few hours than he had in the past ten years. But talking was preferable to silence and the rush of the water caving in on their tiny boat.

He let out a deep sigh and explained the complicated arrangement he had learned about only a few years ago. "Mateo would have married my cousin, Augustina Toth. Nestor told me there had first been a different deal for Mateo's marriage with Lord Dubovic's daughter when he was very young. Lord Dubovic seemed to think for a long time that my brother was to marry his eldest girl. There was a clause in the Dubovic marriage contract voiding it if Mateo was offered a contract with a close relation that first year. My uncle, it seems, offered our cousin as a bride at about the same time." Despite Resi's stunned expression, Mauro continued to explain, "It was convenient that the Count of Toth presided over the legal disputes of the region. He ruled that the second marriage contract with Augustina was the valid one."

"Why was your cousin chosen to marry Mateo? Is that even allowed by the Church?"

"Mateo was my half-brother, Resi. Augustina is a second cousin to me through my mother, but she was not a blood cousin to Mateo. I have met her on several occasions; she is quite nice." He went on to say, "Augustina is my mother's uncle's granddaughter. My mother's uncle was my grandfather's younger brother, but he also married well and was quite wealthy. His first son was Augustina's father, my mother's first cousin." Resi looked lost. "The family tree may seem complicated, but a marriage to Augustina was a favorable alliance for the Barics. My uncle Vladimir is a controlling man, and he wanted to be sure the Baric estate and its name was secure. The Toths and Barics would share titles again, and he could still have some control over it, should Augustina become a widow. But my uncle bet on the wrong son."

The words lingered in Resi's mind. "I thought you admired your uncle?" she finally asked.

"I do. I think he is a courageous and generous man. I have learned a lot from him, and he has been good to me. But one thing I know to be true about him is his own interests come first."

The couple was silent again after sharing such a frank exchange. They sailed pensively into the lagoon. Resi tried not to be troubled by her newly realized constraints. Mauro had kept his fears at bay, but he longed to be off the water, and he concentrated on their destination. He could see the women moving about on the beach. There was smoke rising from the fire pit. Mauro searched for Jero and Fabian, but was disappointed they were not to be seen at the camp.

Ruby had noticed the sailboat coming quickly to shore. She waved cheerfully in their direction and ran down the beach to help them dock their boat again.

Chapter 52

Getting the meal organized had been easier than Fabian had expected. He had given Isabella his knife to cut some onions and a chunk of fat from the ham to tuck into the venison haunch to flavor it. He had showed his sister how to fan the fire and move the embers so the meat could cook slowly. Ruby required only a little instruction on tending the lean meat over the coals. Jero had busied himself cleaning her catch to include with their evening meal. Satisfied that they were not needed on the beach once the meat was cooking over the fire, the men watered their horses and went back into the woods.

Fabian had taken the choice pieces off the skinned deer for roasting that night. The meat left on the bones would spoil quickly in the summer heat, so there was no reason to save it. He would have the chance to hunt again tomorrow. The two carried the unwanted carcass back into the woods to let nature consume the rest.

Having finished their duties, the two men could now relax with some sport before dinner. "This is a good spot to set up a target," Fabian told Jero. "Do you hunt?"

"No, I am sorry to say I have not had a chance to. Lord Lorenc did let me train a bit with a bow. I was a good shot once, but have not held one in years."

"Hmm. Well, we will fix that today. Here, let me show you how this is strung." Fabian took his bow apart again, and then stood closely by Jero so he could watch. "It is a little different from the bows the Barics use."

"Is this a Turkish bow?" Jero asked.

Fabian was impressed that Jero at least knew there was a difference. "Yes, it is shorter and lighter. It is also better than ours, I am sorry to say," Fabian said. "Let me show you how best to draw one. It takes some getting used to." Fabian took an arrow from his quiver and notched it. "It is better to use your thumb, but you will feel what pulls best for you." He demonstrated the technique. "Now you try."

Jero repeated what Fabian had shown him, aimed for the target they had set up in the opening of the trees, and released the arrow. It went off into the brush. He handed the bow back to Fabian.

Fabian notched a new arrow and released it, hitting the target. "You just need a little practice. Here." He handed his bow back to Jero, stood behind him, and showed him where his shoulders should be and the correct stance.

Jero shot several more times, and on the fourth try finally hit the target. He tried once again and hit it dead-on.

Fabian patted him on the back smiling. "There you go," he said.

"Do you use your bow often?" Jero asked.

"Not in battle. I trained as an archer before I joined the army. I prefer the weapon over the others, but archers are not used in the sieges as much anymore. Muskets are more important now. Count Toth did not need more officers for his musketeers, so I was assigned to manage the big cannons."

He and Jero went to collect the arrows from the target and the bushes to practice more. "Bows come in very handy when scouting and in smaller fights," Fabian said. "I like the stealthiness of it. The muskets give your location away with the first shot. A hand gun is heavy and takes time to load. Even for the best musketeers, the aim is rarely true. A good archer, though, can hit a man exactly where he wants: in the heart to kill him, or in the leg to maim him. A skilled bowman can kill ten men and run out of arrows before one musketeer can reload his gun to shoot a second."

They had collected all the arrows, and Jero notched a new one from the full quiver. "Why did you become a soldier, Fabian?" He let the arrow fly; it hit the mark.

"Do you ask because I am wealthy and should just enjoy the lazy life allotted me?" Fabian asked frankly. There was no hostility in his tone. He wanted to know what Jero thought of him.

Jero took a deep breath and told him the truth. "All right then, yes, that is what I am asking. Most men become a soldier because they are called to duty by their lord, or a lord is called to duty by his king. For many men, there is nothing else to keep them at home or on the farm. Soldiering will at least feed him, give a man purpose."

Fabian already knew all of this. Jero notched the next arrow. Fabian watched him. He said thoughtfully, "Maybe I needed a purpose, or maybe I am a fool. I could have lived comfortably in Venice learning my family's trade, but I chose to be camped out on a battlefield free from the duties my father dictated. My father said it is because I inherited my great-grandfather's willfulness."

"Did he choose the battlefield over comfort?" Jero asked.

"He chose to step out of his station in life. He was a self-made man and did what he wanted, not what his forefathers had always done. In his day, if you were smart and acquired the right connections, you did not need blue blood to rise among the ruling class in Venice. Most of those successful merchant men bought some sort of title with their cleverly earned gold. My grandfather rose in rank to the aristocracy that way."

"You are not from the nobility?" Jero was surprised Fabian had admitted this to him.

Fabian chuckled. "We are now, but I am not of noble blood for hundreds of years like the baron is. My father is *Lord* Roberto Carrera, but I am only third in line for my father's title. So, I pledged my allegiance to the Toth Army in service to the Serene Republic of Venice. It has been a good life as a soldier. Mauro has been a good friend and gives me a place to live so I do not need to go back to my father's home between the wars."

"Do you not have your own house?"

"No. I am not cut out for a home life. Maybe one day I will settle down, but for now I am content with just a comfortable bed somewhere."

Jero had finished shooting the quiver of arrows and had hit the target each time but once.

"You are a good shot, Jero. You would have made a good soldier. Let me give you some advice that I was once given." Jero nodded and listened dutifully. "The arrow is a precise weapon. If you ever have to kill a man with one, then kill him."

Jero had expected more wisdom than that. "Well, that is some sage advice," Jero said sarcastically.

Fabian's tone remained serious. "Take it to heart. I have seen men linger for hours, sometimes days, with an arrow wound festering in his belly or his thigh. In a good fight, you do the man a favor and kill him straight out with an arrow to the heart or head, if you can, and end his life quickly."

"I am twenty-five and have yet to own a bow," Jero pointed out. "I doubt I will be faced with that choice, but I will heed your advice, if the day comes."

Fabian nodded, satisfied to have passed on to Jero what he had been taught.

Jero went looking for his stray shot and inadvertently kicked something metal in the underbrush. He reached down and pulled up a half-buried breastplate from a suit of armor. It was rusted and old, but still recognizable. "Look at this," he said to Fabian, holding the steel plate in the air. He looked around the bushes and saw other pieces scattered. He picked up the warrior's helmet with the skull still in it, but dropped it in panic.

"It is best to leave dead soldiers lie. We do not want to disturb their ghosts," Fabian warned.

"Do you believe in ghosts, Fabian?" Jero asked lightly, expecting him to tell him no.

"Do you believe in sea monsters that drag you to the underworld, Jero?" Fabian replied just as lightly. "There is a reason for those tales, and I am not one to doubt there is a grain of truth in it. Now, if you could find the arrow, we should be getting back."

"Yes, you should be getting back," Mauro interjected; he had quietly joined them in the woods. "You have left our women unguarded from the sea. I could have already taken the lot away with me on my pirate ship. Those tales can be real, too."

"Shit, Mauro! Do not startle me like that," Fabian shouted, shaking off his shock. "We are talking of ghosts, and you come creeping out of the trees just like one."

Jero walked over to them with the lost arrow and breastplate in hand. Jero and Mauro greeted each other with a nod and a smile. Mauro told Fabian, "I was not creeping. I walked up to you as plain as day, but you were amusing yourself too much to notice."

"Yes, we were enjoying a little target practice," he said more cheerfully, already forgiving Mauro for causing his fright. "But the question is whether you amused yourself. How was the boat ride, Captain Baric?"

Mauro looked toward Jero, who also waited for his answer. He decided he did not need to gloss the details over because of him. He admitted, "Like any other boat ride, it was miserable. I barely made it to the island. We lost our wind and floated for some time before I had to swim the boat to shore."

Fabian laughed sympathetically. "So have you had enough sailing for one outing? Can I take the boat out tomorrow?"

"I insist you take it out tomorrow, and then my wife will not have a chance to ask me again. The second island is quite nice, though. Once I recovered, we thoroughly enjoyed ourselves," Mauro said sheepishly.

Fabian knew that expression. "Well, Mauritius, I am glad to hear things are happy with the Baric newlyweds again. That will make for a more pleasant evening for all of us. And, I think I can smell our dinner now. Shall we go back and join the ladies?" Fabian picked up his bow, and the three walked off toward the beach.

"I checked in with the ladies after we docked the boat. They are doing a fine job at camp; even your sister is helping. Ruby said she would wait until we were back before she put the fish over the fire. Who caught that?" Mauro asked Jero.

"Ruby did," he told him proudly. "It was ferocious. It took the two of us to land it and Fabian's dagger to keep it from sliding back into the sea."

Fabian laughed at his description and told Mauro, "They were not trying very hard to save the fish, from what I witnessed. I took it upon myself to chaperone the pair and split them up."

"You are too young to play the role of father, Fabian." Mauro patted his steward on the shoulder in sympathy. "I do not think Jero needs a chaperone, do you, Jero?"

Jero blushed. "Thank you. That is what I was saying earlier." He gave Fabian a sideways glance, but Fabian simply shrugged.

"I already told you I was wrong to deny you your bit of fun, Jero. I shall not interfere again." Fabian noticed Jero still carried the old armor plate. "But I will interfere with this. Put that down, Jero, and leave it in the woods. I was not joking about my superstition with ghosts. We all have our little irrational fears, and you will have to allow me this one."

Chapter 53

Resi peeked out of the tent to witness an unexpected, domestic scene around the campfire. She lingered unnoticed near the flap closure of the shelter and quietly watched the friends talk and laugh among themselves as they laid out the food for dinner. When they had left that morning without the usual servants to cook and tend the fire, Resi had wondered how the aristocrats would manage without making too many demands on their only servant, Jero. It seemed they could manage very well.

Caterina had just opened the assortment of small jars and sealed crocks. Resi saw her sample each one before she set it out on the plank table. Resi had seen earlier what Nela had packed for them and knew they would be in for a treat with her marinated goat cheese, pickled onions, house olives, and drunken figs. The young Venetian set out a loaf of black bread and two of Franja's honey cakes for dessert, still wrapped in the parchment to protect them from the hungry insects. Mauro's back was to her, but Resi could tell he was carving the venison joint; it smelled delicious, even from where she stood at the tent. Fabian tended the grilled fish over the smoldering coals to add to the meat offering. Isabella poured wine into mugs from the bottle opened earlier, talking casually to Mauro and Caterina. Resi looked around for Ruby and Jero, who were missing from the rest of the party.

Ruby came out of the trees from the path to the stream with a sloshing pail of water. She noticed Resi waiting by the tent entrance and came over to her. "I hope you feel better after your little nap," Ruby said sweetly.

"I do," Resi replied, reaching out to share her friend's burden. The two walked together to join the merry group, the weight of the full bucket between them. "Mauro insisted that I lay down," she explained. "How long have I been asleep?" The sun still showed above the horizon, but the day was quickly coming to a close.

"You've slept long enough for dinner to be ready," Ruby told her.

They set the water down on the makeshift table. "It smells delicious, and I am starving," Resi said. She took a plump olive from the crock and popped it into her mouth with a smile.

Ruby lowered her voice, although the others were out of earshot at the other end of the long table. "It seems everyone has an appetite. Hunger is a good motivator to the lords and ladies. They have quite a feast ready. It has also brought out the commander in Fabian. He gave the ladies real duties, but they think they are playing house."

Resi liked the result of their efforts. "Where is Jero?" she wondered aloud.

"He went to feed the horses. Here he comes." Jero hurried to join the group now ready for dinner.

Ruby left Resi to check that Fabian had let her fish cook long enough. Resi noticed that Jero followed Ruby with his eyes. She would find out later from Ruby what had happened while she was on the island. Jero's open interest in her friend told Resi that something had.

Mauro finally noticed that his wife had joined the dinner party. He came to her side and kissed her tanned forehead. "Are you hungry?" he asked. "I was just going to wake you."

"Yes, I think the smell of the grilling meat is what woke me. Everyone has been busy while I slept. It is a pleasant surprise."

"Yes, that was my reaction, as well," Mauro said with a chuckle.

Ruby and Fabian brought the perfectly grilled fish to the food table, and the Venetians followed them in their sandy tracks.

Caterina cheerfully declared, "I think I rather enjoy this beach camping, Lady Terese. Our meal looks much better than the food we ate on our carriage ride from Venice."

"Yes, so much better," agreed Isabella. "I wanted to ask you, Fabian, do you eat so well when you are camping in the battlefields?"

Fabian let out a surprised laugh. "We are lucky to fill our bellies, Isabella. We do not have a castle cook to pack us supplies. Maybe the general has special baskets made up for him, or the general's nephew." Fabian winked at Mauro, who shook his head that he did not share that luxury. "The gunners at the rear of the convoy get nothing but bland stew and stale biscuits, or whatever we can steal from the orchards or farmers' fields."

"You stole things?" Caterina was stunned at this revelation.

"In the name of the Venetian Republic, yes," Fabian answered flatly. "Stealing apples is the least of my crimes as a soldier, dear sister." He did not make light of it, like he usually did of most things he told her.

She wanted to know the full details of these other crimes, and at the same time was afraid of what his answer might be. Like most Venetian women, Caterina was kept sheltered from the truth of the world outside their colorful city. She would not know how others struggled to survive each day in times of war, even men of wealth and stature. She did not have a chance to ask further about it that night.

Mauro interrupted her, putting on his pleasant host's smile and said, "Let us not talk of war at our merry party. Let us instead toast to this wonderful feast we have before us."

He handed a mug of wine to his wife and one to Ruby. The rest of the filled mugs were passed around, and then Mauro proclaimed, "I would like to thank Ruby, Jero, and Fabian for providing us with this delicious meal. And thank you, Caterina and Isabella, for presenting it so beautifully." He held his cup toward Resi now and said, "And I especially to you, Terese, for insisting that we take this excursion to the seashore in the first place." She curtsied to the cheering group.

The atmosphere of the meal fit the ambiance of the setting: relaxed and wonderful. They took their time eating the bounty of their smorgasbord and enjoyed light conversation, sitting on the beach together. Mauro had built up the fire in anticipation of the coming night, although the air was warm and comforting without it.

They talked of their leisurely day and what activities might fill their day tomorrow. Fabian praised Jero's potential as a bowman to the small party. He acknowledged that Jero could be relied on to hunt their next meal, if he were not leaving so soon. Jero was happy that the Baric captain had confidence in him already. He regretted that he would miss more adventures with the group, but he looked forward to the ship's voyage in the morning, too.

Mauro took extra pleasure in Fabian's new approval of Jero. The Carreras had many servants at their villa home, but the family rarely interacted with them on a personal level. Fabian did not have conversations with his valet back in Venice like Mauro had with Davor, whom he now considered a trusted confident. Fabian had often cautioned Mauro that he gave his staff too much free choice in how the house was run, and Jero was his most critical example.

Mauro had explained to Fabian that even though he did not make the daily decisions himself, the castle was run exactly to his liking, and Jero was to thank for that. If Jero did indeed steal from him or seduce his wife, like Fabian regularly assumed, Mauro insisted Nestor would relish telling him about it at the first opportunity. This had satisfied Fabian to a point, but Fabian had not managed to let his formality toward Jero go over the years. Today he finally did.

Filled with good food and a second bottle of wine, the chatty group set out blankets in the sand to enjoy the crackling fire. "I will bring the lanterns from the wagon before it gets too dark," Jero said to Mauro when the sun began to fade into brilliant golden hues of yellow and orange. "I am going to lay out my bedroll while it is still light, too." Mauro nodded and Jero excused himself from the group.

Mauro sat down next to his wife on a blanket facing the sea; they leaned against a smooth boulder in the sand. "The setting sun is especially beautiful tonight," he said to her. "I hope that does not mean the weather is changing."

"I don't care if it thunders with lightning, I will remember this peaceful evening for a long time. In Thessaloniki we get beautiful sunrises over the water, but it is not the same as the sereneness of a sunset as the night takes over."

She leaned in to him, and he put his arm around her. She thought to ask him, "When it is fully dark, the ladies wanted to go into the water. Will you give us some privacy to do that?"

The notion of swimming in the black water did not settle well with Mauro. "Will you be swimming with them? You have already bathed in the sea today."

"I can go in the water twice in one day. It is still warm tonight, and it is fun to swim in the dark," she said enthusiastically. She saw his odd expression and added, "Don't worry, Mauro. We will just stay by the dock where it is shallow and we can see the camp."

He was able to find his smile again. "If that is what you ladies want to do, of course we will give you as much privacy as you need. I wanted to remind you, I will be leaving very early with Jero to the harbor. I will be away a couple of hours, so do not worry if I am already gone in the morning. I do not plan to wake you."

~*~

Mauro and Resi's quiet conversation was distracted by a lively discussion between Fabian and his sister. "I can hardly imagine how you did not enjoy camping out with your army, Fabian," Caterina insisted. "Our cookout has been very amusing, and I know I will sleep well in our tent tonight."

"I am not disagreeing with you, Caterina, that this has been the best meal I have enjoyed over an open fire. The company is splendid, and the setting superb. But today is not typical of my camping experiences. There were times when our commander would not allow a fire, even with snow on the ground, and we worried we would freeze to death before we woke. There were nights so black, with neither moon nor stars, that we felt we would be suffocated by the darkness. You could not see the man next to you until he tapped you on the shoulder. Some summers were so hot, you were grateful for the downpour of a thunder shower, until all of your supplies mildewed in the sultry heat."

Jero came back with four lanterns and lit them from the fire while the two discussed the pleasures and miseries of camping. He placed them around the corners of where the group had now settled after their meal. Isabella sat between Fabian and Ruby, and Jero sat down on the sand on the other side of Ruby.

Isabella innocently remarked, "But you traveled with hundreds of men at one time. Surely it was not so grim with so many others nearby for company. There must have been no lack of entertainment along the way to lift your spirits."

Fabian looked across at Mauro. He could see the shadow of a grim memory on Mauro's expression in the fading sunset. Mauro had said he did not want to talk of war, so Fabian thought of a better story to entertain Isabella and Caterina.

"You are right," he said to the group. His voice became animated for the sake of storytelling, and he had everyone's attention. "Sometimes, Isabella, we traveled with an army so large you could only see the heads of men and their horses in all directions. But other times, we were in small bands of only five or six. There was one time, on a night such as this, with little moonlight to help us on our way, and a stiff breeze chilling us, that I shall never forget." He did not have to wait long for one of the women to take his bait.

"What happened, Fabian?" Caterina was the first to ask.

"Were you with him, Mauritius?" Isabella asked their host.

Fabian faintly shook his head at Mauro and gave him the briefest wink. Mauro knew Fabian was going to invent a story for the group's entertainment. Fabian enjoyed telling ghost stories most of all, despite his own superstitions. Mauro wrapped his arm around his wife again to ward off the coming fright. Her attention was already focused on Fabian.

"No, you were not with me, Mauritius," Fabian said. "I was part of a patrol in the northern Empire territories. We had been on our horses from before sunrise and had ridden through difficult tracks in the mountains. We were unsure where we were exactly, although we had expected to come to a small settlement situated along the route by nightfall. We had not seen another soul for days, so deep in the mountains was our crossing. The men and I decided to stop before it became too dark for the horses, even though we must have been near our destination." His body language was animated, but his voice was low and composed now. The others leaned in to listen intently to his story.

"It was not long after we had our fire going that the horses became restless, so I went to check on them. Exactly at that same time, a man in black armor stepped into the light of the camp and bid us a good evening. I will not lie to you; I was startled by his sudden appearance. He had made no sound, even though he was fully cloaked in mail and a breastplate. It was just like the one Jero found today in the trees, just over there." Fabian let the words sink in for the women's sake.

He poked at the fire for a moment until Isabella asked, "What happened next, Fabian?"

Fabian threw the stick into the fire, turned to her, and told her directly, "He lingered in our camp, looking at each man, one by one. I asked him where his horse was, and he said he had left it tied near the road. He told us he was drawn to our fire. He had noticed its glow through the trees. It was a warm fire, like this one we built here tonight," Fabian said to the group. "His comment was curious, though. We had made our camp away from the route so we would not attract unwanted attention. I was sure our fire could not be seen from the road, just like our camp is hidden here." His audience looked at each other and nodded their agreement.

Fabian went on, "Well, you understand, it is a courtesy to offer fellow travelers warmth and a bit of food when you can manage it, and so we did. We would have hoped for the same ourselves, had we been alone like he was." Fabian looked over at Mauro to confirm the expected gesture of hospitality. Mauro signaled that he agreed, falling for Fabian's story now just as much as the others.

Fabian looked directly at Caterina this time and told her, "The man had an odd dress, but there had been many foreigners fighting in these battles. I did not think anything more of it, except to wonder why he was alone on such an isolated route. He sat with us for a time, but did not take our offer for food or a hot drink. He asked us if we were not worried about the spirits that haunted those woods, and we dismissed his cautionary talk," Fabian told them quietly.

He became animated again. "I remember it was odd, though. Just after his warning, the wind began to howl, sounding something like the tide does here tonight. We did not believe it was the spirits he spoke of wandering the woods; we decided it was only the trees moving in the wind."

Fabian took a drink from his mug and waited a long moment.

Caterina asked him, "Did the soldier stay the night with you and your companions?"

He looked at her, then at Isabella, and then explained, "That was the curious thing. The old knight suddenly rose from his seat without so much as a creak of his armor and bid us a good rest of our journey. The five of us watched him walked back into the trees, but not to the path where his horse should have been waiting." Fabian pointed to the woods behind them at their own camp. "We thought we would see him come back out of the woods and down the path to the road, but there was no more sign of him." Fabian looked around at the faces illuminated by the firelight. Even Jero and Ruby were mesmerized by the tale, and Fabian decided he would play a little prank to cap off his story.

"Where do you think he went, Fabian?" Isabella asked softly, afraid of the answer he might give.

"That is exactly what we were wondering, Isabella. We were all grown men and had spent many nights out in woods like these, but we admitted to one other later that an odd chill had come over each of us. It was not from the dark, moonless night, or the wind that had begun to howl despite how pleasant the evening had started.

"We sat around the fire for a few more minutes, I recall. Then, one by one, my companions began to roll up their bedrolls without so much as a word of discussion between them. I joined them, of course. If there were spirits in the trees, as the old warrior had warned, we were not going to sleep waiting for the ghosts to descend on us."

"But you were so tired," Caterina said. "How did you manage to ride again?"

"Tired or not, our horses at least had an hour of rest and some grass to eat. We rode on for another hour, stumbling along the dark trail until we did finally come to the settlement we had been looking for. There was still a light shining in the window of the inn, and we went to see about getting a room to finally sleep for the night. We told the innkeeper of our campfire visitor while we paid him for the lodgings. He went white with alarm at our retelling. He said the old knight was known around those parts." Fabian took another drink of his wine and paused for a melodramatic effect before he continued. "The innkeeper explained that the knight was thought to be looking for his way home, but his search was futile. Those who had encountered him and left like we did, they lived to warn the folks of those mountains. Others were not so lucky, and their bodies were found in their bedrolls near a cold fire. Nothing had been stolen from their packs—nothing other than, perhaps, their souls."

His gullible audience looked at each other for reassurance. "Fabian," Isabella cautiously asked, "are you saying the old knight was a true ghost searching for souls?"

"I believe he was indeed a ghost," Fabian told her seriously.

The group shifted uncomfortably in the light of their warm fire. Fabian stood quietly and stretched his long legs. He set down his mug. He then unceremoniously excused himself from the group with hardly two words and walked into the woods. The others watched him in silence, still thinking about the possibility of spirits among the trees.

Only a few moments passed, and there was a loud banging of metal coming from the trees, and then another clunking noise after that.

Caterina stood and yelled into the woods, "Fabian, are you alright?" The others were on their feet at the noise as well. Fabian did not reply.

"Fabian, was that you?" Caterina called out again. There was another crash in the direction he had just gone.

"That is enough, Fabian," Mauro shouted toward the woods. Fabian came out of the trees on the path to the stream, a different direction from where the noise had come from.

"Did you not hear us shouting to you?" Isabella asked.

"I did, and I came back right away. What is it?" Fabian asked blankly, not giving his joke away.

Isabella was white with worry. She muttered, "The noise in the woods. There was a banging, and . . ."

"It was the ghost, Isabella. The ghost of the old knight must be here," he told her convincingly.

Mauro threw up his hands and was just about to scold Fabian for playing such a childish trick to frighten the women when Isabella swooned and began to fall. "Catch her, Fabian," Mauro shouted.

Fabian rushed the few steps to reach her just as she hit the soft ground. He picked her slumped body up and cradled her against him. Both Jero and Mauro were by their sides, and Resi and Ruby went to Caterina, who was weeping quietly in fear for her friend.

"That was really stupid of you, Fabian. You know she faints easily," Mauro said quietly. "Here, let me take her. If she wakes and sees you, she is going to be extra angry."

"I have her," Fabian told him. "I deserve it if she slaps me, or worse. I did not scare your wife, did I?"

Mauro looked over at Resi with the other women. She and Ruby were smiling and recounting the story, trying to make light of it to cheer up Caterina. "She is fine. They all are fine. It was a good tale, Fabian, but you should have left it at the telling and not played the prank," Mauro said.

"You think I made the noise?" Fabian asked him with a stony expression.

Mauro looked at Jero, who suddenly also had a worried look on his face. The woods were black beyond their lanterns and bright fire. It now seemed possible to the men that ghosts could be hiding in the shadows.

Fabian began to chuckle quietly, not wanting to disturb the limp Isabella in his arms. "You told me you were not afraid of ghosts, Mauro." Mauro gave him an exasperated look. "I am sorry," Fabian said sincerely this time. "No more stories for the rest of the trip. I will put her in the tent now."

"I should come with you. I will hold the light," Mauro suggested, grabbing a nearby lantern.

"No, I want to talk to her when she wakes. I do not need the lantern. There is enough light from the campfire."

The two men exchanged frowns. Mauro knew that Fabian was not over his obsession with Isabella, and he wondered what it was that he intended to say to her when she woke. He agreed to let Fabian handle this awkward friendship on his own terms.

The tent was on a straight path not far out of the reach of the firelight, and Fabian's eyes adjusted to the dimness. Along the way, Isabella leaned into Fabian's grip before she opened her eyes. After a few seconds she realized where she was and who was holding her. "Put me down," she insisted.

He had arrived at the tent already, and he set her feet on the soft ground. She straightened her dress and felt her way to the flap opening in front of them. She changed her mind about going into the darkness alone. She turned to him instead to ask, "Why do you like to torment me, Fabian?"

He reached for her hand at her side and held it while he told her quietly, "I am truly sorry, Isabella. I thought the story would be good fun for everyone, but I went too far. I did not think you would be so scared by it."

"You must have remembered how ghost stories frighten me." She shook her hand free of his. She rubbed the sand off her arm where she had caught her fall and winced from a jab of pain.

"Did you hurt yourself?" he asked kindly. He reached out and lifted her lacy sleeve to examine it.

"Let go," she ordered, and he released her arm. She rubbed it protectively.

He had tried, but her shield against him was firmly in place. There was nothing more to say, he thought, and he held the flap to the tent open for her. She stood in front of the opening looking at him as if deciding on something. She finally said solemnly, "You know I hate you, Fabian. You make me miserable."

"You will be rid of me again in a few days," he replied just as solemnly.

She did not want to be sent back alone to Venice and was angry at him for that, too. "Why will you not let me wait here with Caterina? Why can you not forgive me? Mauritius forgave me."

"It is not a matter of forgiving. You just said that you hate me and never want to see me again, but you cannot stay here without seeing me. *My* life is here, not yours. I am doing you a favor sending you home and out of my life."

She was frustrated and tired, and her arm did hurt. But she did not hate him, not really. "Do not put words in my mouth. I did not say I never wanted to see you again." She was barely audible.

He stubbornly continued the argument. "Well, you were thinking it then."

Just as stubbornly, she held her ground. "What makes you think you know what I am thinking? What do you even know about me anymore?"

"I know more about you than I care to know, Isabella."

"Tell me one thing you know about me for certain."

He took a deep breath and thought for a moment. He answered confidently, "I know that Tuesday, the day after tomorrow, is your twenty-third birthday."

She looked surprised at first, but then scowled. "You were always good with dates; I will give you that."

Caterina and Ruby came toward the tent carrying a lantern, and Fabian and Isabella's verbal sparring match ended in a draw. "Sleep well, Isabella," Fabian said coolly, then turned to walk toward the two women. Isabella stayed by the opening and watched him stop briefly to talk to his sister.

"Isabella is fine, and I apologized," Fabian reported before Caterina could inquire.

"We were having such a good evening together," Caterina pouted. "We were going to have a swim in the sea and maybe play a few games, but now you have ruined it, Fabian."

"You can still go for your swim. There is nothing to fear, Cat. It was a made-up story; there is no ghost here. You are safe with three armed men who will protect you," Fabian promised her.

She was used to her brother's pranks. Now that the fright of the story had receded, she was in a good mood and could not be upset with him. "Maybe we will try to swim tomorrow. I find I am quite tired anyway." Caterina reached on her tippy-toes and kissed her brother on the cheek. "Good night, Fabian." She took the lantern with her into the dark tent.

Ruby had been standing nearby, and Fabian said to her, "I am sorry to have caused you any distress, Ruby."

"You don't have to worry about me, Fabian. I thought your story was very entertaining, but I will retire for the night with the others. Good night." She opened the flap and stooped under to go inside.

Fabian looked out toward the firelight and saw Mauro and his wife talking by themselves. Jero was putting the last of the dinner dishes into a bucket for washing up in the morning. Fabian saw the baroness kiss her husband on the lips, and then she walked in his direction with a second lantern.

He met her halfway and apologized before she had a chance to give him the scolding he deserved. "I am so sorry things have gone wrong for the evening. Please forgive me, Lady Terese."

"Fabian, don't be so hard on yourself," she replied with a sincere smile. "In this one week I have seen Isabella faint twice now. You probably did not know she was sensitive to such tales. How is she?"

"She is unharmed and is going to sleep now. They all are."

"And I will join them, too. Good night, Fabian." She walked past him, toward the glowing tent.

"Shit," he said softly to himself when he was left alone. He went to where Mauro and Jero were talking by the fire. "Have I cost you the company of your wife tonight?" he asked Mauro guiltily.

"You have," Mauro answered, but did not seem to be annoyed any longer. "I am going to put my blanket in the wagon with Jero."

"Not the best replacement," Fabian remarked, lightening the mood a little.

Both Mauro and Jero smiled. "No, but then we can leave in the morning without waking you, if you want to sleep by the fire. We will just saddle my horse and eat our breakfast at the inn with my crew." Mauro looked around the plank table and asked, "Is there more wine?"

"Here is the last of it." Jero handed him the nearly empty bottle that was perched on a rock.

"Should we open another bottle?" Mauro asked.

Jero passed on his offer. "Not for me, thank you. It is still fairly early. I think I will go for a swim," Jero announced cheerfully. He would enjoy his only evening at the seaside, even if no one else did. "Would anyone like to join me?"

Fabian thought about it a moment. "Yes, I will join you. That might be just what I need instead of more wine; a splash of cold water. Mauro, can we convince you to come?"

He poured the wine and shook the last drops out. "No. I already had one rather difficult swim, and that was enough for one day."

Jero left the two men to walk down to the pier, already unbuttoning his shirt as he went. Fabian started to follow, but then turned back to Mauro and asked, "Why would you not tell me about being alone with your brother when he drowned?"

Mauro took a drink from his cup, and then stared at Fabian with his unreadable expression. Fabian insisted, "You could have told me."

"Why are you bringing this up now? It happened twelve years ago, Fabian."

"Because you are my best friend, Mauro. We should know these things about each other."

Mauro looked down the beach at the dark outline of Jero in the glow of his lamp. "Did Jero talk to you about him?"

"He was worried about you. You seemed to have had a bit of a panic attack on the dock," Fabian said firmly.

"There is nothing to worry about. It is all in the past."

Fabian stood in front of his friend and put his arm out onto Mauro's shoulder. Fabian had a pleading stare that Mauro knew all too well and could not ignore. Mauro gave in. "All right, Fabian. The next time I watch someone I care about disappear, I promise to tell you all the details," he said too bitterly. He tried to smile to compensate for it, but Fabian did not smile.

"At least come down with us and sit on the dock. I just told you about ghosts haunting the woods. Do you really want to stay here alone in the dark?"

"Your warrior ghost worries me less than my demons swimming in the dark sea. I prefer to watch you from here." Fabian wanted to protest his choice, but Mauro interrupted him, "I have had to talk about my dead brother today more than I have in years. My wife already asked me a lot of questions about Mateo while we were on the boat. I need a little peace from the memories right now. Can you give me that?"

Fabian reluctantly accepted. "As you wish, Mauro."

Mauro took a seat in the sand and wrapped the blanket Resi had been sitting on around his shoulders. "Go take your swim, Fabian. I can see Jero is waiting for you. I will be fine here."

Fabian gave him a feeble look of disapproval, and then left with a lantern swinging in his hand to the dock. A few minutes later, there were two splashes in the water.

~ * ~

Isabella sat on the blanketed ground in the middle of the tent with Caterina standing over her. "Are you really alright, Isabella?" she asked. "I cannot understand why Fabian had to tell a ghost story. Were you scared by his story, Lady Ruby?"

Ruby stood just inside the flap opening; the lantern Caterina held made the tent glow eerily. "I love ghost stories; I always have," Ruby confided awkwardly.

Caterina told Ruby, "I thought he was telling us a true story, but I should have known better. My brothers still remind me of little boys dressed in their papa's clothes. They will never grow up completely, and Fabian is the worst of the three." She knelt down next to Isabella. "We should have known that he was tricking us, Isabella. It was just a made-up story, so do not be afraid any longer."

"I am not afraid. I am just tired, I think. Can you help me with my gown? I am ready to go to sleep," she said as she struggled to stand again.

Caterina took her arm and helped her up. Both women were undoing the hooks and laces of Isabella's gown when Resi came through the tent opening. "Are you sleeping with us?" Caterina asked her with surprise.

"Yes, I thought I would join you. Strength in numbers, you know, in case the spirits come through the tent," Resi joked lightly. Isabella had been standing with her back to the opening, so Resi did not see her cringe.

"She is no longer afraid, but you don't want to remind her," Ruby whispered to Resi. She then asked the group, "How shall we sleep? It will be tight for all of us in here."

Resi thought a moment how they should organize themselves. There was enough room for the four to stand and move around, but just barely. "My bedding is still outside, but maybe we can make one big bed with the blankets here. It won't be cold tonight. We can put a few on the bottom and throw the other over all four of us. Ruby and I will sleep on the outsides, and you two ladies can be in the middle. How does that sound?" she asked with a forced enthusiasm. They agreed it was the best solution.

They crawled over each other to pull the blankets here and there, and soon they had forgotten about Fabian's prank as they arranged their cozy little bedroom. They carefully draped their garments at one end of the tent so they could easily dress again in the morning. The four took turns brushing and braiding each other's hair, and then they ventured out into the dark woods in protective pairs to relieve themselves. Soon they were ready to curl up together for the night. Caterina was the first one asleep, and one by one their breathing turned into soft snores.

Resi had slept so soundly that afternoon that she could not fall asleep at all. She lay on the edge of the blankets thinking about her day on the island. She sighed softly at how much Mauro had revealed about himself in one afternoon. She should have focused on their pleasurable adventure on the beach, but her mind kept coming back to what Mauro had told her about their wedding contract on the boat ride home. The more she thought about it, the more she realized how heartless their arrangement was. Her dead father-in-law had conceived it with no regard for her, her own father had agreed to it without telling her the unrealistic details, and Mauro had accepted the terms without dispute.

Her internal deliberation did not help her sleep, but she lay there still and quiet so she did not disturb the others. Outside the tent, she heard what must have been Jero walk by toward the wagon. The horses acknowledged his presence with their soft snorts and nickers. The fire popped in the distance, and she imagined Mauro or Fabian was banking it for the night. Then all was quiet again.

Everyone was asleep, or so she thought. She felt a soft tremor coming from Isabella sobbing quietly next to her. Resi rolled over to face her companion and gently put her hand on her arm, trying not to startle her. "Why are you crying, Lady Isabella?" she whispered. "Tell me what is wrong."

Isabella thought the others were all asleep, and that she could finally let her emotions free in private. She looked at the baroness' shadow and told her, "Everything is wrong. My life is over before it even began." She tried to fight back the tears, but they choked her words anyway. "I did everything asked of me, but it did not matter," she sobbed. Resi reached out in the dark and touched her smooth hair; she began to stroke it like she would a child's.

"What was asked of you?" Resi asked gently.

Isabella took a deep breath to gain control over her voice once again. "You could not know. Your marriage was settled from the beginning. You did not have to play the game," she said somberly.

When Isabella did not explain, Resi asked, "What game is that?"

"The game of seduction. I flirted and paraded and danced my way through the courts of Italy, and where did it get me? I have nothing to show for it: no husband, no life to look forward to, and no chance of happiness."

Resi did not know how to soothe her distress. To her, Isabella looked like she had everything to make her happy. "When I despaired, my mother told me once that God has a plan for everyone. Perhaps his plan for you is not yet settled."

Her sobs had quieted now and Isabella replied softly, "It is not God who decides my plan; it is my father."

"My father signed my marriage contract without ever meeting my future husband. It was all done without games, like you say, but the Ottomans practice the art of seduction, too. We have no fancy balls like in the Venetian world, but we do parade our girls just as blatantly," Resi told her. "When my friends were dressed by their mothers in beautiful silks and gold-trimmed veils to attract a suitor, I was still playing in my dusty clothes with my brothers and their friends. I was spared the ritual, but was placed in limbo instead. As a girl with no young men to impress, my mother let me sit with my two brothers when they were tutored in astronomy, mathematics, and Latin. And, at the time, I thought the same thing, Lady Isabella."

She had been listening quietly and asked, "What was that?"

"That at least I didn't have to flirt and be pretty to find the best husband for my father to pick. But I wondered whether I could have even been happy with a different eligible bachelor after all that time waiting."

"Because you knew that there was already a man who wanted you," Isabella reflected hopefully.

Resi was surprised by Isabella's assumption and explained, "No, Lady Isabella. It was made clear early on that Mauro did not want me."

Isabella was puzzled. She could plainly see that Mauritius cared for his wife. "What makes you say that?"

"When I was sixteen, my father wrote to Lord Lorenc Baric that I was of age to fulfill the contract. His reply was that his son was a soldier in battle, and I would be sent for when he returned."

"That is not so unusual. Most girls had to wait for their betrothed to return from war. Did you write to each other?"

"No, my father thought if he was an active soldier, the letters would never reach him anyway. So I just waited. How long does a battle last, I wondered then? My friends married and began to have children, and still I waited to be sent for. Word never came from the Barics."

"How awful for you. What did you do in all that time?"

"At first I did nothing. I was kept in the house away from possible suitors who could taint my reputation. It was important to my family that I be spared for my future husband."

"No! They locked you in your room with no parties, no society, no entertainment? That must have been unbearable."

"It was not as horrible as it might sound. I did sulk in the beginning, but then I decided to use my freedom from chores and children to learn about other things. I read every book I could borrow in Latin, Greek, and even Turkish. I taught myself Croatian from a book our old tutor found for me in the market. I read about music and theater. My brother, Castor, taught me about navigation and how he sails by the stars, even though my father refused to let me go out with Castor on his ship."

"It would not have occurred to me to ask for books and to be educated like a boy. You were very brave, Lady Terese."

"I was stubborn, not brave." They both laughed softly together.

They were silent for a few minutes, then Resi confessed quietly, "I realized something in my solitude, though. Even if Mauro did not send for me, I would never be able to do all that I really wanted to do, not like a man could." There was a long pause, and Resi thought Isabella had fallen asleep in the lull of their conversation.

"So when did you get word from him?" Isabella finally asked softly.

"Almost three years had passed. It was nearing autumn, and I was asked to come in the spring. We would be married at his castle." Resi thought about the arrival of that letter, and how she had dreaded her father opening it.

"Were you relieved the wait was over?"

"No!" Resi said a little too loudly. "I wasn't. After waiting more than two years for my husband to send for me, I had decided I didn't want him. How could I? What kind of a man would neglect a bride like that?"

"But you did come to him that spring."

"I did not come willingly. I left kicking and screaming, sort of like Lady Caterina, I suppose. That is one reason why Ruby came with me. My mother was afraid I would run away, and she knew I would not leave her behind."

"But you loved Mauritius when you met him, did you not?"

Resi thought about what she would tell Isabella. "I would like to have you believe that I did. I wanted to. He is an attractive man to look at and is elegant in his fine clothing. But that cannot be enough. He was obligated to send for me, and he did his duty. He made that clear in how he treated me in the beginning."

"Was he abusive? I cannot imagine Mauritius not treating you well."

"No, he has been gentle and generous, but I was one more complication in his life as a new baron. He had never wished to become a lord. Between the constant battles he was sent to, the family business, and the village affairs, he was too preoccupied to devote any time to a marriage and a new wife. I don't think he knew what to do with me."

"He must have devoted some time to you. You are having his child."

"I was pregnant with another child last autumn, did you know? I lost the first baby."

"No, I did not know that. I am so sorry for you."

"I was still very unhappy with my new life back then, and the miscarriage was an added difficulty to overcome. We had only been married a few months, and I felt like I had failed my husband."

"Why would you say that? Was he angry at you?"

"I thought so at first, but that was because I didn't know him. I think he was just saddened over it, like I was."

"Mauritius seems to love you, Lady Terese. I can see that by the way he looks at you."

"I am sure he does now, but he does not tell me. I would like to hear that from him, just once."

"Men are so thoughtless and hurtful. But you carry on with such a happy spirit. You must have made peace with Mauritius' shortcomings."

"I was discouraged at first and did not know how to tell my new husband my frustrations. Then I decided it was like waiting back at my father's house in Thessaloniki. I began to go on with my new life on my terms. I bought more books for my pleasure, I went riding every day, I played my music, and I made this my new home. Mauro would have to want me to come to him. I would wait for him again, but this time in his house, not my father's."

"And does that work? Will a man eventually come around and love you on your terms?"

"I believe it does, Lady Isabella. He has not tried to change me. We are still getting to know each other, though."

They were quiet again. Resi felt drained after confiding her private thoughts, but she felt content. She began to let a peaceful sleep take her.

"Lady Terese?" Isabella shook her arm a little to be sure she heard her.

"Yes?" Resi asked, half-dreaming already.

"Thank you for telling me your story," Isabella whispered. "You have given me hope. I think I am not afraid of what is to come any more."

"I am glad. Sleep well, Lady Isabella." Resi told her, and she would, too.

Chapter 54

The sun inched its way above the granite mountain range, visible in the distance over the tops of the pines that embraced their camp. The warmth of the dawning sun felt good on Fabian's back when he sat down on the end of the weathered dock. He had come to retrieve his shoes, left there last night after his swim in the dark with Jero. He stuck his sandy feet into the crystalline water to wash them before putting on his shoes. He watched with amusement as the little fish darted toward his toes.

Fabian had a knack for shedding worries and regrets, and he had left them in the water last night. After a dreamless sleep wrapped in his blanket by the fire, he had woken recharged and ready for the day. Sitting in the emerging light, he noticed the abandoned fishing poles and bits of dried bait swept to the side. It had been years since he had dropped a line into the water, and he had the sudden urge to do just that.

Despite his carefree life, there was one nagging worry that surfaced at quiet times like this. Now that the truce was confirmed and his service as an army captain suspended, he was supposed to make a decision about his future plans. He could still remain an army officer, but he was not certain that it would be the right lifelong profession for him. As long as he stayed away from Venice, the pressure to come home only arrived in a weekly letter from his mother or his father. His oldest brother would write from time to time and tell him how he could use Fabian's assistance with the family silk business, although he was sure it was only because of his father that Gabriel wrote to him.

Mauro had offered Fabian continued hospitality to live a bachelor's life at his castle. In return, he gladly helped Mauro train his Guard and patrolled his borders. But was that enough for him? It was like fishing on this lazy morning—relaxing, easy, but with a predictable outcome. Could he just live off fish and not want for more variety in life? He allowed those thoughts to drift into his conscience while he checked the hook the swarming fish had nibbled at. He dropped the freshly baited line back into the water.

He would like to marry, preferably someone he could love, but he did not seem to be destined for love. He had been in love, and women had confessed their love to him, but never at the same time. A marriage was easy to arrange, and his mother wrote to him regularly with suggestions. He had been away for two years and none of the names of the young ladies in her letters had been familiar to him. He would need to go back to Venice to meet the new group of eligible partners, perhaps to stay for good.

A married man needed a more profitable profession to support a family. His father could arrange a seat in the Senate. It was practically Fabian's birthright, since his other brothers had not taken the inherited seat in politics. He might have enjoyed such a dynamic society once, years ago, before he had seen the reality of life outside the capital. The senators did not like to venture beyond their urban villas and walled summer homes on the Adriatic. The threats surrounding their idyllic world were real, and their enemies were still waiting, barely contained at their borders. The ruling party was losing touch with this.

There was a sudden tug on the pole, and Fabian watched the cork sporadically move over the clear water. He waited for the fish to bite the bait completely. Patience—he found he had plenty this morning. The wind lifted his hair; he had fallen asleep with it unbound after it had dried by the fire last night. He tucked it behind his ears, snagging one of the gold loops that he wore in each lobe. The tangled hair would have to wait, because the hungry fish was hooked and struggling on the line. Fabian pulled hard in return and was rewarded with a good-sized catch. "What are you doing so near shore, you big, old fish? You will make a nice meal," he told his prey with a grin.

He let it flop around on the dock while he reached for the stone left from yesterday and put it out of its misery. A good start, he thought. He carefully took the hook from the fish's throat and set the catch out of the way. It was not going anywhere.

The old sausage pieces had worked once, so he would try it once again. He threw the baited line into the water and watched it sink in the changing colors of the clear blue and green sea. A vibration along the planks brought him out of his thoughts, and then the close pattering of feet made him turn around. He saw the barefooted baroness walking toward him, smiling.

She was dressed in the layered robes she had worn yesterday, the lower half salt-stained from dragging in the water. Her long braid kept her hair from blowing in the morning breeze, but wisps of the soft brown strands kissed her face. Fabian was pleased to see that she was alone. He was not in the mood to take charge just yet. "Good morning, Fabian. Am I disturbing you?" she asked politely.

"No, Lady Terese, not at all. I am just trying my luck with Ruby's pole."

She motioned to the fish, with its long silver and blue back glistening in the rising sun, and said, "I see luck is on your side already. Will that be our breakfast?"

"Yes, why not," he answered cheerfully. "You are up early, my lady."

"I suppose I am. I had hoped to find my husband still here. Did they not take time for breakfast?" she asked. "It is barely daybreak."

Fabian agreed with a nod. "Mauro told me yesterday that they would eat something in town before claiming his ship. I did not even see them myself this morning. I only woke because I heard Bacchus."

"Did Jero ride your horse?"

Fabian's horse was temperamental, and there were few who could handle him in close quarters like the crowded harbor streets. "No, they rode double on Mauro's stallion. It is a short ride, only about five miles, but I am sure mine wanted to go with them. Bacchus and Janus are friends; they like to go together."

"That is sweet," she said. She sat down near him on the worn boards. He turned to lean back against the corner post to see her better. "Bacchus is an interesting name. Did you choose it?" she asked.

Fabian was quite fond of his stallion and felt lucky to have acquired him. He proudly told her, "He was already named, but I did choose him. He would have been roasted as our next dinner had I not taken a chance on him."

"Oh, dear. Where did you get him from?"

"He was with a group of horses salvaged from a battlefield a few years ago. Some horses are found riderless, because they were not trained to tolerate the noises and blood of battle, but many of the enemy's horses are still usable. We bring those horses back to the Toth trainers. They were the ones who named him after the Roman god because of the bad influence he had on the herd," he explained with a laugh. "Bacchus was well-trained already as a warhorse, but he was not interested in proving it. He was only interested in corrupting the other captured horses into being difficult. They almost gave up on handling him." Fabian chuckled at his memory of the mischief his horse had caused in the paddock.

"He is a magnificent creature," she said.

"Yes, that is what I thought from the beginning, too. I had lost my own horse in the same battle and had free choice of the new acquisitions. It took a bit of getting used to each other, but we have been together the three years since. When Bacchus met Janus in the Baric stable yards almost two years ago, they had a connection right away. He was not Mauro's horse at the time, but Mauro told me he chose Janus for that reason. He thought it was better if our horses got along well. Mauro is the one who named his."

"Janus is the gatekeeper, is that right?"

He smiled at her; of course, she would have learned about mythology in her boredom. "Yes, but he is also the god of transitions, the god of beginnings. Mauro had only been home a short time when he was shot in an ambush. His horse was wounded in the ambush as well, and it had to be killed." Fabian unconsciously grimaced talking about it. A soldier loved his horse like a fellow soldier, maybe even more. "Stephan and I had just arrived in Solgrad and had agreed to stay on to help Mauro train his Guard. His title as baron had officially been confirmed. Oh, and he had just received your father's letter that you had accepted to come here to marry him. So, when he chose the horse, he thought the name Janus was most fitting."

She nodded, but was speechless. She pondered Fabian's story, and just how much the two men had lived and lost already. Sitting there serenely with Fabian on what promised to be a perfect summer's day, it seemed unlikely that he had already witnessed so much tragedy.

The line tugged again, and both watched the cork bob in the water. Fabian teased the victim by moving the line a little. The fish took the hook and began to fight him.

"That is a fine one," Resi exclaimed.

"Yes, big and strong, the little—" Fabian stopped himself from cursing in front of the baroness. He stood and walked back along the dock. "I need some room to pull it in before he snaps my line." Resi quickly got out of his way. He tugged once against the angry fish, and then once again. After one more solid tug and a heave, the fish lost the battle and landed on the planks next to them.

Resi laughed with delight. "You are a trusted warrior, a capable deer hunter, and a talented fisherman, Fabian. I had no idea."

"I thank you for the compliments, my lady. It should not be a great surprise. I did grow up surrounded by water, you know." He hurried to stun the flopping fish. "I think two fish will do for the five of us for breakfast. What do you think, Lady Terese?"

"I think it will be a feast."

Fabian worked to unhook his prize, and Resi looked out at the calm sea. He took his dagger from his belt and began to clean the fresh catch on the dock, discarding the remains into the water for the scavengers to eat. The crabs came alive at the arrival of Fabian's treats on the tranquil sea floor.

They shared the dock in silence for a few minutes. Fabian worked efficiently to ready the two fish for the fire. "Fabian, I am curious about something, and maybe you can help me," she began.

He leaned into the water and washed his knife before returning it to its sheath, then wiped his slick hands on his dusty breeches. He set the cleaned fish aside and charmingly replied, "With pleasure. How may I help?"

She tapped the planks to motion him to sit with her, and he obeyed her request with a quiet look of surprise. What could she need his help with? he wondered.

"Lord Dubovic mentioned your family to me, and Lady Isabella's as well." She had his attention. "He told me that your father is a powerful councilman in Venice. He wanted to talk to me about them at the ball, but I had nothing to add to the conversation, so I changed the subject."

He hid his true reaction and answered lightly, "Ah, that was clever of you, my lady. Politics is a dull topic to discuss while dancing. A gentleman would never bore a lady with such a subject."

"The thing is, Fabian, it isn't a dull subject to me. Mauro does not talk about the politics he is involved with, but I was curious how it works here."

"I am sure that Mauro has not talked politics with you because he does not want to worry you, Lady Terese. Women do not usually concern themselves with those matters. Some of the details are difficult to explain simply."

"Yes, but if I am to live in this Empire and be a baroness of it, I thought maybe I should understand a little about how we are governed." When he only stared blankly and did not interrupt her, she went on to explain, "I understand the Venetian Republic is an oligopoly, and the citizens are entitled to access to the local councils in the capital. I know the structure of government has us ruled by the Doge and his councilors. But are the citizens here entitled to access to the government? Is there a council or senate held locally in these territories?"

She looked at Fabian with her questioning blue eyes. For all the tragedy of losing his parents the last years, Mauro had received good fortune to be matched with her by chance. Mauro must find her irresistible when she looked at him with that intense stare, Fabian thought. She was captivating, and Fabian was enchanted.

She waited for him to reply, but he only smiled at her. "Have I said something wrong?" she asked. He shook his head and chuckled. "Why are you laughing then?"

"I beg your pardon, my lady. Please be assured that I am not laughing at you. Your question is excellent. It is just, well, politics is decided by men, and women rarely share an interest in it. The only women I have met who have learned about our political system are elderly widows who have taken over the affairs of a dead husband or spinster daughters of Venetian senators who have indulged their children with their own self-importance. You are definitely neither of those, Lady Terese. Now I am the one who is curious. May I ask, who taught you about government and politics?"

"No one taught me. I read about the Venetian Empire and its history in a book in the Baric library. It described how the government is not ruled by a king or a sultan, but the power is divided like an upside-down pyramid. In that pyramid, there should be some choice given to the citizens, like in a democracy. But it is a false democracy, ruled by the few wealthy elite in Venice. If your father and the other councilmen hold the power to decide our fate, what power do we have here to influence their decisions?"

"I will tell you why the answer was not in your book, my lady. The Dalmatian coast is considered by the councilmen to be only a colony of the Republic. The barons are Venetian subjects, of course, as are all the merchants and their servants. The Croat aristocracy does have a local council, and Mauro is a member on that council. The members are allowed to meet and discuss their political concerns, but only with an official Venetian representative present."

"What role does my husband play on this local council?" she asked earnestly.

"He has not been here very long. His father played a large role, I understand, but Mauro is not so interested in influencing the regional opinions. You see, the titled aristocracy here is not given the same advantage as noblemen are in Venice. There is always an undercurrent of discontent in the territories, even among the nobility. Open discussion of their displeasure with the Doge is a punishable offense. Mauro has you and all of the estate to protect, so he is trying to stay out of that undercurrent," Fabian said seriously.

"If Mauro is not on the same political level as you, Fabian, then how can you be so sure he is not keeping some discontent from even you, his dearest friend?"

"You are right, of course. He may have secrets from me, but I have been with him on all of his outings and know where he goes." She raised her eyebrows in surprise at the last comment. "Not because I am spying on him," he clarified, "but because Mauro has asked me to accompany him. I do not think your husband minds me knowing his opinions, and he knows mine."

"So the local council of noblemen cannot make any of their own laws or regulations?" she asked.

"You are correct, my lady. The government mistrusts the citizens outside of Venice. Most of the ruling Venetians are only interested in dining on the delicacies you provide for them at a discount. They line their personal treasuries by reselling the remainder at a profit. They like to summer on your islands and enjoy their hunting sports in your forests. They do not want your input. My father watches over the aristocratic landlords in the territories. That is why he tolerates me living here, instead of calling me back to Venice. My father wants to know of any unrest outside the capital, and then it is dealt with judicially. I am assigned to report what is going on in the villages and with the common folks," he confided.

Resi was seemingly taken aback. "Then you *are* a spy. Surely the Barics are trusted."

Fabian laughed softly at her assessment. "The Barics have been in good standing in Venice for generations, and Mauro's uncle is a favorite family friend, which is how your husband and I first met. It has been advantageous to my father that Mauro invited me to stay at his castle, but there was no obligation for Mauro to do so. In my view, we are all on the same side, so I do not consider my correspondence as spying. Fortunately, there is little to observe here, so little to report back to Venice. I have grown to like these people, and I do not intend to cause them any trouble. There are many Venetians sending reports back to other councilmen, not just me."

She was still dazed at this new insight. "And Mauro knows about this? He does not object?" Resi asked.

"If it were a secret, my lady, I would not be telling you," Fabian said. "As for objecting, my father would ask the same questions of me as a son, and I would probably tell my father as much information in a personal letter to him. I have to admit, I tend to be a bit of a gossip." He winked at her, and she knew he was right.

"Which council is your father on?" she asked, still impressing him with her inquisitiveness.

"The councilmen are elected for short terms of only a few years, but he has been on most of them. He and Isabella's father are on the Council of Ten this term," he told her.

"The Council of Ten? He must have a lot of power in the government."

"He might," Fabian agreed. "Sometimes what is designed as the flow of power in government does not happen in reality. Men with more power sometimes hold a lesser office; many in the lower senate have a great deal of influence."

He did not know how much more detail she expected from him, and he was eager to change the subject. "I have enjoyed our conversation, Lady Terese. I have never had the pleasure to discuss politics with a woman. Did I help you satisfy your curiosity?"

She held his stare and reflected, "I just keep thinking back on what Lord Dubovic said. He seemed convinced that Caterina's and Isabella's presence was more than coincidental."

"To be honest, my lady, it is a bit concerning that Lord Dubovic would discuss it with you at all. If it is any comfort, I can tell you for certain that their arrival is exactly what it appears to be: two silly girls making a stupid decision to run away from their marriage arrangements."

He wanted to make light of her concerns, but her skeptical expression made him decide otherwise. "I can tell you one more thing for certain, Lady Terese: Lord Dubovic comes from an old, wealthy family, like your husband's. The Dubovic name was known to me even before I came to live at Baric Castle. His family has tried and failed over the years to use their influence in Venice. I hope he is not trying a different course this time. Your husband is cautious of him for that reason, and you should be, too, my lady." She understood that Fabian had shared his true judgment, and nodded that she would take his counsel seriously.

Resi had gotten the insight that she had wanted and liked what she had learned from Mauro's dashing friend. He was more than his costumes and charisma. She took a moment to find the right words and then said, "Fabian, I have a confession to make."

He was ready for anything now. "Please tell me, my lady," he said with a captivating grin.

"I suppose I am in the dark about what goes on in the lives of the other men at the castle. I never imagined you had more duties in your day beyond being Mauro's captain. I am glad to know there is more to your life than that."

He had an odd expression as he thought about her confession.

"I did not mean to insult you, Fabian."

"I am not insulted at all, dear Lady Terese. How could you know any more than what you are told? But I do admit I am somehow disappointed to hear you think me so uncomplicated. Not that I would not prefer a simpler life at times."

She smiled at his answer. "I meant to say that I had no idea what you do at other times, on your own time. I know Mauro gives you much responsibility managing his soldiers. Somehow I picture you and the other guardsmen going into the Keep at the end of the day, like the horses to the stables. When you were away, I thought it was a part of your service to my husband."

"Well, that explains it," he assured her quietly. "We do more than eat our oats and go to sleep. And the other officers and I leave on personal business, as well." He thought of another reason. "I suppose you have never been inside the Keep, Lady Terese. The Barics forbid women from coming in, but I do not think the rule was meant to exclude you, madam. It is a part of your home, and the men would not object to your visit. We are a loud, coarse lot, but we are not totally uncivilized. I think you should come see how we live there."

She liked the idea of visiting the Keep. "I was told when I first arrived that I could not go in unaccompanied. But then Mauro never offered to take me."

Fabian shook his head with understanding. "Mauro cannot be relied upon to remember such details; sometimes he needs reminding. It would be my pleasure to show you the tower when we return. It is old and dark compared to your manor house, but you may find it interesting. I do. The view from the roof is especially breathtaking. You might be housed in the Keep one day, should you need protection from an attack. You may want to make some adjustments to your chamber before then."

This was news to her. "I didn't know I had a chamber there. I would like to see it, but I suppose I should ask Mauro's permission."

Fabian knew she was right. Mauro was very protective of her. "Yes, you will need to get his approval, but I am confident he will agree. When he does, I will be your guide."

"Fabian, may I ask one more thing?" she said reluctantly.

He had enjoyed their conversation and found her diverse topics charming. "Of course, my lady," he said without hesitation.

"I would like you to call me Terese, or even Resi, like I am accustomed to by my friends," she said unexpectedly. "I do not call you Lord Fabian, and I would prefer that you not call me Lady Terese."

Fabian was caught off guard for once, and he hoped it did not show in his face. He enjoyed her company here and at the castle, but there was protocol that dictated his friendships. He and Mauro's wife were not friends; they could not be while he was an unmarried man. He did not have to think long about it to answer her honestly. "I am flattered you consider me worthy of such familiarity, but I am unable to accommodate your wish without your husband's permission. You see, it was Mauro who said I should address you as Lady Terese, and he alone can tell me otherwise." She looked confused. "It is a tradition that you may not have in your own culture. I am quite used to it; calling you 'my lady' only shows you how much I admire you and your position. I hope you will understand this formality is not mine or yours to decide."

She had not thought about it that way, but knew he was right. She should have known better than to make such a suggestion.

He sensed her embarrassment and talked his way through the awkwardness. "Lady Terese, I have kept you too long," he apologized. "We have these lovely fish here, and you must be hungry for breakfast. I know I am."

He picked up the fish and hugged the cleaned carcasses against yesterday's dirty shirt. "I shall get the coals going again to start our fire, and you can wake the other ladies for breakfast," he suggested pleasantly.

She nodded and got to her feet. She walked at his side up the dock, both still barefooted, his shoes forgotten on the planks. Fabian watched her as she left him at the beach, walked to the tent, and disappeared into its embrace.

Well, he thought, Mauro might be right about his wife. The old scoundrel Kokkinos did send him something different. She was not like any woman Fabian had encountered, and he had encountered many. He would tell Mauro about their conversation before the baroness could tell him first. He would be sure to mention Dubovic's interest in his own family. But that would all have to wait until later. Now he would get their breakfast started.

He set the two fish down on the end of the plank table and looked in the baskets to find something to add to it. There were some apples and apricots, one more unwrapped honey cake, the bag of almonds and another of raisins, a crock of pickled eggs, and several more loaves of brown bread that could be sliced and toasted. The kitchen servants had packed two metal coffeepots, and he searched the baskets for the ground coffee to go with it. He did not know how to make coffee, so finding the grounds would make no difference anyway. It was a luxury soldiers did without, and at home coffee was poured for him, already steaming in the pot.

Caterina was the first to make her way to their makeshift kitchen. She was wearing a dressing robe and carried her satchel. "Good morning, Brother. Are you in charge of breakfast today?" she asked with a broad smile. She found it amusing that he looked so serious in his new role as cook.

"Unless you wish to be in charge?" he toyed with her. Caterina had never been in the kitchen in their family home; she would be useless this morning. "How did you sleep, Sister? Was the tent everything you expected?" he asked mischievously, expecting her to have found it intolerable.

"Better than expected. The fresh sea air in the cozy quarters made for a good sleep. And now we are going to try the seawater. It should be refreshing," she replied with a youthful innocence.

He looked at her in disbelief. "Ah, you are going swimming. I was wondering why you were so informal in your dressing gown."

She looked him over critically. "At least I am dressed. You look like you slept with the horses."

He pointed to the two fish. "Yes, well, I have had a busy morning already and have not had time to check my grooming. But if you want breakfast within the hour, you will have to tolerate my disheveled state." He winked at her playfully, and she returned a smile. "Shall we have our breakfast first, or do you ladies want to take your swim first? I will leave the order up to you."

"Here come the others. We should ask them." Isabella and Ruby came out of the tent, and Resi came toward the camp from the woods.

"Good morning," they said to one another as they arrived. Fabian exchanged greetings with the women.

"Is there coffee?" Isabella asked.

"There is, but not made," Fabian replied. "I have not found the actual coffee, but Nela did pack two small pots. To be honest, I do not know how it all becomes the final drink."

"Nor do I," Isabella said as she looked over the supplies. She took out a few small apples.

"Be careful of those," Fabian told her pleasantly. "I already ate the worm in mine by mistake." She looked at one with several holes and smiled at him. They could tolerate one another, and she would play her part.

"I can make coffee," Ruby offered, having overheard the exchange. She looked in the basket where the pots had been and found the tied parchment with the grounds. "I have been in charge of boiling the coffee before," she explained. "The young girls usually tended the pot. It is simple, but takes some time to brew." Fabian began to uncover the ash from the weakly glowing coals. He added some of the wood left near the fire pit. "It boils best with the pot in the coals. We could make the coffee now, Fabian, before you add more wood."

"This will burn down nicely into new coals in a half hour or so. Perhaps you should have your swim first, and then we can leisurely enjoy our meal when we are all dressed," Fabian suggested.

Isabella held up one of the two pails of dirty dishes Jero had collected after dinner last night. "We are without our kitchen staff and chambermaids. How will we eat our breakfast on these dishes?"

Fabian laughed and took the pail from her hand. "I will take these to the stream to wash them, along with myself. Caterina can come get me when you are all decent again." Isabella seemed surprised by his unexpected offer, but mumbled her agreement.

Resi grabbed one of the wormy apples Isabella had set out and carefully bit into it. She handed another to a Ruby, and they made their way to the dock. Fabian belted his sword on, collected his own saddlebag, slung his bow and quiver over his shoulder in case he spotted game to shoot, and then grabbed the two buckets of dishes with this remaining free hand. He merrily trudged down the path toward the stream.

~ * ~

After Fabian was gone down the path, Isabella and Caterina followed the Greek women to the dock. "Are you taking off all your clothes?" Caterina asked the baroness, surprised to see that her hostess was stripping out of her undergarment.

"Yes, I want to swim freely," Resi replied. "I swam in my shift yesterday, and it dragged me down. Mauro told me I should swim naked."

"Did he?" Isabella joined the conversation. "That is unexpected of him."

"There is no one here to see us, and Fabian promised to stay away until we call him back," Resi said assuredly before she scooted into the water from the shallow end of the dock. She took one last look at the stunned Venetians, and then plunged under the water and kicked away.

Ruby began to undress and told the worried Venetians, "She doesn't usually swim naked in the sea. In Greece, we wrap our intimate parts with cloth for modesty." She pulled off the last of her clothing. "But she is right. We are quite alone. It is like being in the bathhouse." She slipped into the cool water and waded out until it was deep enough to swim.

Isabella thought it was nothing like being in the baroness' bathhouse. She did not object to public nudity, not even her own. But this was not the same as a drunken dare, jumping naked into a canal after a night of cognac and dancing. This was too exposed in the bright morning light, and it frightened her. "Is it cold?" she called out to Ruby.

"Not at all, especially if you go in quickly. It is wonderful," Ruby yelled back.

They followed Ruby's lead and cautiously removed their lacy undergarments. Caterina stood next to Isabella and held her hand. "I will pretend this is what it would be like with John the Baptist."

"The story of John the Baptist is not the one that crossed my mind, but it is a good thought," Isabella agreed.

The water was cold at first contact, and they hesitated as they scooted off the edge of the planks. It did become warmer after a moment, as Ruby had promised. There was no tide here, so they were not at risk of being knocked over, and the bottom could be seen clearly. But the shore dropped off quickly a few paces from the dock, and Caterina and Isabella did not trust that they could swim back if they went out too far.

"What about all of these fish, Isabella? Will they bite me?" Caterina had not expected to be sharing the sea with so many other creatures.

"No, I do not think they will bother you. Are they not splendid?" Isabella remarked. She walked along the sea floor. "Come over here, Cat. There is a little squid and a starfish."

Caterina shook her head in a panic. "Oh, Isabella, I cannot do this. Things are bumping into me. I do not like it at all." She hurried back toward the dock and clambered out.

"Where are you going?" Isabella called to her.

Caterina hollered back without turning around, "I am getting dressed."

"Suit yourself, Caterina," Isabella shouted back across the water. "I am staying."

She leaned back and floated on the calm surface, enjoying the warmth of the sun on her face. She did not think to bring her hat into the water, but then the beautiful silk and feathers would have been ruined had she dared to float out deeper, as she planned to do.

Ruby swam up to Isabella. "I wish the Barics had a beach on their land," she said, panting to catch her breath. "I never heard Lady Nikolina talk of this spot, but I would be here every day in the summer."

"Where is Leopold Castle? Is it far from here?" Isabella asked.

Ruby was just able to stand on a slippery rock on the seafloor to keep her head above the water to answer. "I have only been there twice. The way we came here looked familiar to me, so it seems like the castle should be close by. It sits on the hill above the town, and Jero said we are only a few miles from the port."

Isabella did not know much about Mauritius' holdings, but she knew he owned quite a sizable estate. "Surely the Barics have a beach somewhere on their land," Isabella wondered out loud.

"Most of the Baric land runs into the valleys behind the first mountain. The waterfront at the village is marshy, where the shallow river flows into the sea. The salt mines make up most of the low shoreline on their land, but I have not been there. The rest of the coastline on the estate is just rocky cliffs."

"I had never thought about it, but I think I will miss the sea when we go to Hungary," Isabella said. She watched the little fish move through the water around her and frowned unhappily.

"I am sure you will return for a visit to the sea with your husband," Ruby said encouragingly.

"I doubt it," Isabella answered. "The first thing that happens when you are married is you become pregnant. After that, you cannot enjoy your new freedoms to travel as a married lady. Perhaps I will be barren, and then I can do as I like without the burden of children."

Ruby was stunned by the statement. "Surely you want children, Lady Isabella."

"To be honest, I have not been around a lot of children. My lady friends who have become mothers are changed by it, though. They grow old quickly. Most lose their looks and their figures by the third child. Their husbands tend to stray after that."

Ruby objected, "My mother still looks beautiful, and she had four children. My father is still very much in love with her." Resi swam up next to them. She had only heard this last part of the conversation and was curious what they were discussing.

"I will take your testimony to heart, Lady Ruby. But if I do have children, I hope they are all boys," Isabella declared.

"You can't mean that, Lady Isabella," Ruby insisted. "I have only sisters, and I helped my aunt raise her little girls. I would wish for lots of daughters."

"In general, I do prefer girls. Their manner and behavior is more pleasant than that of little boys. But I do not want my daughters to have to go through what I have gone through when they come of age. It is not right. My brother was not pushed and bullied to find the richest wife. He inherits my family's fortune, except what is decreed to me for my dowry. Yet I have heard that young ladies have even been sent to the nunnery just because a stingy relative did not want to give her the entitled dowry."

Isabella noticed for the first time that the baroness had joined them. She was especially somber. "Lady Terese, are you feeling alright?" Isabella asked.

"What is the matter, Resi? Do you have a cramp from swimming? What is upsetting you?" Ruby asked with alarm.

"I am supposed to give my husband a boy," she told the two women. "But there is always a chance I may have a daughter, and then what will become of her?"

Isabella brushed off her concerns. "Your daughters will not have that trouble," Isabella reassured her. "Mauritius is a modern man and will be an understanding father. He will not sell his daughters off to the highest bidder. He will protect them."

Resi suddenly began to sob. Isabella looked to Ruby for help. "What did I say?" Ruby shrugged and looked bewildered at Resi's abrupt mood change.

Resi blurted out, "If I have only daughters, we will be sent away. They will never get a chance at anything."

"What do you mean, Lady Terese? Who would send you away? Mauritius?" Isabella demanded to know.

Resi took a deep breath and was in command of her emotions again. "It is in our wedding contract. My husband must have a son, an heir, within five years of our marriage," she said. "He told me about it on the sailboat just yesterday. I asked him what that meant, and he said straight out that he could get rid of me because of it. He would send me away."

Isabella and Ruby exchanged looks of disbelief. "Oh, Resi, you misunderstood him. I am sure the baron would not do that. He must have been joking with you, teasing you, perhaps."

Isabella did not agree with Ruby. "Men are so cold. I have heard of this happening before. They write these contracts like we are a piece of property. And we are to them," she fumed.

"But the baron is not cold. He is different, right, Lady Isabella?" Ruby insisted. She dared to glare at Isabella, who stared back, realizing she had forgotten the baroness' maternal condition. Isabella had said too much already to talk her way out convincingly.

"I think I am done with my swim," Resi suddenly announced. "I am quite tired."

"You were up so early, Lady Terese. Why don't you go lie back down on the blankets?" Isabella told her. "We will come get you when Fabian has our breakfast ready."

"Yes, I would like to go to the tent for a few minutes and rest." She got out of the water and dried off quickly. She slipped her tunic over her head and carried the rest of her clothes in her arms. The two watched her from the water.

"I will have to have a word with Mauritius," Isabella told Ruby firmly. "To tell his pregnant wife that she must make him a son, and she has only less than four years left to succeed? I thought he was different, but they are all the same." She climbed out of the water, and Ruby followed her.

~*~

The rocky stream outside their camp was fast moving, and Fabian looked to where he might best do his washing. A little farther up from the path, the water had been diverted with some boulders and a few fallen trees to make a small pool. He unpacked his change of clothes and pot of soap, and he left them out on a log that surrounded one side of the pool's edge. He would do the chores first. He emptied the dishes, mugs, and utensils from last night into the calm, sandy shallow to let them soak. He cleaned the buckets in the swift water and freshly filled one to take back to camp later. Then he scrubbed the collection of dishes in the stream with sand and rinsed them in the flowing water. He set each item out in the warm sun on the rocks to dry.

He looked down at the clothes he had slept in. He noticed for the first time the bloodstains on his sleeves and breeches from skinning the deer and the ground-in sand from sleeping on the beach. This would not do.

Fabian stripped off his clothes and dunked them into the pool to soak while he washed from head to toe with the fragrant soap he had packed in his saddlebag. The pool was waist deep, and he sank down to rinse his tangled hair. The chilly water shocked his senses at first, but it was invigorating. He took his time lounging in his natural bathtub until he remembered he had not tended the horses yet this morning. It seemed to him there was an endless amount of duties for one man.

He left his dirty clothes soaking in the pool water and stepped out to hastily dry off with the small linen towel he took from his pack. He dressed again to his liking in a clean shirt and fresh breeches, but left the stockings packed for later when he could get his abandoned shoes from the dock. He combed his fingers through his hair; he would let it drip-dry while he got the horses. The sandy path that cut across from the stream to the narrow road where the wagon was parked was scattered with forest droppings and small stones that prickled under his feet. The horses were impatient with him as he untied the first two. He slid onto Bacchus' back and led Ophelia next to him to save the soles of his feet on one of the walks back to the stream.

The baroness had chosen an odd name for a horse, he thought as he held her reins. Maybe Ophelia had a special meaning to her in Greek. Fabian chuckled that Mauro never called the horse by the name his wife had decided on. He still stubbornly referred to her as the gray mare, after having lost the disagreement with the baroness about the chosen name. She was a pretty little mare, though, like her new owner. He hobbled the first two horses, and then went to get the other two, who were neighing restlessly, having been left behind.

With the four beasts finally content at the stream, he dealt with the rest of his own needs. He would have plenty of time while the girls swam and dressed for the day. He set up his small looking glass on the log and filled a clean mug with rinse water for his blade. He began to hum softly to himself as he lathered his face to shave. Fabian grew a full beard when soldiering, just to make his life simpler, but otherwise preferred a trimmed mustache and short goatee on his chin. He had just begun to drag his small dagger over his stubbly cheeks when the horses' agitation signaled that someone was approaching.

He saw in the mirror's reflection that it was his sister coming along the path; she was already dressed. He continued with his task and asked, "I thought you were swimming? Are you done already?"

"I did not realize we would be sharing the water with fish and squid and seagrass. I could not stand things bumping into me in the water, so I got out." He finished his second cheek and rinsed his face. "I see you have found clean clothes," she said casually.

"And I had time to bathe, too. There is a nice little pool there, if you would like to do the same. Oh, I still need to wash the stains out."

He reached across the log and pulled out his shirt. He took his pot of soap and rubbed some on the blood. Caterina sat silently on the log and watched as he rinsed the white shirt once more in the clear water. Then he did the same for his breeches. "I suppose the washing women at the castle will know how to clean these properly later," he said absently. He began to wring them dry and studied his quiet sibling. He knew she had not come there to watch him wash up.

"I wanted you to know, Fabian, that I do love Paolo and I will marry him," she said without prompting. She had not mentioned Paolo to Fabian since he punched her lover in the courtyard. He thought she would want to talk about it eventually.

He laid his wrung garments out on the rocks by the clean dishes. He gave her a sour look and said, "Paolo does not love you, Cat. He only wants your dowry money."

"That is a cruel thing to say, Fabian. You do not know him and how much he loves me. He told me he does."

He came to her side and sat down next to her on the fallen log. He tilted her chin to make her look at him. "It is the truth, Caterina. I talked to Gino, the other solider with him."

"Yes, I know who Gino is," she said quietly.

"They are friends, Cat, but Gino did tell me what your Paolo confided to him. I am sorry, but that is what he said." She hung her head in disappointment. Fabian got up again to put his other supplies back into his saddlebag.

"Do you have a brush, Fabian? I will fix your hair." He found his comb and handed it to her. She stayed on the log, and he sat on the ground in front of her.

"Do you have nothing to say, Caterina?" he asked as she pulled the comb to unknot his nearly dried hair.

"Gino is wrong," she answered, then sulked again.

"Did you sleep with Paolo?" Fabian was compelled to ask. She tugged on his hair a little too hard and he winced. After a moment he insisted, "Well, did you?"

"No, Fabian, I did not. He is a gentleman. It is wrong of you to think otherwise."

"That is good to hear, Caterina, but that does not change my opinion of him. He is not even an officer, and I understand he does not inherit much himself. He needs a wife with a good dowry to supplement his income."

"He does not want to marry me for my dowry, Fabian. Now give me your cord." He handed it to her, and she tied the leather band around his smoothed hair at the base of his neck.

He stood and bent to kiss her on her forehead. "Believe what you like, Cat. I hope it works out for you, but do not count on it." He held out his hand to take the comb back, and she gave it to him.

"Fabian, will you comb out my hair now?" She added sadly, "I miss that."

He smiled tenderly at her. She was his favorite sister. When she was a little girl, he would sometimes brush her hair at night while he told her a story. He walked behind her now, undid her damp braid, and unwound the strands. She had lovely, silky hair, and he untangled it gently. "Will you want a story with this?" He leaned over her narrow shoulder and whispered, "Maybe a ghost story?"

"No stories!" She giggled. Then more quietly she told him, "I just want your company. I feel like we may never see each other again if I am sent to Hungary. I do not want to go, Fabian."

He took a moment to breathe deeply and found his voice. "I know that," he agreed sadly.

He combed her long hair to a glossy sheen. He cleared his throat, then asked, "What do you want done with it, Caterina?"

He only knew how to pin her hair one way, but she liked that he always asked first. She held out her ivory combs to him and answered, "Maybe just a twist."

He twisted the length onto a figure eight and placed the two combs along each side to hold it. He leaned over her and embraced her shaking shoulders. "Shhh. Do not cry, Caterina," he whispered.

He knew she was right. They might never see each other again, but he needed to give her hope to keep her strong. "Your new husband will let you visit Venice after a time, and I will see you there."

"Do you really think so?" She looked up at him, her big, brown eyes pleading for the truth.

"I do," he lied to his sister, struggling to hold back his own tears.

She nodded sadly, wanting to believe him that it would work out. "My hat is in the tent," she said unexpectedly. "I do not want to get too much sun and look brown for my wedding."

"You go fetch it, then. I will take the horses back and then wait here again. Come tell me when the others are ready to start breakfast."

She began to leave down the path, but turned to say, "I had hoped you could fix my troubles for me, but I will not despair. I find some comfort in seeing Lady Terese with Mauritius. They did not know each other. Is it possible that my husband will love me like that?"

What should Fabian tell her? That Mauritius did not want to marry his wife; that it took him nearly a year to fall in love with her; and how Lady Terese had been left alone for much of that time, most likely contemplating her own unhappiness? Instead, he answered, "Father has gone through a lot of trouble to find a favorable match for you. He wants you to be happy, Caterina. You will have to trust his judgment that he has chosen well."

She seemed to regain her strength and nodded again that she would trust him. She turned and disappeared down the path to the beach while Fabian watched her go.

~*~

Ruby and Isabella dressed in silence on the dock. Ruby was anxious to cheer Isabella up, but their attention turned toward Caterina coming back from the beach. Her borrowed sandals clicked on the worn boards as she joined them. Ruby smiled brightly at her. "Hello, Lady Caterina. Did you not like the swim?"

"It was a little too adventurous for me, I am afraid," she said and laughed. "I am ashamed to say that I imagined the fish would eat me, but I am pleased to have tried it. I think I will stay on the beach from now on."

"Well, Caterina, I thought it was the perfect adventure. But I am not sure I will need to go in again either," Isabella confessed.

"Where is Lady Terese?" Caterina asked, looking out at the sea.

"She exhausted herself with her swim. She has gone to lie down in the tent for a moment," Isabella answered. She would tell Caterina the full details of the baroness' troubles later.

"Oh. I was coming to get my hat, but then thought I might lie down as well. Maybe I have gotten too much sun already today," Caterina said.

Ruby didn't know what Resi's mood would be if Caterina joined her, so she said, "Perhaps you could first tell Fabian we want to start breakfast, and then take your rest." Caterina agreed, and Ruby went up to the tent to check on Resi.

Chapter 55

The trip to the harbor that morning had been shorter than Jero had expected. They had arrived in the dawning light with plenty of time to meet the crew for an early meal in their lodging house before their appointment with the navy.

Jero admired how Mauro managed the group of men without insisting on his own authority over them. The captain had brought only ten sailors with him. Under normal circumstances, the two-masted ship would need double that number for the usual six-day round-trip on open waters. But they were only hours from home and would be sailing in fair weather in the daylight.

The ship's crew also worked in the salt production when they were not loading the vessel or delivering the baron's goods. Under Mauro's orders, Jakov Kuzjak and two of his sons had driven the sailors to the harbor town yesterday. Jakov was as anxious to have the ship returned and resume normal work as the baron was. He would be waiting back at the Barics' docks to help land the ship later. All of the men assembled that morning were related to the Kuzjak family in some way; the ship's captain was the one exception.

Branislav Tomsic was not what one would expect of a sea captain. He was small and thin, with a boyish grin when he smiled, and thick curly hair that he let blow unbound in the wind. He was only in his late twenties, but commanded his ship with knowledge beyond his age and size. He knew all the harbors up and down the Venetian and Ottoman coastlines, could sail by the stars, and had a sixth sense for changes in wind and weather. Most importantly, he could dock the Barics' small ship against another to transfer a delivery without a port. He was fair and amiable to his crew, but expected that they worked together the same way. He demanded that each man know all the workings of the boat to be able to fill in for any need, and to work in harmony with the other shipmates. Those who didn't were not allowed aboard again. The men were not confined for long voyages on the *Margaret*, but the seafaring they undertook demanded long shifts late into the night and teamwork.

It was Mauro who had promoted Branislav to captain a year ago when his own father, Ivanoslav Tomsic, the former Barics' ship captain, fell ill with a fever and did not recover fully. The new captain was the former captain's youngest son, who had lived most of his life on merchant vessels and had sailed the last ten years with his father for Lord Lorenc. The two young men found an unspoken connection, having taken over the roles of their own fathers. Mauro knew it had not been his captain's incompetence that had led to his ship being seized. The *Margaret* had been followed into Ottoman waters by the Venetian Navy, tracked down in the storm. Both men wanted retribution.

At breakfast, there was mostly talk of the next cargo run, once the ship was reloaded back at home. Along with salt and wine, this next shipment would transport a special cargo for Demetrius Kokkinos. A smuggling run to the Kokkinos ship was scheduled for delivery every new moon off the western coast of Greece. That would be in five days' time. Branislav had made these runs with his father's crew for years, and he had never asked why they met the Greek ship only on the moonless waters. He had proven to be as discreet and trustworthy as his father had been to Lord Lorenc.

Mauritius Baric owned two ships. The one being held was the larger of the two. The second was used for smaller deliveries across the Adriatic to customers in Venice. It would return filled with supplies for the village merchants and the castle. These runs to the capital were to sustain the farmers, and the baron had little to gain from the sale of their goods. The profitable deliveries for the Barics were made outside Venetian territorial waters, so a larger ship was necessary for the longer voyages in rougher seas.

Both vessels were Venetian made. It was required by law to purchase ships from the Empire. Under normal circumstance, Venetian merchants did not own their own ships. They would hire one from the Empire's vast state-owned fleet. Because the Barics' salt production required special specifications for loading, Fredrik Baric had long ago been allowed to keep his own ship ready with his own chosen crew. Lorenc Baric had been given those same privileges, and Signor Rosso recently signed the papers permitting Mauro to keep his own ships, as well.

Mauro's father had replaced his father's galley ship with a modern sailing vessel. It could hold more cargo and needed fewer men to sail it. The Venetians were excellent ship builders and had sold Lord Lorenc a well-outfitted vessel at a good price, albeit still a small fortune for any merchant. As Lord Lorenc's new steward thirty years ago, Nestor had organized the Baric account books and had found that Lord Fredrik had actually left his son a small fortune, and then some, so the purchase was made.

Purchasing the modern ship had proved to be a good investment, and he named it for his beautiful wife, Margaret. The modern sails allowed the craft to maneuver to their rendezvous point without the laborious oar power of the old galley ship. Oars were still used by the sailors for tight places, but no gang of oarsmen was needed on board. With just two or three deliveries scheduled during the month, it was cheaper to maintain a smaller crew of sailors that could also be employed for the salt production. That is how the Barics' operation ran for decades.

All of the men at breakfast had been aboard the *Margaret* and jailed by D'Alessandro. They were happy to share the baron's pleasure in meeting him at the harbor that morning. Jero walked with the crew to where the ship was docked at the end of the long pier, and Mauro met the lieutenant at his office to sign the paperwork. The harbor was already alive with activity from small fishing boats to larger ships tied for unloading. Men of all races brought wares on and off the docks, and to and from the warehouses located across the harbor's main street. The Baric vessel was moored next to two naval warships. Two more warships were anchored in deep water near the edge of the bay, ready to sail into open waters when called upon.

Jero had traveled by ship only twice in his lifetime, and only as a passenger. The easygoing commander and Jero knew each other from the many times they had coordinated the manifests for the shipments last year, and he welcomed Jero aboard like an old friend. Of all the times Jero had visited the Barics' small harbor, he had only met with the captain on the loading pier. He eagerly walked the gangway onto the ship's deck. This was not his world, but he was glad to finally be invited in.

The crew immediately busied themselves inventorying the cargo, as Mauro had requested, so the baron could correct any wrongdoing on the navy's part before they sailed. Weeks ago Jero had written the manifest that went with this cargo. He read the list again today to the men as they counted the barrels and bundles onboard. Most were goods from Mauro's tenant farmers: dried apricots, pressed olive oil, salted fish, bales of wool, and tanned hides. Sealed containers of salt were loaded in the bottom as ballast; most containers were presold to be off-loaded along the way. The men noted that many of the bundles and crates had been opened and poorly reclosed by the Venetian inspectors. Upon closer inspection, Jero and the men agreed that nothing had been taken out of the hold.

Mauro, Lieutenant D'Alessandro, and Captain Toselli came up the plank walkway as Jero climbed the ladder back onto the ship's deck. Although Mauro kept his expression in check in front of the Venetians, Jero could tell he was very relieved to have this annoyance behind him. Mauro had told Jero he would not make the same arrogant mistakes again.

The two had talked the entire way to the harbor that morning. They had speculated how Mauro's grandfather, Fredrik, would have handled D'Alessandro. Jero was convinced the elder Baric would have also resolved it with a grand party. Jero had heard as many stories about Lord Fredrik growing up as Mauro had, and they had laughed together on their morning ride as they retold some of the tales they remembered of his extravagance and his generosity.

Jero's thoughts came back to the present as Mauro casually introduced him to the lieutenant. "You might remember my steward?"

Lieutenant D'Alessandro looked him over once and said, "Of course. Good to see you again, sir." Jero nodded and tipped his cap in respect, but said nothing to the officer. Upon seeing Mauro board the ship, Branislav came to join the four.

He gave the naval officers a quick glare of resentment that the lieutenant ignored, and then Branislav told the baron, "The cargo has been inventoried and everything is accounted for. We are ready to make sail on your command, my lord."

Mauro turned to the lieutenant and waited for permission from the naval officer. "Yes, your ship is free to go," he acknowledged. Then D'Alessandro turned to the seaman and warned, "Captain Tomsic, and I use that title lightly, I hope you can find your way home. If we discover you off course again, you shall be named yourself for your crimes next time. Pirating is more than frowned upon, it is illegal. I suggest you heed my warning."

Branislav's expression was unreadable. He simply nodded once to the lieutenant, and then returned to his crew and began giving orders to get underway.

"My captain is employed by me and is under my orders. I do not like being accused of pirating, Lieutenant. It is untrue, and there is no basis for it," Mauro said coldly.

"I apologize if you thought I was accusing you of anything, Lord Baric. One thing tends to lead to another, and a friendly warning is sometimes required to keep an *employee* in check." He lowered his voice and told the baron, "I feel I owe you a bit of privileged information. There *is* basis for my warning, sir. I have learned that your man, Tomsic, may also have another employer besides yourself. He is suspected of captaining a ship recently stolen from a local nobleman. I have no proof, but I will eventually get it. You will want to look for a new captain when I do."

He let the words sink in, and Mauro did not argue with him this time. Mauro glanced at Jero, who had silently listened to the conversation along with Captain Toselli.

"A local nobleman, Lieutenant? Was it Lord Leopold who was the victim of this crime?" Mauro asked with clear concern for his friend.

"No, Lord Baric, he was not the victim," the lieutenant reported. "This would generally be confidential while still under investigation, but since you are neighbors and have long ties with this family, I am sure you will remain discreet. It was Lord Dubovic's merchant ship that was pirated."

"Shocking," was Mauro's reply. He was indeed shocked. Pirating happened too often in open waters, but they did not generally take the ship, only the cargo they had wanted. He did not believe Branislav would steal a merchant ship, especially not from Baron Dubovic.

D'Alessandro cleared his throat and then said lightly, "I have no intention of sailing with you to your home port, so I will leave your ship in your hands now, Lord Baric. Good day to you, sir."

"Good day, Lieutenant."

Mauro watched him and Captain Toselli disembark. He walked closer to Jero's side. The crew was done with the preparations for casting off, and he said quietly, "I will find time to ask you about this later. I do not believe the lieutenant suddenly has my best interest at heart, but if you can, keep your ears open for me about this stolen ship."

Jero nodded; he understood the importance of it.

Mauro was anxious to get off the swaying boat. He smiled at his old friend. "Well, Jero, I will leave you to your fun. I wish you a safe passage for the short journey."

Jero grinned and replied, "Just sailing the harbor would be just as exciting to me. You know that I have never been on your ship."

"I know, Jero. I am glad you are looking forward to it. I will make haste now back to camp and see you in a few days back at the castle." He patted Jero on the back for good measure and hurried down the gangplank and onto solid ground. Two of the Baric sailors slid the planks back onto the deck.

Mauro did not linger to watch them sail off, but mounted his horse, which he had left at the naval headquarters, and rode slowly through the crowded streets.

Chapter 56

Ruby moved the coals with the thick stick to make a well on the edge of the large fire pit. "This is how my mother taught me," Ruby said. "There are two pots. Would you like to take charge of one, Lady Isabella?"

"Yes, I would," Isabella volunteered. She looked smugly at Fabian, who was also at the fire tending the fish. He raised his eyebrows at her unexpected acceptance of the job, but said nothing.

Ruby explained, "Nela put a packet of sugar in the basket. I put a few spoons of sugar in the water already. We will let it boil, and then we will add a few spoons of the coffee."

Isabella was not impressed. "Is that all there is to it? No wonder children make the coffee in your home."

Ruby chuckled softly at her remark. "Well, the only trick is that you have to watch it carefully," she explained. "You cannot let the coffee boil over, or you will lose your drink to the fire. It needs to steam and lightly bubble, but you don't want it to get bitter by cooking it too quickly."

"The fish are done," Fabian announced and moved them from the fire onto a clean board on the table. He came back to where the women were crouched. "They will need a few minutes to cool. Should I call for Caterina and the baroness?"

Resi had been asleep when Ruby had checked on her earlier, and Caterina said she was going to do the same. "Do you think you can watch both pots, Lady Isabella?" Ruby asked. "I can go get them in the tent, Fabian."

Isabella did not get the chance to answer. "I will watch the second one," Fabian offered. "It looks like the water is boiling now. Should we add the coffee?"

"Thank you, Fabian. Yes, add two spoonfuls and stir. Remember, it should simmer, not boil. And don't let it bubble over. I will be back in a few minutes." Ruby hurried off to wake the sleeping women.

The charcoal popped. "Be careful not to get too close, or you will singe your gown." Isabella moved back, closer to Fabian. "How did you enjoy your swim?" he asked casually, looking down at his task.

She concentrated on her duty as she told him, "I was surprised we had to share the water with so many fish, but once I learned they would not harm me, it was very nice."

He finally looked over at her. It would not change anything, but he felt like talking. "We swam in the dark last night, and the fish were asleep. You will have to try swimming again tonight."

"Maybe I will. I would like to try a lot of things while I am here." She had little time left, she thought.

"You were always adventurous when you were a girl. Do you remember when you took my bow and wanted to learn to shoot?" Fabian asked. He took the pot off the coals to let the bubbles subside, then put it back on.

She stirred her pot absently and recalled, "I think I tried to shoot you with it."

"Yes, and you almost succeeded. I will give you another chance this afternoon, if you like," he offered with an easy smile.

"To shoot you?" she said and laughed.

He laughed with her. "To shoot a target," he clarified. "I hope you do not want to still shoot me?"

She could see he was trying to apologize. "Maybe," she teased. She was not supposed to be enjoying his company, but she had already forgiven him. "Caterina can also join us."

"I am not certain if it is a good sport for her. The bow is almost as tall as she is."

Isabella looked at him seriously. "She is grown up now, Fabian. She is stronger than you think."

He matched her stare. "Yes, I know that, but I can still worry about her. I *want* to protect her, Isabella, but I cannot. It was wrong of you to suggest she come here."

"It was not my idea," she declared firmly.

He raised his brows in surprise and challenged her. "No?"

She shook her head. "No," she said flatly. She did not want to begin another argument with him.

He was getting bored with their simple job and uncomfortable with the conversation. "Do you think this coffee is done?"

Isabella was not bothered by the task. "We will wait until Lady Ruby comes back."

There was a comfortable silence between them as they each focused on their little brewing pots. Isabella asked him something more personal this time. "Do you prefer it here, Fabian?"

He looked up from his chore. "Yes, I actually do," he answered honestly.

"Do you not miss the society and the luxuries at home? Carnival time, parties, the midnight boat rides?"

He took the spoon from her hand and stirred his coffeepot while he thought about it. "Sometimes," he admitted. "The ball this week made me realize how different things are for me here. It was an exceptional evening, not an everyday invitation, like in Venetian society. But I like the quiet. I especially like the freedom."

"I can see it suits you," she told him pleasantly. "And do you have a sweetheart, Fabian?"

He had expected this question at some point. He looked into her eyes and replied, "No. I have no one of consequence in my life. I like it that way for now."

"Good for you," she said cheerfully. In his distraction, he did not observe what she had noticed. "You are boiling over, Fabian."

He picked up the handle of the little coffeepot. "Shit, that is hot." She should not have laughed at him as he sucked his burnt finger, but she did anyway. "That will be my lost coffee then," he declared.

"We will make it stretch." She took the folded rag and carefully removed her pot from the fire, too. She set it on the sideboard with Fabian's pot. "Caterina does not like coffee anyway."

"But this is a special coffee, made by her brother. She may never have a chance to taste my coffee again, because I will not be cooking it next time. Ah, here she comes now." He bowed to the three women while still nursing his blistered finger. "The coffee is done, ladies, and so is our fish. We can eat."

They were all famished by the time they sat down to enjoy their hard-earned meal. The pleasant conversation turned to the subject of their good fortune at the ball and the baron getting his ship back.

Caterina complained, "It was a shame that we missed so much of the dancing. We were so preoccupied with Lieutenant D'Alessandro's pleasure. I only danced a few dances, and they were all with him."

Fabian corrected her good-humoredly, "I believe we shared a dance or two, Sister."

"Which dances would you have wanted to dance?" Isabella asked her. "Fabian can make it up to you." Isabella looked his way with a coy smile.

"Here and now?" Fabian feigned his objections.

"Yes, of course here and now," Isabella insisted. Resi and Ruby cheered him on. Fabian enjoyed dancing, and he would gladly oblige her.

He stood and set his empty dish on the plank table. He wiped his fishy fingers on the rag they had used at the fire, and then went to his sister and gallantly offered her his hand. She stood and curtsied gracefully to him.

"Which dance shall we dance, my lady?" Fabian exaggeratedly crooned.

Caterina thought for a moment, and then chose a lively dance, one with many twirls and kicks. The three Venetians all sang and hummed the music to her choice, while Fabian and Caterina put on an entertaining show. When it was over Resi asked, "How do you remember all the moves, Fabian? That was quite good."

"I always told him he should have been in theater," Isabella said. "He remembers every detail, and he loves an audience. Fabian was my first dance partner. How old were we then?"

"Twelve and thirteen," he recalled quickly. "And I think you were taller than me," he added.

Caterina was catching her breath when she said, "You are both beautiful dancers. Show us one of your favorites, Fabian."

"Well, all right. I actually prefer the slower dances, and then I do not get so hot in my costume. Do you remember this one?" he asked his sister.

He began humming an intricate tune, and Caterina picked up on it and began to sing the melody. He stood in front of Isabella this time, and she took his offered hand with a smile. She knew this dance. It was her favorite, not his.

They moved about in the sand in front of the shore while Caterina sang the sweet song and Isabella hummed along. Fabian had the tune in his head without their added efforts, and he glided the capable Isabella around their camp; both were barefooted, but floated just the same.

Resi was intrigued watching them. She felt that she was intruding on two lovers. There was something too familiar, too intimate between them. Did they not notice their own connection? He gave Isabella one last twirl and then bowed to her at arm's length. The three women in the audience clapped at the end of their dance.

"That was beautiful," Caterina declared.

Fabian released his grip on Isabella's soft hand, and she curtsied before saying, "You have outdone yourself, Fabian. And as a reward, we shall wash the dishes this morning." She quickly gathered the plates for something to do, so she would not have to look his way again.

Resi and Ruby were surprised by the abrupt ending to the dance party. They stood and joined Isabella at the sideboard. She was flushed, but it was not from the dancing. "Would you like to take a boat ride around the lagoon this morning? I think all four of us could fit on the benches," Resi asked the two ladies.

Caterina looked anxiously at Isabella. "Not out to the island?" she asked.

"Not if you don't want to. We could just sail around here," Ruby interjected what she hoped would sway the ladies to join them.

Isabella did not hesitate and exclaimed, "We are here for an adventure. I am willing." She turned to Fabian and said, "We will wash up quickly and then take our boat ride. Perhaps we can shoot your bow after lunch."

He accepted her peace offering. "Yes, I will show all of you how to shoot later. Hurry along now. I will pack up the rest of breakfast."

The ladies took the pail of mugs and an armful of plates with them down the path to the stream. Fabian looked at the small pile of logs left and set them over the coals to bank them for the day. He would chop more wood while the ladies enjoyed their sailing excursion.

Fabian had begun to tidy up the sideboard when he heard the horses in the distance. He instinctively reached for his bow leaning against the plank table. Then he heard Bacchus' greeting to Janus; it must be Mauro. He saw his friend come out of the trees onto the path near the tent. Fabian set the weapon down again and waved; Mauro waved back, smiling.

Mauro made his way onto the beach. "That was quick. Did you get your ship off alright?" Fabian asked eagerly.

"Yes, it was a success." Mauro looked around at the remains of their morning feast. "Do I smell coffee? Is there anything left from breakfast?"

Fabian laughed at the sudden change of subject. "I thought you were getting a meal in town?"

"We did, but that was hours ago." Mauro turned his attention back to Fabian. He looked at his usually well-attired friend and chucked, "What have you been doing this morning? You are not even dressed."

"I have yet to retrieve my stockings and shoes, but at least give me credit that these are clean clothes, Mauritius. I have been busy with my morning chores," Fabian said defensively.

"Is that right?" Mauro replied cheerfully.

"Yes, I caught two fish for breakfast, washed all the dishes from our dinner, took care of the horses, bathed, washed my bloody shirt from yesterday, made coffee, and danced with the ladies." Mauro laughed at his list of achievements, and Fabian went on to tell him, "They swam in the sea earlier, and we have just finished our meal."

Mauro picked up a knife to cut a corner off the remaining chunk of honey cake. He took a bite; it was still moist and sticky. Fabian handed him a mug half-full with the last of the coffee. Mauro said with a relaxed smile, "It seems I missed quite a morning then. Thank you for taking care of things."

He looked around the camp, then out over the lagoon. He saw the sailboat was still tied to the dock. "Where are the ladies?"

"They were feeling domestic themselves, and they have taken the breakfast dishes to wash in the stream."

Mauro drank the cold coffee. "I wish you could have been there to see D'Alessandro's face when he handed me the papers reversing all of the charges."

Fabian leaned against the table with his arms crossed, imagining the officer's discomfort. "Yes, I would have liked to have seen that. And will he behave in the future?" Fabian asked.

Mauro took a hunk of the fish in his fingers to eat, and then replied, "The lieutenant assured me it was just navy regulations, and he hoped I understood that he was only doing his duty, etcetera, etcetera. You know how he can talk his way out of anything. But the ship was quickly handed over, and my crew was there waiting for us. The boat was still loaded, and everything checked off satisfactorily. There is a good wind this morning from the south on the Adriatic, so I imagine Jero will be back with no troubles."

"And is Jero seaworthy?" Fabian asked, meaning to poke fun at Mauro's fears again.

Mauro laughed. "Very. He was like a ten-year-old boy eager to take his first voyage. I am glad I brought him. It was satisfying to see that bright smile on his face."

Fabian felt an unexpected twinge of jealousy looking at Mauro's happy expression. "Is that why you keep Jero as your steward? Just to see his bright smile?"

"And if I do, what is wrong with that?" Mauro admitted out loud for the first time.

"You are not in the same social standing, and yet he is like a best friend. You need him, don't you?" Fabian asserted, and the mood suddenly changed.

"What do you want me to say, Fabian? Yes, I need him. He is a good man, an honest man, and without him I cannot run my estate. I like him, too. Is that so hard to accept? We have a long history together."

"That is all fine, Mauro, I like the man well enough, too. He is growing on me. But he is just too good to be true, and I do not trust that. I have warned you before about servants. You let them get too close, and they can extort money from you, or worse."

"You do not know Jero like I do. He does not care about money, and he is loyal to the Barics."

"For now," Fabian warned.

"Now is all I have."

Each looked at the other earnestly for a long moment, and then Fabian shook his head and laughed. "All right, Mauro. You keep whatever pets you like. I have said enough. I will not talk of it again."

"Thank you." Mauro finished his cup and said, "I'll just settle in Janus and be back for some more." Fabian nodded and went back to his task.

~*~

Mauro had just unsaddled his horse when his two soldiers rode up the sandy track from the main route. They stopped next to their commander and reported, "We have been searching for you, my lord. There is news about your visitors."

"Have they arrived?"

"Yes, my lord."

Mauro led the two scouts out onto the beach as the women came down the trail with their cleaned dishes.

"Mauro, you are back!" Resi eagerly greeted him. The couple embraced with a soft kiss before Resi realized that he was not alone. "Who are those men, Mauro?" she asked quickly.

"Those are two new recruits of mine, Denis and Teodor. They were on border duty and have brought us news."

"Patricius," she said to herself with a smile.

"Yes, your brother was seen coming out of the valley pass at first light," he told her.

She was excited at the news, and Mauro tried to be happy for her.

Fabian walked up to the two to ask, "What is the word? Will we be ending our campout early?"

"I hate to call the party off, but it looks that way." He put the question to his wife, knowing the answer already. "Unless you want to stay, Resi? Your brother and his gang will be welcomed at the castle without us and taken care of for the next few days. We can finish our outing here at the seaside."

"No, we must leave at once."

"Very well," Mauro said agreeably. "But maybe after we dress first?"

She was still in her salt-stained robes from yesterday. "You are right, Mauro. I cannot meet Patricius looking like this." She dashed away, back to the tent, with a confused Ruby following after her.

Mauro turned back to Fabian and relayed what the scouts had briefly told him. "My new brother-in-law and four others were spotted this morning coming out of the mountains along the wagon road. Goran rode ahead to warn Simeon, and Denis and Teodor came to get us. They were having a hard time finding our hidden beach, but they saw me turn off here in the distance when I rode in."

Caterina and Isabella had watched the scene from the path, unsure of what it all meant. They had not been forewarned that their excursion might be cut short. Isabella and Caterina approached the two. "What is going on?" Caterina asked.

"Good morning, ladies," Mauro greeted them. "There has been a change in plans, and we will be returning to the castle. If you can gather your things, then we will get the wagon packed."

"Oh, but this is so sudden," Caterina protested. "We had such a wonderful morning planned."

"I am sorry to have ruined our outing, but my wife will explain the new circumstances to you. She is changing in the tent." Feeling abruptly excused, the ladies hurried away, speculating quietly between themselves.

The young guardsmen approached their commander at the campfire and waited for instructions. "Help yourself to whatever you find left from the meal before we have to pack everything up. The fish is delicious, and there is fresh water and some mugs. Eat the last of the cake, too." The men thanked him and eagerly followed his suggestion.

"I need to gather my things at the stream," Fabian said. "I did bring a proper wardrobe to change into, just in case. I will help you pack up first, and then we can change."

"There is not much to pack. The scouts can lend a hand with the tent and loading the wagon after they finish eating." Mauro looked around at the cozy camp. They would try this again another day, under other circumstances. "I have my bag here. I will go to the stream with you."

Fabian said, as they walked along together, "Just think, this evening you will have an enjoyable meal with your wife's favorite relation and his four best friends. This will be a full day, indeed."

"I am going to believe it will not be so bad," Mauro declared cheerfully.

"You are quite the optimist today, Mauro. What has happened to you?"

Mauro smiled back. "Can a man not be happy in life?"

Fabian patted him on the back and exclaimed, "Yes, please, be happy, my friend. Who am I to interfere with that? I just hope your new visitors feel the same."

Chapter 57

After Mauro left them, Jero turned his attention back to the ship's deck. The captain was signaling to secure the oars to move the ship out into the open harbor to set the sails. With no waiting vessels restricting their maneuvering, they were out on the open sea within the hour.

Halfway through their journey home, Branislav motioned to Jero to come to the port side to see something special. "Sometimes we have companions. Do you see those? They are called dolphins," he told Jero excitedly. Jero watched in amazement as a pod of fifty or more dolphins swam alongside the ship in the clear water.

"What a remarkable sight," he said, almost to himself. He and Branislav watched the marvelous creatures swim in tandem with them for another few minutes, and then the pod split up and dove into deeper waters.

Jero found he loved being out on the sea. The ship was on a steady course up the coastline. The wind was in their favor, coming from the southwest, so the crew had time to show Jero the workings of the ship while it almost sailed itself. After a time, he began to recognize the landmarks, and knew they were close to home.

"Do you enjoy captaining?" Jero asked Branislav.

"I do, even when it is not ideal weather like today. This trip is easy. Many are not, and the baron has us sail at night for the deliveries with the Greeks," the captain told him.

"What did you do while the ship was held by the navy?" Jero asked lightly, thinking now of the pirating accusation. "Did you work with the Kuzjak cousins?"

"Me? No," he answered in a friendly manner. "I am not good with manual labor. Well, not on land, at least. We had the baron's small cargo run to Venice, and then I met up with some friends and helped them with another odd job before I sailed back to Solgrad with his purchases. I did not think the baron would object to my staying away a few days longer."

"No," Jero agreed, "why would he expect you to just sit around the docks? Your cabin is on the ship, right?"

"Yes. I don't even have lodgings on land right now. I could stay with my father, but he lives with my aunt on one of Lord Dubovic's farms. I did visit him there, but I am not a farmer. He isn't either."

"How is your father?" Jero thought to ask. The former Baric sea captain had almost died of his illness last year.

"It is not so much his body troubling him anymore, but his mind. There is no reason he should not be fully recovered. He is able to get about now with no trouble, but has little will to go on. I am trying to save some money to get us a small house on the sea, so he can spend his days looking out onto the Adriatic that he loves, not the fields. That is why I helped my friend out with a job that he has now and then." Branislav had forgotten that he was talking to the baron's steward, and not just a new hand. He clarified, "Not that I am not grateful for the salary Lord Baric pays me. I just need a bit more to secure the new lodgings for my father."

"Do not worry about telling me this," Jero reassured the captain. "I think it is good of you to try to offer your father a life by the seashore again."

They were both quiet for a moment. Jero noticed the men were climbing the rigging and securing a sail as they approached the entrance to the Barics' little harbor. Jero brightened again. "What can I do to help?" he asked Branislav.

The captain motioned to the bow of the ship. "Andrej!" the captain shouted across the deck. The sailor turned for instructions and Branislav waved him over. "Show our friend what is needed to dock his master's ship." Branislav winked at Jero, who nodded and followed Andrej across the deck to a group of men working the lines. The captain got to work giving orders to the others.

When their ship docked a quarter hour later, Jero thanked the captain and said his goodbyes to the crew. There was a saddled horse waiting for him at the small stable at the top of the hill. Had there not been one, he would have gladly run the distance to the castle; he was full of adrenaline from his maritime adventure.

Jero looked back at the docked ship from the top of the horse trail. Branislav had given Jero an open invitation to sail along on one of their weekly deliveries in the future. Jero wanted to take the offer, but was not sure if Mauro would be as agreeable to the idea. The baron kept Jero very busy at the castle, and already had reluctantly let him go to Rijeka for a week. Maybe he would get his courage up to ask the baron at the end of the summer, when all the guests were gone, and life became predictable again.

The trade route back to the castle was surprisingly empty. At this time of day there were usually carts coming and going along the well-traveled road. The horse that was left waiting for him at the dock, Blaze, was a young gelding with a reputation for his speed. This long stretch of road from the salt port to the castle crossroads was smooth and free of holes. Jero took off his felt cap and tucked it into his belt. He held tightly to the reins and gave the horse a kick-start to send him flying home. It was all he could do to keep from hooting at the pleasure he felt today. The horse seemed to enjoy the release of energy, too, and galloped steadily with no further prodding.

Up ahead, in the blur of the landscape, Jero could see a group of horses coming into view. They seemed to be at a leisurely pace, blocking the road. Jero would catch up with them quickly at this speed, and they had already turned to look his way. He slowed Blaze to a trot as he closed in on them. The five equipped riders had two spare horses with their group. They were strangers, foreigners for sure, and their extra horses were loaded with shields and other makings of weapons. Panic washed over Jero. They could only be the expected Kokkinos warriors, and there was no way Jero could avoid greeting them.

He summoned his courage and said loudly as he neared, "Good day to you, gentlemen."

They watched him with stern expressions as his horse slowed to a stop. He pointed to the crossroad just up ahead of them. "You will be wanting this road to the right for Baric Castle."

"Are you from Baric Castle?" one of the men asked. The man was dusty from their travels that morning, and his long, brilliant blue jacket was dirty from wear. But his face was freshly shaven, and his wavy brown hair was neatly tied under his low cap. He had unusual blue eyes that matched the baroness'. Jero was certain this was Patricius Kokkinos.

The men looked at Jero intensely as he answered, "Yes, I live at the castle. I am Lord Baric's steward. My name is Jero." He tried to sound casual as the five men surrounded him with their horses to hear him better. "The baroness has been expecting you. She is not at home, but I can escort you there."

"And how do you know if she is at home or not? You do not seem to be coming from the castle this morning," her brother said in a skeptical tone that made Jero think twice about how he would answer the mistrustful men.

"Yes, well," he anxiously explained in too much detail, "I was with her and the baron on an excursion to the seaside until this morning. The Baric scouts will have found them and notified them of your arrival. Lord Baric said he would return home immediately if you arrived while they were gone. Your sister is only a few hours away."

"We saw your scouts along the hills," the dark-skinned man told him. He had a smooth accent when he spoke in perfect Latin.

Jero had not expected such fluency from the stranger. He thought the man must be from African lands, but perhaps he had once been a slave to a nobleman to have learned the language so well. He was not as black as the slaves Jero had seen before, but he was too dark to be an Arab. The other brown-skinned man would be the Persian that Lady Terese had spoken of. The tall, blond man would be the Dane. The last was a small European man, with dark hair and a neatly groomed mustache. He reminded Jero of Stephan. This man spoke to him next.

"How fortunate for us to have met you here on this crossroad. Will you escort us then, Signor Jero?" he asked in an oddly familiar, yet different Latin. The man was definitely Italian, but not from Venice, or he would have used the Venetian dialect that they spoke. Where had Jero heard that accent before? Was it in Tuscany?

"Jero is my given name, sir. It is just Jero," he clarified to the Italian.

The Persian said something to Patrik in Greek, and Patrik asked Jero, "Are you a relation to Mauritius Baric?"

"No, I am employed by the Baric family." Patrik looked at Salar Nassim and shrugged. "But I can see that you are a relation to Lady Terese. You have her eyes and her coloring. You must be Patricius Kokkinos," Jero added.

"I am," her brother replied. "I am known as Patrik, and this is our commander, Salar Nassim. Next to him is Soren, to his right is Bem, and on my left is Cyro." They remained tall and still on their horses, each glaring at Jero.

A slow cart with three local men rode slowly by them, keeping their distance on the far side of the road. Jero nodded to them, and the farmers tipped their hats nervously at the familiar Baric steward.

"Do you usually travel alone, Jero?" Patrik asked. He had a deep, accented voice that was both calming and menacing.

Surrounded by the group of foreign men, Jero felt a sudden sense of danger. His hand instinctively went to his sword belted by his side.

"There is no need for that, Jero. We are here as invited guests of the baron, and we will not harm you," Patrik unconvincingly assured him. He stared with the same eyes as the baroness'. Jero knew how kind she was. There must be some kindness in her brother, too, he thought.

"Yes, well, I am counting on that," Jero replied honestly, and the men smiled for the first time since their encounter.

Jero had the urge to be behind the protective walls of his home, so suggested, "Shall we be on our way?" He put on his cap again and nudged the impatient Blaze to continue on.

The five mercenaries followed Jero to the turnoff. The baroness had told Jero that her brother and his gang fought against the Ottomans, but he thought they still had the look of their origins, despite the mix of European garments they wore. The Croats lived on the crossroads of many cultures; their borders had been drawn and redrawn over the centuries. There were no displaced foreigners left in the Barics' barony, but his new companions reminded him of Ottomans he had encountered in other parts of the region.

Jero had always thought that a band of soldiers united through one, uniform look—like Baron Baric's soldiers dressed when they left together. But each of these men had an independent style. Patrik and Cyro both wore high knee boots—Patrik's a bold red and Cyro's a faded brown. The others had shorter, heeled riding boots of different heights. They were barely noticeable, though, because they wore loose leggings to their ankles instead of breeches. Their long, varied coats seemed out of place in the hot summer sun, but they were made of linen and broadcloth; more for protection along the trail than for warmth. Each man was clothed in varied colors of blue, gray, black, red, and brown. Only Cyro had a broad-brimmed hat; the others wore caps of different shapes and colors perched over their long, bound hair. The Persian had his black hair wrapped with a coarse scarf of crimson red. Despite their intimidating looks, Jero now saw the tiredness in their faces. Even warriors needed rest.

They proceeded up the ascending, castle road without speaking and stopped in front of the shut gate. Simeon and Eduard were at the guard post with crossbows pointed at Jero's unlikely friends. Patrik counted six more guards staring down at them atop the impressive ramparts, also armed with muskets and bows.

Jero was shocked at the show of aggression from the guardsmen, and he knew the baron would not approve. "Stand down," he shouted in disappointment. His sudden order was enough to make the Baric men lower their weapons. Jero added in a voice of authority and frustration, "Open the gate for us. These are the baroness' visitors you were asked to welcome." The gate began to open.

Jero led the group across the expansive courtyard and to the stables. Alberto came to greet Jero from the outside paddock, where he had been exercising some horses. Geoff came through the stables' double doors, but ventured no farther when he saw the mercenaries. The Baric soldiers went to war with their swords and shields, and some with muskets and spears, but Geoff had never seen their horses laden like this. The visitors had special saddles with holders to secure their pieces of equipment. Along with their weapons, each man had a blanket roll and saddlebags strapped behind their seats. It was the mix of sizes and colors of the men that surprised Geoff more than their baggage. Not just their clothing, but the color of their skin was a new sight to him. Geoff had never seen a black-skinned man, although he had heard they came from a place across the sea. He tried not to be frightened, but he worried that his mistress may not have known such men would be arriving with her brother.

The great gate closed behind them, and more soldiers began to come out of the tower to see who had arrived. The mercenaries did not like that they were so obviously outnumbered by their unfriendly welcoming party. Patrik turned to Jero, who had dismounted and handed his horse over to Josip. "Where did you say my sister went; on an excursion?" he asked.

"Yes," Jero answered cheerfully, glad to be safe within the walls. "It is a long story, but I believe the outing was meant to celebrate the Barics' first year of marriage. The wars had made for a difficult year, and then the ship was confiscated, which was the reason for the party. With the arrival of the other guests, well, that made things complicated. But the ball was a success, so the baroness wanted the Venetian ladies to join her and—Oh." Jero realized he was rambling and made no sense to his audience. He took a deep breath and started again. "We were a party of seven at the seaside. I came back early because of an errand. I have been asked to make you comfortable until the baron and baroness arrive," he explained more simply.

Nestor walked up to Jero's side. "Ah, good, here is Nestor. He is Lord Baric's estate administrator," Jero explained to the mercenaries. "Nestor, this is Patrik Kokkinos." Jero singled out Patrik among the group of horsemen, having already forgotten all the other names.

Nestor calmly bowed. "At your service, sir. The baron asked me to show you to your quarters so you can get settled while you wait." Nestor waved his arm toward the expansive stables. "You can bring your horses to the grooms there."

The warriors remained stone-faced and did not dismount. "We will wait here with our horses until my sister arrives," Patrik informed him.

Nestor was unfazed by this, but Jero was concerned they did not understand that the Barics would not be arriving anytime soon. "Baron and Baroness Baric will be delayed several hours," Jero explained. "They will have to pack up camp and are riding with the women by wagon. In the meantime, you could wait on the terrace and have some refreshments." Jero pointed across the courtyard.

"We do not require refreshments," Patrik stated coldly.

"Well, your horses will want to be watered. Would you not like to unpack their burdens?" Jero politely offered. None of the other four had even glanced at Jero while he spoke; they were watching the Baric guardsmen.

Patrik told him, "The horses are fine."

Jero did not know what to do to make them feel welcomed, but Nestor decided Jero had done enough. Nestor looked over to Simeon and Hugo, who stood armed at the double doors to the armory, and announced loudly to the courtyard spectators, "The Baric men may go back to their duties. Our guests will wait here for his lordship."

Simeon was not sure he should take orders from Nestor, but Nestor held his earnest stare at the captain. Simeon nodded, put his sword back into its sheath, and walked back toward the steps of the Keep to sit on the bench there; Hugo followed him. The other guardsmen disbanded, still within shouting range if needed, but no longer openly confronting the new arrivals. The visitors took their hands off their sword handles as well, but remained perched on their mounts.

Nestor turned his attention back to the mercenaries. "Should you need anything, Jero and I will be in the manor house."

Nestor began to walk away. The speechless Jero bowed to their guests and followed him. When they were out of earshot Jero asked, "What will the baron say when he comes home to find the guests waiting here like this?"

"I extended his offer of welcome, and it was refused. It is now in the baron's hands."

~ *The End of Part One* ~

A Discussion Guide for Reading Groups can be found at:
www.JillianBald.com

Books in This Trilogy:
The House of Baric Part One: Shields Down
The House of Baric Part Two: A Brother's Defense
The House of Baric Part Three: Widows and Weddings

Acknowledgements

Many thanks to Lourdes Venard for her keen editing eye. www.comasense.net

Thank you to my beta readers, especially my sister, sons and husband who now know the Barics better than anyone.

With special acknowledgement to the artists who turned ideas into pictures:
Map illustration © 2015: Tim Paul ~ www.timpaulmaps.com
Sketch illustrations © 2015: Jeff Meyer ~ www.anaseer.com
Digital artwork contributor for 2015 cover: Trevor Heinsohn
Shield original design: "Guyra" ~ www.swordofmoonlight.com
Croatian wall photograph: Jillian Bald

Shutterstock.com provided the venue for the following art contributions. All components were used by permission and licensed. Credit goes to the artists who helped make the book cover complete:
Girl sketch: @moschiorini
Dress fabric: PK55's portfolio
Lace overlay: smash338@gmail.com

About the Author

A go-getter from a young age, collecting deposit bottles from neighbors with her sister for spending money and babysitting after selling Kool-Aid on the corner, the business world called her name. With a degree in Management, and another in French, Jillian Bald found her niche in international trade. Jillian lived, worked, and traveled throughout Europe for many years. Certified fluent by Goethe and her husband in his native German, her hard-learned French has been mothballed to the archives in her head. After a homelife of master gardening and raising two sons, chickens, and a wonderful dog, Jillian now focuses her time on writing fiction in her native Oregon. *Shields Down* is Jillian's first novel.

Made in the USA
Lexington, KY
25 August 2018